CW00468874

The Artist,
the Farmer
and the
Ancient Oak

by Gill Buchanan

Visit my website at www.gillbuchanan.co.uk

Printed in the United Kingdom
First Printing: GB Books
ISBN – 9798375505695

This book is dedicated
to all the farmers
who listen to the land

CHAPTER 1

Wanda considered that her latest art work was safe, accessible and a far cry from what she really wanted to express. Was it the disapproving Taylor family, that she had married into, that stifled her creativity? Or simply the demands of the gallery that she sold her work through.

She heard Adrian's voice in her head: *The art we sell is a bit more light-hearted; beautiful in an obvious way; not too demanding of our customers.* Wanda had looked around the town gallery at the time and wondered who these compliant artists were.

The poppy seed heads before her looked innocent enough. She'd used her watercolours and a blending brush to allow grey green to run into pale aubergine with darker accents where the seeds containing the milky sap of opium caused the sphere to bulge slightly. She had fancied using a more diverse palette, perhaps some yellow ochre, even a hint of magenta, but Adrian's casually delivered remarks held her back. His tone might be light but his words were carried heavily by Wanda.

Her mobile rang. She had forgotten to switch it to silent mode, something she usually did when she was hidden away in her makeshift studio, which was originally an abandoned farm shed tucked away in

Rachel's Covert.

'Dad, everything okay?'

'Wanda, my love, am I interrupting important farm work?'

'You've caught me having a sneaky cup of tea.' *Why did she lie to her father?*

'Your mother says...'

'Why, oh why doesn't Mum phone me if she has something to say?'

'Ah, yes. Good point. She's busy at the moment.'

Wanda pictured her mother signalling that she was unavailable. Ever since she had retired, she had thrown herself into church bell ringing (she must be the shortest bell ringer in the country – they even had to build a platform for her to stand on) and all sorts of craft activities. She excelled in producing highly undesirable objects. She had once wrapped up a fluorescent pink knitted tea cosy as a Christmas present for Wanda, even after Wanda had been offered the ugly thing and rejected it.

'Anyway,' Graham's voice faltered, as he went on slightly nervously, 'she was just wondering if you're going to the Farmers' Wives meeting this evening. Apparently, Fi says you've not been going recently.'

'My dear mother-in-law is right. I've not been going for quite a while mainly because they treat me like some sort of freak and I'm bored out of my mind.'

'Oh Wanda, that's not good.' He lowered his voice to a loud whisper. 'Your mother thinks you should make the effort to fit in. Wouldn't hurt, would it? Once a month.'

'I take it Mum and Fiona have been discussing my inadequacies over a cosy coffee.'

'No, no, nothing like that. She just wants the best for you.'

'But Dad, I'm fifty-two.' She raised her voice in frustration. 'How old do I have to be to know myself, what is best for me?'

It was moments like this that she could not help pondering the life-changing day many years ago when the family camping business had passed, with very little discussion, to her brother, Ben. He was the first born but, more importantly, she was considered unlikely to be capable of running such a venture. It was ironic really when it was her who had helped out after school and weekends to run the reception desk, answer the phone and even clean the shower block. Meanwhile her brother Ben was far too important and busy to do anything but study, pass exams and attend worthy activities like the debating society.

'I'm not going Dad. Sorry, but it's not for me.'

'Okey dokey, I'll tell her you can't make this evening but you'll try and make the next one.'

'Dad, that's a lie.'

'Yes, I know. Keeps me out of trouble though.'

'Oh Dad! I love you.'

'Love you too. I'll let you get back to the farm.'

As soon as she hit the end call button three texts screamed at her from her husband. She saw that it had gone four o'clock at the top of the screen and didn't need to read the messages.

'I'm sorry I'm late, okay?'

Glen wouldn't even look her in the eye. 'Huh!' he yelled and shoved the iodine cup at her before storming off. The cows seemed to have picked up on Glen's agitation and were mooing loudly and jostling for position to be the next in line to be milked. Wanda sighed and tried to work out which cow he had got to. She always felt trapped in the milking pit surrounded by two hundred impatient cows, their udders at eye level – at least they were for people seven inches taller than Wanda. The air was damp and smelt of urine and crap. She stood on her wellington boot toes to reach up to each and every teat. There was a block somewhere for her to stand on but she couldn't see it and she couldn't keep the girls waiting. Was she really expected to do all this on her own? *Where was Lee?!* He should be helping her out. Milking was a two-person job as far as she was concerned.

The murmurs and grunts in the shed were getting louder filling her with horror. She really didn't need crazy cows on top of everything else. Her head was beginning to throb. It seemed like a never-ending task. She would turn off the loud pop music, that the cows supposedly enjoyed, when she let the current batch of twenty-eight go back to their pasture.

Her mind drifted back to her painting. She *would* add a hint of magenta. She didn't want to be a safe painter. One of the cows urinated with the force of a power shower and she didn't manage to get out of the way in time. 'Thanks a bunch, Daisy,' she cried out. She called all the cows Daisy. It wasn't the first time she'd been covered in wee but today she just wanted to cry. *Where was Lee?* Fair enough she was half an hour late and apparently this was totally unacceptable to the cows who could tell the time. But she wasn't usually expected to do all this on her own.

Finally, two hours later, with all the cows milked, she trudged up the track, following the last of them back up to the pasture. It was a beautiful May evening; the sun was low and still bright in the big Suffolk sky. If only she was shower fresh and wearing a floaty dress with a gin and tonic in her hand. But no, she was covered in mud, poo and urine and still had the milking shed to wash down.

Glen appeared in the kitchen almost immediately after she got back to the farmhouse. He sat at the table.

'Sit down Wanda,' he ordered. Over the last year his hair had become more grey than dark and he had the beginnings of a beard through lack of shaving. He was as handsome as the day they had met with his dark brown eyes and he had a great physique; that was down to the hard life of a farmer.

She found some newspaper to put on the chair before she sat opposite him and, after leaning on the table with her elbows and putting her head in her whiffy hands, she looked up at him.

'We can't go on like this,' he said simply. His eyes flicked from her to the table.

'Look, I was just a bit late. I've said I'm sorry. I forgot to put my watch on... and... well, I...'

He was looking at her as if she was a lost cause. 'Well if you don't wear a watch.'

Wanda felt her naked wrist, even though she knew she wasn't wearing one. She didn't want to be ruled by time.

'I suppose you were up at Rachel's Covert in your fancy shed?' he continued.

'Okay, fine. I forgot the time. But where's Lee? I can't milk two hundred cows on my own.'

Glen looked shifty now. 'Look, I'm struggling to pay the lad. I've had to reduce his hours.

'You didn't ask me what I thought about it.'

He glared at her with contempt. 'When you pull your weight, you can have an opinion.'

'I'm doing my best!' She stood up despite the disbelief in his eyes as he stared back at her. 'Right now, I want to have a shower and pour a glass of wine, is that a crime?'

'I just don't believe you! You don't get it, do you? We're facing financial ruin. If it wasn't for the EU subsidy, which is fifty per cent of our income, we would be going down. And now we've voted to leave, goodness knows what the government will replace it with.'

'Brexit isn't my fault!' Wanda exclaimed.

'But it's our reality and we have to plan for it. Look, this farm has been in the Taylor family for three generations and now Dad's retired it's down to me.'

'But Martin still interferes; he's full of advice. It's a pity he doesn't help out a bit more if things are that bad.' Feeling weak, she sat back down again.

'He's seventy-five! Give the man a break. Do you want him to go the same way as a lot of farmers and keel over in the yard before he has any time to enjoy a retirement? Is that what you want?'

'No! Or course not. I'm just saying he's always got an opinion on everything.'

'You have no bloody right to say that when you're so hopeless. I honestly think this farm's days are nearly over. And it will be all my fault. All because I married you!'

Wanda gasped. 'Well, you'd better get yourself on the *farming-find-yourself-a-wife-dating-site* then, hadn't you?'

'You're being ridiculous!'

'You're being a monster and now I'm going to have a shower and then I'm going to Saffy's to get drunk!'

His face froze, his expression shocked. She walked out, feeling his eyes drilling into her back.

CHAPTER 2

Saffy had that look that said, *You really shouldn't be here*, as she showed Wanda in to the kitchen.

'Oh Wanda,' Ben said with a deflated tone. He was sat at the table. He didn't hug her. 'We've just finished our supper.'

'Don't worry it's a glass of wine I'm after.' She couldn't go back home now after her dramatic walk out. Saffy and Ben were looking at each other like married people do when they don't have to say anything, they just know what the other one is thinking.

'Glass of wine, I can do,' Saffy said a bit brighter now. She grabbed a couple of glasses and a bottle of white from the fridge. 'Let's go and sit in the lounge; Ben's got work to do.'

As soon as they were settled Wanda asked, 'Have I called at a bad time?'

'Not for us, no. But what about you? I'm taking it you've had a row with Glen?'

Wanda couldn't help feeling that this was a little disloyal. 'He started it. I do my best. You know that. I did the afternoon milking all on my own. It nearly killed me. Glen's reduced Lee's hours apparently. I was totally exhausted when I finally finished and what does my husband do? Sit me down for a telling-off.'

Saffy's expression changed. 'You poor thing. You didn't deserve that.'

'He has been quite understanding in the past, but recently he's got really tetchy. It's the farm; it's just not making enough money. And now with vote to leave last year, we've no idea what that's going to mean for our subsidy.'

'That doesn't sound good. But will we really leave the EU, do you think? So many are against it.'

'They might be but the EU Bill went through in March. I can't see it not happening now.'

'Perhaps you need to make some changes.'

'Martin won't let us. He just orders Glen around without lifting a practical finger. He says, "Now, if I were you, I'd ring chemical solutions, or whatever they're called, and get some advice on which pesticide you should be using on the rapeseed," and that basically is a thinly disguised order to get on the phone and get spraying.'

'Have you told Glen how you feel about his father's interference?'

'Just today. It didn't go down too well. Apparently as I'm such a useless farmer I have no right to complain about anything.'

Saffy topped up their wine glasses. 'I can see why you need this.'

Wanda sighed and settled back on the sofa. 'I don't know. Maybe I'm just not cut out for this farming life? When I was in the gallery in town the other day – you know the one on Angel Hill? – Adrian said they are looking for a receptionist stroke salesperson.'

'That would be right up your street.' Saffy looked thoughtful. 'But wouldn't you be leaving Glen in the lurch?'

'That's the trouble. But then I would be bringing some money in. He could pay Lee more and increase his hours.'

'You've thought this through.' Saffy looked concerned.

'I know it's a hare-brained scheme but can't I do what I want? Just for once?' Wanda put her glass down. Her head was beginning to swim. 'I do envy you. I'd love to run this place; I love how you've turned it into a glamping site.'

'I'm so sorry you're not here. The camping site shouldn't have automatically gone to Ben. I always feel bad that we got the house too.'

Wanda swallowed hard. It was an injustice she lived with. 'I try not to think about that.'

'You must hate us.' Saffy shrank away from her.

'Don't be silly. You know I love you both.'

'We should sort something out. With our will, I mean. So that your girls benefit as much as Toby and Jemima. It's only right.'

'I have broached that subject with my mum, actually.'

'Oh, and did she agree?'

'No! Don't be silly. I married a Taylor. Apparently, that means Abi and Lily will be fine – they'll inherit the farm! Or at least a share of it as Aunty Jane has two children, even though they've barely set foot in the place.'

'I don't suppose Abi or Lily are too keen on taking the farm on, are they?'

'I very much doubt it. Lily is doing really well now in London. It was so lucky she was able to buy that little flat with her gay friend, Liam.'

'Yes, it's pretty amazing to get on the property ladder at her age. How about Abi? She is still working as a make-up artist, isn't she?'

'As far as I know. It all seems to be a bit sporadic – you know, a BBC contract here and then another Channel 4 contract there. That's television for you.'

'It's a shame she hasn't had her lucky break into acting yet.'

'Yes, I think she's a bit too much like her mum. Doesn't believe she's good enough. You're lucky that Jemima is settled with a lovely husband and a great job.'

'Well, yes, but she is up in Cumbria so we don't see her as much as we'd like. And we're not sure what's going on in Toby's life. He's in his second year of uni but doesn't seem to know what he wants to do for a career.'

'It's funny isn't it how the oldest child flourishes while the youngest seems to struggle a bit. I'm the youngest; must explain why I ended up in this mess.'

'Oh Wanda. Don't be so down on yourself.'

'Well, I'm so fed up. Everything I do is wrong. I feel like running away.'

Saffy bit her lip. Wanda pushed her wine glass away. 'If I don't eat something, I'll keel over.'

'You should have said.' Saffy jumped up. 'There's some lasagne left if you don't mind it re-heated.'

'Sounds wonderful.'

*

Wanda held one of the Goldline hens in her arms and stroked her red brown feathers, lightly kissing the top of her head. The mild fresh air felt good this morning; it helped to clear her head after a bit too much wine with Saffy last night. She still hadn't seen Glen; he had been out milking the cows when she got back. It was horrible to think that they had rowed and said some terrible things to each other.

'You like it out here, don't you, Delilah?' She put her down so that she could waddle off and join the others, foraging in the field. She had noticed that when the hens were outside, they weren't too interested in the feed she was supposed to be giving them. They seemed more absorbed in exploring, pecking at the ground as they went. Looking out over Hungry Hill and beyond, she could see the water of Pond Meadow glistening in the sunlight.

'Don't go too far, Snowball,' she called out as a Light Sussex turned to look at her. 'Nothing wrong with your hearing.' She smiled as the hen held her perky head high displaying its bright pink comb.

Reluctantly she left them to roam and went back into the barn. Feeling her way in the dark, she could just about make out where the eggs were. Turning off the bright artificial lights, that were supposed to be on all the time, was just one of things she did that irritated the Taylors. After a while her eyes adjusted and she was able to place the eggs carefully into large trays. There must be around two hundred which was quite enough for one day as far as Wanda was concerned.

Back outside, she was so tempted to leave the little waddlers to wander until dusk. She could come back then to make sure they were all safely in for the night.

Martin appeared from the distance. He was rushing towards her as if there was some great emergency.

'What are you doing, Wanda?' He was out of breath as he reached the barn.

'Hello Martin,' she said not rising to his alarmed state.

'What are the hens doing out here?' His tone was reproachful.

'Enjoying a bit of sunshine on this beautiful spring day,' Wanda said lifting her voice despite the disappointed look on his face.

'But they are barn hens. Not free range.'

Wanda took a deep breath. 'Anything else?' she asked.

He stood there defiantly. 'You need to get them back in the barn.' He was looking straight at her now.

'I was just about to, actually.' Wanda smirked at him.

'You'll need a hand.'

'No! Thank you,' she said loud and clear.

He stared at her with contempt and didn't move.

'Don't let me keep you,' Wanda said and finally he stomped off, his head darting round, looking at how far the hens had got, every few paces.

Delilah was at Wanda's feet again and she picked her up and cuddled her. 'See what I put up with, just so you can escape the barn for a bit.' The hen settled in her arms and purred.

Back at the farmhouse, Wanda smiled to herself as she placed her mobile down on the kitchen table and sat back in her chair; her conversation with the gallery had gone well. Just then her mother, Rita, burst through the back door. She had her hands on Abi's shoulders in the way you might present an errant child to a headteacher. Wanda's daughter looked rather sheepish.

'This one called me at nine o'clock last night. From Ipswich station! She had got the train up from London. Apparently, she tried to call you but no luck.' Rita was good at making Wanda feel like an unfit mother. In fact the evening with Ben and Saffy had greatly improved after Saffy had warmed up the lasagne for her. The three of them had shared a lively conversation leaving her feeling so much better about life. And she had slept really well in their spare room.

'I'm sorry my angel,' Wanda said. 'Thank you, Mum, for picking her up, that's really good of you.' Then she turned to Abi. 'So, what's happened?' she asked gently.

Abi looked close to tears. Rita had her arms firmly folded now. 'She's split up with her boyfriend,' she pronounced.

Wanda gave Abi a hug. 'Sorry to hear that.' She was trying to make eye contact but Abi had her palms covering her face.

'And as if that's not bad enough, she's out of work at the moment.'

'Hang on a minute, Mum; Abi is twenty-seven, she can speak for herself.'

Rita sniffed. 'Shall I make some coffee?' She went over to the kettle.

'Good idea.' Wanda turned back to Abi and now her daughter did make eye contact uncovering her red blotchy face.

'I was between contracts. I had something lined up with the BBC – that costume drama I told you about – but they shelved it at the last minute.'

'I see. But isn't it always a bit like that? I mean contracts come and go.'

Abi exchanged a sideways glance with her grandmother.

'I think some time here at the farm is what Abi needs,' Rita said.

'But surely you need to be in London in case any jobs come up?'

'Mum, will you leave it. I've just split up with Gavin. I'm devastated.'

'Of course you are, but you know life goes on.' Wanda tried to keep her tone light.

Rita rolled her eyes. 'Surely you can indulge her at the farm for a week or two; the poor girl's heartbroken,' she said placing a mug of milky instant coffee in front of Wanda and handing one to Abi.

'I don't drink instant, Mum, you know that.' Wanda said it quietly in the hope it wouldn't offend.

'Oh, for goodness' sake. We have a family crisis and you want freshly ground coffee. Get real.'

Glen came through the back door. 'Abi? What are you doing here?'

'She's broken up with Gavin and has lost her job,' Rita enlightened him in brutal fashion.

'I'm sure you've got places to be, Mum. Thank you for bringing Abi home.' Wanda looked at her mother expecting her to take the hint.

'Charming! Is that all the thanks I get. You know I picked her up from the station last night. You weren't answering your home phone or your mobile.'

Glen caught Wanda's eye. It was the first time they had seen each other since their horrible row. But as usual they were both too wrapped up in their busy day to even acknowledge what had happened.

'Right, well I was over at Ben and Saffy's. My mobile battery had gone.'

'Aunty Saffy could have charged your mobile for you,' Abi said and Wanda felt a pang of remorse.

'I was out checking on the cows,' Glen said. 'But still, you're here now. Will you be staying a few days?' he asked.

Abi looked to Wanda for an answer. 'Yes, she'll be staying.'

'The tractor's fixed. Fancy helping me spray the carrots out on Sally's Grove? You look like you need a bit of fresh air.'

'Dad! Please! I'm not here to work!'

He looked nonplussed. 'Any chance of a coffee before I go back out?'

Rita handed him the coffee she had made for Wanda. 'Here, you might as well drink this since it's not good enough for your wife.'

'Oh thanks.' He drank it down in a few gulps and handed the empty mug back to Rita. 'See you later then,' and he was gone.

Wanda sighed deeply.

CHAPTER 3

'I can see the sense in moving the cows each day to a new section of pasture but isn't it using up too much acreage?' Martin's presence around the dining table was somehow larger than everyone else's. His elbows were held out wide resting on the table and his chest was puffed up.

'It's easily done though, Dad, with the track and gate system we've put in place. The cows know where they've got to go after milking.' Glen was looking straight at his father's troubled face. 'Of course, I bow to your better judgement.' *If he had a forelock, he'd be pulling it.*

'But moving them daily means we don't need to use fertiliser to help the grass grow back,' Wanda chipped in. She tried to keep her tone light. She actually hated these family meetings but felt obliged to attend.

Martin's mouth twitched to the right and he screwed his eyes up. 'What about the bull we're using to mop up the cows that we've missed with the A.I.?'

Wanda was never sure if artificial insemination was a better method of getting the cows in calf or whether a more natural method would improve the chances.

'We've hired Sampson again.' Glen said.

'The Jersey bull?'

'Yes, best for milk production I reckon with the Montbéliarde.'

'And we've used Sampson before,' Fiona, Glen's mother, pointed out before picking up a biscuit from a plate in the middle of the table.

'Sounds like you've made your mind up for this year, anyway.' Martin tapped the end of his pen on the table over and over.

'It's a pity because you really should be growing more veg.' He raised his voice. All three of them waited for his words of wisdom as though frozen in suspense. 'We've got to make more money somehow.' He leaned back in his chair. Everything about him was self-assured.

'He's got a point.' Glen looked straight at Wanda. 'We simply must become more profitable before we come out of the EU subsidy scheme.'

'But won't the UK government create a new scheme?' Fiona asked.

Wanda felt a strong urge to leave the room and sprang out of her chair. 'More tea, anyone?

'Do you need a hand?'

'Don't be silly,' Wanda said but Fiona got up anyway and followed her into the kitchen.

'We'll make a pot; they'll want a cup when they see it. And a few more biscuits.' Fiona was a feeder. She saw people and fed them. 'Where's Abi this evening?' She always had a slightly troubled expression as she looked around what was now Wanda's kitchen. It had taken Wanda years to persuade Glen that it needed modernising. While all the home interior magazines displayed Agas and even bread ovens, elevating them to prized possessions, Wanda was all for practical and easy. She had never had much time for cooking, let alone baking.

'She's gone to meet an old school friend; she's been here a week now; I'm beginning to think she doesn't want to go back to London.'

'Well, if that's what's right for her now while she gets over her boyfriend. But there's not much here for her, is there? It's a pity she doesn't show much interest in the farm.'

Wanda poured boiling water from the kettle into the tea pot a bit too quickly and some splashed on her hand. She didn't complain but stuck it under a running cold tap to ease the pain.

'Have you burnt yourself? Where's the first aid kit I used to keep in here?'

'We've got stuff in the bathroom cabinet.'

'Always better to have it in the kitchen. And in my day, of course, I used the Aga which meant I'd always have one of my gloves on.' Fiona looked smug as she turned to go upstairs.

Wanda's mobile rang. She turned the tap off and picked up her mobile with her dry hand. 'Lily.'

'Mum, what's happening with Abi? I've had Gavin on the phone.'

'Really? She says they've split up. Anyway, she's here with us at the moment.'

'Gavin says this month's rent hasn't been paid on their flat.'

'Can't he pay the rent for now. He's earning quite a bit at that accountancy firm, isn't he?' She winced and put her burnt hand back under the tap.

'But they've split up and he's moved out.'

'Suddenly I've gone right off Gavin,' Wanda said. Something else she could do without right now. She reached to put a jug of milk on a tray with her free hand.

'What are we going to do?'

'Lily, darling, we're in the middle of a family meeting about the farm. Grandad Martin and Granny Fi are here. Can I call you back?'

'Sounds serious.'

Fiona appeared looking triumphant with a tube of something and a plaster.

'Got to go Lily.'

Back at the table, Fiona poured tea and placed mugs very obviously in front of the two men who took no notice.

'I think you're right, Dad,' Glen was saying, 'we should try this new pesticide on the rapeseed. We must have lost forty per cent of the crop last year.'

'I think it's your only option. I mean it's very expensive but I've heard from the NFU that it works very well.'

Fiona manoeuvred the newly refreshed plate of biscuits in front of Glen who didn't take one.

'And you think we should expand the veg acreage?' he asked his father.

'Ideally, yes. You see in my day, we had a smaller area for pasture so we had more room for root crops.'

Glen took a moment. He looked like a troubled man. Wanda knew he was at breaking point with his workload. 'I think we should get Bartletts involved for any additional work,' Wanda suggested and Glen looked at her with an encouraging smile.

Martin twitched but then conceded. 'I can see you're stretched. We can still make it pay even using the contractor if we have the right terms.'

'What does that mean?' Glen asked looking anxious.

'Well, perhaps it's time to renegotiate with them. Even look at rivals to compare fees.'

Alarm bells rang for Wanda. Even Fiona was looking nervous.

'We've used Bartletts for many years and we know we can rely on them. I'm sure their fees are competitive.' Wanda wasn't sure of that at all but the thought of going to new contractors to tender for the work was soul destroying.

'I think Dad, we stick with Bartlett's. I really don't have it in me to start changing our contractor right now.'

Martin looked disappointed. He took a deep breath before saying, 'Okay

I understand. But there's the important point of where you're going to put this new veg. I mean where, apart from the dairy pasture, will you get a bit of land from?'

'We could try and get Hungry Hill up to scratch and incorporate that bit of field in front of the hen shed,' Glen suggested.

'Oh no!' Wanda couldn't help herself. 'No, that bit of field is where I let the hens out.'

'I keep telling you, they are barn hens.' Martin lent forward showering his solemn expression over the whole table. 'What about a potato crop to go in now and then we'll plant up oilseed rape come September. That would work but of course you wouldn't be able to let the hens out at all. They'd cause havoc with the crop.' He sat back and darted a disdainful look at Wanda.

'That's not fair!' Wanda cried out.

'What do you mean?' Glen actually looked at his wife.

'The hens love to go out especially if it's a nice day.' Wanda's hands were clammy. She knew she was sticking her neck out.

'But that isn't a policy that has been agreed, Wanda.' Fiona reached over to gently stroke Wanda's arm. Wanda snatched it away and looked at Glen with a sense of bewilderment.

'We've got to weigh up what's best for the farm,' Glen said simply and averted his eyes. A red rash started to creep up his neck. 'We'll get on and cultivate Hungry Hill. It's going to need irrigation and fertilisers to get it up to scratch.'

'I think it's time we address the figures,' Martin said looking expectantly at his son.

'Oh, yes.' Glen shuffled some papers about and found a spreadsheet. He handed the one and only copy to Martin who poured over it pulling faces as if perhaps he was in pain. 'The milk just isn't making enough money, is it?'

He looked up at Glen.

'No, but the carrots did okay. It's just a pity the price from the supermarket has been rock bottom of late. Rejection rate is pretty high too.'

'We still have the Nairobi variety of carrots, I take it?' Martin asked. 'They were great little performers in my day.'

'Yes, it's still the Nairobi. Just that the supermarkets get more and more fussy about what they'll take.'

'What happens to the rejects?' Wanda asked. They all looked affronted by her question.

'We're not allowed to sell them elsewhere,' Glen said dismissively.

'Not allowed to?'

'That's the contract.'

'That's ridiculous. So what actually happens to them?'

There was an awkward pause. Wanda looked round the table wondering what terrible fate befell these not so perfect carrots.

At last Glen spoke. 'I gave the last lot to a pig farmer I know.'

Wanda poured herself another cup of tea and decided she didn't really want it. Her bladder wasn't so robust these days.

'Moving on, I think we have to talk about what we do with Lee,' Martin said avoiding anyone's eyes but his son's.

'What do you mean? What do we do with him? He's a great worker.' Wanda glared at her father-in-law and getting no reaction she nudged Glen. 'Darling, what is this about?'

He shuffled in his chair. The red rash had crept higher and up to his cheek. Fiona wet her forefinger and dabbed up some biscuit crumbs from the table. Martin turned his spreadsheet over so that the problematic figures were hidden from his sight. Glen turned to her.

'Look, we're going to have to let Lee go. I'll help you with the milking when I can. Then there's Abi; she could help out while she's here.'

'But she doesn't want to! You just don't understand your own daughter, do you?' Wanda said raising her voice and Fiona shrank back in her chair. 'And anyway, I think she needs to go back to London so she can get another job.'

'Well, while she's on the farm, I think she should put some hours in.'

'You can't force her!'

'You'll just have to make her see sense,' Martin added unhelpfully, as if we were still living in the dark ages.

Wanda's hands flew up in frustration and she knocked her mug of unwanted tea over. The beige liquid was spreading over the table fast and heading towards Martin's lap. He jumped up.

'Look what you've done now!' he shouted. 'The table will be ruined!'

Fiona ran into the kitchen. Glen sighed.

'I can't do this any more!' Wanda shouted. She got up and left the room meeting Fiona coming back armed with dishcloths and kitchen towel.

'That oak table has been in the Taylor family for many years,' she said looking sternly at Wanda.

'Arrrgh!' Wanda headed straight out of the back door and into the cooling evening air. She didn't stop walking, just kept going down the track as fast as her little legs would carry her. She shivered and shook her head as she tried to rid her mind of Martin's overbearing presence and the carnage she had left behind.

When she got to Low Meadow she stopped for a moment to take in the scene. The sun was low in the sky, a warm orange. It really was a beautiful landscape. But then she thought of the hens stuck in the barn under the eye-popping lights being forced to lay to meet maximum production targets and was very tempted to go and let them all out.

At Glenham field she waved to the Montbéliarde cows who stared back at her. They were content as they munched the green grass. 'Evening

Daisy,' she called across to them and tried to lift her voice; it was an effort when it seemed like the whole Taylor family were against her. Where the track divided she chose the path up to Rachel's Covert and, from there, she headed into Lucas Wood.

Walking through the ivy-covered trees she heard blackbirds sing joyfully in chorus and her pace and breath slowed. A baby wren, round and brown, darted around the forest floor looking for food, flying off as soon as Wanda got near.

Reaching the ancient old oak tree in the thick of the wood she stopped and looked around her. Spring green buds and leaves burst from branches; some trees already had a green canopy. The sun had dipped below the horizon and the light had faded. She was all alone. She leant against a nearby birch beside her and rested the side of her face against the smooth white bark, taking comfort in the certainty that no one would come looking for her here in this peaceful haven.

She listened to the sounds of the wood, a low rustle in the breeze, the flapping wings of a tawny owl nesting in the distance. Suddenly there was a loud snap, crackle, thud! Wanda looked around her for signs of life, her eyes peering into the dusk. Then came some disgruntled mumbling and from behind the big oak trunk an old man emerged in an ungainly fashion from the undergrowth, staggering to his feet. He turned to her and now she could make out his face.

'Gilbert?'

'Wanda Taylor?'

'Thank goodness. You had me worried there, for a moment. You okay?'

'Me? Of course, I am.' He straightened himself out, shaking the debris off his old mac. He always seemed to wear the same old clothes whatever the season. Strangely, his eyes were darting back and forth from Wanda to the oak tree.

'Are you sure you're okay, Gilbert?'

'I come here every now and then,' he said sniffing and turning his nose to the sky. Then his eyes brightened. 'Did you know that Suffolk folk used to go a-maying on the first of May? They collected foliage and flowers and stuff.' He held up a white wood anemone and its delicate head drooped. 'Anywise, they took it back to their homes. It was to show that ordinary folk and nature should co-exist.'

'What a lovely idea.'

'Not an idea, Wanda Taylor, it's what folk did.'

Wanda smiled. It was so refreshing to talk to this old Suffolk boy. His world was somehow simpler than everyone else's. 'Gilbert, why do you always call me Wanda Taylor?'

'That be your name. And the Taylors, well, they've farmed this land for many a year.'

'Well, yes, but you must know I married into the family.'

'You're not one of those burn-your-bra-feminists are you, that won't take her husband's name?'

Wanda laughed. 'I'm just saying, you could call me Wanda. I'd be happy about that.'

He thought about it. 'Right you are, Wanda Taylor.'

They both basked in the moment; Wanda could hear bird song in the distance. Gilbert's face lit up. 'The song of a nightingale,' he said lyrically lifting his head to the sky.

A tear fell from Wanda's eye. She hugged the birch tree she was stood next to.

'All not be well in Wanda's world,' Gilbert said steadily as he approached her now.

Wanda sniffed.

'Ah but you feel better for being in this place of solitude,' Gilbert continued, 'far from the madding crowd.' A deep throated chortle came up from his lungs. 'All nature around you,' he added, a twinkle in his eye.

'Now I think about it, yes, I do.'

'So what brings you up here, and at this time?' Gilbert asked. Like Wanda, he didn't wear a watch, just looked up to the sky to gauge the time.

'Oh, I just needed to get away. Those Taylors are hard work at times. Everything seems to be going wrong with the farm.'

Gilbert was thoughtful and stood back from the old oak peering up into its branches as if looking for something. Wanda gazed up too.

'I'm telling you, Wanda, you must listen to the land.'

She was intrigued but didn't know how to respond.

'Listen to the land; it will tell you what to do.' Gilbert looked straight into her eyes now.

And as she stood here in this magical place, she wanted to believe him.

Wanda found Glen asleep in front of the television when she got back to the house. She stood there, at the lounge door, watching his chest rise and fall, his mouth gaped open. She crept over and sat beside him taking a limp hand to hold in hers. He shuddered, stiffened and blinked.

'What?... Oh.'

Wanda looked into his eyes as he came too. She waited until he straightened his back and then she said gently, 'What has become of us?'

'What do you mean?' He looked disconcerted.

'Do you not know?'

Looking downwards he sighed. 'I know things are difficult, but Dad reckons we can get through this bad patch if we pull together.' He paused for thought. 'Where did you go?'

'Up to Lucas Wood.'

'What on earth were you doing going up there at this time?'

'I felt strangely safe amongst the trees. And Gilbert was up there.'

'What? Old boy Gilbert? What was he doing? He's trespassing.'

'Oh, come on. He's not doing any harm.'

She placed her head on Glen's chest and his arm closed around her and they stayed like that, still for a few moments. Then Wanda sat up to face him. 'I don't mind helping out a bit more on the farm but your dad can't have all his own way. I need a voice at the table.'

'But he has years of experience. I need his help right now.'

'You have a lot of experience too!'

'And it's still *his* farm really.'

Wanda sat bolt upright now. She wanted to scream. He just didn't get it. 'Then I'm not sure how long I can stay,' she said her voice breaking.

Glen looked shocked. 'Don't leave me. We're good together, aren't we?'

The situation seemed hopeless to Wanda. 'I can't do the milking on my own. We need to keep Lee on.'

Glen frowned. 'I wish we could afford to keep him. But I promise, I will milk with you. Whenever I can.'

'Exactly, I will be expected to do it on my own each time something urgent crops up which, let's face it, will be most days.'

'No, no, I will make the effort. I'll make sure.'

'Not enough,' she said simply, meeting his anxious expression.

'Don't leave me,' he begged. 'Tell me you'll stay. We'll work something out.'

Wanda stood up. 'I'm going to bed now.' She walked slowly away feeling nothing but despair.

*

Wanda felt weirdly doomed for the following few days. Glen turned up for afternoon milking every day and did the lion's share of the work. They

25

were civil to each other and actually worked well as a team but there was nothing warm about their relationship. One morning Graham turned up at the farmhouse unexpectedly.

'Dad! What are you doing here? Is it raining? You're wet.'

'Never mind that, you look terrible, love.'

'I've only just got up. I've had a migraine overnight but I'm okay now.' She was very aware she was underplaying what a bad night she'd had.

'Sit down and let me make you a cup of tea.' He led her gently to the kitchen table with his hands on her shoulders and lowered her into a chair. He said nothing as he put the kettle on. Wanda took a deep breath and held her head in her hands.

With the mug of tea in front of her, she said, 'You not having one?'

'Your mother has made me three cups today already. I'm like a leaky tap.'

Wanda smiled. He had a kind face, the sort that made you feel better just by looking at it.

'So, what's going on love?' He peered into her eyes as if the answer might be there. 'I know you get headaches when you're stressed.'

Wanda caught sight of the wall clock. 'Oh no, Dad, I'm supposed to be feeding the hens.'

'You're not going anywhere until you've drunk that.' He opened the back door and looked out onto the yard. 'Where's Lee these days?'

'Gone. We can't afford him. Glen's had to call the vet out again for two of the cows.'

'For goodness' sake.'

'He thinks they might need antibiotics which means we won't be able to milk them for a while.'

'Are you really that strapped for cash?'

Abi wandered in. She was wearing tartan pyjama bottoms and an old greying T-shirt. 'Granddad,' she said looking surprised to see him.

'Abi, have you only just got up?'

'Don't have a go. I had a late night.'

'All right for some.' Graham watched her pour cornflakes into a bowl followed by milk and make her way to the door.

'Where are you going?' Graham asked her.

'Upstairs,' she said clearly annoyed. 'What?' she asked turning to face him.

'Just sit here a minute will you lovey. Your mum's had one of her migraines.'

'Sorry to hear that Mum,' she said and sidled into a chair. 'I'm not feeling great myself.'

'Hangover, is it?' he asked.

'No! I'm devastated. I can't believe it's over between me and Gav.'

Graham raised his eyebrows. 'How about going to feed the hens? The fresh air would do you good and you'd be helping your mum.'

Her eyes widened; she looked quite confused. 'I'm not a farmer, Grandad. I'm an actor waiting for my big break.'

'Well, you're not going to be spotted as the next Keira Knightley sitting in your bedroom, are you?'

'Charming!' She looked to her mother for backing.

'He's right, my love.' Wanda lent over the table and stretched an arm out to try and reach her daughter. 'We need to have a conversation about when you are going back to London. It's either that or you help out on the farm.'

'But I've got nowhere to live in London. I've had to give up the flat. Gav won't pay the rent.'

'You could move in with your sister, just temporary,' Wanda suggested and met an outraged glare.

'I think that's a great idea.' Graham pursed his lips and looked slightly nervous.

'She won't want me!' She stood up now, holding on to her bowl of cornflakes. 'Anyway, it's a two-bedroom flat and I'm not sharing so I'll be on the bloody sofa, won't I?'

'A bit of hardship focuses the mind,' her granddad told her.

'You're unbelievable!'

'Why don't you just talk to Lily? See what she says?' her mum suggested.

'No!' She was halfway to the door.

'You'd better feed the hens then,' Graham raised his voice. She groaned and disappeared.

'That went well.' Wanda let out a giggle.

'Listen, I'll do the hens,' Graham said standing up.

'I tell you what, Dad, let's walk up there together. The fresh air will do me good.' She peered out of the window. 'It looks like it's stopped raining.'

As they approached Hungry Hill, they could see someone driving a tractor trailing a plough that was churning up the ground behind it. Wanda's heart sank.

'What's he doing?' Graham asked.

'Must be Colin from Bartlett's. He's turning over the soil so he can drill potatoes.'

'What here, on Hungry Hill? But this is for the hens.'

'Believe me, Dad, I was dead set against it. I can't believe that Delilah and Snowball and all the others are going to be confined to that barn day in day out.'

'I thought this field wasn't any good for crops? Hence the name, Hungry Hill.'

'Oh, don't worry about that Dad; the Taylors will load it with lots of expensive fertiliser to bring it up to scratch.'

'Seems crazy. I feel sorry for the hens.' He looked genuinely gutted. 'Surely there must be a better way.'

CHAPTER 4

The tranquillity of the dark night, with little moon for light, was broken at dawn with a gale force wind from the cold North that whooshed through the trees of Lucas Wood and sent ripples running across the pond. A fox lay dead in a sheltered resting place and a buzzard circled overhead. There was a smell of aniseed coming up from the ground elder and an uneasy feeling in the air.

The old oak tree, Quercus, to those who knew him, creaked with exhaustion. These strong winds were getting more common. They just had to stand and bear it. But there would be casualties: weaker branches ripped from trunks; possibly whole trees going over.

The fungi network below ground was frantic with activity, messages speedily streaming through plant tissue and up the roots of trees. Distress calls came from Hungry Hill where the soil had been hacked into, turned upside down, inside out, violating its bug population. Earthworms are thrown to the top, exposed to a vicious light and trampled on by a ten-tonne tractor. Nasty substances added by man sat heavily, awkwardly, leaving every living organism damaged if not dead.

Quercus, feeling weighed down by the chemical bombardment that has only come about in the last seventy years, wonders when this madness will stop and the miracle of nature will rule once more.

The trees of Lucas Wood all got on pretty well with just a few exceptions, the beech over towards Rachel's Covert being one of them which he referred to as *beneath*. It was a team effort to keep the canopy joined up so that they had their own ecosystem to keep them all safe from extremes of heat and cold. It also kept it nice and humid which meant that they had a better chance of reaching a grand old age. And looking their finest, of course.

Now Quercus was just a hundred years into his resting period. He liked to take life at a leisurely pace; after all he wasn't going anywhere. Not that he wasn't always shifting, balancing his weight and responding to his environment and the plant life around him. At about four hundred years old (he didn't count the repeating cycle of seasons too fastidiously these days) he had to admit he was middle-aged and he had history. He was acutely aware that he was already wiser than any man could imagine. And so, he could see that he needed to organise the sending of nourishment and messages of calm back up to Hungry Hill even though they were experiencing very threatening behaviour from man.

On the same morning Gilbert woke up at Wisteria Cottage with a start. It wasn't usual for him to be awake so early. Something was amiss. His cottage sat just a mile away from Lucas Wood on the edge of Capel Green.

The dawn chorus was fighting strong gusts of wind but he could still make out robin, then blackbird, song thrush, chiff chaff and willow warbler – all singing their hearts out as if their tweets were needed to soothe an unsettled land.

He sat up and swung his legs over the side of the bed wincing; his arthritis was bad today. It had been such a calm and warm evening; he'd slept in just his pyjamas and bed socks with the window wide open. But overnight the air must have turned cold and somehow it had got into his joints. He struggled to his feet and moved slowly across the room, dragging his right foot where he felt pain today. Reaching the window, he leant heavily on the frame with one weather-worn hand and slammed the window shut with the other. He sighed. Getting old was no fun.

The cows were livelier than usual this afternoon. Probably their hormones, Glen thought, knowing that many would be pregnant by now. The fact that Sampson, the bull they had hired from Woodstock Farm, was in the field with them doing his stuff was likely to be a factor too.

He sighed. It was hard holding everything together. Farming was all he knew; he'd taken to it from a very early age. It was different for Wanda and he did understand where she was coming from, but managing the lion's share of the work single-handedly was taking its toll on him. It was all such a worry. At least they had managed to drill a potato crop in on Hungry Hill. He'd had to fork out for more fertilisers to get the soil up to scratch but the turnaround time for a first crop was quite fast.

Yet whatever he was doing, the fact was the farm was losing money daily. When he looked to his father for help, he just didn't seem to hear what he was saying.

'I managed in my day,' Martin would say. 'Mind you, your mother was a great support to me. What you've got to remember is that the Taylor family have been farming this land for generations. Now it's up to you to take the baton and run with it.'

His sister Jane had it cushy being a doctor as far as Glen was concerned. Funnily enough she'd always shown more of an interest in the cows than his younger brother, Robert. When Martin had found out that Robert was gay, he'd closed down, saying nothing at first. It had taken him a long time to process this revelation. Glen had even overheard his parents at the time questioning how this could have come about. *Which side of the family was responsible?* Martin had asked.

'Oh, but we still love him just as much,' Fiona protested while Martin remained mute on the point most of the time and seemed to spend more time than ever out in the fields, avoiding the farmhouse. It wasn't long afterwards that the pressure on Glen to man up and commit to taking over from his father was deepened; it didn't even seem to be an option for him to turn his back on the farm.

Glen felt weary as he started the afternoon milking. He struggled to focus and couldn't remember what he'd done with which cow. He let out a long breath and decided to call Wanda. She'd hate it, especially after he'd promised her the afternoon off, but he needed her today.

'Love I'm struggling. Can you come over?'

'I'm waiting for the egg van. Shouldn't be too long.'

'Can't you call him and tell him you won't be at the hen shed; he knows where to go.'

'I'll try. If it's the usual driver, I suppose...'

'Please, just get here.'

'Are you all right Glen?' she sounded worried.

'Just knackered, you know.'

'We need to get Lee back.' *How many times had she said that!*

'If only. I'll crack on.'

The cows were mooing loudly, impatient to be milked. Glen went through the motions. He realised he'd forgotten to turn the music on but didn't care. It took all his concentration to get things right. The last thing he needed was an infected tank of milk and more money down the drain.

Wanda came quickly. She looked anxious. He told her where to start and she got on with it without complaining.

'Calm down Daisy,' she called out soothingly. Normally that would annoy him but today he was just so pleased to have her by his side.

Finally, they were all milked.

'I'll take them up to the field; you wash down, okay?' he said to her.

'You sure? I like the walk.'

'Not with Sampson in the field, no.'

'Okay then, mind how you go.'

It was a trickier operation with the bull in the field. Luckily Sampson was over the other side of the pasture. He had seen them but was waiting patiently. When the cows were all lined up filling the track, Glen opened the gate and they surged forward and onto the green grass and started to munch straightaway. With the last ones in he closed the gate and locked it. It was then he noticed that one of the girls was walking lame. She probably had a stone in her foot and would be in pain. It was rare with this particular breed, but he couldn't leave her like that. He let himself in and carefully made his way over to her. Luckily the bull was still some distance away.

'There, there, come on girl. We need to get you back to the shed.' He started to push her from behind but she wasn't having it. 'Come on, for goodness' sake.' He looked into her eyes. She was obviously in pain. 'There, there, I just want to help you.' She seemed to understand at last and slowly started making her way, limping as she went.

'That's good, good girl.'

They were nearly at the gate and Glen had just begun to feel relieved when the first blow to his ribs knocked him flat. He looked up and saw Sampson swinging his head for another aggressive blow and instinctively tried to protect himself. But not content with flooring him, the bull headbutted him over and over, knocking him around on the ground, kicking up dusty mud. Glen was winded, unable to get up. He cried out, 'Wanda' but it was feeble, pathetic. He thought, *Is this how it ends?*

Wanda had washed down the milking shed and headed back to the farmhouse. A text from egg man assured her that he had managed to collect the eggs as usual. But she was surprised that Glen was not back already. He had looked pretty terrible today, pale and almost shaky with exhaustion. One thing was for sure; they couldn't carry on like this. She decided to try his mobile. No answer. She grabbed a jacket but only got as far as the yard when she saw Gilbert hovering there, looking agitated.

'You haven't seen Glen, have you Gilbert, by any chance?'

He held still, a look of alarm about him. 'Oh, Wanda! Wanda Taylor! I have a bad feeling.'

'What do you mean, Gilbert?'

'Where is he? Where is he right now?' His head darted from side to side as he looked around the yard and up to the pasture land.

'I don't know. He went to take the cows back. He's not answering his mobile.'

Gilbert's eyes widened as if they might pop out of his lined face. He started up the track at quite a pace for old legs, his walking stick pounding the ground as he went. Wanda was astonished but followed him up through Low Meadow. It wasn't until they got to the cows that they saw Glen, lying there motionless in the field. Was that blood on his overalls?

'Oh my God! Oh no!' Wanda started to open the gate, struggling with the latch that she had opened thousands of times before. She called out, 'Glen! Glen! Oh darling, don't tell me...' The gate was released but Gilbert grabbed her arm and pulled her back. 'Don't Wanda. It's not safe.' He pushed the gate shut.

'But... but I can't just leave him there.'

'We need to call 999. Where is your mobile phone?'

Wanda shed desperate tears. She feebly handed her mobile to Gilbert.

'I don't know what to do with these things,' Gilbert said, handing it back to her. 'Here, you'll have to do it.'

She wiped her blurry eyes and tapped in the number., speaking as soon as the operator answered. 'We need help right now. Capel Farm. Please come – my husband has been badly hurt.'

'Tell them there's a Jersey bull in the field. Nasty, them Jerseys.'

'The bull, he's...' Wanda couldn't hold it together.

Gilbert grabbed the handset. 'We need armed police and air ambulance. Please be quick. Capel Farm on the Capel Road. We're up in Glenham. Just look for cows!'

'Just get here,' Wanda wailed. And Gilbert displayed a rare moment of affection and patted her back.

'Now, Woodstock Farm,' he said handing the mobile back and urging her to keep it together. 'You can do this.'

'Why've I got to call them?'

'Sampson is their bull. We need to inform them. He'll be shot by the end of the day.'

The rotor blades of the helicopter chopped through the air with a deafening noise as the craft landed on Rooked Meadow hurling the vegetation around and alarming the cows who ran as far as they could across Glenham towards the track and away from the commotion. Luckily, they stopped in the near corner and didn't try to scale the fence. The bull was going nowhere and strutted around letting out low angry growls. Gilbert and Wanda looked at each other.

'It will be all right, Wanda. Help is here. When it's safe I'll go over to the cows; see if I can't calm them down a bit.' Did he mean *after* they had shot the bull? It seemed so brutal.

Suddenly the place was a hive of activity. A fearsome team of armed police set about dealing with the bull without hesitation. Gilbert assured

Wanda that they would tranquilise the bull first, before they shot him. The paramedics worked quickly and efficiently. One intubated Glen while another attended to a leg wound. Wanda was now at his side. He stirred and opened his eyes. 'Oh Glen,' Wanda cried. She felt so helpless.

'We're going to anaesthetise you, Glen, okay?' The paramedic spoke loudly but without alarm. 'And then we'll put you in the air ambulance. We're taking you to hospital, okay?'

'Is he going to be all right?' Wanda asked even though it seemed like a stupid question.

'A lot of his ribs are broken, possibly his collarbone and he's got a serious leg injury. We need to get him to A&E,' the paramedic replied then looked up at Wanda and said, 'I think it's best if you follow behind in a police car.'

'It's all right; I'll drive myself,' she said confused.

'No, Mrs Taylor, you're in shock, you need to let this police officer take you.' He signalled to a woman in uniform who had a sympathetic smile.

The time at the hospital left Wanda weary and exhausted. At first, they had to simply wait in corridors on moulded plastic chairs. Martin and Fiona arrived very soon after Wanda had called them. He couldn't settle and fired questions at Wanda every now and then, needing to know every detail of the day. It felt like an attack to Wanda; a witch-hunt to apportion blame for the terrible accident. It was almost as though he thought that it should have been her who took the cows back to the pasture. She should have insisted because Glen was tired and struggling with the day. When her dad turned up and hugged her, she buckled under the strain and broke down in tears. Thankfully, Graham's presence was enough to silence Martin.

'I've told Abi and Lily what's happening; they both want you to call them,' Graham said to Wanda. 'Abi wanted to come in with me but I said it's going to be a lot of waiting around.'

'Of course.' She looked at her mobile screen. 'My battery is low.'

'Here, use my mobile.'

She walked away to make the calls. She couldn't tell them anything they did not already know; it was even hard to offer them the reassurance they desperately wanted. All she could say was that she didn't know what was happening yet.

When Wanda returned to the group Fiona was sobbing into a handkerchief. Eventually Martin sat next to his wife and said, 'We never should have got a Jersey. I nearly said to him, not a Jersey bull again. But he seemed so sure it was the right thing for the herd.'

'Don't blame yourself,' Fiona said arching her back and wincing.

'It should have been me,' Martin said gazing ahead of him at nothing in particular. 'I've had my time.'

It was then a doctor appeared. Finally, some news. But all he could say was that Glen was settled in intensive care and he was stable. They could go in and see him. Two at a time. That was at least something.

The first patient that Wanda noticed, as she wandered up the intensive care unit, was an elderly man who lay very still with luminous white skin as if he was about to fade away from this world. The other patients all seemed to be much older than Glen. They all lay deathly still as nurses attended to their every need through the machines and drip feeds they were connected to.

Fiona walked nervously beside her and finally there was Glen. Soft bleeps and the sound of the ventilator, providing the mechanics of breathing, were reassuring somehow. He was asleep and had tubes coming from both arms through cannulas as well as the tube going into his mouth. Wanda looked round for a nurse who appeared almost straightaway. She worked calmly checking screens, making adjustments here and there.

'What's happening? How is he?' Wanda asked.

'We're keeping a close eye on him. He has pain relief.'

Fiona looked horrified at the sight of her son lying there so still and lifeless. 'Will he wake up soon?'

'He's heavily sedated but you can talk to him. He'll be able to hear you.'

Wanda couldn't help doubting this but decided it was worth a try. She managed to find his free hand under the bedclothes and held it gently.

'Glen, darling, we're here for you. Me and your mum. You've had a nasty accident but you're going to get better. They are going to make you better. I know they are.'

'Yes, and we miss you desperately,' Fiona added. 'You are Capel Dairy Farm; we can't manage without you. You need to get better very soon and we'll get you home where you should be.'

Wanda looked her mother-in-law squarely in the eye. 'It's going to take time, Fi, you do realise that.'

'But how will we cope without him?'

'I don't know.'

Fiona started sobbing again. She said to Glen, 'I'll go now and let your dad come and see you.'

CHAPTER 5

It was nearly midnight when the taxi dropped Wanda off at the farmhouse. She decided to make herself a cup of tea; she did not feel hungry. There was a note from Abi telling Wanda to wake her when she got home. Wanda smiled; it was tempting but she would let her daughter sleep. She knew her mind was too busy to go to sleep right now, so she sat outside in the garden and the cool night air and sipped her drink. The sky was clear and she could see the moon and the stars. It was magical and calming after such a difficult day.

Finally, lying in bed, she willed herself to sleep. She had left the curtains open so that she could still see the stars. If only she could stop the endless anxious ruminations whirling through her mind. Would Glen live? Would he be permanently disabled? How would they manage? Would they have to sell the farm?

Her mobile phone was right next to the bed and plugged into its charger in case the hospital called. She checked the screen over and over. Perhaps she'd missed something. But no, there was no message, no call. No news was good news, wasn't it?

It was just beginning to get light when Abi drifted in and climbed in to bed with her mother. Wanda wrapped her arms around her and held her tight. They lay there still together for some time, she may even have dropped off briefly, then she heard her daughter's voice, feeble with sadness.

'Dad's going to be all right, isn't he?'

'I hope so, darling.' She felt Abi's warm tears on her chest, through her T-shirt. Abi clung to her and Wanda was so grateful that her daughter was with her at that moment.

The next thing she knew it was nearly nine o'clock. She leapt out of bed, checking her phone for messages. There were none. Abi was still asleep so Wanda grabbed some underwear, jeans and a sweatshirt and crept out of the room. She thought briefly about the cows but she knew she didn't have the physical strength to milk them right now. She would have to get some help.

She had just put the kettle on when her mobile rang. She answered it even though the screen read, unknown caller.

'Hello Mrs Taylor, I'm Mr Davies. I'm a cardiothoracic surgeon at the hospital.'

'How is Glen?' Wanda asked in a daze.

'He's stable at the moment. But we need you to come in. We need to talk to you about an operation we want to carry out today. You and any other members of the family you think should be present.'

'I'll come in. Shall I come in now? I'm just about to make a cup of tea but what does that matter? I can just come in now.'

'Mrs Taylor.'

'Wanda, please,' she interrupted him, hating the formality he was insisting on.

'Wanda, do you have anyone with you?'

'Yes, my daughter's upstairs but she's asleep.'

'Is there anyone you can call; anyone who could drive you to the hospital?'

'Don't be silly, I can drive myself.'

'Please don't come on your own. Wake your daughter up. Will you inform Glen's parents?'

'Do I have to?

'Yes, I think it would be better if they could come in as well. And any other family members who are available.'

'He's going to die, isn't he?' Tears burst from Wanda's eyes.

'He's in a critical situation. Let's talk about it when you get here.'

'Okay,' Wanda said feebly and gripped the worktop beside her, turning her knuckles to white, for fear of collapsing. The cows would have to wait.

The four of them gathered in the family room next to the intensive care unit.

'What's going on?' Martin demanded. Wanda had told him as much as she knew on the phone.

'We're waiting for Mr Davies.'

Abi had the expression of a bewildered child across her bare face. Fi went up to Wanda and glared at her, placing her hands on Wanda's shoulders and shaking them angrily. 'What's happening? Why was he in that field on his own?'

'Fi, please. It was an accident.'

Fiona broke down in tears. Wanda held her in her arms until her mother-in-law was reduced to a sniffle and she blew her nose on a tissue which looked already sodden.

Mr Davies appeared. He was calm, solemn and smartly dressed in a suit. Wanda knew from his demeanour that it was going to be bad news.

'Please,' he said signalling the seating in the room and they all perched hesitantly on the edge of chairs. Mr Davies took a tub chair and placed it in the centre of the uneasy semi-circle they had formed.

'Right now, Glen is in a critical condition as you know.' He lent forward with his hands pressing down on his thighs his expression earnest. 'He has breaks in most of his ribs, a broken collar bone and a serious gash to his left leg, but only bruising, nothing broken there.'

Wanda swallowed hard.

'So...' It was a long drawn out *so*, followed by a hesitation. 'So we are recommending that we operate to pin titanium plates to all his broken ribs which will,' he paused looking thoughtful, 'help us to speed up the healing process and reduce the pain. It should also decrease the risk of any further complications.'

'Sounds like the best thing to do,' Martin said as if it were case closed.

'But,' Mr Davies said very definitely. Of course, there was a *but*. Wanda took a deep breath. 'There are risks with this procedure.'

'What sort of risks?' Martin asked.

'This will be the second major trauma to Glen's body in two days. He may not survive the operation.'

Fiona gasped.

'What are the odds?' Martin demanded.

'It's difficult to say as these cases are so rare.'

'And if he doesn't have the operation?' Wanda asked.

'At the moment Glen is stable but he's on a ventilator and he may have to remain in that state for the rest of his life. If we don't operate.'

Fiona stood up and cried out, 'No! No! This isn't happening.'

Tears streamed gently down Wanda's face. The thought of him being on a ventilator for the rest of his life was unbearable. Unthinkable really. And Glen wouldn't want that. No one would.

She said to the surgeon, 'We have no choice, do we?' He pursed his lips as he looked at her but didn't reply. 'Will you be doing the operation?' she asked.

'I will be involved. We have a specialist in this area coming over from Papworth Hospital in Cambridge as we speak. We'd normally do the operation there but we dare not move your husband. Also, I don't wish to put pressure on you but time is of the essence.'

'You've already decided!' Fiona yelled hysterically. Martin took her arm and tried to calm her.

'We'll go ahead,' Wanda said taking command. 'I want to see him before you take him to the operating theatre.'

Fiona looked horrified. 'It's not your decision! We're his parents. We'll decide. We should ask Jane for a second opinion; she's a doctor you know,' she said wagging her index finger at Mr Davies. He didn't react.

'Fi, love,' Martin put an arm around his wife, 'this man is a cardiothoracic surgeon; he's an expert in this field. Jane is a GP.' Fiona burst into tears as if this meant that there was no hope left.

Wanda said nothing at first but then stood up, placing her handbag over her shoulder. Abi sat there staring into space with a look of disbelief.

'Come on Abi, let's go and see your dad.' She took her daughter's hand and they walked slowly back into the quiet careful environment of intensive care and up towards Glen's bed. Just before they got there she stopped and turned to look at Abi. Her poor daughter looked terrified.

Wanda said softly, 'Let's try and put on a brave front. I know it's hard but I would hate to think that he knew he might die during the operation. I'm sure that wouldn't help him.'

'Lily isn't here. She should be here. Shall I call her?'

'Oh darling, it would take her hours to get up here even if she did drop everything at work. Let's call her later, when we're home.'

'But Mum, this might be the last time we see Dad alive?'

Wanda hugged her daughter tightly. 'Let's try and be positive. They have a specialist coming from Papworth. He's got a fighting chance; I'm sure he has.'

They both looked across the room to Glen and walked over to his side.

He lay there pale and comatose, the ventilator still breathing for him. Wanda and Abi looked at each other.

'Are you sure he can hear us?' Abi asked.

'Absolutely, every word,' Wanda replied and turned to Glen taking hold of one hand. 'Glen, it's me and Abi is here. We want you to know how much we love you.'

'Yes, Dad, we really do. You must get better,' Abi chimed in.

'We're sure you will get better in time. We can't wait to have you back home again.' Wanda was fighting back the tears. 'We know you're strong and you're going to have the very best doctors looking after you.'

'We'll be here when you come back, Dad.'

Martin and Fiona appeared. Fiona was red in the face but calmer.

'We've signed the consent form,' Martin said with despair in his voice.

'Thank you,' Wanda said.

'We'd like a moment with our son,' Fiona said not unkindly.

'Of course.' Wanda gave Glen's hand one last squeeze and kissed his forehead. 'I'm going back to the farm to do the milking.'

'But you can't,' Fiona said, 'you can't leave him.' She looked horrified.

'The operation is going to take several hours and the cows haven't been milked today. Besides which I need to do something.'

'The cows will be a bit rowdy,' Martin warned, 'I should come with you.'

'You're going nowhere,' Fiona said sternly.

'I'll help Mum,' Abi said and Wanda hugged her daughter.

'Thank you.'

Graham was at the farm when Wanda got home.

'Dad, you're here.'

'Yes, when I got your text message I thought I'd better come and help you out.' He was pacing the kitchen like an expectant father. 'How long will the operation take, do they think?'

'Hours and hours. They don't know really. Martin and Fi have stayed there.'

'Gosh, that's a lot of that dreadful machine coffee and those bloody uncomfortable chairs.'

Abi laughed. 'Granddad, you can't say that.'

'Ooh I can. Now, are we going to milk the cows? They're making quite a racket.'

'Are you going to help Dad?' Wanda couldn't quite believe it.

'Oh, you won't need me then.' Abi headed for the door. 'I'll call Lily.'

'Hang on a minute missy; we're going to need all the help we can get.' Wanda said grabbing her daughter's hand.

'But what about Lily?' They could hear the cows from the farmhouse, rowdy and mooing, jostling for position at the gate.

'I'll phone her as soon as we've done the cows.'

In the milking shed the cows were all pushing to get to the front of the queue and boisterous with it. Big beasts that they were, they could be quite scary when they were unruly. They had carried their heavy udders for too long.

Wanda told her assistants not to worry; the cows would settle down when the milking started. She gave them a course of instruction, making it very clear that if they missed anything out, like disinfecting the teats, the whole batch of milk would be no good. Graham's memory was not as it had been and he kept forgetting what he was doing. Abi kept an eye on him.

'Granddad, don't forget the iodine cup.'

'We forgot to put the Abba soundtrack on,' Wanda remembered. It felt good to be doing something positive even though thoughts of Glen were never far away.

'They need calming down, not geeing up,' Graham suggested.

'Got any whale music?' Abi said. 'That might be better for us humans too.'

'You might have a good point there.' Wanda was so pleased her daughter was helping.

When the milking shed was washed down and all the cows were back and in their new pasture, munching away on the green grass of late spring, they all headed back to the kitchen and Graham put the kettle on.

'I'm shattered,' Abi cried slumping on a kitchen chair. 'But it wasn't too bad. I thought it was going to go on forever at one point but then the time went quickly.'

'It's a lot of work. Hard work,' Graham said. 'I don't know how you do it on your own?' He looked at his daughter.

'It completely does me in. Goodness knows how I'm going to manage now.'

'Love, you need help.' Graham put a mug of tea on the table in front of Wanda. 'How about getting Lee to do the morning shift?'

'Yeah, I think I'm going to have to. But how do I pay him?'

The phone call to Lily was difficult.

'But why didn't you tell me this morning? I can't believe it!'

'I'm sorry darling.' Wanda decided not to make excuses.

Lily's voice quietened. 'Actually, I was in a meeting with one of my clients but you could have texted me. So, he's actually being operated on now? Having these titanium plates put in him?'

'That's right.'

'Should I come home? It won't be easy; I'm buying winter fashion for the store at the moment and working to a deadline but... What do you think?'

'Up to you.'

'What time will he come out of theatre?'

'We don't know but it's a lengthy procedure.'

'Will you call me as soon as you know.'

'Of course I will.'

Wanda kept herself busy with farm work to try and take her mind off Glen but the fact that he was having life-saving surgery hung heavily over her. She tried to persuade Abi to come up to the hen barn with her but her daughter was intent on moping round the house.

It was a cloudy day, the sun barely breaking through, but it was mild and the hens seemed happy enough to leave the barn and toddle around pecking at the ground. She collected the day's eggs, tears leaking from her eyes as she imagined the worst outcome. The thought of him dying was unbearable. What would become of her? And the farm?

It was six o'clock in the evening when Wanda received the call.

'Martin, what's happening?'

'He's coming out of the operating theatre. He'll be back in intensive care soon. We can see him in about an hour. You'd better get back here.'

'Do we know anything about how the operation went?'

'They are saying it went well. He's still alive; that's the main thing.'

'That's amazing news.' Wanda burst into tears.

'Hopefully this Mr Davies will be able to tell us more when we see him.'

'Okay, we'll be right there.'

Late that evening, Wanda and Abi were side by side on the sofa, each with a bowl of oven chips.

'I've eaten nothing but junk for two days now,' Wanda declared.

'You're allowed to, at a time like this,' Abi said taking another chip.

'Yeah. Maybe I'll become a vegetarian tomorrow; they must have a healthy diet.'

'Vegan, Mum.'

'You can't be a dairy and egg farmer and be vegan; it just doesn't sit well.' Wanda laughed.

'You have a point.'

There was a relaxed silence as they both sat with their thoughts.

'I called Lily,' Abi said. 'She said she'll come up as soon as she can. She's got some big fashion show she's organising for the store.'

'That's okay,' Wanda said. 'I'm grateful that you're here to keep me company.'

'I'm pleased too.'

There was a thoughtful pause before Abi asked, 'Do you think Dad's going to be okay?'

Wanda took her time to answer. 'I hope and pray he is. He's too young to die.'

'That Mr Davies, the surgeon chap, did say the operation had gone well.'

'Yes.' Wanda's voice faltered.

'But?'

Wanda sighed. 'It's just he did keep emphasising that your dad is still critical and it will be a long road back.'

'Yeah.' There was another long pause before Abi added, 'but he has to be okay. I just can't bear to think he won't be. He's my dad.'

Wanda put an arm around her daughter and cuddled her. 'I have a strong feeling that he will pull through. But as for the farm..'

'You'll have to take over, Mum. I mean who else is going to do it?'

'Your Granddad?'

'What Granddad Martin? But he's retired.'

'I have a feeling that won't stop him.'

CHAPTER 6

Ben turned up the next morning as Wanda was eating a piece of toast and making some fresh coffee.

'Morning.' He gave her a wide-eyed look of concern and an awkward embrace. As he stood back, he said, 'Cavalry's arrived.'

'You're going to help me with the milking?' she asked thinking how wonderful that would be.

'Dad said he wasn't very good and Abi's not usually up at this time. I said I'd have a go. We're pretty damn busy but Saffy's holding the fort at Meadow Glamping.'

'I love you! I love you bruv! I was just thinking that I really can't face it alone today.'

'How's Glen doing?'

'He's a tiny bit better this morning, apparently. I spoke to the sister on the ward.'

'Good.' He looked at his watch. 'Should we get started? What time are they normally milked?'

'Forget that. In Wanda world they will be milked after my breakfast which today happens to be,' she looked at the wall clock, 'seven-thirty.' The cows would be agitated again with heavy uncomfortable udders but she was doing her best.

It didn't take long for the cows to fill the milking shed and for the first twenty-eight, fourteen each side of the pit, to get into place. Ben seemed to pick up the routine pretty quickly. The girls were noisy.

'Right, I'll go and fill the troughs with their treats; that should quieten them down.' Wanda went over to where they stored the pellets but the cupboard was bare. She went back to help Ben.

'No pellets. I'll have to order some. Glen's been off his game for a while. I should have noticed. Well, I did notice but... I should have done something.'

'It's not your fault,' Ben said.

Wanda focused on the job in hand; it was good to take her mind off everything else that was going on. The cows settled down after a while; Ben and Wanda worked well as a team. With all the cows milked, Ben insisted on cleaning down the shed before he left to get back to Meadow Glamping. Wanda walked the last cows up to their new pasture and made sure the gate was closed behind them. It was raining quite hard now but Wanda had a little bit of hope in her heart; Glen had survived the operation. She was sure that her brother's help would have been prompted by her father or possibly Saffy, but it was still good of him to come.

Thoughts of Glen lying there in intensive care were never far away. It was too awful and still hard to believe the events of recent days. Part of her felt guilty because, if she was being honest with herself, their relationship had been uneasy, fragile even before the accident. It was like their marriage was held together by the constant demands of the farm, leaving them no time to think about anything else. Glen had been weary with work and his usual bright eyes were looking pale. It had pulled at her heart to see him like that but, while he stubbornly refused to stand up to his father and find a better way, they were stuck in this nightmare place. And now the accident. Where on earth would they go from here?

When she got back to the farmhouse Martin was pacing up and down outside the back door. He came to an abrupt standstill when he saw Wanda. Her heart sank. Maybe the hospital had rung.

'Martin?' His expression was its usual mixture of anxious, slightly confused and offended. 'Any news?'

'He's the same. I've just got back from the hospital; Fi's stayed with him. She's taken it hard you know.'

'I spoke to the sister this morning and asked her to call me on my mobile if there is any change at all. I'll go in later to see him.'

Martin nodded before saying, 'There's something else.'

'Oh?' Wanda braced herself.

'I've been thinking about our insurance policy. I'm pretty sure we have personal accident cover for Glen.'

'That's a good point. I'll look out the policy.'

'Yes, if you would. Actually, I could come up to the office now, if you like?'

Wanda felt uneasy. 'It's all right; I'll look it up.'

'Don't delay, will you. I think you have to put a claim in right away.'

'Okay.' Wanda thought about all the other jobs she had to do and how making a claim might be quite involved. 'Actually, would you be able to handle it?'

'I'd be happy to. More than happy.' Martin followed Wanda inside.

'Coffee?' she asked. She was gasping and felt she had to offer him one. 'Please, go on up. It will be in the filing cabinet.'

'Yes, to coffee.' He disappeared up the stairs.

As Martin had not reappeared when the drinks were made, Wanda went up to the office. She put the two mugs on the desk.

'Oh thanks.' Martin was at the laptop looking at a spreadsheet.

'Not sure you will find it on there,' Wanda said. *What was he doing?*

'Sorry, yes, just having a quick look at the latest forecast figures.'

'Did you find the policy?'

'Er, no, not yet.'

Wanda went over to the filing cabinet. It didn't take her long to find the relevant file. She pulled out some papers. 'I think this is it.' She dropped the bundle onto the keyboard in front of Martin.

He looked up at her. 'Good, yes. I'll take that with me.' He picked up his mug of coffee to drink but carried on staring at the screen.

'So now you've got what you came for,' Wanda said with emphasis and he took the hint and turned the laptop off.

As he was leaving, he said, 'Wanda, about the milking. It really needs to be done at six.'

'Martin, I'm doing my best; you have to understand that. Things won't run exactly as they did but I'll muddle through somehow.'

'I see your brother helped out today. I hope he knew what he was doing. We don't want an infected batch of milk.'

'Of course, I showed him the ropes. We did it together.'

'So, is he going to be helping you every morning?'

'Er, that's a bit much to assume. He does have a glamping business to run.'

'Well, whatever, you really need to start at six at the latest.'

She didn't respond. He was looking at her, waiting for her compliance.

'The thing is it's going to affect milk production if you don't,' he added.

'I'll see what I can do,' she said avoiding his gaze and very pleased that he was leaving.

Lee was slow to answer her call.

'Hello Lee.' Wanda was relieved he had picked up.

'Heard about Glen. Nasty business. How's he doing?'

'Well, he survived the op that they said might kill him.'

'Bloody hell.'

'He's in intensive care.'

'He's a tough old boot. He'll pull through, you'll see.'

Wanda's eyes filled with tears. She grabbed a tissue. 'I hope so, Lee, I really do.' She blew her nose and composed herself. 'Anyway, the reason for my call, I was wondering if you could come back and help out? With the milking? What do you say?' She was practically praying. It went very quiet. She took a deep breath and then said, 'Lee? Are you still there?'

'Yes,' he said, in no hurry to give her an answer. 'Yes, I'm here.'

'Okay. Look, I know Glen let you go. Believe me, I was dead set against it.'

'Trouble is, can you afford to pay me?'

'Yes.' Wanda wanted to sound convincing even though she didn't know how she was going to find the money.

'You sure? What's changed?'

'Lee, I really need you. Please, I'm begging you.' It went quiet again. 'How about cash in hand after each shift?'

'Sounds good. You can do that, can you?'

'Totally. How about you start with the morning milking tomorrow?' She screwed up her face in hopeful anticipation.

'Okay, you're on.'

The next day Wanda drove round to Saffy's first thing.

'Wanda?' Saffy looked surprised to see her. 'It's not Glen, is it?'

'No, no, he's the same; I saw him yesterday. The hospital are saying it's a case of wait and see. Sorry to turn up like this and so early.'

'That's okay, I can spare half an hour. Cup of tea?'

'That would be lovely but...' She looked at her watch. It would probably be another hour before Lee finished the milking. 'Okay, yes, a quick cup.'

Saffy put the kettle on and looked at Wanda, raising her eyebrows in expectation. 'So?'

'I've had to take Lee on again. I really can't manage the farm without him.'

'Of course.' Saffy signalled to Wanda to sit down at the kitchen table.

'I need to ask a favour. I'm really sorry. I'm just so desperate. I'm not coping and...'

Saffy walked over to her and put an arm round her shoulders. 'Hey, it's all right. I understand. Now sit down for a few minutes while you can.' Wanda did as she was told.

'You're the only one. Well apart from my dear old dad.' Wanda sniffed.

'So, what's the favour?' Saffy was pouring boiling water from the kettle now, into a china pot.

'The thing is I had to beg Lee to come back and he kept going on about the money side of things so I said, and I know I shouldn't have, but I said I'd pay him cash in hand at the end of each shift.'

Saffy smiled. 'Oh dear,' she said almost laughing.

'It's not funny, but there is good news.'

Saffy sat down at the table. 'I'm all ears.'

'I've got that job at the gallery in town. Adrian called me yesterday. Three days a week from ten until four.'

'How's that going to work with Glen in hospital?'

'Oh Saffy, please don't ask difficult questions. You know I'm struggling. Martin turned up yesterday; he's going to see if we can make a claim on Glen's personal accident insurance. But in the meantime, I can pay Lee out of the money I earn at the gallery. That will mean that the milking is taken care of at least. And the money will go into my own bank account; the one I use for all my art sales.'

'Sounds like you've got it all sussed. Sorry, I know you're in an impossible situation.' Saffy got up again to pour the tea.

'I'll still be able to manage the hens.' Saffy looked at her, eyebrows raised. 'Okay, it won't be ideal when I'm at the gallery but...'

'Which days are you working?'

'Thursday, Friday and Saturday. I start on Friday.'

'So, tomorrow?' Saffy was thoughtful as she sipped her tea. 'How about I try and come over on those days to check on the hens.'

'That would be brilliant. But are you sure? What about Meadow Glamping?'

'Friday and Saturday tend to be busier days but I can always get Ben to pop over if I'm tied up.'

'Of course, weekends are your changeover days. I can't ask you.'

'Listen, we'll work something out. It's the least we can do.'

'Maybe Dad can do Fridays. He was a bit hopeless with the milking but the hens are a lot easier.'

'What about your mum; surely she wants to help?'

Wanda rolled her eyes. 'Wonder woman, Rita? Newly elected to the W.I. committee and bell ringer extraordinaire? The village of Ixworth would no doubt collapse into chaos without her, if you were to believe my mother.'

Saffy stifled a laugh.

'Anyway,' Wanda shuffled nervously in her seat, 'I was wondering, – I know it's a lot to ask – if you could lend me some cash so I can pay Lee today? It's only until I get paid by Adrian and he's promised to pay me weekly.'

Saffy looked uneasy. 'Okay, yes. Of course, I will. But I'm not sure how much I've got on me? I suppose there's the business float.' She went off to the office. Wanda crossed her fingers and found that she was holding her breath.

Saffy appeared again holding some ten pound notes.

'Thank you so much! I'll pay you back every penny.'

*

On Sunday Abi appeared in the kitchen at lunchtime. It looked like she'd washed her hair and she had a bit of make-up on.

'Are you going out?' Wanda asked her.

'I'm coming to the hospital with you this afternoon. Don't you remember?'

'Right. Maybe. My head's full of all sorts.'

'Lily's train gets in just before two so we'll need to go to the station first.'

'Lily's coming? But I thought...?'

'Yes, I know. But she did her fashion show yesterday so she's free today.'

'Great, is she staying overnight?'

'Yeah, course. I think she has to get an early train tomorrow, though.'

Wanda rolled her eyes. At least Lee would be doing the milking.

'Mum, Lily just wants to see Dad. He might be dying.'

'I thought we were being positive.'

'Well, yeah, but even so.'

'Perhaps you'll go back to London with her?' Wanda said without thinking. Since the day of Glen's operation, Abi had not lifted a finger on the farm. She said she was too busy with her job search.

'Mum! I've got nowhere to stay. We've had this conversation.'

'We have and we talked about you staying with Lily just while you find a job and can get your own place again.'

Abi was red-faced and sulking now. 'You just want to get rid of me,

58

don't you? I'm your failure of a daughter. Lily is doing so well and I'm just a hopeless waste of time.'

'I've never said that. I've always supported you both in whatever you want to do.'

'Well right now I just want to see Dad get better.' She burst into tears.

'So do I, Abi.' Wanda softened her tone. 'But in the meantime, I'm having to work all hours to keep the farm running.' Abi didn't respond so Wanda added as gently as she could, 'And I don't see you helping out.'

'I'm not a bloody farmer! How many times. Anyway, I'm applying for jobs online. I'll get something soon.'

Lily was talking into her mobile as she emerged from the station. It sounded like a work call. Wanda stood outside the car and waved at Lily as she walked over, acknowledging her mother but simply climbing into the back. No hug. Was she being oversensitive? Abi turned from the front passenger seat to smile at her sister.

'We might as well get going to the hospital,' she said to her mum and Wanda got back into the car

They only allowed two visitors at a time in the intensive care ward. Abi said she had a call to make to Channel 4 about a job so Wanda went in with Lily first. Before they reached Glen's bed Wanda turned to her younger daughter and reached up to put her hands on her shoulders.

'Listen.' Lily looked worried but Wanda continued. 'You need to know he's on a ventilator and he's sleeping most of the time.'

'Abi's told me.'

'Right, okay then.'

Wanda was relieved to find that it was Staff Nurse Annie on duty today. She had been kind to her.

'Hello Wanda, how are you?' Annie smiled at Wanda. 'Is this your other daughter?'

Lily was looking down at her father with an expression of sadness and confusion.

'Yes, this is Lily; she's up from London for the day.' Wanda turned to look at Glen. 'How is he today?' His skin still had a grey pallor and his eyes were shut.

'He's stable, he really is.' Wanda believed her because she really wanted to. 'We're keeping a close eye and all his vitals are good.'

'When will he be able to come off the breathing machine?' Lily asked.

'Soon, we hope.'

'Gosh, Mum, he looks dreadful.' Tears filled Lily's eyes.

'He's been through a lot.' Annie smiled at Lily. 'But you know, he's over the first hurdle and the signs are encouraging.'

Wanda put an arm around Lily and held her tight. Lily put her arm around her mum.

'Don't forget to talk to him; he can hear you.' Annie walked away.

That evening Lily cooked a chickpea curry insisting that the health benefits were amazing.

'Has it got lots of hot chilli in it?' Abi asked with a dubious look on her face as she poised her fork over the orange-looking dish.

'No, just some smoked paprika, garam masala and...' Lily thought for a moment, 'root ginger.'

Abi took a small tentative mouthful. She looked relieved. 'Not bad. So are you vegan now?'

'Not exactly. This has yoghurt in it actually.'

'Not cream?' Wanda asked surprised.

'No, not cream. I'm definitely eating more veggie though. Liam's a bit of an eco warrior and I suppose it's rubbing off on me.'

'Actually, it's really lovely, darling,' Wanda said and meant it.

'Thanks Mum,' Lily half smiled now.

'How's the job hunting going?' Wanda asked Abi.

Abi played around with her food, moving her fork around her bowl, before she said, 'There's quite a bit of work. Make-up only; Channel 4 would probably give me something if I was in London. But no auditions I like the look of.'

'Best to get some make-up work then,' Lily said and Wanda was secretly pleased.

'Yeah, I know, but the thing is, I've got nowhere to live.'

'Couldn't she come and live with you, Lily?' Wanda said bravely.

'Mm... Not sure, I mean we don't have a spare bedroom.'

'No, you see, it wouldn't work,' Abi was quick to chime in.

'Mind you we do have a sofa bed in the lounge. We got it for friends staying over.'

'There you are. Perfect.' Wanda felt triumphant. Abi looked annoyed.

'I don't fancy sleeping on a sofa bed for more than a couple of nights.' She screwed her face up in horror at the thought.

'It's quite comfy actually,' Lily said, though Wanda considered that Lily had probably never actually slept on it given that she had a perfectly good bed.

'But I'd be in the lounge. I'd have no privacy.'

'It would just be until you got a flat share organised.' Wanda tried to sound casual.

'I don't know.' Abi pulled a sulky face.

'The thing is,' Lily said, 'you need a job and you need somewhere to stay.'

'It wouldn't be for long.' Wanda was practically crossing her fingers.

'Stop ganging up on me!' Abi's face went red.

'We're just trying to help.' Wanda tried to squeeze Abi's hand but she was having none of it.

'I suppose if you're staying here for a while, you could help Mum out with the farm. With Dad in hospital there must be masses to do.' Lily placed her fork in her empty bowl.

'Look,' Abi was agitated now, 'just because I'm a farmer's daughter doesn't mean I want to be a farmer.'

'Well, have I got news for you,' Wanda said, 'I married a farmer thinking he would run the farm while I pursued my own career.' Her daughters looked at her nonplussed.

Lily was first to share her considered opinion. 'Perhaps you should have realised, Mum? I mean isn't it obvious; you were going to be living on a farm.'

'I was very young,' Wanda said in her defence. 'At the time Granny Rita made me feel like it was my only option. She never took my art seriously.'

'Don't blame Gran for your mistakes,' Abi said as if she'd got one over on her mother.

Wanda swallowed hard. 'That's harsh.' She stood up and started to clear the bowls away. 'The way I see it, Abi, is you have two options, stay at the farm and help out or go back to London.'

'That's not fair!' Abi screamed.

'Well, I'm sorry but you can't stay here scot-free long term.'

Tears sprang from Abi's eyes. 'This is my home! You are so horrible to me! All that rubbish earlier about always supporting what I want to do.'

'The trouble is, Abi, right now you don't want to do anything.'

'Huh!' She stormed off.

Wanda sat down and took a deep breath. Her heart was racing. Was she a bad mother? Lily appeared thoughtful. For a moment neither spoke then Lily said, 'I'll talk to her, persuade her to come back with me.'

'Thank you.'

CHAPTER 7

The American was very tall with broad shoulders and had dark curly hair. He wore fashionable thick-rimmed glasses as he peered at each piece of art in the gallery. Holding a notepad and pen, he occasionally jotted down his thoughts. He must be serious about buying. Wanda's mobile bleeped. Adrian was approaching her so she ignored it. He came right up to her and in a lowered voice said, 'Just popping out; I'll be about an hour. You're okay here I take it?' He raised his eyebrows and nodded in the direction of the American. She had only been working there for a week but she was sure she could handle it.

'Yes, fine thanks.' Her mobile buzzed again and she wished it hadn't. She smiled at Adrian and he left looking a little uncertain. As soon as he was gone, she checked the screen. Three messages from her dad and two from Saffy. She got halfway through the first message from Graham.

Nothing to worry about Wanda but some of the hens

The American was right in front of her. She smiled at him, inviting a question.

'Hi, me again.' There was no one else in the gallery. No chance of confusing him with another customer.

'How are you getting on?' she asked.

'I wonder, do you know this artist?' He moved over to one of the paintings and screwed his eyes up trying to read the signature in the bottom right-hand corner. 'Wanda, it looks like.'

She joined him next to the painting. 'Er, yes.' *Why was she embarrassed?* 'Yes, actually I am the artist for this painting. It's a watercolour.' Why was she stating the obvious? It was her *poppy seed heads* and now she looked at it with fresh eyes, knowing this important-looking man was interested in it, she decided it was one of her better efforts.

'Oh really! How fortuitous.' He looked down at her and then at the painting. She wished she'd worn high heels but they would have made her feet ache by lunchtime. Eventually he said, 'I like it. I guess you've worked that out.' He was laughing now.

Just then Wanda's mobile, which was still on the desk, started ringing. 'Oh, I'm sorry about that.' She willed it to stop.

'No, please, do answer it. Might be important.'

'If you really don't mind.'

'Not at all.'

The mobile stopped ringing as soon as Wanda got to it so she opened up her messages again.

... have escaped and I'm looking for them. But most I'm sure are safely in the barn. Hope the arty job is going well. Dad x

I've found a white one and I can see a brown one, not too far away

The egg man has turned up and I can't find the trays. There seem to be quite a few eggs though

Wanda decided not to read any more. She went back to the American. He was looking at another painting. *Damn.*

'Everything okay?' he asked jovially.

'Oh fine.' Wanda forced a smile. She looked at the painting which was of Lake Como and rather clichéd and stylised in Wanda's opinion but then she remembered she was being paid to sell all the pieces in the gallery, not just her own. 'Do you like this one?' she asked with little enthusiasm.

'It's not really my thing,' he looked apologetic, 'but I just know back home this will sell. Us New Yorkers just love the Italian lakes, you know.'

'Well, they are stunning,' Wanda matched his ludicrous grin as she remembered all the times she had tried to persuade Glen to go on holiday somewhere a bit further than Cornwall and failed.

'Yes, I think I'll take this. That's a fair price.'

'Excellent. Would you like to complete the transaction now or would you like me to take some details and mark it sold with a little red dot?'

'Oh, the latter. I'll come by tomorrow to collect, if that works for you?'

'Absolutely.'

'And I'll take the poppy seed heads too. That will be for my personal collection.'

'Well, I'm honoured.' She wanted to dance with glee.

'It's so great to meet you. My name's Aaron by the way.'

'Right.' Wanda wasn't sure how to respond to that.

'I don't suppose you fancy a drink later; I'm staying at The Angel Hotel just opposite here.' *Casanova alert.*

'Oh, that would be lovely but I really can't. I have places to be.' She envisaged herself chasing around the farm trying to catch hens.

'Of course.' He didn't seem too gutted. Perhaps he had several other options.

By four o'clock Wanda was desperate to get away. The gallery was empty but Adrian had suddenly become very chatty. He was obviously pleased that she had sold two paintings.

'I've got a new artist's work coming in next week. Interesting. Abstract.'

'Great.'

'I don't suppose the farm can spare you another day a week? I'm thinking Wednesday.'

'I'm really sorry but with Glen in hospital we're quite stretched.'

'Yes, of course.'

'In fact, it's actually time for me to go so...' She was looking up at the clock and had her handbag over her shoulder.

'Oh, gosh, yes, look at the time.' Adrian seemed preoccupied.

'Yes, so I'll see you tomorrow.' Wanda was at the door now.

'Yes, if you must go. Good day's work today, Wanda.'

As she walked to her car in the long stay car park, she couldn't decide what she should do first. The hospital was only five minutes away and so it made sense to visit Glen first, and then drive home to the chaos her father seemed to have created. But the hens never flew very far. Maybe some of the younger ones might get a bit adventurous. Hopefully they wouldn't lose any. The most recent text message from Saffy had said she was helping Graham and not to worry. Damn it, she would go to the hospital first.

She calmed herself, taking a deep breath, before entering the ICU; this was never easy. Ever since her first visit she had made a point of not looking at the other patients as she made her way over to Glen's bed; it was too distressing.

To her surprise, he was sat up in bed, propped up with lots of pillows. His eyes were more alive than they had been for a long time. There was something different. He was no longer on the ventilator, freeing his mouth from that tube. He managed a brief smile as Wanda leant over him to place a gentle kiss on his forehead.

'Hello,' she said as gently as she could, stroking his brow. 'This is a surprise.'

He was peering at her but said nothing. Had he forgotten how to talk?

'How are you feeling?' she asked him.

He coughed as if trying to clear his throat. 'They're still pumping me with painkillers.' His voice was scratchy.

'Does your throat hurt?'

'It's the pipe I've had down there.'

Wanda felt full of love for him. 'Things will get better now, I'm sure. It's so nice to be able to talk to you.' She smiled into his eyes.

'How's the farm? Is Abi still there?'

'She's still with us. Lily tried to persuade her to go back to London with her but she won't budge.'

'Will she help out?'

'No, not really. She's been a bit of a nightmare to be honest.'

'So, the farm? Are you managing to keep things ticking over?'

Wanda hesitated. 'Yes, more or less.' Seeing his concerned expression she added, 'Nothing to worry about anyway.'

'Have your mum and dad been in to see you recently?' she asked.

'Yes, I hear Lee's back,' Glen said raising his eyebrows.

'Well yes, he is.'

'How are you paying him?' he asked. She was not ready to tell him about her job at the gallery.

'Your dad's putting in a claim on the insurance. He seems hopeful that they are going to start paying out soon. Enough to cover your loss of earnings. So we can use that money to cover Lee's shifts.'

'Yes, Dad did mention it. It had crossed my mind too. So, if they pay up will you hire someone to manage the farm?'

'I'm not sure about that. We'll just have to see how things pan out.'

'What? If I actually make it out of here? If I'm unable to run the farm any more?' He sounded bitter.

'Listen,' she pleaded, 'you need to stay positive and concentrate on getting better.'

'What else am I going to do, just lying here?'

'Can you listen to music? Radio?' she asked hopefully.

'*Farming Today*,' he said and smiled properly this time.

'Well, not necessarily that.' It occurred to her that farming really was his whole life. It wasn't like he played golf occasionally or liked the cinema, theatre, a comedy club even. There was nothing but farming. He had only had a passing interest in their daughters as they grew up and that was mainly wondering if either of them would take up the farming mantle. Succession was a subject that reared its difficult head from time to time. First of all, they didn't have a son and then they had two disinterested girls. Comments were often made along the lines of, if Abi and Lily took after their mum, there was no chance of them eventually running the farm. It was just yet another failing of Wanda's.

So, what was Glen to think about all day long, lying in bed unable to move too much?

'Would you like me to see if I can get some headphones for you so you can listen on your mobile? I could download some podcasts.'

He took his time but then ignored her question and asked, 'Are all the rest of the cows pregnant yet?'

As she drove out of town the streets quickly turned into countryside. It was a beautiful early June day and the sun was shining in a big blue Suffolk sky over the gently undulating fields. She took calming deep breaths to quell her anxious mind. But she couldn't help feeling guilty about being absent from the farm at all. Her father was obviously not up to it. It was just so sweet the way he really wanted to help her out. She drove round to the courtyard at the back of the house and found two Goldlines pecking away to their heart's content. At least they were safe. She rang her dad.

'What's happening?' she braced herself.

'Ah, Wanda, yes, well, it's been a bit of a day. I'm back home now; we did what we could and locked up the barn.'

'Okay, so tell me, Dad, how many hens are in there?'

'Ah, well, quite a few. I would say most of them. I haven't actually counted them.'

'There should be two hundred.'

'Gosh, I'd never be able to count two hundred. They keep moving about.'

'Oh Dad, what are we going to do? I've got two of the hens here. Goodness knows how I'll get them back up there.'

'What about the carrier we used to use for our cat; we've still got it. Not sure why. I'll bring it over.'

'That's not a bad idea.' As she said it, she realised that there was a car she didn't recognise in the courtyard.

'Dad, do you know anything about a small blue car?'

'No. Nothing.'

'That's weird. Right, well, I'd better go in.'

'Yes, be careful, love. I'll be over shortly with the carrier.'

Wanda went through the back door and into the kitchen only to be faced with Gavin in just a pair of underpants taking two bottles of beer from the fridge. When he saw her, he put the bottles down and placed his hands over his private parts even though they were the only bit of him covered in fabric.

'Ooh, sorry Wanda. We didn't know you'd be back this early.'

'What are you doing here?' Wanda couldn't help being amused but at the same time this seemed like an unnecessary intrusion in her life.

'We've er, well, Abi and I have got back together.'

'I see; consummated the reunion too, have you?'

'What?' He looked confused.

'Never mind. I don't suppose you've been involved in finding hens?'

'Hens? No, nothing to do with us.'

'Well perhaps you should put some clothes on.'

'Er, yes.' He looked uncertain but scurried off.

Wanda called Saffy. 'Please tell me something I want to hear.'

'Oh Wanda, I think we got them all back, maybe with a few exceptions.'

'Yes, well there's two right here in the courtyard.'

'Oh good. Hopefully that's the lot.' There was a pause before Saffy added, 'I hate to say this but I think it's all a bit much for your dad.'

'I'm getting that message loud and clear. Did the egg man get anything?'

'No, Graham told him he'll have to have today's eggs tomorrow.'

'Oh no! They won't be as fresh tomorrow. I'll try and call him. See if I can't get him back.'

'I'd come over but I've got glampers turning up in about ten minutes.'

'No, don't be silly, you've done enough. And thank you so much for helping out. Did you get the cash I brought over the other day? I left it with Ben.'

'Oh, yes, thank you. I wasn't expecting you to pay me back so soon.'

'I went to the cash point actually. Got some out of my own account.'

'That was kind. Did you get to the hospital today?'

'Yes, and good news, he's off the ventilator. We could actually talk to each other.'

'Oh, Wanda, I'm so pleased. Things are looking up.'

'Well, yes. Except that Abi's errant boyfriend has just turned up.'

'What Gavin?'

'Yes, it's all back on apparently. I've just had a conversation with him in the kitchen; he was practically naked.'

'Lucky you.' Saffy giggled.

'What has my life become?'

'Interesting. Challenging,' Saffy offered.

'Crazy more like!'

Saturday was very quiet in the gallery. Adrian seemed uneasy.

'I think we need to do more posting on social media. I mean it is Saturday. Where is everyone?'

Wanda looked out of the window; it was pouring with rain.

'It might brighten up later,' Wanda said uncertainly shuffling a few papers on the desk she was sitting behind. She'd given up with weather apps; they were nearly always wrong. Especially when she was farming.

Just then Martin burst through the door. Adrian looked pleased until he had a good look at him. Although her father-in-law was still agile, he was pretty weathered by years of the outdoor life. Farming seemed to age you. Yet another reason to avoid it. Martin made a beeline for Wanda, confirming that he wasn't there to browse the art.

'Wanda.' He kept his voice lowered at least, but his tone was agitated. 'Wanda, what are you doing here?'

Adrian cleared his throat loudly and raised his eyebrows. He positioned himself in front of the desk and looked Martin straight in the eye. 'I'm sure you are aware this is a gallery, so unless you are interested in looking at our current collection?'

'Excuse me,' Martin raised his voice now, thank goodness there were no customers, 'but this is my daughter-in-law and she is supposed to be running Capel Farm right now.'

'Wrong!' Adrian pronounced, very sure of himself. 'Wanda is working for me until four o'clock.' He sounded condescending at the best of times.

'Listen, you don't know the half of it. My son is in intensive care. Who's going to see to the hens and the veg, not to mention the forage and muck spreading?'

Adrian looked horrified. 'I am aware of the situation, actually.'

'I know all about the hens escaping and wreaking havoc on Hungry Hill.' Martin was trying to look past Adrian and at Wanda. 'That potato crop has only just been drilled a couple of weeks ago!'

Wanda felt her cheeks flush. She had thought she'd got away with that one. Just then the American walked in. Could things get any worse? Wanda got up from her chair and went to greet him.

'Hi Aaron. Your paintings are all wrapped up.'

'Well thank you, Wanda, that's just great.'

Martin turned to Wanda. 'Listen I've just about had enough of all this nonsense. I'm taking you back to the farm.'

Aaron's eyes nearly popped out of his head.

'I'm terribly sorry,' Wanda said to Aaron, acutely embarrassed. 'Don't worry I haven't been sold to the slave trade; this is, in fact, my father in-law.'

'I don't care who he is,' Aaron said outraged. 'Listen sir, you shouldn't talk to Wanda like that. She's a fine artist; not a farmer!'

'I see! I see what's going on here. You two are up to no good.' Martin turned red in the face and squared up to Aaron. 'Shame on you, Wanda, when your husband is fighting for his life in hospital.'

'There is nothing going on!' Wanda said emphatically. 'Aaron is buying two works of art. He's here to collect them.'

'Yes, and one of them, Wanda's *poppy seed heads*, is for my own personal collection,' Aaron added unhelpfully.

Martin looked like he was about to explode and sneered at the American.

'I'm going to have to ask you to leave.' Adrian stepped forward and actually took Martin's arm trying to manoeuvre him to the door. Martin was having none of it and threw him off.

'Don't you dare!'

'I'm sorry Mr Taylor but this is my gallery and I would like you to leave now.'

Martin stared at Wanda in disbelief. 'Wanda, say something!' he demanded.

'I think you'd better go,' she said without raising her voice. Her father-in-law looked bewildered and hesitated but then left, slamming the door behind him.

'I'm terribly sorry about that,' Wanda said to Aaron.

'Not at all. What a dreadful man.'

Adrian was quiet after the commotion caused by Martin. Wanda said sorry too many times and then felt silly.

'It's not your fault, Wanda, but I simply cannot afford disturbances like that again. I mean what must Aaron have thought?'

'He still bought the paintings,' Wanda said hoping this might make up for the awkward incident.

'It's repeat business we need. The gallery relies on that.'

Wanda considered that Aaron lived in New York. How much time would he actually spend in this little Suffolk town?

She felt flat as she left at four o'clock. It had clouded over and was spitting with warm rain. She started down Angel Hill towards the car park, wishing she had her waterproof jacket on, when suddenly Aaron appeared in front of her.

'Oh!'

A large colourful umbrella shot up and over her. He held it so it sheltered her but hardly himself, rather awkwardly given the height difference between them.

'What's this? You are my knight in shining armour, are you?' She saw his face light up with a smile and regretted her words immediately.

'I figure you need rescuing with a father-in-law like that terrible man.'

'Martin has his reasons. And the fact is I am married to a farmer. It sealed my fate.' The rain was coming down harder now; the umbrella was actually very welcome.

'No! That's not fair. Listen before we get very wet, how about a drink at The Angel Hotel? Look, it's right there.' He waved his hand at the imposing Georgian façade which was covered in bright green foliage with pops of purple-pink flowers at every window and above the grand pillared entrance. Wanda was conflicted and didn't know how to respond. Perhaps she could justify it on the basis that repeat business from this client would make Adrian very happy. It was practically part of her job.

'Well, just a quick drink then.'

'Excellent.'

Inside the hotel, in the lounge, it was all rather lovely with art-deco style furnishings and a very relaxed ambience. Halfway through her first cup of tea Wanda was warming to this American man. He was actually quite sweet and seemed pretty straightforward. Perhaps he just got a bit lonely on these art dealership trips.

'So do you have family back in New York?' *Would he talk about a wife?*

'Er, yeah. Well, sort of. I have an ex-wife and two sons, both grown up and living in Washington now.' He looked thoughtful.

'Sorry, painful divorce, was it?'

'No, no, no. Well, yes, but it was a few years back now. And with all the travelling I do, it's actually easier being single. Less nagging to be home the whole time.'

'Sounds wonderful,' Wanda said.

'So, you live on a farm?' He had an expression of incredulity.

'Afraid so.'

'And your husband, he's...?'

'Usually running the place but currently in intensive care in the hospital in town here. In fact, I'm going there next.'

'Oh, yes, I do recall your father-in-law mentioning something. I'm sorry to hear that. Is he going to be all right?'

Wanda swallowed hard. 'I'm hoping so.' She sighed and there was an awkward pause which for some strange reason she filled with, 'Is there any other work at the gallery that you might be interested in?'

He looked confused at the sudden change of subject but shook himself. 'Actually, I was going to ask you if I could commission another painting by your good self.'

'Gosh, yes! I'd love that.' Her mind whirred. *How would Adrian react if he knew. Perhaps he didn't need to know.*

'Do you have any work in your studio I could look at?'

Wanda thought about her glorified shed and grinned.

'What's funny?'

'Nothing. Actually no, I don't. I would have to paint. I don't really have the time at the moment. When are you going back to America?'

'Well actually I might be able to help you there because I'm doing a trip up north to Manchester, so I could call back here on my way home.'

'Are you sure?'

'Very sure. I actually love this quaint little place.' He sat back in his chair.

'I just don't know.' She knew she was sounding flaky. How could she commit with the farm to run? But it was so tempting. And she would make some money.

'Okay, I'll do it then. What had you in mind?'

*

Three days later Gavin was still at the farmhouse. He and Abi were behaving like a couple of lovesick teenagers. Apparently, Gavin had taken a week's leave so he could be with Abi. This meant that her daughter had the perfect excuse to not engage in any farm work; not that she had any intention of doing so anyway. Her attitude and behaviour were beginning to grate on Wanda's nerves.

That evening Wanda had helped Lee with the milking and got back to the farmhouse to find them canoodling in the kitchen whilst apparently cooking a fried breakfast. Every surface was covered with open packets of food, a milk bottle, discarded egg shells, dirty dishes and cutlery, a bag of unopened shopping, even some laundry which looked like it hadn't made it to the washing machine yet. They had the decency to look a little embarrassed when Wanda walked in.

'What the hell's going on?' She couldn't take any more of their selfishness.

'All right, Mum, keep your hair on.' Abi looked as if she was ashamed of her mother's presence. Gavin started serving up fried eggs, overdone bacon and black-looking mushrooms from a pan on to two plates that were already on the kitchen table probably because there was no other space.

'How dare you! You treat this place like a bloody holiday camp while I'm working all hours. I've had enough! It ends here!'

Abi was red-faced. Gavin stopped what he was doing and looked uncertain.

'Mum, you need to calm down. Let's just... Let us just eat this food

77

and—' She was a determined madam.

'No! No more!' Wanda was shaking with anger.

'Mum, why don't you go and have a shower?'

'Yes, yes! That's what I'm going to do. I'll go and have a shower and when I get back this kitchen will be spotless! Do you hear!'

'Mum, we'll clear up, of course we will, but it's going to take time and we're going out this evening.'

'Forget it! You're clearing up this place and then we're going to have a sensible discussion about whether you leave here tomorrow or start paying rent.'

Abi looked shocked; Gavin nervous. Wanda went off for her shower having to tell herself that she had done the right thing. By the time she came back downstairs there was no sign of the errant couple. The kitchen had been tidied in a hurry with grease marks still smearing the worktops. It was a lovely sunny evening; she would walk up to the hens in the hope of leaving her troubles behind.

Her heart sank when she saw the white feathers of a Light Sussex strewn across Hungry Hill. As she got nearer to the carnage it felt like she was being stabbed. The poor hen was no more, not even a discarded body remaining. The fox must have taken it away. Of course, it wasn't the first time it had happened but still tears streamed from her eyes. Please God, don't let it be Snowball. It must be one of the hens that had escaped on her dad's watch and wasn't rounded up but she couldn't blame him.

Wanda was eager to get into the barn now but she found herself staring at what appeared to be a brand new padlock on the doors. That was strange. Perhaps Lee had done it. But why? She tried her usual key but it didn't fit. She could hear the hens inside clucking away and she could make out through the cracks that the artificial lights were on even though it was still broad daylight. Why couldn't she get in? She phoned Lee. He was just as baffled at first.

'Thinking about it, Martin did appear this morning when I was milking. He asked me if I was being paid. And I said, of course, cash in hand, like we agreed. He seemed pretty crazy at that point; something about you had no right to hire me.'

Wanda closed her eyes and sighed.

'Right. Probably him responsible for the lock then.' Wanda felt defeated. How was she going to carry on with Martin lording it over her all the time?

'I know a good locksmith if you want me to call him. Chap named Arthur. He's quite reasonable.'

Wanda took a deep breath. 'Thanks Lee. I'll have a think about it.'

'Yeah, course. Will I see you in the morning?'

'Yes, the morning.' She tried to sound upbeat but was really unsure if she could carry on like this.

'Thanks Wanda. I do like working at Capel Farm. Your cows don't cause no trouble.'

'That's good to know,' Wanda said gulping back a tear.

As she walked back to the farmhouse, she felt overwhelmed by everything life was throwing at her. Glen was still in a critical condition. What would happen if he died? What would become of the farm? There was so much she wanted to say to him but it was hard when he was lying there, so helpless, in hospital; their lives seemed to be such a mess; where to start? She was even unsure how long their relationship could last with Martin a constant dark shadow hanging over them.

Glen would pull through. They said he was making good progress. She had to believe her. But it would be weeks, months even, before he would be able to return to work. Wanda felt emotionally and physically drained. She couldn't carry on. Something had to give.

CHAPTER 8

Carolyn placed two drinks in tall tumblers on the low-level table in the lounge of The Angel Hotel.

'Looks like a lot of fuss for a tonic water,' Wanda said looking at her drink embellished with lime and something leafy.

'Cheers,' Carolyn said with a mischievous glint in her eye.

Wanda knew immediately. 'This has gin in it! I told you I'm driving.' Even so she giggled.

'Well, just look at you. You need cheering up. You can crash at my place tonight. I'm in the Medieval quarter, just a five-minute walk up from here.'

'You know that is so tempting. But what about...?'

'It's Friday; can't you let your hair down on a Friday evening?'

'But I'm working at the gallery tomorrow.'

'All the more reason to stay at mine. Just relax,' Carolyn interrupted her.

'You always were a rebel. Remember that assignment at the London Met when we had to produce a piece in acrylic and you flatly refused and chose oil instead.'

'Gosh, yes, and the silly thing was that Mr Jacobs, far from marking me down, gave me an A!'

'He fancied you! Must have!'

They laughed together and Wanda felt herself relax. This was fun.

'So, Wanda, tell me all; it must be twenty odd years since I saw you. Wasn't it fortuitous coming across each other on Facebook?'

'Where to start.'

It was past eleven o'clock when they staggered up Abbeygate to Carolyn's place. It was a Georgian terrace on Whiting Street painted Suffolk pink and looked very small from the front but was cosy and beautifully decorated inside.

'So, what have you got here, one bedroom?' Despite the fact that they had ended up eating in the hotel restaurant, Wanda was definitely tipsy and so driving home wasn't an option.

'Two, actually. The previous owners went up into the attic, so I've got a master suite up there.'

The kitchen was tiny but had large glass windows on to a pretty courtyard garden. 'This is perfect for one person,' Wanda said. Right now, the thought of escaping the farm for a bijou place of her own was bliss.

'Or two,' Carolyn replied playfully.

*

The following morning Wanda overslept; Carolyn's guest bedroom proved to be very comfortable. The first thing she did when she woke was to look at her mobile screen. One thing was for sure, there wasn't enough time for her to dash back to the farm and pay Lee for the morning milking before her shift at the gallery. As she sat up she realised her head felt tight; one too many drinks last night. Carolyn appeared with a cup of tea.

'Tea in bed. That's a first for me.' Wanda sat up, still wearing her T-shirt from the previous day, and smiled at her friend.

'Thought you might need a gentle introduction to the day.' Carolyn placed the mug on a bedside table.

'Lovely, but I'm going to be in so much trouble.'

Carolyn sat on the side of the bed. She looked thoughtful. 'You know, from what you told me last night, you just can't win with those Taylors. It's appalling the way they treat you.'

Wanda did not respond; what choice did she have?

'And changing the lock on the hen house; it's like they are shutting you out.'

'I know.'

'What would happen if you just upped and left?'

Wanda laughed nervously now. 'Goodness knows. Martin would do his nut. He's already mad with me.'

'So, you're going to carry on slaving away for them for no reward?'

'When you put it like that.' Wanda yawned and stretched her arms; she definitely had a headache. That second glass of wine last night was a very bad idea; she wasn't used to drinking so much. 'Trouble is, where would I go?'

'Here,' Carolyn said as if it would be so easy.

'Oh, but I couldn't. I mean I just... no! That would be...'

'Good fun? Close to the gallery where you work? Close to the hospital where Glen is?'

'My God, you're right! I would be, wouldn't I? I'd be able to call in and see Glen every day. It would be amazing but...'

'But?' Carolyn was wide-eyed, eyebrows raised. 'At least think about it. Now,' she got up from the bed, 'Drink your tea; I'm going to find you a blouse to wear to work today. What would you like for breakfast?'

As Wanda walked down Abbeygate in a rather lovely peachy floral blouse, she called her dad's mobile but her mother picked up.

'Wanda, it's me. Your dad has gone out and left his mobile. Honestly, he's so forgetful these days.'

'Right, er well, I need a favour.' She prayed for a positive reaction. 'I need someone to pay Lee for me. He'll be at the farm now.'

'So where are *you*?' Her mother was clearly outraged.

'I'm just about to get to the gallery in town for work.'

'Honestly, Wanda, what are you playing at?'

'I've just had a good night out with an old uni friend and I stayed over. She lives in town.'

'All right for some.'

'For goodness' sake, Mum, give me a break.'

'I'll remind you that your husband is in hospital while you're off galivanting.'

'Yes, Mum, but will you pay Lee for me? Please. I'll pay you back straightaway.'

'I've got a W.I. committee meeting. I can't just drop everything. Can't Lee get his money tomorrow?'

'He may well have to. After all, what's more important than the Ixworth village W.I.?'

'There's no need to belittle what I do, Wanda.' Rita sounded genuinely offended which disarmed Wanda momentarily.

'Sorry Mum, but believe it or not I'm going through a difficult time and a bit of support would be nice.'

'I'll ring Fi and ask her if she can pop over. She's nearer than us.'

Wanda could see the fumes coming out of her mother-in-law's ears at the prospect. She stifled a giggle. 'You do that Mum. And thanks.'

The gallery kept Wanda busy that day and she ended up leaving a little later than usual. She had to explain to Adrian that she needed to get over to the hospital to see Glen before she could go back home. So it was just coming up to seven-thirty in the evening when she walked into her kitchen. She was starving but there sat at her table were Martin and Fiona. It was as if the farmhouse didn't actually belong to her and Glen, but they were just allowed to live there, having to put up with any intrusive visits the Taylors cared to make.

'I didn't realise you still have a key.' She knew there was an edge to her voice.

Fiona looked a little embarrassed. 'Well, we do, actually. Only for emergencies. But it was Abi who let us in.'

'Is that girl really still here? I don't believe it.'

'I think she's going back to London soon. Something about a job she's got and moving into Gavin's new place.'

'Good. So, to what do I owe this pleasure?' Wanda asked wondering what they were going to hit her with.

'Wanda, we feel we need to talk properly. I mean round the table.' Fiona gestured to an empty seat opposite her. Martin was staring at her. Wanda stayed standing.

'Why are you so late?' Martin asked as if he had a right to know.

'I've been to see Glen,' she said simply.

'I saw him this morning,' his mother said as if trying to point score.

'Now Wanda, we need to have a serious discussion about the farm. I'm not happy about the way things are being run.' Martin had a self-righteous expression.

'You've never been happy with the way I do things, let's face it.' Wanda met his stare.

'The chap I'm dealing with,' Martin said, ignoring what she had just said, 'at the insurance company, Alan, he says we need evidence of the income Glen took from the business and then they will start paying out.'

'Right, well that's good news.' Wanda decided she would sit down after all; she was feeling quite weak after a long day.

'I've had a look, but can't find any paper bank statements in the office showing the income he takes.'

'What, you've been rooting around in the office looking for our personal bank statements?' Wanda was shocked at the level of intrusion this man was willing to go to.

'But you agreed that Martin would manage the claim,' Fiona butted in.

'I didn't agree to you coming in to my private space while I am out, searching for our bank statements.'

'I think you're being a bit ridiculous,' Martin said. 'There is another way of doing it. You could call the accountant, Richard, and get him to sort it. I tried but he wouldn't deal with me direct.'

'Fine, I'll call him.' Wanda closed her eyes and took a breath.

'The sooner that is sorted, the sooner we get the weekly payouts and we can hire in some help,' Fiona added as if that justified their earlier actions.

'But I have already hired Lee to do the milking. Surely the money would go towards paying him?'

Martin looked awkward. 'We really need a farm manager, someone on Glen's level. I mean you could potentially take over the milking, couldn't you?'

'No! I'm sorry, but it's my decision to work at the gallery so I can pay Lee to do the milking. It's worked well for the last two weeks.'

'But then you're absent from the farm for three days a week. That won't do.'

'For goodness' sake!' Wanda paused to compose herself. 'Listen, I'm running the farm now on Glen's behalf. You have retired and it is my decision to hire Lee.'

Martin's eyes almost popped out of his head. Fiona looked terrified.

'But hang on a minute, I'm willing to be more involved,' Martin said. 'I've already assigned Fi to manage the hens.' His wife dutifully nodded.

'Ah, that's why you put a new padlock on the hen barn.'

'I had to. I had no choice after Graham caused havoc the other day. And we've lost birds thanks to him.' He heaved himself upright in his chair, straightening his back. 'The important thing is that you leave that silly job you've got in town and get back full time on the farm. I will direct you so you get things right. I understand your lack of experience.'

'No! Not happening. It's thanks to the money I earn that I can pay Lee to do the milking.'

'It's not just milking though, is it. There's the veg. The carrots haven't been sprayed. There's a cow gone lame, though luckily Lee spotted that.'

'You see, Lee is good with the cows; he knows the herd well.' Wanda interrupted Martin's flow.

'But what about the cows that still aren't pregnant. Have you thought of that? I walked up to Mill Field the other day and there's definitely a problem with the sugar beet. There's a lot that's been neglected and this cannot continue.'

'Fine. You do it then! But don't expect me to be your skivvy.' Wanda sprang out of her chair. She wanted to scream.

'Wanda, dear, we're not going to resolve anything if you don't just sit down and let us talk about this.' Fi had a sickly smile on her face.

'No! I'm not sitting down. This isn't a discussion! This is you dictating to me how you want this place to run.' Her in-laws looked at each other in horror.

'It's just not possible to reason with you.' Martin's face was red with anger.

There was nowhere to go with this. 'I want you out of here. This is my house and I've had a long day so please go and leave me alone.' She waved an arm in the direction of the back door. But they both sat tight. There was a dreadful minute when nobody moved.

'Wanda, please, will you sit down?' Martin was demanding now.

'Right, that's it. If you won't go, I will!' Wanda was shaking as she walked out of the kitchen and up the stairs. She had no idea if she was doing the right thing but felt compelled to pack a bag and leave.

CHAPTER 9

Wanda parked on Mill Lane on the far side of Lucas Wood. The road was rather narrow there but she dared not risk going down to the farmhouse for fear of bumping in to Martin. This way she could get to her art studio unnoticed and make the most of one of her days off from the gallery.

She still could not quite believe what she had done. It had only been a few days and she had considered more than once that perhaps she should go back, but the fact was she had left the farm. Abandoned it. Her main concern was the animals. What hope was there for her hens now? It broke her heart to think of them locked in that barn, subject to the fluorescent light, day in day out. It might mean that Capel Farm ended up with a few more eggs to sell but, in her mind, happy hens were better layers every time. She was even rather fond of the cows.

Carolyn had welcomed her with open arms which was incredible as, apart from one tipsy evening, they had not seen each other since the eighties. She had recently been through a messy divorce; her husband, Gerard, going off with another man which was somehow harder to swallow. Wanda could see that it would leave you questioning your whole marriage. It certainly seemed to have knocked Carolyn's confidence and she seemed very grateful for Wanda's company.

This new life felt strange; it had all happened so suddenly. And she had not planned it. It was like a force had overtaken her and powered her on, to maintain her own well-being. She was definitely running away from an existence she really could not cope with any more. The scary thing was she rather liked where she had ended up.

She was still angry with Martin for his unremitting hold on the family farm and his unrealistic demands on her. He had always had unreasonable expectations of Glen too. But at the same time, the thought of him and Fi having to manage on their own was quite terrifying. Of course, they had done it in the past but they were much older now. What if Martin had a heart attack? She would, no doubt, be blamed. But he had made it impossible for her to stay.

Since she had made the radical move of leaving, her father-in-law had been sending text messages several times a day, asking her questions she simply did not know the answers to and pointing out what she had done wrong or had failed to do in the first place. For a man in his seventies, he had a pretty agile texting finger. She had decided not to reply. What was the point?

At least living in Bury, Wanda could easily call in to see Glen each day. She had sorted out an arrangement with the nursing staff so that she could avoid any times that her in-laws were visiting. So far it had worked. But making conversation with Glen wasn't easy. Would she admit to him that she'd up and left Capel Farm, leaving his elderly parents to manage alone? He wouldn't like that. It seemed like ages since they had talked properly about anything, years even. Running the farm rather conveniently got in the way most of the time, making it easier to avoid any intimate topics or share their true feelings. After all, farmers didn't seem to feel anything except a compulsion to get out there and farm.

It was a lovely summer's morning and there was warmth in the sun and a high humidity in the air. As Wanda walked through Lucas Wood she started to tune in to her surroundings and forget about her troubles. She needed to be in the right frame of mind to be creative when she reached her art studio on the other side of the wood. She was excited about producing a new work for Aaron but at the same hadn't a clue what she would paint. His brief had been vague: something in nature.

She came to a clearing in the wood with a large pond. The sight of a moorhen, alongside her comical young with their miniature dark grey, powder-puff bodies and red faces framed with flame orange feathers, made her smile. The mother, sleek and black, picked up speed when she noticed Wanda. Her five offspring frantically swam following after her to the far edge of the water where they clambered out and scurried through the reeds. The chick bringing up the rear didn't make the bank on the first attempt but fell back into the water causing a splash. Wanda cried out, 'Oh no!' and willed it to try again. Was it because it was the story of her life? Left behind and always struggling. With a valiant effort the chick made it on the third attempt, just in time to catch up with its siblings. Had she ever caught up with Ben? He was running a thriving glamping business, married to the lovely Saffy, and living in a delightful home that had been handed to him by their parents without any thought for Wanda. Her fate was closely sewn up in her marriage to Glen. A decision she had been cajoled into by her mother. How had she allowed her mum to have so much influence over such a big decision? She hadn't thought about it like this before, but it was true that her entire existence was a result of marrying a farmer. She shook herself back to the here and now and moved on from the pond.

The sounds of the wood were magical with a blackbird singing out loud, *Look at me, I'm here!* Leaves rustled in the gentle breeze and the sun cast dappled light over the woodland floor.

She had made it to the ancient oak tree now and gazed up to see that there were bright green leaves bursting out through its maze of sturdy branches. The sun was lighting up the canopy and it was a glorious sight.

'It's all right for you, tree,' she said out loud feeling sure she was alone in the wood and no one would hear her. 'I suspect you don't have a care in the world.' She laughed at herself. 'Look at me! Having a Shirley Valentine moment, talking to a tree!'

'Ahem, I can hear you, you know little lady. Wanda, isn't it?'

Wanda stood back in amazement and searched around for another human being. Although it hadn't sounded like a human voice in many ways. It was deep and echoing. She was amazed but somehow curious rather than freaked out.

'Is that you, tree?' she asked peering up at the large gnarled trunk hardly believing what she was saying.

'Quercus, actually, if you don't mind. I am the oldest specimen in this wood, you know. You could say I'm in charge of this rabble, although there's a beech tree near Rachel's Covert that wouldn't agree with you. Stubborn young thing it is; can't be more than a hundred years old.'

Wanda blinked several times, her eyes wide. *Was this really happening?*

'You're wrong you know!' The voice bellowed and made her jump.

'About what?' she asked timidly.

'I have plenty of cares in this world, thanks to you farmers.'

'Oh dear. But we've left the wood alone. Martin was all for cutting it down years ago but it wasn't allowed – thanks to the ancient trees like your good self.'

'How so very kind of you, homo sapiens! All I have to worry about now is sudden oak death.'

'That doesn't sound good. What causes that?'

'It's complex. But you humans have been killing so many organisms in the last seventy years, it's all a bit of a struggle for us to survive. You see we all rely on each other.'

91

'It's not me. I don't even kill flies.'

A deep bellowing laugh came from Quercus. 'Flies, huh! What about the bacteria, the fungi, protozoa, nematodes, arthropods and earthworms, all up on Hungry Hill?'

'That might have been Bartletts, cultivating and drilling potatoes. Anyway, how do you know about that all the way over here?'

'Let's just say I can feel it in my fungi.'

Wanda felt a little nervous now. 'Actually, I must go. I have to paint.' She started to hurry away.

'I'll be seeing you again,' the tree roared. 'I have much to complain about!'

Wanda picked up speed up the path to Rachel's Covert and the refuge of her art studio. She went straight in and shut the door, standing motionless trying to take in what had just happened. Perhaps with all the drama in her life she'd started hearing things. That was a rational explanation but she knew deep down it didn't ring true. Perhaps she was going mad and in this crazy state she'd entered the wonderful world of nature like never before and could not only gaze up and marvel at the ancient oak tree but hear his wise words too.

Listen to the land, Gilbert had said. *Was that what he'd meant?*

Had she really just talked to a tree?

*

Martin felt weary as he walked up to Glenham. He stopped and leant on the gate looking out over the meadow where the Montbéliarde cows grazed. He could picture his own father, John, beside him. John had always had a bit more weight on him, despite the hours he put in, and his face bore the lines of an outdoor life. Martin could remember the cooked breakfast his mother made for his father daily after milking, always with streaky bacon.

All that fresh air gives you an appetite she'd often said with a knowing smile. Martin had started milking at the age of four. He took to it; it was just a way of life. They drank the raw milk at home; *full of goodness,* his mother pronounced. He had realised when he went to school that not everyone was a farmer but to him it was the most natural thing in the world.

Martin had insisted that John retired when he got to sixty-five; it was only right as his health was suffering. And thank goodness Martin had because it was only seven years later when his dad had a massive heart attack and died. All those years of hard slog. He never complained. Martin's mother Ruth hadn't lasted long after. She'd sort of given up, almost as if she just wanted to join him.

It was a history that Martin didn't want to ignore and one that Fi reminded him of often. But what choice did he have now? He felt physical pain when he thought of the farm going to rack and ruin on his watch. His son was lying in intensive care and he would not let him down. As for Wanda he simply did not understand the woman. The thought of her carrying on with that big American guy was too much to bear. She'd been quick to deny it; perhaps he had got the wrong end of the stick.

Martin had planned to turn Lee away that morning when the lad turned up for milking. Funnily enough he had found it quite easy to jump out of bed at five o'clock. It had taken him years to break the habit and still now he found it hard to sleep past six o'clock.

Lee had been quite angry when Martin suggested that they didn't need him on the farm.

'But I have an arrangement with Wanda.' He had raised his voice and seemed agitated. So Martin had agreed they would do the milking together that day and left it at that. There had been a bit of an atmosphere between them but they worked well together, both knowing exactly what they were about. Lee was faster than Martin, he had to admit that.

Around one hundred cows down, Martin had felt a twinge near his heart and was forced to sit down on the floor of the pit and take a breath. He had clutched his heart and tried to slow his breathing. Lee had looked quite concerned.

'You all right old man?' he'd asked.

Martin had not answered. After a couple of minutes, his breathing had returned to normal and he'd felt better. But he had been overcome with a feeling of immense sadness. It was no good; he would have to keep Lee on.

The hens were noisier than usual. They seemed troubled. Fiona shouted out, 'Calm down girls. Let's see what you have for me today. I hope it's an improvement on yesterday.' Despite raising her voice she failed to drown out their din. Sheltering her eyes from the fluorescent lighting, she started collecting up the eggs. It had been one of her favourite jobs when she was in residence on the farm. She would always hope for a good number so that Martin would be pleased. Today it seemed a more arduous task and the lights bothered her more than they normally would. She ploughed on and when she really couldn't find any more she counted up the rows in her six-by-six trays. She had five complete trays and a few more, so over one hundred and eighty eggs. But there were around two hundred hens and they should be laying one a day under the lights. Perhaps Graham had lost more hens than they had previously thought. She looked around the barn making some vague attempt to count them. That was when she noticed that some of the Goldline hens were scratching at the door as if they wanted to get out. She went over to try and shoo them away and as she did several of them started pecking at her feet and ankles. She had a light pair of trainers on, not the wellingtons she'd always worn when this was her daily job.

'Ow!' She looked down. One rotter had drawn blood, two even, maybe three. Others were still pecking at the door and the din was deafening now.

'For goodness' sake!' she yelled but they just kept on. She kicked her legs to frighten them away but still they came darting around with their active beaks. They were menacing. She needed to get out but they were right by the door. If she opened it, they would escape and after last week's fiasco she couldn't let that happen. She tried moving away from them but they simply followed her. It was relentless. Panicking now, she reached for her mobile in her pocket and rang Martin. It rang and rang but he didn't answer.

'Help!' she cried out even though she knew no one would hear her.

Just then the barn door opened and Gilbert appeared looking puzzled. 'You all right, Fiona Taylor?'

'Oh Gilbert! I'm being attacked.'

'Attacked by hens!' He started laughing.

Some of the Goldlines were already outside. 'Quick! Get them back in,' Fiona cried.

'All right, Fiona Taylor.' Gilbert sounded as if she was making a fuss about nothing.

'But they're escaping!' More and more were headed out. She went out herself and tried to shut the door on those that were left, nearly trapping and killing one in the process. There must have been twenty, thirty even, now out on Hungry Hill.

'The potato crop,' she cried and she knew she sounded hysterical but she felt totally out of control.

'Don't worry yourself, Mrs Taylor. Wanda lets them out all the time.'

'But they escaped the other day! We lost some to foxes.'

Gilbert calmly walked amongst the hens that had made their way on to the field. 'Best to leave them for a bit; I'll keep an eye,' he said.

'But, but...'

He walked back to her and said in the gentlest of voices, 'Mrs Taylor, why don't you go back to the farmhouse and have a nice cup of tea. I'll get these hens back in; don't you be worrying.'

It was a tempting thought. 'Are you sure? You will get them all safely in?'

'Of course.'

'Thank you, Gilbert,' she said, her voice still shaking, and started off back down the hill taking a calming breath as she went.

CHAPTER 10

Wanda was sitting behind her desk in the gallery when Fiona walked through the door. As she approached, Wanda felt like a sitting target exposed to anyone who fancied having a pop at her. At least Fiona had the decency to look a little nervous.

'Hello Wanda.' Her voice faltered. 'Can we talk?'

'Fi, I'm at work as you can see.' There was no one in the gallery at that point. Not even Adrian.

'It won't take a minute.' Wanda braced herself. 'The thing is, we've had to keep Lee on, what with Martin's blood pressure, well, we've had no choice.'

Wanda was secretly pleased. She really didn't want her father-in-law having a heart attack on top of everything else.

'I think you've done the right thing,' she said smiling at Fiona.

'Yes, but the thing is, we desperately need the money to pay him. We've had to use the farm account for the last week since you left. And we know you were paying him out of the money you earn here.'

'That's right,' Wanda said thinking fast. It was a cheek, it really was, but actually it was still her husband's farm. The question of rent hadn't come up at Carolyn's but Wanda was increasingly uncomfortable about not paying her way. 'Yes, I was, but things have changed.'

'They certainly have changed with Glen, and now you, not working on the farm. We need to keep Lee on and hire a farm manager to keep things going.'

'But won't the insurance money cover that?'

There was an awkward pause. Then Fiona said, 'Martin says it will cover getting someone to replace Glen, but not Lee as well. We need your money for that. And don't forget Martin is giving his time freely to make sure everything runs smoothly while Glen is in hospital.'

Wanda sighed. Her mother-in-law looked desperate and she did have a point. 'Listen, I'll give you what I can. I've sold a painting recently.'

'Thank you.' Fiona was gracious now. 'Will you transfer the money to the farm account?'

That sounded scary. 'How about I get some cash to you? Lee likes to be paid in cash.'

'Okay, will you drop it off at the farmhouse? Martin and I have had to move in.' Fiona looked embarrassed. 'Just so we're on hand to look after things,' she added.

'I don't suppose you could pop in here tomorrow?' Wanda asked.

'If I must.' Fiona turned and left without another word.

It was raining, warm summer rain, as Wanda walked up Abbeygate to Whiting Street. Passers-by smiled at her perhaps because she didn't have an umbrella. She bobbed into the porchway of a café and looked up at the sky. It was heavy with grey and unforgiving. Her thoughts turned to her current predicament, living at Carolyn's – not that she had been anything other than welcoming. But it wasn't the same as having your own place. Knowing that her in-laws were definitely in residence at the farmhouse somehow made it worse. The rain was showing no sign of easing so Wanda decided to make a dash for it. She arrived at her temporary home, wet.

'Oh goodness, Wanda, didn't you have a brolly?' Carolyn was in the kitchen putting the kettle on. 'Sit down, I have some news.' She seemed elated.

'Let me just go and change and dry my hair off,' Wanda said making her way upstairs. When she came back down there was a mug of tea for her on the breakfast bar.

'Thank you,' she said feeling very much like a house guest.

'Is everything okay?' Carolyn asked.

'Fine,' Wanda said knowing that probably wasn't enough to allay her friend's concern. 'You said something about good news?'

'I did. I've got a little part-time job. Something to get me out and about.'

'Well done.' *Would this mean she wouldn't want any rent?*

'Don't laugh, but I'm going to be doing viewings for Sheridans, you know, the estate agents.'

'How wonderful. They're quite upmarket, aren't they? Posh houses are us.'

'They certainly have houses at the upper-end price bracket. Anyway, I start tomorrow. Weekends are their most popular times.'

There was an awkward silence. Probably the first since Wanda had moved in.

'Do you fancy going out this evening to celebrate?' Carolyn asked.

'Oh, I don't know.' Could she afford it now that she was paying for Lee again?

'Come on! That's not like you. Don't deny me a bit of fun.'

The Angel Hotel lounge bar was buzzing. The art-deco elegance was the perfect setting for a gin cocktail evening. Wanda felt horribly under dressed and rather hot (not in a good way) in her jeans even though Carolyn had lent her another pretty blouse which was more like a tunic on Wanda. She realised that as a farmer's wife she simply didn't have the right wardrobe for such a sophisticated town setting. And now she'd agreed to give Fiona some money, she didn't feel she could splash out on new clothes. Not until the thorny issue of paying rent was dealt with. As Wanda looked across the room, she noticed a beautiful young woman in a floaty silver metallic dress. She was throwing her head back as she laughed, nearly spilling her drink, which made the moment all the more hilarious for her and her beautiful young friends. Wanda sighed.

'Cheer up!' Carolyn placed a gin and tonic in front of Wanda. 'It's Archangel Rhubarb,' she added gleefully.

'Wow.' Wanda held her glass up examining the concoction. 'You have to wonder what this might do to you.'

'Let's hope it puts you in a better mood,' Carolyn said with a slightly manic look.

'I'm sorry, I just…'

'Evening ladies.' Aaron appeared from nowhere. He was wearing a smart blue jacket over a yellow shirt and jeans and seemed to fit right in.

'Well, hello.' Carolyn's eyes lit up. 'Do join us for a cocktail,' she said sitting upright and arching her back seductively. Wanda thought it would be wise if Carolyn wore a *recently divorced* badge to warn unsuspecting males.

'I'd love to,' he said and sat down. 'You didn't tell me you have a very attractive friend, Wanda?'

Wanda let out a sarcastic snigger. 'Well thank goodness you two have finally met.'

'Hang on a minute, you know each other?' Carolyn was putting two and two together.

'Aaron has bought one of my paintings.'

'And commissioned a second,' he added with a broad smile. 'How's it going, by the way?' he asked Wanda.

The truth was that she had got nowhere with this promised work so far. Her first trip to the shed had proved to be a barren den of frustration where she had finally painted something that she had promptly decided was rubbish and torn up. Maybe it was her encounter with Quercus that had thrown her. Or perhaps she just was not in the right frame of mind right now. *It's in the procrastination stage*, she wanted to say but that would be not be wise.

'I'm off to Manchester next week,' he added as if he could read her mind. 'So you have a little time. But I'm expecting great things on my return.'

'My best works are born out of adversity.' *Why did she say that?*

'Poor Wanda,' he said. 'Let me get you both another drink.'

The next day Wanda was with a customer who was interested in the new abstract artist that Adrian was so keen on. The gallery currently had five of this particular artist's works on display and the customer loved them all and simply could not decide which one she would buy.

'Why not buy all five?' Wanda knew she was being flippant but really this woman's long-winded deliberations were becoming tiresome. She forced a smile at her. Just then she noticed Fiona hovering at the door; she was almost pleased to see her.

'Would you excuse me for just a minute?'

The woman looked slightly confused but then said, 'Yes, I need a bit of time to think about this. It's such a big decision.'

'Of course,' Wanda said and went over to Fiona as she came through the door.

'Morning Fi,' she said breezily.

'I take it you've got the money.'

'Er, yes.' Wanda reached for her handbag under the desk and took out the notes from her wallet. It all felt very clandestine. She braced herself as she handed it over.

'How much is here?' Fiona was already scowling at the amount and waving the notes around. The customer looked over and Wanda could feel herself blush.

'Fiona, would you put the money away please and lower your voice. This is an art gallery.'

Fiona was wide-eyed with astonishment. 'But, but this can't be enough!'

'It's enough for one week. The best I can do right now.'

'But surely you earn enough to give me more than this?'

'Sorry, I have other outgoings.'

'Really! What would they be? Drinking gin at The Angel with your new fancy man?'

How on earth did she know? It must just be a silly presumption on her part. Wanda took a deep breath before saying, 'Please keep your voice down.'

The customer appeared looking very concerned. 'I'm terribly sorry,' Wanda said to her and then, turning to her mother-in-law, she glared at her. 'Fiona is just leaving.'

'Martin will have something to say about this,' she said looking as if she was close to tears as she turned to leave.

Wanda ignored her and gave her full attention to the customer. 'I'm dreadfully sorry about that. Have you made a decision?' When the customer didn't answer Wanda added, 'What are your thoughts at this stage?'

*

On Sunday, Wanda made her way over to Lucas Wood with a newly bought blank canvas under her arm. She wouldn't be able to tear this one up. She parked up, as before, on the narrow lane and started to make her way through Lucas Wood. The sun was out today and Wanda imagined using her easel to paint under the shade of a tree. She just needed to find the right inspiration.

After a warm wet spring all life was rampant: masses of elderflowers with their pretty creamy white sprays; deadly nightshade with its tempting purple star flowers; rich green ferns with feathered leaves; violets spreading over the woodland floor. She could hear the buzz of bees high in the sky and the song of a willow warbler.

She used her thumbs and forefingers to create a view finder holding it up to anything that caught her eye. But nothing seemed special enough. Was she being too fussy?

When she reached the large pond, she stopped and took in the scene. Reeds and yellow irises were now in a tangled mass around the pond. Green algae sat on the surface of the water and all was still until suddenly a couple of mallards appeared in flight, swooping down onto the pond, their raucous quacks interrupting the harmony. They made a bit of a fuss and then calmed down. Wanda found herself looking for the moorhen and her chicks and was ridiculously disappointed that she couldn't see them anywhere today. But then the female appeared from some undergrowth and slipped into the pond. She was alone; perhaps the chicks were in their nest. Reluctantly Wanda moved away and walked on further into the wood.

She considered giving the old oak tree a wide berth but curiosity got the better of her. When she reached Quercus, she stopped and gawped as she gazed up at its magnificence, the darkness of the twisted lined trunk and the luscious green of the canopy as the sun shone through it.

'You're back then,' said a disdainful voice.

'Yes, well, passing through, on my way to my studio, well shed actually.' This still felt really weird.

'On the edge of Rachel's Covert. I can see it from here.'

'Quercus, do you mind me asking, do you talk to everyone you see? I mean this is all a bit strange for me.'

'You don't have to join in.' The tree sounded offended. 'Huh! Homo sapiens, never happy are they!'

It was a good point. How should she respond to that?

'You have an aura about you,' he said more gently this time. 'You don't often see it in humans.'

'I have an aura about me and that's why you talk to me?'

'Correct. You see I know it's safe when the aura is present.'

'Goodness.' Wanda thought about this. Perhaps it explained why she had found Gilbert up here. 'Does Gilbert have an aura?'

'I'm not one to gossip. Let's just say I'm beginning to think you are cleverer than you look.'

'Praise indeed.' Wanda laughed. 'So, what does it mean, if you have this aura?'

'It means, little lady, that you have an empathy with nature; I can trust you.' Raising his voice he added, 'I *can* trust you, can't I?'

'Yes! Of course.' She wasn't quite sure what she needed to be trusted to do but she quite liked the idea. She was the chosen one for once. It made a change compared to the rest of her life when she was made to feel useless.

'What meaningless task are you doing in your shed?' the tree asked.

She held up her canvas. 'I need to do a painting for an American guy and I have no idea what to paint.'

'But you're painting that thing in your hand. What's the problem?'

'Yes, but what am I painting *on* it? What subject? Do I paint a flower, pond life, elderflowers? I'm just not sure. I can't think of anything that might impress him enough to buy it.'

'Ask him. Ask him what he wants. I hear Americans are forthright folk.'

'Nature was the brief. He has already bought one of my paintings; it was of poppy seed heads.'

'Well, if that wowed him, you're on to a winner with this American. He's easily pleased if you don't mind me saying.'

Wanda laughed again. 'I like you, Quercus. No airs and graces.'

'What does that mean?' The tree was ruffled now.

'You know, no pretention, down to earth.'

'Down to earth! I'm that all right.'

'I'd better go. I've got to get on with this painting somehow.' She felt deflated by the thought.

'It strikes me that hiding in your shed is the last thing you should do.'

'What do you mean?'

'Well, nature is here, all around you.'

'Yes, you're right. I should bring my easel out and my paints.'

'I have an idea,' Quercus said sounding pleased with himself, 'it's a particularly good idea.'

'Really? I'm all ears.'

'You're not all ears. You have two of them only.'

'You're right. I meant I'd be pleased to hear your idea.'

'Do a painting of me. Right here where I can keep an eye on you.'

'There's a thought,' she said contemplating the notion.

'You should know my trunk was much smoother a few hundred years ago and less lined, so perhaps you could bear that in mind; show me off to full advantage.'

'Oh no, I'd have to paint what I see. Anyway, it's beautiful, your wizened bark, the twists and turns of your trunk, your huge canopy...'

'No need to carry on. You have my permission to paint my form on your white board.'

'Thank you, it's an honour.'

'I will, of course, want something from you in return.'

'Ooh.' That was surprising. 'I can't imagine what that might be.'

'You will find out in the fullness of time. In the meantime, you have much to learn, Wanda.'

CHAPTER 11

The following day Martin woke early. Was it because he was back at the farmhouse? He lay their trying to go back to sleep but it was no good. So he got up quietly leaving Fi to sleep. He needed to get a grip on this farm and get it working properly.

As soon as he'd had a bit of breakfast he went out into the yard and saw a girl walking towards him. What was she doing here?

'Mr Taylor?' she asked.

'You're not Colin,' he said to her. Her dark hair was tied back in a ponytail with a peak cap over it and she wore jeans, a T-shirt and a waterproof jacket. He had to admit she looked like a farmer.

'No, Colin's on another job so they sent me. My name's Tanya.'

'But I need a big strong lad to help me with the baling. Bartletts didn't say anything. I'm not supposed to be working, you see. I'm just helping out, well, running things really, while my son is in hospital.'

'So I hear. I might not be a lad but I'm strong enough to drive the tractor.' She looked at him with a confident air. Martin decided that if she was not up to the job, it would soon become apparent.

'Okay, well you'll need to prepare the storage barn first; it needs a good clean out.'

She raised her eyebrows. 'You'd better show me where this barn is then.'

Fi was staring out of the kitchen window when Martin got back to the farmhouse. She had a dressing gown on and her hair was unbrushed. He watched her for a moment hoping for some sort of acknowledgement.

'You had your breakfast, love?'

She turned and looked surprised to see him there. 'Breakfast. No. Not yet. I made a pot of tea. It might still be warm.' She placed her palms over the pot. 'Oh, cold.' She sighed.

'I'll make another pot,' Martin said kindly. 'Do you want a piece of toast?'

'Toast? Yes, okay. Not really that hungry.'

He put the kettle on, looked in the fridge for the bread and found the end of a sliced loaf, a crust in fact. He rammed it into the toaster and looked over to his wife expecting a look of disapproval but she hadn't noticed. She was sat at the table now looking blankly at her phone.

'Are you going into the hospital today?' he asked.

There was a long pause before she looked up and said, 'I don't know what to say to him.'

'Tell him about the farm, he'd like that.'

'Shall I tell him I was nearly pecked to death by the hens?'

'Oh love, it wasn't that bad. It's your nerves. You need to take it easy. I'll deal with the eggs today.'

'This isn't what we had planned for our retirement, is it?'

The toast popped up emitting a swirl of smoke from a burnt ridge on the edge. 'Ah. I'll scrape that bit off.'

'I'm not hungry really.'

'Do we have any more bread?'

'I don't think so.'

Martin went over to the table and sat next to his wife. 'Look love, we've just got to get through this. I know it's not easy.'

'Have you taken anyone on yet, to fill in for Glen?'

Martin shifted awkwardly in his seat.

'You said you would, you promised.' Fiona was close to tears.

'Hey, don't fret. I have as a matter of fact. There's a young lad, Conor, who looks promising. He's coming over later as it happens.'

'Young? Does that mean he's a farm hand, not a manager?'

Martin was slow to answer. 'He's sort of an experienced farm hand. We'd be able to give him quite a bit of work.'

Fiona looked at him suspiciously; she knew her husband too well.

'Look, I'm just going to be overseeing things.' Martin took her hand in his. 'Nothing too strenuous, with Lee and Conor, not to mention Bartletts, we'll have all the labouring covered. I will be sort of desk based, directing things.'

'I suppose the insurance money will cover both wages then? It would be great not to have to go cap in hand to Wanda.'

'Ooh, I'm not sure about that. Listen, Wanda's left the farm and taken that job in town so I think it's only right that her wages pay for Lee.'

Fiona looked anxious. 'Don't fret love,' Martin tried to reassure her. 'I'll deal with Wanda if you like.'

Quercus was strangely quiet as Wanda approached with her paints and her easel today. It was breezy with white fluffy clouds going over so that the sunshine was intermittent. It wasn't ideal for painting with the changing light but as it was a day off from the gallery she really needed to crack on. She stood by the mighty trunk gazing up and wondering if she'd dreamt the last two encounters with this talking tree. Did trees sleep?

She set herself in the same place as her last visit and looked at her canvas. *Mm, much to do.* Immediately she wanted to change the texture of the bark, add in a wider array of green tones, the background needed something. *What?* She set to work feeling slightly ill at ease as Quercus was not with her in the way he had been previously. *Was it something she had said?*

Good progress had been made on her canvas when she heard, 'Hello, little lady.' The voice sounded old and tired.

'Quercus, I thought maybe you were sleeping.'

'Resting actually. I started my resting period about a hundred years ago. It's what we oaks do in our middle age.'

'Gosh, so how old are you, if you don't mind me asking?'

'Why would I mind? I'm proud of my four hundred and twenty years.'

'That's incredible. To think you have been around for all that time. You've certainly seen some changes.'

'It was a fine life on the whole until about seventy years ago. That was when it all started to go horribly wrong.'

'Oh dear. What happened then?'

'Nasties. That's what happened. Nasties in the soil, in the air, killing off organisms; even the fungi network has been badly affected!'

'Do you mean fertilisers, pesticides?'

'Anything with nasty chemicals. Man waging war on nature, that's what it is.'

'Seventy years ago. That would have been after the Second World War. There was food rationing for about fourteen years. That was why they started intensive farming.'

'Intensive, huh! No wonder I'm exhausted. Anyway, why oh why did you decide that intensive was a good thing?'

'Well, they were worried about having enough food for everyone.'

'Homo sapiens. That's what concerned them?'

'Well, yes, now you mention it, it was quite selfish. But they didn't realise that what they were doing would cause harm.'

'Ignorance is bliss. Do you realise what your actions have done to the wildlife population?'

'I'm beginning to think it's not been great,' Wanda said apologetically.

'Not great! It's been a disaster!'

Just then there was a lot of commotion in the trees behind them. Wanda turned to see Gilbert covered in foliage and barefooted as was his wont when he was in Lucas Wood.

'Wanda Taylor! What are you doing here?' He approached with caution and peered at her painting. 'Interesting,' he said.

Wanda looked up at Quercus and then at Gilbert with raised eyebrows. There was an expectant silence. Eventually Quercus spoke.

'I'm pleased you've turned up, Gilbert. I think we need to teach Wanda a thing or two.'

Gilbert shuffled his feet looking anywhere but at Wanda or Quercus.

'It's all right,' Wanda said gently.

'This must go no further,' Gilbert said gravely.

'Our secret is safe with me.' Wanda smiled mildly.

'If you say so,' Gilbert still eyed the scene suspiciously. Eventually he took another look at the painting.

'Have you seen this work of art?' he asked Quercus.

'I don't need to. I know what I look like.'

'It's not a mirror image.' Wanda knew she was being precious about it probably because she was so worried that it was not up to the mark.

'I should hope not,' Quercus retorted. 'You should be showing me off to full advantage.'

'It's good,' Gilbert said slowly. Wanda could feel a '*but*' coming. 'But it needs something more.'

Wanda positioned herself so that she had the same view of the painting as Gilbert. 'But what?' she asked, telling herself it was a perfectly competent painting and what did this old man know about art anyway.

Gilbert scratched his head. 'I think it needs to be more... magical.'

'I'm not sure if my client is looking for anything fantastical. He likes nature.' Wanda knew she sounded defensive.

'And you don't think there's magic in nature?' Gilbert asked simply.

'Of course there is,' Quercus roared. 'Nature is magical.'

'You have a point.' Wanda smiled a knowing smile. She thought about it. Perhaps it could work? Perhaps it would bring the painting to life? At the moment she was broadly happy with it; how she had caught the light coming through the canopy and the darkness of the aged trunk where the roots went deep into the ground. But was it enough to wow Aaron? What would Aaron think of a magical tree?

'That's your answer,' Gilbert said brushing his palms together as if that was that.

'I'll have to think about it,' Wanda said still feeling uncertain.

'After all, you are a woman,' Quercus said and both humans looked up at the tree with raised eyebrows. Gilbert stifled a laugh.

It was coming up to eleven o'clock when Martin approached the field where Tanya was working with the tractor and baler. He watched her from the gate as she harvested the straw and formed the round bales that would feed the cows in the winter. He could not fault her. She was clearly doing a good job. Probably as good as Colin if not better. She had made a decent job of the barn too. He had checked. It might be safe to leave her to it.

By mid-afternoon, Martin had managed to get a few jobs done and had collected the eggs and handed them over to the egg man. Hopefully Fi would be up to doing it again tomorrow, although he had his doubts.

As he walked back towards the farmhouse it started spitting with rain. He looked up at the sky. There was enough greyish cloud cover to cause a problem. He hotfooted it up to the straw barn and sure enough Tanya had brought the tractor in and was just dismounting.

'That's it for today,' she shouted across to him. 'It will be too wet after this shower.'

Martin looked into the barn. The bales were neatly stacked from one corner, right up to the roof. 'Good job,' he said.

'For a girl.' She smiled at him.

'Sorry, I was just expecting Colin.'

She turned to go. 'I'll be back when the straw is dry again.'

'Hang on a minute. I'd like your opinion on something. Can you...?'

She turned back. 'What sort of thing?'

'Will you walk with me? There's a field I'd like to show you adjacent to Lucas Wood.' She looked surprised but followed him anyway. 'It's called Rooked Meadow. We've not done much with it for many a year. You could say it's gone a bit wild.'

The kitchen was full of delicious food aromas when Wanda walked in to Carolyn's.

'Wow, something smells good.'

'Chicken tagine!' Carolyn's face lit up as she said it.

'You shouldn't have.' Wanda was feeling bad about all this free hospitality.

'Well actually,' Carolyn dipped a teaspoon into the saucepan and pulled it out, waving it in the air gently to cool the sauce, 'Aaron is coming for dinner.'

'Aaron! Isn't he in Manchester?'

'Mmm,' Carolyn was twirling around and fluttering her eyelids, 'not quite yet. He decided to postpone his trip.'

'What? What does that mean? Do I need to speed up the painting?'

'Oh, I shouldn't think so. His trip to Manchester might be a little shorter that's all.'

'Are you two an item then?' Wanda asked.

Carolyn affected a look of innocence. 'I'm certainly hoping so.'

'But Carolyn, you haven't even got your decree nisi.' Wanda was wondering why that mattered even as she said it.

'Huh! My ex was having an affair a year ago. With a man!'

'Yes, that must have been quite weird. But what I mean is, are you ready for a new relationship after all the heartache and messiness you've been through.'

'Oh Wanda, I just want a little fun. Let's face it, Aaron lives in New York. It's hardly likely to last.'

'You're right. Perhaps you should keep it platonic.'

'Are you jealous?'

'No! Don't be ridiculous. I'm married.'

'But, Wanda my dear...' Carolyn came over to her now and put her hands on Wanda's shoulders, looking straight in to her eyes, 'you never talk about your relationship with Glen, your marriage. I mean I know he's in hospital but even so.'

Wanda was thrown by this. The truth was that she had no idea if her marriage was going to last after all the turmoil of recent times. She was finding the daily visits quite problematic as she didn't feel she could talk freely about what her life had become and Glen's only interest was the farm. 'It's difficult,' she said meekly, blinking away a tear.

'It must be. Very difficult. But you don't talk about it.'

'I think I'm frightened of the truth. You see our marriage was on shaky ground before the accident. The farm business is in trouble and Glen wanted me to do more and more; he saw it as a way to fix things.'

'That's not fair on you.'

'That's what I thought. I was close to walking out.'

'Oh, Wanda, you poor thing. So you want out but he's laid up in intensive care and you've got to play the super-concerned wife.'

Just then the doorbell went.

'I'll make myself scarce,' Wanda said.

'No, you won't. Stay and have some fun. We can fight over him!' Carolyn laughed as she went to answer the door.

Aaron's tall, broad-shouldered frame seemed to fill Carolyn's bijou dining area. Every now and then throughout the meal he moved awkwardly, trying a different position for his long legs. He could not be comfortable. Wanda could almost feel the stiffness in his hips.

'So, Wanda, how's my work of art coming along?' Aaron asked as Wanda put her knife and fork down neatly on her plate.

'It's going well, thank you.'

'You sound very sure of yourself.'

'Not really, I'm just happy about the way it's shaping up.'

'Are you going to tell me what it is?'

Wanda considered this. 'No, I think it's best to wait for the big reveal.'

'Coffee anyone?' Carolyn asked.

'I'll make it.' Wanda jumped up.

'Great, we'll go through to the lounge,' Carolyn said reaching for Aaron's hand so she could drag him in there.

Wanda delivered two coffees to the lovebirds. 'Here you are.' They barely looked up. 'Listen, I'm going for a walk.'

'Oh, no, you don't have to do that,' Carolyn protested. 'It'll be dark soon.'

'Honestly, I'll be fine. I feel like a walk.'

'Don't be too long then and take your mobile,' Carolyn ordered.

The rain had stopped leaving a fresh breeze which carried white fluffy clouds across a blue sky. Wanda made her way down Whiting Street, turning right into Abbeygate with no particular plan. The independent shops and cafés were all shut but the restaurants were alive with customers who had spilled out on to this pretty pedestrianised street. There was laughter and optimism amongst the tables as they enjoyed the warm summer's evening. When she reached Angel Hill, she couldn't help noticing that there was a light on at the gallery. Strange. Maybe Adrian was working late. She dismissed any concern and decided to have a walk round the Abbey Gardens.

The floral display was impressive as always, a carefully orchestrated spectacle, symmetrical every which way, with a footpath forming a cross between the grassed areas. Purple salvias towered over lime green euphorbias and yellow marigolds and in other beds rich red oriental poppies sang amongst silver foliage and café au lait dahlias.

She thought of how this scene contrasted with Rooked Meadow on the farm. For some reason she was not sure of, the meadow adjacent to Lucas Wood had been left untouched for as long as she could remember. Maybe the soil was too poor there. And yet she had noticed that it was a riot of wild flowers in spring, summer and even autumn. The butterflies and the bees feasted on the pollen and birds were frequent visitors. These formal gardens didn't seem to attract insects and bird life in the same way. Was it because it was in the centre of a town? Or was there too much intervention from man?

Wanda walked further into the park and down to where the ruins of the Abbey stood. Where once there had been a rich and powerful Benedictine Monastery, now only misshapen stone forms remained. She tried to imagine what it would have looked like back in the twelfth century, a magnificent building no doubt with many monks in brown habits walking gently around the grounds. It was a walled community, separating itself from the townsfolk and the wall remains along with the abbey's gate. Looking at the floral display in front of her, Wanda considered that they probably grew vegetables in the monks' day.

Back on Angel Hill she decided to walk past the gallery this time and peered in only to see Adrian staring back at her through the window. She smiled apologetically and waved. Should she go in and ask if he was okay? He appeared at the door.

'What are you doing here at this time?' he asked.

'Just having an evening stroll.' He looked troubled, his forehead lined. 'Everything okay?' she asked lightly.

'Fine. Yes. Absolutely fine. Enjoy your walk.' He seemed to be in a hurry to get rid of her. 'Make sure you're home before it gets dark,' he added.

'I will,' she said knowing there was little chance of that.

From there she turned up Churchgate Street and, lost in her thoughts of what her life had very quickly become, she weaved her way through the town and up to the hospital. It wasn't until she arrived outside the building that she realised what she had done. Should she go in, now she was here? Would Glen be pleased to see her? What had become so apparent since his accident was that they had been growing apart for years. Were they ever right for each other? Perhaps they should not have married in the first place?

It was getting dark now and the well-worn sixties hospital building was lit with harsh lighting. She was at the entrance, watching people anxiously rush through the doors towards loved ones, no doubt. Others were leaving with serious expressions, or getting frustrated by the car parking payment machines which never seemed to work smoothly.

She was still ambivalent. Then she remembered. Of course, Glen had just been moved from intensive care to the post-op ward where visiting hours were limited. Was it afternoons only? There was a part of her that wished she had a strong enough desire to go inside, walk up to the ward, barge in and insist on seeing Glen and then to relish the few moments they had together. But deep down she knew that if she did, she would leave disappointed. She'd have to go back to Carolyn's. *Surely by now Aaron will have made his move and they will be in bed or he will have gone home.*

She turned and looked up at the night sky. Suddenly she felt insecure. What was she doing here? Everyone else was leaving in cars. There were no taxis, just ambulances and she could hardly justify being taken home in one of those. She would just have to walk.

Halfway up Cullum Road she felt vulnerable and alone. It was a big wide road, with areas open to trees and common land. Perfect places for a nutter to wait and pounce. She quickened her pace. Was someone following her? She glanced round. No one was there, it was just the leaves of the trees rustling in the breeze. At last she could see the roundabout at the top of the hill, which gave her hope; from there it was not far to the top of Whiting Street. Somehow, when back in the Medieval quarter, she felt protected. And she would be nearly home.

The house was quiet and dark when she got back. Was Carolyn on the top floor with Aaron having her bit of fun? Did Wanda wish it was her? Of course not. Aaron must be twice the size of her; they would not be a good fit. She smiled to herself. She would make a cup of tea and take it up to bed.

As she put the kettle on her thoughts turned to her painting for Aaron. Perhaps she *would* make Quercus magical.

CHAPTER 12

Martin stood looking out over Rooked Meadow towards Lucas Wood. It must be a couple of acres in total, a riot of wild flowers and buzzing with insects in the late June sun. He could remember playing here as a kid, building dens and exploring, the weeds towering over him in jungle-like fashion. Had his kids not done the same? He had no memory of it. Too much television, he supposed, and Jane always had her head in a book.

He had never really questioned why they did not put the land to good use or use it for pasture. He remembered his dad dismissing any ideas of cultivating it and saying it was best left alone. But why? Surely, they could make some money from it? They were supposed to be getting the maximum yield from every inch of land they owned. And they certainly needed to do something to get them out of this financial pit. The insurance was paying out now and with Conor on board, they had the resources to do it; any improvements they could make on the farm would help.

Tanya's reaction the other day was interesting. She talked about the indirect benefits that this wild area brought to the rest of the farm. Martin failed to understand what she was saying but he was not going to admit it. If they went ahead and cultivated, Bartletts would have more work. Why would they turn that down? She had mentioned pigs. Martin had no experience of rearing pigs and certainly was not keen to get involved with any new enterprise at this stage of his life. But what might Glen think of pigs? Apparently, they would eat the vegetation and it would be a natural and cost-effective way of clearing the field. They would have to put an electric fence round it, to stop the pigs wandering everywhere. And then what would they do? Breed? They would need arcs for that not to mention a boar. He sighed. It would be easier just to cultivate it and grow crops. He needed to find out what Glen thought about it. And maybe get Colin over from Bartletts for his opinion. Tanya was good at baling but she did not seem to be too hungry for more work.

Fiona was a shadow of her former self. She looked like she had aged over the last month, her skin was pale and dry and her hands looked sore and pink with nails broken down to nothing. Wanda reached across the café table and placed her hands gently around her mother-in-law's.

'Fi, are you all right?'

'Yes, yes, I'm fine. You have to be, don't you?'

'Well, yes. But you're allowed to be fed up with everything.'

'What, like you walking out on us and leaving us to manage the farm on our own?' She stared at Wanda who released her hands and recoiled back in to her chair. They had a table outside the No. 5 café and looked out over Angel Hill with the abbey gate opposite. It had clouded over and looked like it was about to rain.

'I rang the insurance company,' Wanda said and Fiona looked shifty. 'Apparently they have started paying out.'

'Yes, that's right.' Fiona spoke so quietly that Wanda could hardly hear her.

'So has Martin hired a replacement for Glen?'

'Yes, something like that.' Fiona would not meet Wanda's gaze.

'What does that mean?'

'It means he's hired someone!' Fiona raised her voice now as if she was annoyed. 'His name is Conor.' She had barely touched her coffee; it must be cold now.

'Shall I get us another latte?' Wanda asked deciding not to push her mother-in-law any further.

'We still need the money to pay Lee,' Fiona said ignoring Wanda's question and then she added, 'I'm worried that he's going to leave if he doesn't get it.' She looked close to tears.

'I'm sorry Fi. I did give you some last Saturday.'

'I know but it just feels like I have to come cap in hand to you all the time.'

'Okay, I'll draw out some money from the cash machine as soon as we leave here. How much do you need?'

'How much have you got?'

'Fi, I need some money to live on.' She wouldn't mention the spending spree she'd had on clothes in Phase Eight recently so that she could stop looking like a farmer all the time. She had felt guilty at the time but it was getting embarrassing having to borrow Carolyn's clothes all the time.

'But you're staying with a friend.'

'Yes, but I have to contribute for food, maybe rent. I'm not a permanent house guest.'

Fiona bristled when Wanda said the word permanent. Obviously, it wasn't forever.

'Listen, I'll give you a week's wages for Lee for now and more as soon as I can. I'll even drop it in to the farmhouse.' She could do that after a visit to Lucas Wood to work on her painting.

Fiona looked like she was in an anxious trance. 'That will help. But I just can't see a way out of this mess.'

'But Fi your son is on the mend; he really is. They are optimistic he'll make a full recovery in time. Surely that gives us hope.'

'But what about the two of you. What's happening? Are you leaving Glen and running off with this big American chap?'

'What?' Wanda sighed with frustration. 'Fi, I'm doing a painting for Aaron for which he will pay me handsomely. If you really must know it's my friend Carolyn who has started a relationship with him.'

'How disappointing for you.'

'Now that was uncalled for. I might not be living at the farm right now but I visit Glen every day pretty much.' The way her voice trailed off gave her away. The truth was that, as they seemed to have very little to talk about, she was finding the visits excruciating at times. All he wanted to know was what was happening on the farm. She had been on the verge of telling him the truth more than once but each time she decided it was better that he did not know; he would only worry.

'I haven't told him that you've moved in to town,' Fi said with a look of disappointment.

'Probably for the best.'

Fi had said that visiting time started at two. Martin made sure he was there on time but the car park seemed to be full. Eventually he spotted someone leaving and nipped in to their space. He hadn't visited his son much since he was out of danger. The farm had demanded a lot of his time and Fi had been in to see Glen quite a bit. But today he had a spring in his step as he walked through the corridors following the directions that the woman on reception at the entrance had given him to the ward Glen was now on.

Glen was up and dressed and sat on an armchair next to his bed.

'Son, good to see you up.' Martin pulled up a chair opposite him and patted him on the knee.

'Dad,' Glen said, his voice quiet. He looked a shadow of his former self but at least he was out of bed.

'You look well.' Martin thought it was better to be upbeat. 'Feeling better, are you?'

'It was a major op, Dad, but I'm not too bad. Still on some heavy painkillers which make you want to sleep all the time.'

'Probably best for you right now. Can't be much fun stuck in here. I bet you can't wait to get back to the farm.'

Glen's expression didn't change. 'I certainly would like to be home again.'

'Of course, you would. We're looking after the place for you, me and your mum.'

'What, you're popping in each day?'

'Living there actually. Sorry, I thought you knew. We had to, son. The thing is Wanda would never manage on her own.'

'Makes sense,' Glen said. 'So, what's happening? Are the cows milking well? Wanda doesn't tell me anything.'

'It's all ticking over. Managed to get the straw in. They sent a girl would you believe? Anyway, I wanted to talk to you about something else.'

'Oh yes.' Glen eyed his father suspiciously.

'Nothing to worry about, son. You know Rooked Meadow?'

'We don't touch it. It's wild.'

'Well yes, it is. But we could do something with it.'

'Granddad always seemed to think it was best left. I've never questioned it.'

'Maybe we should. He had some funny suspicions, did John. Not sure where he got all that from. But anyway, just think, we could make some money out of it.'

Glen was looking puzzled now. 'How? What are you thinking? It's terribly overgrown.'

'Pigs are a possibility.'

'Pigs? Since when have you wanted pigs on the farm?'

'I thought it was a bad idea at first but Tanya, she was the girl they sent, she suggested it. She said they would clear all those weeds for us for starters.'

'And then what?'

'Well, we could get a boar in, try and breed or just rear weaners.'

Glen looked flustered. 'Can you pass me that glass of water?'

Martin reached for the glass and passed it to him. He sipped from it.

'Sorry son, I didn't mean to bother you.'

A tear appeared in Glen's eye. 'You have no idea how difficult this all is for me. I don't even know if I'll be able to farm again. I'm thinking I might just be able to do the milking one day, with some help. But pigs? We know sod all about pigs! What are you thinking?'

'Forget it. I'm sorry. It was Tanya's mad idea. Just forget I said anything.'

Glen glared at his father but said nothing. The look he gave him reminded Martin of when Glen was a boy and he'd hurt himself.

'Look you must concentrate on getting better. That's the main thing. I'm sorry I came.'

'You're sorry you came?' Glen raised his voice. A nurse appeared.

'Everything all right here? Glen needs to stay calm.' She looked pointedly at Martin before heading down the ward.

'Sorry, I'm really sorry. It's not easy for any of us.' Martin stood up from his chair and hovered.

'You're not stuck in here!' Glen shouted and something inside Martin snapped.

'No, I'm not but I'm running the farm single-handed. I'm supposed to be retired.'

'What do you mean, single-handed? What about Wanda? And Mum for that matter.'

'Well, to be honest your mum's nerves aren't very good and as for Wanda...' He looked down at the ground. He knew he'd said too much.

The nurse appeared again. 'I think you'd better leave now,' she said and stood there waiting.

'What do you mean, "as for Wanda"?'

'I'll be on my way.' Martin turned to leave.

'I think that would be best,' the nurse reiterated.

'Tell me! What's Wanda done? She's my wife, I have a right to know.' It sounded like he was straining his voice.

Martin turned back. 'She's left the farm. We didn't tell you because we didn't want to worry you.'

'Left the farm! So where is she?'

'I think you'd better ask her that yourself.'

The nurse looked like her patience had run out.

'I'm going now,' Martin said and walked away.

Wanda got herself all set up with her easel in position but, instead of sitting down to paint, she stood back to look at the painting from a couple of metres away. It was amazing what a difference that made, especially with today's fresh eyes. At first, she could only see little things that irritated her and she wanted to put right. But then she remembered the light was different today. She had a photo on her mobile which she had taken when she'd started this painting which showed the light coming through the canopy. She searched for it now, so she could take a look at it. Yes, she'd got it right.

'What are you looking at?' Quercus sprang to life.

'You, of course. My painting of you.'

'Is it finished?'

'No!' She raised her voice more than she'd meant to.

'Don't blame me.'

'Sorry, I'm finding this bit hard.'

'What bit?'

'Well...' *Should she tell him? It would be sort of committing to the idea.*

'And?' the tree roared.

'Making you look more magical.'

Quercus fell quiet. Wanda desperately wanted his help. But you couldn't rush an old oak tree.

At last Quercus spoke. 'It is midsummer's day today, Wanda. Over sixteen hours of sunlight.'

'Yes, of course, the summer solstice. Well, if nothing else I have plenty of time.'

'And I simply *am* magical as is all of nature. Exhausted, admittedly, but still magical. Even if I am in my resting period.'

'What happens after your resting period?' Wanda was curious.

'The gradual decline follows. Three hundred years or so if I'm lucky.'

'Wow.'

'See that tree over there.'

Wanda looked around her wondering which one he meant.

'South of your easel.'

'South, which way is south?'

'Look where the sun is!' Quercus sounded exasperated. 'Actually, you're facing in the right direction.'

'Do you mean that one, with its lower branches on the ground?'

'Yes, as I explained to Gilbert, with the walking stick, that ancient oak tree has put out stabilisers to stop it falling over through its declining years. Do you see?'

'I do, yes. How wonderful.'

'Strong winds, which are coming more and more, are harder to withstand as you get older.'

'So the stabilisers help to keep the whole tree up.'

'Yes. Very wise, unlike humans who sometimes think it's a good idea to cut off the lower branches.'

'Why do they do that?' Wanda was suddenly outraged.

'Why do you do a lot of things?' Quercus sighed deeply. 'You have so much to learn.'

This was all very interesting but she had yet to paint a stroke.

'What makes you magical?' Wanda asked the tree. That was what she really wanted to know.

'Everything about me,' Quercus replied.

'Yes, but what in particular? Just give me one amazing fact that will help me to make this painting magical.'

'It is difficult to name one thing as I am extraordinarily amazing, not to mention far wiser than humans.'

Wanda smiled. 'Just one thing,' she pleaded.

Quercus was quiet for a minute. 'I know. This will probably surprise you. I have well over two thousand species living within and on me and—'

'Over two thousand?' Wanda got closer to the trunk and peered at it looking for signs of movement.

'The amazing fact is that three hundred and twenty of those species can only survive on a mature oak tree such as myself.'

'That is truly amazing, Quercus. What exactly am I looking for?'

'Insects, bugs, lichens and mosses; they live off my bark. I've even got birds nesting in me.'

With a closer look she could see how the bark had loosened and where crevices had formed. 'And creatures nest in these holes?'

'If you must call them holes. I had a very smooth trunk once, you know.'

'You may have mentioned that Quercus.'

'There are bats, of course; you'll catch them at night.'

'Bats! How wonderful.'

'I even had a barbastelle once. They are extremely rare.'

'How exciting. What do they look like?'

'You should know. Don't humans know everything?'

'You're always telling me I have so much to learn.'

'Yes, I'm forgetting. I think I need a rest.'

'You rest Quercus. I'll google it later.'

'Google it? No, don't tell me. I'm not up for another human idiosyncrasy right now.'

And with that he fell silent.

Carolyn could see that it was Gerard calling. *What on earth did he want now?* She remembered back to the last time they had met up in a small café in London. He had actually been kind to her briefly with an appealing look on his face that she couldn't quite fathom.

'Gerard,' she said putting on a confident air now, as if it would fool him.

'Carolyn, how are you?'

'What do you want?' *After all they had been through, what could it possibly be?*

'Just checking you're okay.'

'After all that bitchy behaviour, you want to know if I'm okay?' She didn't hide her outrage.

'I forgive you,' he said and she could tell he was sniggering down the other end of the air waves. 'You clearly felt justified in being bitchy.'

'*Me!* You rat!' Everything in her being told her to cut him off. But curiosity got the better of her. 'What do you really want?'

'I'd like us to be friends,' he said so simply it was ludicrous.

'Friends! No thank you.'

'Hear me out. Look, I'm sorry it all got a bit messy. I know it was a terrible shock to you that I'm gay. Well, bi-sexual actually. The thing is I'm coming up to quaint little Bury St Edmunds and thought it would be nice to meet up. You know, for old times' sake.'

'What brings you here of all places?'

'That little gallery near Angel Hill looks interesting. And well, with you in town, I'm not adverse to a bit of nightlife.'

'Nightlife! I tell you these days I'm enjoying my nightlife with a rather fine gentleman from New York, an art dealer, in fact.'

'Gosh, sounds exciting. Would he fancy a threesome?'

'He is not gay!'

'Only teasing.'

'Why are you really coming up here?' This was worrying.

'To see you. To forget about all those silly arguments; after all you got a good settlement, didn't you? And just to be friends again.' He was incorrigible.

'Has he left you?'

'You mean Maurice? Not exactly.' His voice faltered.

Cryptic as ever. Carolyn closed her eyes and prayed. 'Listen Gerard, just leave me alone!'

'I'll be staying at The Angel Hotel this weekend,' he blurted out as she cut him off.

Damn. It was Wednesday already; how was she going to avoid him.

Carolyn took a deep breath and sat with a cup of herbal tea, her mobile on silent so there were no distractions for a good fifteen minutes. She had promised herself faithfully that she wouldn't chase Aaron and she'd let him do all the running. It was a good insurance policy against getting hurt. She had ruminated endlessly on their evening together just a few days ago. He had seemed really keen on her and the sex was amazing. But he hadn't called or texted since. Had he used her?

He had said he was going to Manchester very soon. When she'd asked which day, he'd said, 'Not sure of the exact day but soon.'

Carolyn felt deflated now. What was wrong with her? She'd kept her looks, just about. She looked after herself; plenty of exercise and healthy salads. Okay, she drank quite a bit, but didn't everyone?

The temptation to look at her mobile was too much. She picked it up. And there was a text from Aaron.

Are you free this evening? xx

Carolyn leapt up from her seat and laughed out loud as she swirled around the room with glee.

Pea Porridge turned out to be a charming little restaurant tucked away on a small residential square. Carolyn had not heard of it, even though it was only a ten-minute walk from her place. Aaron had assured her that the restaurant came recommended.

She looked at him, sat opposite her, as he poured them both a glass of the red wine he'd chosen, saying, 'I think you'll like this Pinot Noir, not too heavy.'

He always dressed smartly but this evening she had the feeling that he'd made an extra effort. And his aftershave smelt divine. She must manage her expectations though, not get too carried away. With the North Atlantic between them, this liaison could only be brief.

'How's it going at Sheridans? Sold any real estate yet?' he asked.

'I really quite enjoy it, actually. Some of the clients are a bit non-communicative. But that's fine. I have to ask them at the end of the viewing what they think of the property so I can call in my feedback.'

'Has anyone said they hate the place?'

'Gosh, no! We British just keep quiet if we don't like anything. I asked one guy what he thought of this place on Southgate Street and I might as well have asked him which sexual position he preferred. The look on his face before he made a run for it!'

Aaron was laughing. 'Maybe he had the hots for you.'

'No, I don't think so. He was just the nervous type.'

'What sort of place was it?'

'Old. Let's just say it needed updating.'

'Your place is old but it's lovely. Really cute. In the Medieval quarter as well. Must have been big bucks. Was it like that when you bought it?'

'I did some work, actually. A lick of paint here and there to lighten the walls and I had the wood flooring put in downstairs. Luckily my divorce settlement left me with a little spare cash.'

'Good to know!' Aaron said with a big smile on his face leaving Carolyn wondering. 'On the contrary,' Aaron continued, 'my divorce settlement left me with a lot of work to do to raise some cash. That's why I decided to go it alone and start up my own art dealership.'

'And is that working out for you?' *Surely if he could afford to stay at The Angel Hotel he must be fairly well off. But, of course, it was none of her business. And why should she care?*

'It's going really well. I've managed to secure the use of some exhibition space in Brooklyn recently. It's a great opportunity.'

'That sounds amazing. So what takes you up to Manchester?' She was pleased with herself for weaving this question into the conversation at a relevant point.

'There's a guy up there with a gallery, near the castle, and some interesting contemporary works. I just thought as I'm this side of the pond.' Their eyes met; the conversation paused. He was smiling at her and she almost felt herself blush.

'Would you like to come with me?' he asked. *How did she answer that?*

'What really? Well, I...' She couldn't think fast enough. 'The thing is, Sheridans...'

'What days do you work for them?'

'Oh, it's the end of the week, Thursday to Saturday.'

'Perfect, so we travel up on Sunday. But only if you want to.'

This was not fitting well into her plan of keeping this relationship casual. Would they be sharing a hotel room? She should say no. But then again, it would be fun. And she might even be able to avoid Gerard's visit to this town that she had come to love.

'Do you know what, I'd love to come. And actually, we could go up on Saturday as soon as my last viewing is done, if you'd like? It could even be mid-afternoon.'

'Excellent. Okay if I drive you up?' he asked.

Brilliant. She could leave Gerard high and dry.

Wanda got back to Carolyn's to find an empty house and a hand-written note. She was out having dinner with Aaron. Lucky her. But actually, that was good as Wanda needed some time to herself.

Talking to Quercus had been inspiring. He was opening up a whole new world to Wanda. Knowing that this magnificent oak was riddled with living creatures gave her an idea for her painting. She just needed more detail; she would go on to Google and find out more. She sat on Carolyn's sofa and opened up her laptop.

Just then her mobile rang. It was Glen. She hadn't managed a hospital visit yesterday and now she was too tired to go out again today. It was so important that she got this painting right and it was taking up all her time.

'Glen, how are you?' She put her laptop to one side and stood up.

'The same. Are you not coming in today?' He sounded hurt.

'I am so sorry; I've been busy.' She began to pace.

'Busy doing what?' Somehow she knew that was a loaded question.

'Well actually I have a commission for a painting. It will bring in a decent amount of cash so...'

'You're painting and not working on the farm.' *Did he know?*

'Today, yes.'

'Every day,' he said sounding deflated rather than angry. *How had he found out?*

'Look, darling, I'll come in tomorrow to explain everything. I promise.'

'So you expect me to lie here with nothing to do but wonder what on earth is going on.' There was an anxious pause before he said, 'Dad's told me you've left the farm.'

'Right.' It was a relief in some ways to know that he knew. Especially as he wasn't actually shouting at her. Although his throat hadn't been the same since the ventilator; it had weakened his voice.

'So it's true?' She could hear his disappointment.

'Your mum and dad just moved in to our home and took over. I wasn't even there. Did you know they have their own key? I couldn't bear it. Your dad was already bossing me about and then...'

'Where are you living? Why didn't you tell me?'

Wanda closed her eyes and took a calming breath. 'Listen, I'm sorry, I'm really sorry. That's all I can say.' She sank back on to the sofa, throwing her head back on to the soft cushions.

'Do you plan to come back to the farm when I come out of hospital? Where do I stand? Are you leaving me?'

Wanda felt tears bursting from her eyes. 'No,' she spluttered unconvincingly. 'No, it was all too much for me and I just needed to...'

'Leave the farm,' he said clearly not wanting to understand her side of things.

'It was more to do with your dad and the way he treats me.'

'He's seventy-five. He's supposed to be retired and he has high blood pressure.'

'I know.' Wanda was shaking and her breath was getting shorter. 'But he's so horrible to me!' She was crying now and couldn't hide it from Glen.

'He's not that bad. His heart's in the right place.'

'Yes, that's right, you defend your father. Make me out to be the bad person. You always have taken his side. You do realise you are married to me!' she shouted out in frustration.

'How could I forget. I've put up with a lot over the years but every time I make allowances...' It was even worse that he spoke slowly and weakly. It was if he had time to consider every word and mean it.

'Ah yes, you make allowances because I'm not good enough for you. I'm not the perfect farmer's wife.'

'No one expects you to be perfect. We've given up on that long ago. But you could make an effort. Especially when times are hard like right now.' His voice was getting scratchy. Wanda could hear a nurse telling him he should rest now.

'I've got to go,' he said and he was coughing, choking even, as he ended the call.

Wanda cried loudly and unashamedly now as she sat there all alone. It was horrible to hear Glen distressed and perhaps in pain. It made her feel all the more guilty about leaving the farm. But it also hurt to hear his disappointment of her loud and clear. Was it really so wrong for her to pursue her own dream of being an artist? Did marrying a farmer condemn her to a life of farming at the cost of her own happiness? If so, perhaps this should have been pointed out to her at the tender age of twenty-one before she said *I do*. She had been so naïve to think that she was marrying Glen and not signing up to the hard life of a farmer. For many years she had mildly accepted her fate even blaming her own inadequacies. But now she was older and wiser she could see that the Taylor family had put her in a very difficult situation. They were dictating the way the farm should be run and she was expected to work hard without questioning a thing; without complaint. It simply wasn't fair. She knew then, without a doubt, that even if it meant the end of her marriage, she could not return to the farm unless there was some sort of change. She thought of Glen in hospital again– she did love him – and fresh tears burst from her eyes.

CHAPTER 13

Adrian was in the room at the back of the gallery fawning over a new Chinese artist called Chu Hua which apparently meant chrysanthemum, a flower that Wanda had never been fond of. He had made a point of telling Wanda what an exceptional artist Chu Hua was and how excited he was that she might consider exhibiting her work at his gallery.

Before her arrival he had insisted that the place was pristine, even roping Wanda in to help with emptying bins. *Would this artist be looking in the bins?* Wanda couldn't help noticing there were a lot of empty takeaway cartons in the little kitchen they used to make drinks. Also a microwave had been installed. All this reminded her that she'd seen Adrian in the gallery on the evening she had walked round the town to avoid playing gooseberry. Was he camping here? Had his wife thrown him out?

It was Saturday and there were quite a few people casually browsing around as if they had come in on a whim. Wanda had tried to engage in conversation with some of them but none of them seemed to be serious about buying anything. She rather missed Aaron's presence. He was quite good fun. But there was no chance of him walking in. Wanda had been surprised to hear from Carolyn that she was going with him to Manchester for the weekend. So much for just a bit of fun. Was this getting serious?

Wanda sighed. Why should she deny her friend some joy? At least the painting was going well. As she added the touches of magic, she was beginning to love it. She still had no idea if Aaron would be pleased. Perhaps Adrian would put it in the gallery if Aaron rejected it. That is, if there was space for it. Obviously, Chu Hua was the artist of the moment.

Wanda stayed until five o'clock when the gallery closed even though she could have gone at four. It had got quite busy in the end with a couple of potential buyers.

'Not a bad day,' Wanda said to Adrian as she tidied the desk.

'An excellent day. I'm very excited by Chu Hua Wang's work. I think this collection will generate a lot of good PR for us in the art world.'

'And there was a woman from Highgate interested in two or three paintings. She said she'd call on Monday,' she reminded him.

'Yes, she may well call. Pity she didn't take them today.'

'She wanted to consult her partner. She took photos of the three she liked.'

'Good.' He looked at her and there was an awkward pause.

'You off home soon yourself?' Wanda asked, looking out of the window. Dark clouds were coming in replacing the earlier blue sky.

'Er... not just yet. I think I'll check the week's figures first.'

'On Saturday evening?'

'Yes, well.' He looked shifty and then asked, 'Do you have any plans yourself?'

'I've got stuff to do,' she said, not wanting to mention the painting she was working on as she was not selling it through the gallery.

'I see.'

'Is everything okay Adrian?'

He pursed his lips and hesitated before he said, 'If you must know, my wife's thrown me out.'

'Oh no. I'm sorry to hear that.'

He shrugged his shoulders. 'It happens. She's never really understood what I do.'

'So where are you staying?'

'Oh, here and there.'

Wanda decided she wouldn't get too involved. 'Well, I'd better go,' she said putting her handbag over her shoulder.

The clouds were menacing and threatened rain. As usual Wanda didn't have an umbrella. By the time she was halfway up Abbeygate the rain had started and quickly became fast and furious. She ducked into the entrance of a café and looked out on to the street. Some people were scurrying away, others not bothering to quicken their pace, resigned to their fate. At least it was warm summer rain.

A man just inside the café was mopping the floor as they closed up. He looked at Wanda but didn't say anything. After a few minutes there was no sign of the rain abating so she decided to make a run for it. She stuck to the side of the street where she could but still her thin cotton skirt and blouse got wet and her hair was dripping. Her wedge sandals slowed her down and she was tempted to stop and take them off but any delay would just make her wetter. By the time she arrived back at Whiting Street she was soaked through. She struggled to take off her sodden sandals, the buckles proving stiff and making a squeaking noise as she forced them open to release her feet.

She would dry herself off and change her clothes; she'd be okay. She would wait for the rain to stop before venturing out again that evening. She padded through to the kitchen, aware she was leaving footprints, and looked in the fridge to see if there was anything she could eat. Nothing but half a carton of milk, a small piece of cheese and some broccoli. Broccoli pasta with grated cheese? She really needed comfort food. And wine. It was her own silly fault for not going to the supermarket.

She laughed at her own misfortune and went upstairs to change. That was when she saw the water dripping through the ceiling of her bedroom. It was almost missing the side of her bed but the carpet was drenched and the duvet damp. She went straight up to the top floor where Carolyn's room was and, sure enough, there was water coming through the roof and at quite a rate.

She ran all the way down stairs to the kitchen and frantically started looking for a bucket, opening cupboards and closing them again. When she'd run out of cupboards, she opened and shut them all again as if she might get a different result the second time. All she could find was a washing up bowl. This was hopeless. She went back up to the top floor and placed the bowl under the drip. Except it was a bit more than a drip now, more of a running tap. She looked out of the window. There was no sign of the weather abating. Maybe having a bowl in place would stop the water going down to her room at least. But how long would that bowl last?

Just then the doorbell went. She had a horrible feeling it might be Adrian. Had she mentioned Carolyn's address to him? She had definitely referred to Whiting Street. She went down, her wet skirt chafing her legs which was becoming uncomfortable now.

As she opened the door she saw a man she didn't recognise. He was wearing a bright yellow kagool and carrying a supermarket plastic bag. Water dripped from his face.

'Hello, is this where Carolyn lives?'

'It is, yes, but she's not here.'

'Are you sure? She knew I was coming. Gerard, her ex.' He held out a wet hand and Wanda reluctantly shook it.

'Ah. Wanda, I'm just staying with Carolyn for a while.'

'Oh, I see. Are you expecting her back soon then?'

'Not until after the weekend.'

'Really? But she knew I was coming.'

'That's odd. She didn't say anything to me. Anyway, she's gone to Manchester.'

'You're kidding.'

Just then a car went past, its wheels splashing up water making Gerard even wetter. He wore a pleading expression and Wanda felt compelled to let him in even though she just knew it was a bad idea. The slightest gesture as she stood back from the door was enough.

'Oh, thank you,' he said sounding genuinely grateful.

'Perhaps you could stay until the rain stops.' *Why had she said that? It might rain all night.*

They both stood there for an awkward moment and then Wanda said, 'Actually, I've got a bit of a crisis; I think the roof's leaking.'

'No! That's awful.' He looked up to the ceiling.

'I can't find a bucket. Carolyn doesn't seem to have one.'

'Do you want me to help you look? Being her ex I might...'

'There aren't many places to look. This is a pretty small house.'

'Ah.' He bit his lip. 'Sorry but do you have a towel I could use?'

'Yes, of course.' She went off to find one. This wasn't the evening she had planned and she knew she should be going to visit Glen to try and clear the air.

When Gerard had dried himself off, he said, 'What about the neighbours? Might they have a bucket?'

'Worth a try.' Wanda didn't know what to make of him now. Carolyn had painted a picture of him as a good for nothing, selfish idiot.

'I'll go if you like,' he offered. They both looked at his soaked kagool. 'Do you have an umbrella I could borrow?'

'Oh, yes.' Luckily there was one hanging up right by the door. It was pink and covered in a pattern of roses, one of Carolyn's. She handed it to him. He opened the front door and put up the umbrella. 'Excellent, my favourite colour,' he said as he stepped out.

'Good luck,' Wanda said laughing as she pulled the door to before deciding to check on her bedroom again. There was less water coming through now. She moved her bed away from the leak and wondered how she would dry the duvet out. Perhaps she'd use her hairdryer. But first she needed to change out of these wet clothes. She quickly dried herself off and threw on the first dress she laid her hand on in the wardrobe. It was actually one of her recent purchases, a red tunic dress which was amazingly flattering.

Gerard got back with not one, but two buckets.

'Well done.' Wanda couldn't quite believe it.

'I was lucky, both sides had a bucket. Trust Carolyn not to have one. She was never very practical.'

'Right. I'll put one in each room and put some towels down on the carpet. Then, hopefully, we'll be able to relax a bit.'

When she got back downstairs, she found Gerard unpacking his shopping bag. He had a bottle of Chablis which Wanda knew was Carolyn's favourite wine, and a large ready meal of paella.

'I don't wish to be too forward but I bought these for Carolyn. I don't suppose you want to share them with me?'

Gerard turned out to be surprisingly good company. After all the drama, that first glass of wine went down very niccly. As far as Wanda could tell, his only real sin was that after twenty-six years of marriage he had realised he was gay and had an affair with another man.

'I don't suppose she's been very complimentary about me?' he asked with a resigned smile.

'She has made you out to be the bad guy,' Wanda said carefully.

'I know I hurt her badly.'

'Still, if you suddenly realise you prefer men.'

'It was not even that, actually. I mean I'm bi-sexual. It just took meeting Maurice.'

'Sounds like you're happy.'

'Actually, it's not that straightforward.'

'You don't regret what you did though, do you?'

He waved his head from side to side as if undecided. 'I sort of do. But still, too late now.' He looked thoughtful and then asked, 'What's Carolyn doing up in Manchester?'

Wanda wasn't sure if she should tell him the truth at first but couldn't be bothered to come up with an alternative version. 'Well, actually she's gone with an American art dealer. Aaron. He lives in New York but is over here on business.'

'She mentioned him on the phone.'

'So she really did know you were coming?'

'Yes.' Gerard paused before he added, 'she did make it clear she didn't want to see me.'

'Looks like I've been stitched up,' Wanda said laughing.

It was gone ten o'clock when Gerard headed off back to his hotel. The buckets upstairs had both been emptied and put back in place and the rain had stopped for now. Wanda looked at her weather app. There was a forty per cent chance of precipitation forecast for the early hours of the morning. She would just have to hope that the buckets didn't fill up again. She thought about texting Carolyn to let her know what was happening but then imagined her having a romantic time with Aaron and decided to wait until the morning.

Wanda was painfully aware that she hadn't visited Glen but what with the heavy rain and leaking roof she had good reason. She decided she would send him a text message to explain and promise to go tomorrow.

On Sunday morning the sun was out and the bucket on the top floor only a quarter full. Wanda called Carolyn.

'So this happened when? Why didn't you call me?' Carolyn didn't take the news well.

'As I said, it was yesterday evening. When I got back from work.'

'And what's happened? Did you manage to stop it?'

'Gerard turned up and he managed to get some buckets from the neighbours.'

'Gerard! What the hell was he doing there?'

'He came to see you. Apparently, you knew about it.'

'Oh God, I didn't think he'd actually come to the house.'

'Well, he did. Turned out to be quite fortuitous as there was nothing in the fridge.'

'You mean he brought food?'

'And Chablis.'

'You didn't spend the evening with him? Tell me you didn't.'

'I did actually.'

'Wanda! You slept with him, didn't you?'

'No! Don't be silly. He went back to his hotel when the rain stopped.'

'Have you called anyone to fix the roof? Is it going to rain again?'

'No, I haven't contacted a roofer. Carolyn, this is your home. Don't you think you should be doing that?'

'But I'm not there!'

'Are you not coming back today?'

Suddenly Carolyn was sheepish. 'Well, actually, we were planning on staying a couple more days.'

'How lovely for you. Bit of a romantic break.'

'No need for the sarcasm. I don't suppose you could find a roofer to come out?'

'On a Sunday? How much are you prepared to pay?'

'Oh God, I can really do without this.'

'Funnily enough it's not much fun for me.' Wanda felt that Carolyn was being a little unfair.

'You know Wanda, I'm just going to have to start charging you rent. I mean to pay for this.'

Wanda gulped. 'I see,' she said meekly. There was a very awkward pause.

'Look, I'm sorry that wasn't the best way of telling you but you have been staying with me for two weeks now and I know you have been contributing to the food budget but still, it has crossed my mind; I mean if this is going to become a long–term arrangement.'

'Fair enough,' Wanda said as her mind whirred with ides. Where else could she live? On the streets? Should she throw her in–laws out of the farmhouse and move back in? Perhaps she just had to bite the bullet and live with them. Suddenly she felt very hot.

'First things first, we need to deal with this leaking roof. Would you mind terribly seeing if there's anyone local who can come out? And check the forecast. If there isn't any rain expected today, it could perhaps wait until tomorrow.'

'Of course I will.' Wanda responded obediently.

'Right, well perhaps you could update me later today.'

'Absolutely.'

'Text me. Anytime.'

Wanda's first thought as the call ended was that she must visit Glen.

When Wanda reached Glen's ward she found him up and dressed and chatting with one of the other patients. She stood at a distance and waited patiently. Glen noticed her but did not smile.

'I'll see you later, Bill,' he said and walked slowly, slightly awkwardly, towards Wanda.

'There's a visitor lounge,' he said and started to make his way along the ward. The effort involved was etched on his face. Wanda followed him not daring to say anything.

They sat at one end of the lounge on a couple of armchairs which were side by side. Wanda thought about moving her chair, so that she was opposite him, but decided against it. There were a couple of family groups at the other end of the room having a much easier time of it by the looks of things.

'I wasn't sure if you would come.' He gave her a sideways glance and then rested his eyes back in his lap.

'Did you get my text last night?'

'Yes, I did.'

'I think we need to talk,' she said gently.

'Where are you living?' he asked. 'Dad said he didn't know.'

'Carolyn's. She's an old uni friend. She's lives on Whiting Street in town.'

'How long have you been there?' He seemed intrigued.

'It's been...' What should she say? She had to tell him the truth. 'A couple of weeks.'

'I've only been in here for five weeks.'

'It wasn't straightaway. It was when your mum and dad moved into our home. Uninvited.' She tried to keep any malice out of her voice.

Glen took a deep breath. 'So you'd like them to go home?'

Wanda couldn't actually imagine that her in-laws would ever leave.

'Or is this about us?' Glen turned and looked at her properly now and their eyes met.

'After the accident I did my best to keep the farm going,' Wanda started to explain. 'Of course it wasn't easy. Martin kept turning up and telling me what I was doing was wrong. He criticised me at every turn and I just couldn't take any more.'

'I'll talk to Dad and tell him to back off a bit.'

'Thank you,' Wanda half smiled. 'In actual fact I think I'd like to go back home now. Things have got a bit difficult at Carolyn's.'

'Oh.' He raised his eyebrows.

'It's one of those Georgian houses in the Medieval quarter and the roof started leaking yesterday when we had that heavy rain.'

'That's your friend's problem, surely?'

'Well actually she's away for a few days so I've had to deal with it.'

A man walked into the lounge carrying a couple of takeaway drinks and took them over to a woman on the other side of the room.

'I don't suppose you'd go down to the café and get me a decent coffee?' Glen asked. 'The stuff we get on the ward is pretty awful.'

She stood up and smiled at him, putting her handbag over her shoulder.

'Cappuccino, please.' His face had softened now. She was beginning to remember what she loved about him.

By the time she got back with the coffees, she knew what she had to say to him.

There was a note on the doormat when Wanda got back to Carolyn's. It was from Gerard. He'd managed to find a roofer who would come out on Monday morning. All Wanda had to do was call him; that was kind of Gerard. There was a P.S. suggesting they might have a drink together at The Angel Hotel around sixish if she was not busy. Maybe she would. But first she needed to do some more work on her painting.

Gerard was wearing a silk scarf over a navy-blue T-shirt with a beige linen jacket. He leapt up when Wanda walked in to the lounge of the hotel. She had changed into another tunic dress, this time white with a floral print, mainly so that she didn't feel out of place in this trendy venue.

'Any luck with that roofer?' Gerard asked.

'Yes, thank you for that. He's coming at eight-thirty tomorrow.'

'And have you reported back to Carolyn?'

'I sent her a text.' Wanda sipped her gin and tonic. It tasted good.

'Have you told her what his call-out charge is?'

'No.' She smiled at him.

He laughed and relaxed back in his armchair. 'She won't like that.'

'Yes, she's already replied to my text with words to that effect. I just wonder what her last slave died of.'

'You're looking at him,' Gerard said and they laughed together.

'Anyway, she's made it perfectly clear that she's going to start charging me rent so that she can cover the cost.'

'Ah. How do you feel about that?'

'Well, now I've been in to see Glen and we've cleared the air, I've decided that there's a chance we can make our marriage work. At least it's worth a shot. So I'm hoping to move back to the farmhouse.'

'I'm pleased for you. What made you change your mind?'

'It wasn't so much changing my mind. More, that I wasn't sure there was any hope before. But he's agreed to talk to his dad and get him to back off. And most importantly to ask them to leave our home, the farmhouse. So now I've got somewhere to live.'

Gerard sipped his drink and smiled broadly. 'Carolyn won't like that.'

'Actually, I've decided I am going to give her some rent. When Aaron pays me for this second painting, I will have some money. Anyway, hopefully she'll be all loved up with him and won't care.'

Suddenly Gerard looked serious.

'Sorry, have I said the wrong thing.'

'No. No, you really haven't. In fact, this whole experience is reminding me of what, no doubt subconsciously, pushed me away in the first place. I had thought that it would be nice if we could be friends again but I now realise it's far too soon for anything like that.'

They sat in quiet contemplation for a moment.

'Is it over with Maurice?' Wanda asked carefully.

He was staring at the low table in front of them in some sort of trance. 'I think possibly it is. Or at least we want different things from the relationship.'

CHAPTER 14

Martin's mobile rang waking him.

'Who the hell is that?' Fi almost shouted. They were lying in bed back-to-back; he hadn't realised that she was awake already. Martin grabbed his handset from the bedside table.

'It's Lee. Better answer.' He swung his legs out on to the floor and sat on the side of the bed.

'Lee? Everything all right.'

'I'm not up for milking today. Not feeling too good.'

'But Lee, this is short notice, isn't it?' He looked at his watch. Six o'clock already.

'You've not paid me for the last two days.'

'We will pay you, I promise. It's just cash flow.'

'Sorry but I won't be coming today.'

'Lee, we need you. We're desperate.'

Fi was out of bed now. Her hair was stuck at odd angles on her head, her long T-shirt once white now greying. 'You're going to have a heart attack at this rate,' she said to Martin. 'Tell him that.'

'No need, I heard,' Lee said. 'Pay me and I'll come.'

'I'll have all the money we owe you at the end of your shift if you just come now.'

There was silence at the other end.

'Please Lee; the cows have got to be milked.'

'I'm calling Wanda. She will pay me.'

'Don't call Wanda now.' He couldn't get the words out fast enough. 'You'll wake her and it won't help. I'll contact her.'

There was an audible sigh from Lee. 'Right, well, you'd better have the money.'

'We will, definitely.'

As the call ended Fi was hurriedly throwing on some jeans and a T-shirt.

'What are you doing love?' Martin looked puzzled.

'I'm going to do a bank transfer into Lee's account. We've got the insurance money and I'm fed up with scrounging money off Wanda.'

'Don't do that!' Martin implored her but she ignored him. 'Look I'm still going to get the money from Wanda.'

'If you must,' Fi said, 'but I'm sorting this now.'

Wanda had just put the kettle on when Martin called. Carolyn was due home tomorrow, Wednesday, so she still had the place to herself which she rather liked. After her conversation with Glen on Sunday, she felt it would be safe to at least talk to her father-in-law.

'Wanda, sorry to call so early. We need some cash to pay Lee. He wasn't going to do the milking this morning but I managed to persuade him.'

'Right, okay, well I was planning to come over to Lucas Wood anyway so I'll bring it then.'

'We could really do with enough for a week's wages.'

Wanda stopped herself from reacting. If she was going back to the farm, she needed to keep Lee sweet.

'Has Glen spoken to you?' she asked casually.

'Fi saw him yesterday. He said you'd been in.'

'Right. But you haven't spoken to him.'

'About what? You've got me worried now.'

'Never mind. I'll be over mid-morning.'

'I need to catch Lee at the end of his morning shift.'

'Looks like I'll be there a bit earlier then.'

'Thanks Wanda.' That was something she didn't hear very often.

Wanda made her tea and sat at the little table to drink it. It was obvious that Glen hadn't said anything to his father yet. Her move back to the farm depended on it. At least the roof was fixed now and the chap had said he would send an invoice. A lot was resting on her painting for Aaron; he had to love it and pay her handsomely for it. Then she would be able to give Carolyn some rent before she left. She decided to send Glen a text.

Have you managed to speak to your father yet? xx

Martin was at the farmhouse when Wanda called round. It felt odd walking in to her own kitchen as a visitor. She noticed that certain things were in a different place including the coffee machine which had been shoved into a corner. There was an unwelcoming smell of bleach.

Martin counted the notes. 'This should be okay for now. A regular bank transfer would be better really. It would save a lot of bother.'

Wanda considered how she should respond to this. 'Martin, will you go in and see Glen this afternoon, please? I know he wants to talk to you.'

'What about?'

'Visiting starts at two.'

'I know it does. There's lots to do on the farm as you well know.'

'I hear you've hired Conor to do Glen's work? Wanda looked straight at him.

'Yes, we've had to. That's where the insurance money is going.' He averted his gaze.

'So why are you rushed off your feet?'

'I need to manage everything. You can't rely on a temp to know exactly what they are doing. And Fi's not her usual self,' Martin continued. 'Ever since the hen-pecking incident.'

'What incident?'

'Nothing. The hens got a bit excitable.'

Wanda thought about her girls, Snowball and Delilah; were they still alive?

'Anyway, it's not easy all this.'

'No,' Wanda agreed. He was looking at her expectantly.

'I'd better go,' she turned to leave.

'What are you doing up at Lucas Wood?'

'Painting. I'm painting a picture of an ancient oak tree up there.'

'Fat lot of good that will do us.'

'Actually,' she turned and looked straight at him not hiding her irritation, 'it's the money I am earning from my art that's paying Lee.'

When Wanda reached Quercus, she set herself up, securing her canvas to the easel. She had decided with a certain amount of trepidation that this had to be her last session working on this painting. After all she had spent many hours refining it and she did not want to overwork it. She grinned to herself as she had that thought. It was a well-used phrase in the world of art – *to overwork a painting*. Despite having had some success as an artist and selling numerous works, she still struggled to believe in herself.

Quercus was quiet. She always waited for him to speak first, imagining that he might be asleep if trees did in fact sleep. But today she wanted company. She wanted to share her woes. It felt like she was at some important juncture in her life. Would her in-laws move out of her home so that she could move back in? What would happen when Glen came out of hospital? How would they manage? The outlook seemed impossible whichever way she looked at it. She needed Aaron to love this painting and pay her a generous amount just to get through the next few weeks.

'Still working on that small square thing?' Quercus sounded subdued today.

'It's a work of art, Quercus.' Wanda smiled to herself. 'Anyway, today's the last day. I'm going to show it to Aaron tomorrow.'

'Americans are easily impressed.'

'You think so?'

'Your American seems to be.'

'I'm not so sure. I think he's either going to love this or hate it. It's a bit out there since I added the magic.'

'Out there?'

'Different in a crazy sort of way.'

'Not a true representation of me.'

'That's interesting. In many ways it is true to you. Revealing even. All those creatures that live within you. I particularly like the barbastelle bat that I've put in.'

'You've seen it?' Quercus was amazed.

'Only on the internet.'

'The inter-what? Humans are very confusing.'

'Sorry Quercus.'

'I'm not sure why I like you. Although you do seem to be willing to learn and understand why the nasties have to stop.'

'I agree with you totally. I wish it was my decision to go organic. But, unfortunately, I'm outnumbered by Taylors.'

'How many Taylors are there?' Quercus sounded incredulous.

'Well, there's Glen and his parents. The rest don't get involved.'

'Four of you in total. And you are one. That makes one quarter in favour of organic.'

'Interesting way of putting it.'

'Just stating a fact.'

'So I'm outnumbered three to one. They are not good odds, Quercus.'

'No, but if you could persuade one Taylor to be in favour it would be two against two.'

That was true. How astute this tree was. But what were her chances of persuading Glen to go organic?

'I'll bear in mind what you have deduced my wise friend.'

'Good.' There was a long pause and then Quercus said, 'Will you still be coming to see me now that you've finished your painting?'

Wanda thought about it. 'Yes, I will. Why not? Actually, you always make me feel better about life.'

'That will be the pheromones I give off. Any tree can do it but I'm especially good at it being a mature specimen.'

'I appreciate that.'

'And that means you will come here to this spot?' Quercus was quite insistent.

'Yes, I will come.'

'You have a lot to learn Wanda Taylor, little lady. I'm relying on you.'

Wanda looked right up into the canopy of the ancient tree and just then a cloud moved out of the way of the sun and the blue sky shone through.

'It really is magical this place.' Wanda hadn't meant to say that out loud but she was pleased that she had.

Martin was agitated when he reached the hospital. He should really be doing the eggs but apparently this was important. If only Fi would join in; she didn't seem to have the energy for anything. She just was not her usual self.

He got to the ward and a nurse approached him.

'Martin Taylor?'

'That's me. Everything all right, is it?'

'Yes, your son Glen is in the visitor's lounge.' She showed him the way.

Glen was stood looking out of the window, not that there was much of a view.

'Feeling better son,' Martin said as he went over to him.

'Yes, I'm not too bad. There's talk of me coming home.' He sounded like he didn't believe it.

'That's marvellous. Oh, I'm so pleased. I knew you'd pull through.'

'It is good news but Dad, to begin with, I'm going to need some looking after. I'm not going to be back to farming for a while yet.'

'It'll be great just to have you home. Your mother needs a lift.'

Glen went over to some chairs and sat down. There was a change in him today which Martin didn't quite understand. He sat beside him.

'But Dad, will the insurance still pay out when I'm home?'

'Yes, Alan says that if you are only able to do clerical work that it's a partial disability – that's just what they call it – and the insurance still pays out. It's up to two years if necessary.'

There was a long pause. Martin wondered why he was really here. Then Glen spoke.

'Dad, I've been talking to Wanda about her coming back to the farm.' Glen looked directly at him now.

'Really? She didn't say anything this morning.'

'No, well, I said I'd talk to you.'

'Well, the sooner she gets back and helping out the better. To be honest your mum's not really doing anything at the moment; it's all been on my shoulders.'

'Dad, can you hang on a minute?' Glen interrupted him. Martin looked at his son; there was something in his tone that alarmed him.

'Yes, of course I can. What is it?'

'The thing is, Wanda won't move back while you and Mum are living in the farmhouse. It's time for you to go home.' This was a blow Martin was not expecting; he was managing to keep everything going quite nicely now that the insurance money was coming through.

'Won't she now! Little madam! She knows she can't cope on her own. And you said yourself you're not going to be able to do much.'

'I know, I know. But it's the only way I can persuade her back.'

'I don't think you're thinking straight, son. We have to think about what's best for the farm.'

'Wanda says she'll manage.'

'And you believe her?'

'She might not do things your way but she'll cope. Especially with Lee and Conor on board.'

Martin stood up and walked over to the window. He stared out over the car park, saying nothing. Glen went over to him.

'Dad, it's for the sake of my marriage. I've got to do this.'

'You're putting that woman before the farm.'

'I'm putting my wife first; I don't want to lose her.'

'You're crazy.' Martin was shaking his head from side to side. 'I suppose I'll just have to manage her from a distance.'

'No, Dad, no. She wants to be left to manage on her own.'

'Now you really have lost your marbles. I can't let you do this. Being in here, it's turned your head.'

'No, it hasn't. But it has made me realise what's important.'

'The farm and your family; that's what's important.'

'And that includes my wife,' Glen said gently but still his words tore at

Martin's heart.

'I really don't know what to say to you. You've obviously made up your mind.'

'I have, Dad. Thank you for all you've done for me while I've been in here. Now it's time for you and Mum to go home.'

Martin stood in stunned silence for a moment before walking away. Glen sat back down in his chair and sighed. Perhaps with a bit of time his dad would come round.

Fiona walked up to the hen barn and stood outside the door, taking a few deep breaths. She told herself that she had been in thousands of times before over the years and thought nothing of it. She took the key for the padlock from her pocket and went to open it but her hands started shaking, she could feel her heartbeat accelerating. She stopped and took a breath but it was no good; the thought of going inside terrified her.

Why had she lost her confidence? It was soul destroying not being able to help her husband when he was clearly struggling. They could not carry on like this. She turned and walked slowly back to the farmhouse. She was a failure. A hopeless failure.

Martin was in the kitchen when she got back.

'You been up to the hens?' He smiled, looking pleased with her.

'Yes, but...'

'Great news.'

'No, no I didn't go in.'

'Oh.' He shook the frown from his face. 'Still, you went up there.'

'Not much good, is it?' She sat down at the kitchen table. 'How was Glen?'

'I'll put the kettle on.'

'He's all right, isn't he?'

'Yes, yes, he's doing well actually.' Martin filled the kettle from the tap. 'He was asking about the insurance claim, you know, how long they will pay out for.'

'Does he know when he might be able to come out of hospital?'

'He said quite soon. He seemed positive. Anyway, I need to tell you what he's saying about Wanda.'

'Wanda? What's she done now?'

'Nothing. Well, not nothing. She wants to move back in here.'

'That's good.'

'Yes, but she wants us to move out.'

Fiona thought about it. It would be nice to be back in her own home. The farmhouse was much larger than their two-bedroomed place. It meant a lot more cleaning. Also, it would be less of a worry if they were away from the farm. It might be like an ostrich putting its head in the sand but she was ready to have the weight of responsibility lifted. 'And Wanda would run the farm again?'

'That's the trouble.' He poured boiling water over two tea bags in two mugs and went to sit next to her.

'We are supposed to be retired.' She reached out a hand to touch his. It wasn't something she did very often but she had been worried about him of late. All the strain of running the farm with his blood pressure.

'I want to take it easy, of course I do, but the farm...'

'We've always put the farm first, just like your parents.' She was trying to catch his gaze.

'It's the right thing to do.' He got up again to attend to the tea.

'They didn't have much of a retirement did they, John and Ruth, just seven years together.'

'I'll never forgive myself for that.' As he turned towards her she could see a tear in his eye.

'It wasn't your fault!'

'That is why I find it very difficult to deal with Wanda.' He was angry now. 'She's so selfish. All she cares about is her stupid painting.'

'Martin, love, she does at least make some money from it. And if she's offered to come back and run the farm, I think we should take her up on it.' She sat back in her chair and prayed.

'But she'll never cope! Glen's not going to be able to do much. And I don't know how long we'll be able to keep Conor on. The farm could go to rack and ruin.'

'We have to let go. They've got Bartletts and Lee to do the milking.'

He had his head in his hands. 'But how can we?'

'We can and we will. We'll just walk away. It's Glen and Wanda's farm now. It's all down to them.'

'But what would my dad say if they mess it up?'

'You can't think like that.'

His hands fell from his face to the table. 'So that's it now?'

'We're going home, Martin. It's the proper start of our retirement.'

'Glen will still need my advice though, won't he?'

CHAPTER 15

Wanda was shaking as she turned her canvas around to reveal her painting of Quercus to an audience of two. She had set up her easel in the lounge after dinner, a modest pasta dish cooked by Carolyn; apparently, she and Aaron had overindulged over the weekend. Throughout the meal Wanda had been on tenterhooks knowing what would follow. And she had been bored silly hearing of the vaguely amusing happenings of the lovers' city break.

Carolyn peered at the art looking unhelpfully confused. Aaron stood back with a quizzical expression but said nothing. Wanda prayed. She needed the money. Still, he said nothing.

'Interesting.' Carolyn had to speak first even though the painting was not for her.

Aaron shuffled from foot to foot. Then he zoomed in on the golden bat before standing back again to take in the whole painting. He took his eyes away from the canvas and beamed at Wanda. 'I love it.'

Wanda could breathe again. She smiled back. 'Really?'

'Totally! It's... it's magical.' He was excited now. 'It's this amazing wizened old tree and then you look closer and you see it's crawling with life: huge fungi at the base, fluorescent green mosses, creepy crawlies, birds and, best of all, is that a bat? A golden bat?'

'It is.' Wanda couldn't hide her joy.

'And it's called Quercus. What does that mean?' Aaron said looking at the signature. She had signed it, *Quercus by Wanda Taylor.*

'Quercus is the Latin name for oak tree,' Carolyn advised.

'I love it even more.'

'It's brilliant Wanda,' Carolyn said now and Wanda sensed she was just agreeing with the American.

'It is truly amazing.' Aaron sank down onto the sofa. 'Wanda, you are such a talent. I can't believe I have made the acquaintance of such an amazing artist.'

'It's great that you've persevered with your art, Wanda. I let mine slip years ago,' Carolyn said.

Aaron couldn't take his eyes off the canvas. 'This calls for Champagne!'

'I don't have any in the house,' Carolyn said bluntly.

'Champagne at The Angel, what do you say Wanda?'

'Don't mind if I do.' *She deserved this after all her hard work.*

'Oh, I'm really not up for going out, Aaron,' Carolyn said sinking down onto the sofa next to him. 'I'm quite exhausted after our trip.' She laughed at her own admission.

Aaron stood up. 'You won't mind if I take Wanda then, will you?'

Carolyn looked taken aback. Wanda nearly jumped in and said that he did not need to bother but then she thought, *This is my moment, I won't let Carolyn spoil it.*

'No, of course I don't mind. You two go ahead and have some fun.' She waved them away with her hand.

'Thank you,' Aaron said graciously.

The lounge at The Angel was lively with a hen party at one end: a lot of pink on show, a silver wand and the odd high-pitched squeal. Aaron steered Wanda to the opposite corner and using his tall presence quickly managed to flag down a waiter.

'So, what are your plans, Wanda?' Aaron seemed genuinely interested.

'It's all a bit up in the air at the moment but I think I might be going back to the farmhouse soon.'

'That's where your art studio is, isn't it? Where you paint.'

'Well, yes, when I get a chance. Glen should be coming out of hospital soon.'

'That's good to know. Good man, he'll be back in charge.'

'He won't be able to do much manual work to begin with.'

'I see. But they're not expecting you to do it, are they?'

Wanda let out a nervous laugh. A bottle of Champagne arrived providing a useful distraction. Once they both had a flute in hand he said, 'Here's to my artist of the moment,' and clinked her glass.

'Thank you,' Wanda said and took a sip.

'Wanda, you must paint.' Aaron had an intense expression. 'You have talent.' He looked like his mind was whirring. 'I'm thinking...'

He paused looking around the room. The women in the hen party were all falling about laughing. 'I have an idea. I don't want to say too much but...'

Wanda couldn't help thinking that she had pretty much committed to Glen, which meant the farm, so whatever scheme he was cooking up, it would have to be *no*.

He continued, 'Oh damn, I've got to say this. I feel sure it's the right thing to do.'

Wanda braced herself.

'New York,' he said emphatically.

Wanda could only think that New York was a very long way away. 'New York?'

'Yes, Wanda Taylor, New York. The big apple. What are you thinking?'

At this point she was totally confused. 'What are you talking about?'

'Wanda, I've got this exhibition space in Brooklyn. It's across the bridge from Manhattan but it's a popular gallery – in that neighbourhood, anyhow.'

Wanda felt nervous and excited at the same time. 'A New York gallery for what?'

'For your work.'

'Oh my God! Really?'

'Yes, really. If you can produce a series of paintings of the same theme and quality as *Quercus* then... we have an exhibition.'

Wanda gulped down her Champagne and Aaron topped up her glass.

'What do you think?' he asked her.

Wanda could only think about the hens and the daisies and how busy she would be with the farm. She tried to think beyond that. Could she really find some time to paint? Perhaps if she gave up the gallery. Yes, that would help enormously. But then she would need the money to pay Lee. And then she dared to dream of herself in a New York gallery with her paintings on display. This was a dream that could come true.

'Wanda, what do you say?'

'It's an amazing opportunity but I need to work out how I can do it. I'd have to give up my job at the gallery so I have the time to paint.'

'Of course. So is money an issue?'

'I'm afraid so.'

'Listen I'm willing to give you two thousand pounds for the *Quercus* painting and a further three thousand as an advance for the exhibition. That would be returnable if the exhibition didn't go ahead, of course. But I know it will. I'm prepared to take the risk, Wanda.'

'Wow. That would certainly help.'

'Wanda, do you have ten or twelve more *Quercus*-style paintings in you?'

'You don't want them all of Quercus, do you?'

Aaron laughed. 'Anyone would think that the tree was actually called Quercus and not just a name you've given some random tree.'

Wanda felt strangely offended on Quercus' behalf but said nothing.

'The point is,' Aaron leaned forward, 'I love the magical theme. They must all be magical.'

Wanda had no idea of what she would paint but perhaps Quercus could help her. This was a crazy idea to commit to. What would Glen say? Would she be able to keep it from him? There were so many questions but she knew what her answer had to be.

'Yes, yes I will paint for your exhibition and they will all be magical works of art.'

Aaron put an awkward arm around Wanda's shoulders and kissed her on the cheek. 'Brilliant!'

CHAPTER 16

Wanda's waking thought was *What have I done?*

The Champagne had gone to her head. An exhibition in New York. That was ludicrous. Perhaps she should back out now. Then she remembered something Aaron had said to her about getting funds to her today which totalled five thousand pounds. Five thousand pounds! She would have to persuade Glen that they needed the money and that this would be the last art exhibition she would do. Not to mention the first.

She got up and dressed ready for the gallery and found Carolyn downstairs staring into a mug of tea. 'Oh, there you are. I did wonder if perhaps you'd spent the night at the hotel.' There was an edge to her voice.

'Don't be silly.' Wanda went over to the kettle and filled it from the tap.

'Did Aaron say anything?' Carolyn asked. 'Any message for me? "Wham bam thank you ma'am, I'm off back to the big apple now".'

Wanda ignored the histrionics. 'He said that as you were tired, he'd get a room at the hotel.'

'Is that it?'

Wanda was confused and said nothing. Carolyn stretched her arms above her head and yawned. 'Did he say when his flight is?'

'I think it might be tomorrow.'

'Right, I might see him today then.' She sounded thoroughly

disillusioned with life.

'I'm sure you will,' Wanda said, perhaps a little too dismissively. She had too much important stuff on her mind.

'It's my fault. I knew this would happen.' Carolyn began to pace the kitchen as best she could in such a small space. 'I promised myself I wouldn't get too involved. Why can't I be more like you and not give a damn about men? You seem to have them falling at your feet.'

That was just silly. 'I do give a damn, actually. About my husband.'

'Oh? But Wanda, it doesn't look good from where I'm standing. I mean you two are as good as separated.'

'Actually, you are wrong about that. Things have changed between us. We have an understanding. And Glen will be coming out of hospital any day now.'

'Is he going back to the farm? Won't he need looking after?'

'He will need some help. That's why I'm going back to the farmhouse.' She said it as gently as she could.

'What, so *you're* leaving me too?' Carolyn sank onto a chair at the little dining table just off the kitchen.

Wanda finished making her tea and went to sit next to her.

'I am really grateful to you for taking me in, in my hour of need.'

Carolyn wore a worried frown despite Wanda's kind words.

'Listen,' Wanda continued, 'I have to do this for the sake of my marriage.'

'I understand. I'm sorry.' She put a conciliatory hand on Wanda's arm.

'Me too.' Wanda didn't want to leave on bad terms.

'I don't suppose you could back pay just a little bit of rent so I can cover the roofer's bill? I'm rather short after my mini break. I insisted on paying half of everything in some sort of women's lib attempt. Stupid really.'

'Of course I will. As soon as Aaron has paid me for his painting.'

166

'Yes, you must be quite flush now.'

'Well, actually I've been paying for Lee to do all the milking while I've been here, so not really.'

'I see. I thought you'd put the farm behind you.'

'It's not that simple.'

Scurrying down Abbeygate, Wanda called Aaron.

'Good morning, Wanda.' He sounded very bright and breezy.

'Aaron, morning, listen, it might be better if you don't tell Carolyn about our arrangement yet. Especially the financial aspect of it.'

'I wouldn't divulge that kind of information anyway.'

'Right. Good. But if you tell her that you've offered me a New York exhibition she might start asking questions.'

'Don't worry, I can handle Carolyn. Listen Wanda, I've got a flight back tomorrow morning so we will need to set up some Skype meetings to track progress.'

'Yes, okay. Listen, be nice to Carolyn, will you? She's quite a sensitive soul.'

'Of course, yes.'

'When do you plan to hold the exhibition exactly?' She couldn't remember any particular date being mentioned.

'Just over eight weeks' time. 26th August. It's a Saturday. Obviously, you'll have to be there.'

Wanda stopped in her tracks. She suddenly felt a little faint. Eight weeks to produce how many paintings? Ugh. How was she going to manage to go to New York without Glen noticing?

'Right,' she said unconvincingly.

'You can do this, Wanda, I know you can.'

Fiona rang at about eleven o'clock. It was deathly quiet in the gallery and Adrian was busying himself at the back, so Wanda answered.

'We are leaving the farmhouse on Saturday,' Fiona announced. She sounded quite upbeat.

'I see. Thanks for letting me know.'

'What time do you think you'll come over?'

'Er, well… it will have to be after work. So, it will be about five. Will you have gone by then?' *Should she have asked that?*

'We'll wait until you get here.'

'Okay then.'

There was an awkward pause. 'For a handover sort of thing.' Fiona sounded apologetic now.

'Good idea,' Wanda said wondering how an earth her life would pan out from here on in. She was setting herself up for almost certain disaster.

'I think Glen will be out of hospital next week,' Fiona said. She was definitely brighter.

'Yes, it looks like it.'

'That's such good news, isn't it?'

'Excellent news.' Why did the thought of him being back at home terrify her?

'If you like I'll pop over to the farmhouse to help look after him a bit. Just until he's able to do more for himself.'

'That might not be a bad idea, Fi, if you don't mind.'

'Of course, I don't. You're going to have a lot on your plate with the farm.'

'Yes,' Wanda laughed with a definite note of hysteria.

'And thank you,' Fiona said.

'What for?'

'Agreeing to take the farm back on. I know it's a lot of work. But Martin and I really do need to start our retirement now.'

'Absolutely.' She wanted Fiona to feel that she was doing the right thing even though Wanda was not at all sure how she was going to cope with everything.

After the call Wanda took some deep breaths to try and calm herself. She had one hand on her belly and had just breathed in when a customer walked into the gallery. She smiled through her exhale as he looked over at her, his expression one of concern.

By four o'clock, after much wrestling in her mind, Wanda had decided that she really should give up this gallery job. Otherwise, there was no hope of being ready for this New York exhibition. Every time she thought of it her heart skipped a beat. Adrian appeared as if on cue. 'Quiet day.'

'Wasn't it? Actually, I've been thinking.'

'Oh? You have an idea of how we could get more clients in?'

'Er, no. No, not exactly. Listen, as it happens, I'm simply not going to have time to continue with this job for much longer. I'm so sorry.'

He looked more interested than annoyed.

'You see I'm going back to the farm. Glen's coming out of hospital so he'll need me.'

'I see. It's quite understandable.' He managed a half smile.

'Thank you, Adrian, I appreciate that.'

'Well, I've liked having you working here; I mean you've done a good job.' He looked as if he was processing this as a revelation. 'So, do I get some notice?'

'Would it be okay if this Saturday is my last day?'

'That's just two days. Let me see what I can do. I suspect it will be.'

Carolyn was looking very chic, in a pink linen dress with a flowery silk scarf thrown around her neck, when Wanda got back to Whiting Street.

'Going out?' she asked smiling at her friend.

'Aaron's taking me to Maison Bleue,' Carolyn said gleefully. 'He's coming here first for a drink.' She starting plumping the cushions on the sofa.

'I'm pleased,' Wanda said even though it occurred to her that no one ever took *her* out for dinner.

Carolyn came right up to Wanda and put her hands on her arms. 'Sorry to ask this, but I don't suppose you could make yourself scarce?'

'Throwing me out now, are you?' Wanda was laughing as she said it.

'Well, you did say you were going back to the farmhouse soon.'

'On Saturday. That's two more nights.'

'Okay, so if you could just pop out for a couple of hours now and then perhaps be in your room when we get home.'

'Fine.' Wanda was seriously miffed now. Carolyn disappeared off to the kitchen and returned with a bottle of Champagne in a cooler. 'Wow, you are really pushing the boat out, aren't you?'

Carolyn blushed. 'Just making the most of our last evening together and you never know...'

'Never know what? Are you expecting an invitation to visit him in New York?'

'No, no, although that would be rather good, wouldn't it?'

Wanda feared for her friend; disappointment mainly. 'What time is he coming?'

Carolyn frantically looked at her watch. 'Not for another half an hour.'

'Right.' Wanda went upstairs to her bedroom and packed up her things. She had accumulated quite a lot during her stay but luckily her car was just down the street. It took three trips but she managed to cram it all in to her small car. Carolyn didn't even seem to notice what she was doing or perhaps she was pleased. When Wanda was ready to go she said, 'We need to sort out the matter of rent.'

'Yes, yes, we must. Let's talk about it tomorrow.'

'Okay. Have a lovely evening,' Wanda said and walked away feeling quite sad that her stay in Whiting Street had ended in this way.

Her brother's driveway was empty when Wanda pulled up and parked. She looked around her. It seemed very quiet. Perhaps she should have called ahead. Her luggage was mainly hidden in the boot of her car but some had spilled onto the back seat. She got out and, taking just her handbag, went up to the back door. Still no sign of life. She walked round the back and towards the kitchen garden where she was relieved to see Saffy in the distance, picking sweet peas.

'Hi Saffy!' She waved and Saffy turned as Wanda made her way over to her.

'Well, this is a surprise. Everything's all right, is it? With Glen, I mean.'

'Absolutely, I popped in to see him after work. It looks like he will be coming out of hospital soon; it's really cheered him up.'

'Oh, that it such good news.' Saffy placed another stem with a delicate lilac flower in a bucket of water. 'Just cutting these to decorate the yurts.'

'They are so pretty. Sorry to just turn up like this but Carolyn wanted me out of the way this evening. Long story.'

'It's lovely to see you.' Saffy gave her a hug.

'I'm going to be moving back into the farmhouse on Saturday.'

'That's great. I've really missed you round here.'

'Are you fully booked?' Wanda looked across to the glamping site; it looked very peaceful.

'Yes, it's great. Going really well. Keeping us busy.'

'I was hoping you might be able to put me up. Just for a couple of nights.'

'Ah. That could be a problem. You see Toby's staying here for a few days; they've broken up for the summer holidays already.'

'I see.' *Damn.* 'Doesn't that leave one spare bedroom? I don't mind the smallest room.'

'That room's the office now. We moved the desk and stuff up there so we have more room downstairs.'

'Of course.' Wanda felt deflated. 'The sofa?'

'Why don't you make yourself comfortable in the garden, it's a lovely evening. As soon as I've delivered these flowers, I'll sort out some drinks.'

Martin rifled through the filing cabinet in the farmhouse office looking for invoices. It looked like Glen had changed everything and he couldn't find one bit of paper that told him anything useful. When Martin had taken over the farm from his father, he had been happy to keep the same systems in place. If it ain't broke, don't fix it. But oh no, Glen had seen fit to bring in some newfangled ways. Or was it Wanda?

He had found the financial spreadsheet on the computer that they used for forecasting but was struggling to update it. He was tempted to print it out and just scribble the new numbers all over it. But first, he needed all the invoices. Fi appeared holding a mug of tea.

'What are you doing?'

'I'm just trying to update the numbers for the forecast.'

'You can't do that. Leave it. Glen will have it done in no time. Or Wanda.' She handed the mug to him.

'Thanks love. But I feel I should at least have a go. I mean it's not going to be easy for him when he comes out of hospital.'

Fi sighed and sat on the side of the desk. 'I agree, but we need to leave them to it. They'll manage somehow. I've already offered to come over and take care of Glen until he's a bit stronger.'

Martin slammed the filing cabinet drawer shut. He hadn't managed to find one invoice. 'For goodness' sake!'

'Come and have a seat downstairs. Look it's gone six o'clock.'

'I suppose so. But I'm worried. I can't help being nervous about the state of the farm and with Wanda in control, God help us all.'

Fi ran her fingers through her hair. 'Just leave them to it!'

'But it's not fair on our son.'

'He married her.'

'Why? Why did he marry Wanda, of all women? He's a handsome chap; he could have had anyone. I've always wondered about Wanda; whether she's some sort of witch and she cast a spell over our poor son.' He sat at the desk and rattled the mouse around with his hand to bring the screen alive. 'Now I've got to put the bloody password in again.'

'Stop right there!' Fi put her hands on his shoulders. 'You're being totally ridiculous. Just stop. We're going downstairs.'

'You don't understand!' Martin yelled out in anger. Fiona flinched and stepped back. He had his head in his hands, his elbows on the desk and he started to cry, shaking as he broke down, tears wetting his cheeks. Fi hugged him and laid her head gently on his.

'It's going to be all right. I promise you; it will be.'

As an orange sun sank below the horizon beyond the yurts, the embers of the barbecue were still glowing and giving off some warmth. It had been such a relaxing evening, it had made Wanda realise that she had always been slightly on edge at Carolyn's. Being back here in Saffy and Ben's garden felt right, in the same way as being with Quercus in Lucas Wood left her feeling good. Perhaps she was not cut out to be a townie.

'What does Glen think about this New York exhibition?' Ben asked. He was almost horizontal in his chair, looking up at the sky.

'I haven't told him. And you mustn't either,' she said sternly.

'But sis, he's going to have to find out sometime. Anyway, won't he be pleased? Sounds like decent money.'

'Just let me handle it.'

Saffy gave Ben an annoyed look to shut him up.

'I've just realised that the lesbian couple that were supposed to be coming today are not coming until Saturday; something to do with a work commitment one of them had.' Saffy smiled at Wanda.

'So, one of the yurts is free?' Wanda felt quite excited. She'd been convinced she'd be on the sofa.

'Yes, that's lucky, isn't it?'

'You homeless, sis? I thought you were driving; I'd have given you some more wine.'

'No, I'm fine thanks. Had a bit too much Champagne last night actually with Aaron. Anyway, I need to be back at the gallery by ten tomorrow morning.'

'That's sorted then.' Saffy squeezed her friend's hand.

'I've never slept in a yurt.' Wanda was beaming.

'With a bit of luck the cockerel will wake you up,' Ben sniggered and Wanda whipped the side of his leg with a napkin.

Wanda lay supine in her huge bed looking up through the central crown at the top of the yurt, gazing at the stars in a midnight blue sky. It was a clear night giving her a perfect view. She felt blessed. It was a moment in time which would mark the end of one phase of her life and give her a chance to pause before the next chapter. She had no idea how events would pan out – the farm; New York; Glen – but nothing could take away this special moment.

Tiredness overcame her and she turned to curl up on her side, cosy under her duvet. She heard a tawny owl calling out, once and then again, before falling into a deep sleep.

CHAPTER 17

It was gone five o'clock before Wanda got away from the gallery on her last day. It had been a particularly busy time with two paintings sold and much interest from another buyer. Carolyn had popped in too and Wanda was pleased that they had quietly agreed a reasonable amount of rent; she would make a bank transfer in the next few days. As Wanda gathered herself to leave, Adrian tried to persuade her to go for a drink with him.

'That would be lovely, but I'm already running late,' she blurted out only to watch his face fall. Was he only asking because his wife had thrown him out? At least Fiona had been understanding when she'd replied to Wanda's text, warning Fiona that she would be late.

It felt strange as she drove into the farmhouse yard and parked outside the back door. Fiona came out to greet her and gave her a hug.

'So sorry I'm late.'

'That's okay, you're here now. I'll make you some tea.'

'Lovely. I'll unload the car later.'

Wanda sat at her own kitchen table as Fiona put the kettle on. The place looked very clean and tidy. The coffee machine was still in a tight corner and certain things seemed to have a new home.

'I haven't had time to visit Glen today,' Wanda said as she felt a pang of guilt.

'Don't worry, I went in earlier. I told him you had a busy day. He's cheered up now he knows he's coming home.'

'Yes, I'm not surprised after everything he's been through.'

'I don't know where Martin is; he's just disappeared.' Fiona poured boiling water into a teapot, one that Wanda did not recognise.

'Oh. Perhaps he's saying goodbye to the daisies.'

Fiona raised her eyebrows and laughed lightly. 'Yes, I suspect so.' She brought the pot over with two mugs and a milk jug.

'So, how have you been?' Wanda thought her mother-in-law looked a bit brighter than the last time she had seen her.

'Fine. We're fine. At least Martin will be, when I've managed to persuade him to relax a bit.'

Wanda did not know how to respond and there was a long awkward pause. Then she asked, 'I take it Lee is still doing the milking?'

'Yes, yes, we've managed to keep him on. In fact, you've just missed him for today but he'll be back in the morning. I've told him what's happening.' Fiona stared into her mug and then added, 'He didn't say too much but I suspect he's pleased.'

'And what about this Conor chap?'

'Yes, he's been managing the veg, the muck spreading and the silage. Martin says he's a good worker.'

'Great, that must be an enormous help. Is he staying on for now?'

'Yes, if you want him to. The insurance pays out until Glen's fully back to work. I think it's for up to two years. I've written Conor's mobile number on this pad, along with a few other notes.'

Wanda nodded. There was hope for her yet and she might just be able to find time to paint for this exhibition. 'And the hens?'

'Yes, that's all going okay. I don't go up there but Martin has been collecting the eggs and topping up the feed. He cleaned the barn out this morning. Egg production isn't great; he's been talking about increasing the stock.' Fiona glanced at her anxiously. 'That will be up to you now.' She managed a half smile. Wanda knew she would never increase the number; in fact, she was pretty sure they were at their limit for the size of the barn. No point in saying anything though.

Fiona pushed a key over to Wanda. 'For the hen barn; there's a new padlock,' she said.

'Thank you.'

'I think the sugar beet needs spraying. Oh, and we need to make more silage. There's grass and maize to harvest and ferment. But Conor should know about that. You might need to manage him, though.'

'Right, okay.'

'Martin deals with Bartletts so...' Fiona stopped suddenly and asked, 'Do you want a biscuit?'

'No, it's okay, thanks.' She gave Fi a warm smile. 'I'll contact Bartletts and get up to speed with them tomorrow.'

'Martin should be here.' She tapped her fingernails on the table over and over.

'Don't worry.' Wanda covered Fiona's hand with her own to bring it to stillness. 'I tell you what, why don't we walk up to the cows now?'

Fiona looked her up and down. 'In that dress?'

'I'll change my shoes.'

'You still have your farm clothes, don't you?'

'Of course. I've come straight from the gallery, Fi.'

'Yes, of course you have.'

Martin was not with the cows. It was nice to stand and stare at them for a few moments as they munched away on the grass; Wanda had missed them. She looked over towards Lucas Wood, wondering how Quercus was today. It was then she spotted a lonely figure on the edge of Rooked Meadow.

'I think I can see him.' Wanda pointed. 'What's he doing there?'

Fiona looked doubtful and said nothing. They made their way up the main track, turning left at the top. When they reached him, it was clear that he was deep in thought so they stood quietly next to him. After a few moments he looked round, blinking his eyes. Had he been crying?

'Wanda, you're here.'

'Yes, Martin. How are you?'

He coughed. His expression said he didn't want to tell her. 'Fine. This field, Rooked Meadow; we should do something with it.' He waved an index finger at the field.

Wanda raised her eyebrows and smiled at him. She said nothing.

'Martin, it's down to Glen and Wanda now.' Fi put an arm around his shoulders.

'Well, yes, I suppose it is.'

Wanda felt quite sorry for her father-in-law as the two of them drove off and away from the farm. He was a shell-shocked shadow of his former self. Fi had clearly persuaded him to leave. She walked back through the back door and into the kitchen and stood there looking at the place. Her two nights in the yurt had been amazing; an oasis for a wonderful, if brief, moment in time. Now, back in the farmhouse, the place that had been her home for many years, reality was dawning on her and it felt scary. She picked up the key that Fi had given her and left the house.

The evening was warm with a fresh breeze and it felt good to walk up the track to the hen barn, the gentle incline making her slightly breathless. It occurred to her that she had probably put on a bit of weight living in town. Those farming trousers were going to be tight. Looking over to

Sally's Grove in the distance she could see a figure; perhaps that was Conor? She would meet him soon enough.

Reaching the barn door, she unlocked the padlock. It seemed like a long time since she had been here. She left the door wide open and walked carefully in, shading her eyes from the bright lights. The smell was strong, despite the fact that Martin had cleaned that morning. The hens were either subdued as if defeated or calling angrily to her. There seemed to be more than the usual two hundred. Was she imagining things? And were Delilah and Snowball amongst them? Would she ever know? Actually, she did know and it was probably for the best that they had not lived to see this day. It was odd that none of them had decided to venture outside. She released the locks on the second door and pushed it wide open too. Then she decided to switch the lights off. Slowly the hens made their way cautiously out into the sunlight. Just a few at first, but then more followed. Soon there were hens all over Hungry Hill pecking away and Wanda was beaming to herself. Happy hens. This was the sort of farming that felt right. She knew, of course, that Martin would be horrified by this sight; hens jabbing their beaks here and there, all over his precious potato crop. But what harm were they really doing? She looked at them more carefully now. They were smaller than she remembered, not as agile, not as lively. She shouted out, 'Snowball,' and then, 'Delilah' in a vain hope that one Light Sussex and one Goldline would look up at her. Nothing. She shed a tear and then a white hen, with its black collar and deep pink comb on its perky head, approached her steadily and looked up at her.

'Are you my new Snowball?' She bent down and gently lifted it from the ground and into her arms. It sat, content and purring away. 'Yes, Snowball, it's me now. Everything is going to be all right.'

The sun was low in the sky and the view over the farm was glorious. Wanda had a thought. Perhaps the hens would provide one of the subjects for her art exhibition. They were certainly magical creatures to her. But right now, they were not in the slightest bit interested in going back into the barn so she decided to leave them. It felt a bit reckless but she would return at dusk when, with a bit of luck, their homing instincts would kick in.

Back at the house, she unloaded the car and started to settle back in to her home. With everything unpacked, she realised she had not eaten for several hours. She opened up the fridge and was not disappointed. Fi had left some cold chicken and salad and a crusty loaf of bread. Perfect.

*

Abi was so pleased to be home. It had been an exhausting day. The female presenter of the programme she was currently working on was just horrible to her. She seemed to think that, with a bit of make-up, Abi could make her look like Tess Daly. The fact that the woman was only five foot two seemed irrelevant. And while she was quite pretty, she was no model. Abi had quietly done her best using every trick in the book and was actually quite pleased with the result. The presenter had just scowled at her image in the mirror before standing up and saying with a deep sigh, '*Please God, let me have another make-up artist tomorrow. I simply can't continue to go on camera looking like this. My audience are going to think I'm ill with some dreadful disease.*'

Abi made herself a coffee and slumped on the sofa. No sign of Gavin. She had hardly seen him all week and she missed him. She reached for her mobile. No messages. She sent him a text.

Will you be home soon? Need a cuddle and a glass of wine xx

She finished her coffee and decided to ring her mum. No answer. Perhaps she would try her dad. It was good that now he was on the ward he had his mobile with him; she had spoken to him several times and it was such a relief that he was getting better. But again, no answer. She could text him but she was never quite sure if he got her messages as he didn't reply. She looked across to the kitchen which was at one end of the living room; this new flat they were in was tiny, all they could afford in London. Lily's flat was lovely, a Victorian conversion with a huge bay window and so stylishly decorated throughout in shades of grey. That girl had all the luck.

Abi just sat there feeling deflated and not knowing quite what to do with herself. Still no reply from Gavin. She felt a thud to her stomach as she had a strong sense of déjà vu. She had only been back in London for three weeks and doubts were already creeping in about their relationship. She knew he'd had a lot of work on, doing the accounts for a major new client, but it was Saturday. The last time he had been absent all the time it had turned out he was seeing another girl. All that crap about *This time it's for keeps, honestly babe.* Maybe he had gone into work and put his phone on silent. She would call him. Why not? It was far from cool to phone but she needed to know.

'Hello.' The girl's voice was uncertain.

'Who's that?'

She heard the same voice say, *Gav, phone call.*

'Who is that?' Abi demanded.

Gavin's voice next. 'All right babe?' He sounded flustered.

'Where are you?'

'Just in a bar, you know, having a drink with a few mates. I thought you were working.'

'I was. I told you I'd be back by seven. Didn't you get my text?'

'Right. Well, I'll be home later.'

'Really? Is that after you've shagged your latest girl?'

The silence on the other end of the phone was so thick that Abi had to scream. *He rang off! He bloody well rang off. Total bastard. Total waste of space.*

She went over to the fridge, pulled out the remains of a bottle of wine and poured it into a glass. She searched for some peanuts or maybe crisps, anything; she was starving. All she could find was half a stale packet of Pringles. She started eating them anyway, glugging back the wine in between munches.

Her life was crap. She couldn't carry on like this. She wanted to see her dad; after all, he had nearly died. It was so awful. Thank goodness he was over the worst. She looked at the calendar on her phone. She was due back at the studio at four tomorrow to work miracles on the stroppy cow. Maybe they would find someone else. That would be fine by her. She would go home to Suffolk. London wasn't all it was cracked up to be.

The bottle of wine was empty. She grabbed her bag and flat keys and headed for the convenience store at the end of the road. She needed food and another bottle of wine to get her through the evening.

The next day Abi woke up with a sore head and an empty space beside her in the bed. Gavin had been out all night. That was it. Her mind was made up.

CHAPTER 18

Wanda saw the text message from Martin on her mobile as she sat down with her first cup of tea of the day. It took the edge off what might have been a tiny highlight. She had been pleased with herself for being up at seven. On a Sunday as well. The message read: *The potato crop needs spraying ideally before the weather breaks. Order from our usual contact, Karl. Let me know if you need help.*

There was a knock at the back door. Wanda shouted, 'It's open.'

Lee appeared in the entrance to the kitchen.

'Come in, Lee.' She got up and looked for her handbag which she found in the hallway. She opened up her wallet.

'You're all right I'm up to date at the moment. Mr Taylor sorted it until Tuesday.' He smiled.

'Oh!' she put her wallet away. Of course, she had forgotten.

'Just wanted to say welcome back, you know.' He hovered on the spot he was standing on.

'Thanks Lee.'

There was an awkward pause.

'Everything okay,' Wanda asked. 'Do you want to sit down for a minute? I could make you a cup of tea.'

He looked pleased and sat at the other end of the table. 'Tea would be good. Sorry, I'm a bit smelly after the cows.'

'Have you finished for today?' Wanda asked as she put the kettle back on and found a mug for him.

'Just got to wash down.'

'Are the cows back?'

'Yes, all okay. No problems today. Although there are two that I've isolated in the shed with what might be mastitis. I put a call in to the vet. He should be here later this morning.'

'Okay, thanks for letting me know.

'Actually, there's a fence down on Low Meadow. Needs fixing before tomorrow when I move them down again. I did tell Martin, but...'

'I'll sort that too then,' Wanda said.

'Thanks Mrs T.'

'Lee, will you call me Wanda, please?' *What had come over him? Had Martin insisted on being called Mr Taylor?*

'Sure.'

She took the mug of tea she had made for him over to the table.

'Nice,' he said.

Wanda sat down too. 'Have you met Conor yet?'

'I've seen him around.'

'Right.'

'Actually, he came over to the pasture when I was securing the cows in the other day. He was complaining.'

'Complaining?'

'Yeah, just said he was expected to do a hell of a lot for the wages he was paid.'

'I see.'

'Old Mr Taylor has him doing most of the work Glen used to do, bar the milking, see. And he's only a young farm labourer.'

'Right, I get the picture. From what I can gather from the notes Fiona left me there's quite a lot of outstanding work for Conor. But that would explain it. I'll talk to him but would you be up for doing a few more hours?'

Lee's phone bleeped and he looked at the screen. 'The vet's coming at midday now.'

'The vet?' Wanda's mind had gone blank.

'The mastitis, two of the cows.' He seemed agitated.

'Of course, yes. So, are you completely busy or could you fit in a bit more for Capel?'

'A bit. Maybe. Isn't Glen coming home soon? That's what old Mr Taylor said.'

'Yes, we're hoping he'll be home soon but he won't be back to farm labouring for quite a while.'

'That's not good.'

'No, so what do you say?'

'Are you sure you can pay me?'

'I'm sure.'

'S'ppose so then.'

'How are you fixed today?'

'Today? No, but I can start tomorrow.'

Wanda decided to make a second cup of tea before bracing herself to call Martin. She hated having to call him so soon after they had left but she needed to find out precisely what she should order to spray the potato crop. This was the sort of thing that Glen would normally handle. Martin welcomed her call, almost sounding jubilant, and told her very precisely what she needed to do. That was when she found out he meant the crop on Hungry Hill. She asked him what was in the pesticide.

'What do you need to know that for? I've told you the brand.'

'I'm interested. What's in it?'

'It's a weed killer, glyphosate. Everyone uses it,' he answered dismissively. 'Anyway, the point is, the sooner they are sprayed the better.'

'Right and how do you spell that word?' That really wound him up.

'For goodness' sake! Are you sure you don't want me to ring Karl myself? I don't mind.'

'Don't be silly, Martin,' she said. 'I'll manage.'

As soon as she was off the phone, she decided to put the word *glyphosate* in to Google. An image appeared of the pesticide containing this chemical and showed a menacing black skull and cross bones on the label. The price of it was eye-watering. Before long she was reading about the harmful effects to farmers who used this chemical. Then she read:

Animals exposed to products with glyphosate may drool, vomit, have diarrhoea, lose their appetite, or seem sleepy.

No way was she spraying that all over Hungry Hill where she let the hens out. The potatoes would just have to cope with whatever nature threw at them. And the farm would save some money.

The makeshift repair Wanda had made on the fence up at Low Meadow looked remarkably sturdy. Her mobile rang.

'Abi, everything all right?'

'Finally,' her daughter said.

'I answered, didn't I?

'I've been texting for ages.'

'Oh, sorry. Maybe the signal's not too good this morning. But you're okay, are you?'

'I'm on the train.' Abi sounded irritated, as if her mother should just know where she was.

'I see. It's a bit early for you, isn't it? Where are you going?'

'Ipswich, of course! I'm coming home.'

'Oh.' Wanda hesitated as she tried to process what this actually meant in the scheme of her new life.

'So will you pick me up?' Abi asked in a demanding tone.

Wanda really needed to start on a painting today if she could find the time. It would take her about an hour to get to the train station if she went her preferred scenic route and forty-five minutes the other way.

'Can you get a train to Bury?' she asked guessing what the answer was likely to be.

'Mum! Why can't you pick me up from Ipswich?'

'Well,' Wanda said, thinking fast, 'I'm running the farm single-handedly; there's a lot to do.'

'Can't Lee help you? Can't you just get in the car and drive?'

'I'm sorry, darling, no. It's about a two-hour round trip and I can't spare the time.'

'Oh for goodness sake. I'm always the last person you are bothered about.'

Wanda said nothing.

'I suppose I'll have to call Granny Fi.'

'Ooh, not a good idea. They've only just got back to their own home and, well, it's been a bit emotional for them.'

'What?' Wanda could picture her daughter's frustrated face. 'Granny Rita then.'

Wanda smiled at the thought of Rita having reason to assign Wanda to unfit mother status yet again. 'If you like.'

'I'd rather you came to pick me up,' Abi said sulkily.

'See you soon then.'

Wanda got back from dealing with the hens in time to see the vet at midday. He confirmed the cows had mastitis and said he would be back with antibiotics.

'They will need to be hand-milked before treatment. And, of course, keep them isolated from the rest of the herd.'

'What are their chances?' Wanda asked.

'Pretty good, I'd say. Fingers crossed. Right, I will go and check the rest. Where are they?'

Wanda took him up to the cows and left him to do his work. 'I take it you will invoice us at the end of the month?'

'Yes, afraid so,' he said and they exchanged knowing looks.

Back at the farmhouse she was making herself a quick coffee when Abi walked into the kitchen with Rita close behind.

'It's all right for some,' Rita started. 'I thought you were rushed off your feet.'

Wanda paused to take a breath. 'Hello Mum, thank you for picking Abi up.' Her mother gave her a sarcastic smile which Wanda decided to ignore. 'Everything okay, Abi?' She had a strong feeling she knew what the answer was simply by reading her daughter's demeanour.

'It's all over with Gavin.' She seemed angry rather than upset. 'This time for good.'

'I'm sorry.' She hugged her daughter. 'I really am.'

After a moment Abi pulled away and said, 'Have you got anything for lunch?'

'There's not much in the fridge, I'm afraid. Cereal? Sorry, I wasn't expecting you.'

'Great!' Abi shot her mother a wry smile.

'Abi, I've only just got to the farmhouse myself. Your Granny Fi kindly left me a bit of food for last night. I haven't had time to get to the supermarket yet.'

'You'll have to come home with me,' Rita said. 'I can make you a nice sandwich.'

'That's okay, Gran, I'm not that hungry.'

'Suit yourself.' Rita flicked up an indignant nose.

'I just want to stay here with Mum,' Abi explained.

'I see. Well, if that's all the thanks I get for dropping everything to come and fetch you all the way from Ipswich, then I'll be off.'

'Thank you,' Wanda said. Rita looked unimpressed.

'Thanks Granny.' Abi gave Rita a hug which softened her features a little.

After she'd gone and Abi was munching her way through a bowl of muesli, Wanda sat down next to her at the kitchen table.

'Abi, darling, what are you going to do? I mean how long do you think you'll be staying?'

'I thought I'd stay a while. Don't you want me here? You're going to need help with Dad, aren't you?'

Wanda was amazed. 'Well, yes, I will.' She decided to say it. 'And the farm really.'

'I'm not milking.'

'No, no, I've got Lee for that.'

'Maybe the hens? Do I just let them out?'

'If you could look after the hens that would be really helpful. But it's a bit more than letting them out. We have to feed them and collect the eggs up each day in time for the egg man who comes at four. Then the barn needs to be kept clean. And we need to make sure they are all safely in at dusk. I was lucky last night they had all gone back in when I went to close up the barn.'

'Doesn't sound too bad.'

'Okay, well let's do it together this evening and in the morning and then you can take it on. It's seven days a week you know.'

'I know,' Abi protested but the look on her face said that she was surprised she wouldn't get weekends off. 'I don't have to get up ridiculously early, though, do I?'

'No, but the earlier the better for letting them out. The poor things don't like being locked in all day.'

'I heard they attacked Granny Fi.'

'Who told you that?'

'Your mum.'

'Sounds like malicious gossip. If you love them like I do, they'll love you too.'

Abi laughed at that. 'You're weird Mum!'

'Right, I'm off to the supermarket. I've had enough cereal for one day.'

'Can I come too?'

'Of course you can.' Wanda looked at her daughter with enquiring eyes. 'Are you sure you're my daughter?'

'Ha, ha. Look Mum, I'm here to make a go of it. I've had enough of London. And I really want to see Dad and spend some time with him. All that's happened, well, it's made me think.'

Wanda felt a tear in her eye. 'That's lovely to hear. And actually, it's really great to have you back.'

Glen called when they were in the supermarket.

'I'm coming home on Tuesday. All being well.'

'That's good.' Wanda's mind was whirring; that was just two days' time. *What did she need to do before he came home?*

'Where are you?' he asked.

'The supermarket. There's no food in the house. Abi's here too.'

'Abi's there?'

191

'Yes, she's come to stay for a while. To help out, actually.' She winked at her daughter who laughed.

'Good. Are you coming to see me today?'

'We're quite busy,' Wanda said screwing up her face and praying that would satisfy him.

'I know. Mum rang to say they're back home. She seemed quite pleased. I think she's worried about Dad's health, though. Trouble is, he's worried about the farm.'

'I can't help that.'

'No, but, well…' he paused and Wanda braced herself for what might come next. 'It would be good if you could keep him updated. Just so he knows everything's getting done.'

'No way Glen, that's too much to ask. Honestly, there aren't enough hours in the day.'

'But you've got Abi. And Lee and Conor.'

'Mm, turns out Conor is a labourer, not an experienced manager. And your dad has been paying him farm-hand wages.'

'I see.' Glen seemed to be taking that piece of news in. 'Dad did say that he needed managing but it looks like he hasn't been entirely honest with either of us.'

'Let's talk about all this stuff when you're home, shall we? I'll call you later today. I need to know if you will be able to get upstairs, things like that.'

There was an awkward pause before he said in a rather deflated tone, 'Okay then.'

'I'm sorry I have to go. I'm in the middle of the supermarket and Abi's rapidly filling the trolley with I don't know what.'

'I miss you,' he said. *Where had that come from?*

'I miss you too,' she said.

'And me!' Abi chimed in as she added some fresh tagliatelle to the unstable mound piling up in the trolley.

Back home, they began to unpack the shopping and Abi started to make a tuna salad.

Wanda's mobile rang. It was Martin. Damn, he was checking up on her. It wasn't fair.

'Martin.'

'Sorry to bother you Wanda but I was wondering...' There was a pause and Wanda heard a door open and close. He sounded shifty.

'Where are you?'

'I'm at home,' he said, 'just making sure I'm out of reach of Fi's ears.'

'Martin, you should really be taking it easy, not phoning me every five minutes.'

'I just wanted to say that you really need to crack on with more silage making and you should get on to Bartletts first thing tomorrow unless you can do it. That would be ideal.'

'What about Conor?'

'He'll be able to help out but you can't leave him to do it on his own.'

Wanda rolled her eyes.

'And another thing,' Martin continued, 'I'm pretty sure all the cows are in calf now but can you just get the vet to check.'

'Yes, okay. That's good.'

'It is but you do need to check them.'

'I will!'

'Have you ordered the pesticide from Karl?' Martin was relentless today.

'Yes,' she lied.

'Good, well that's one thing. Would you like me to come over tomorrow? I might be able to get away for a couple of hours.'

'No, Martin, you mustn't.' She took a breath. 'Listen, I do appreciate you pointing out what needs doing but you really need to leave it to me. And Glen. He'll be home on Tuesday.'

'Oh, that's marvellous. Yes, he'll be able to direct things.'

'So, there's no need for you to worry.'

'I will worry. I can't help it.'

'Listen, Martin I have to go.'

'Yes, all right then.' He sounded dejected as he hung up.

Wanda turned to see Abi holding two plates each laden with what looked like an interesting tuna salad and a buttered bread roll. Half the shopping was still packed in bags but it would have to wait; they were both famished. 'Let's sit in the garden.'

'Good idea,' Wanda said thinking she might collapse if she did not sit down soon.

The garden was just a small strip at the side of the house but it was fenced off and, as the house was set back from the road, it was quite pleasant. The sun fell on to a little patio area where there was a bistro-style table and chairs. They sat in quiet contemplation as they ate, Abi keeping in the shade of the umbrella. Wanda considered that the garden was neglected and very overgrown but looked quite pretty. It was alive with butterflies and bees buzzing around looking for pollen and was giving her ideas for her art. That made her think that now was probably a good time. It would make it easier if Abi was onside.

'Abi, I've got something to tell you.'

'Oh God, that sounds ominous. You're not leaving Dad, are you?'

'No, don't be silly.' Wanda paused to gather her thoughts. She needed to handle this carefully. 'Listen darling, I would rather you kept this to yourself.'

Abi frowned.

'It's nothing terrible. Quite the opposite. I've been offered an art exhibition for my paintings.'

'That's brilliant.' She was smiling and looked genuinely pleased for her mum. 'Who by?' she asked. It was a reasonable question. 'Not that man from America that Granny Rita was going on about?'

'Was she now. What a bunch of gossips this family are.'

'So, who then?'

'Well, actually, it is Aaron.'

'So where will the exhibition be? Not in America?'

Wanda panicked. 'London, in London.' *It was okay to tell a white lie. She had to leak the information out slowly over time so that no one freaked.*

'Blimey, that's pretty amazing. I thought it was just your hobby, painting.'

Wanda didn't rise to that comment. 'Anyway, I'm going to have to produce some paintings in the next few weeks, so you see...'

'Bad timing, Mum. What does Dad, say?'

'Well...'

'You haven't told him!'

'I didn't want to worry him.'

'Mm. This is going to be really tricky.'

'Well, yes, but look, I've persuaded Lee to do more round the farm, from tomorrow.'

'That's good but how will you pay him?'

Wanda decided to bite the bullet. 'Aaron has already bought two of my paintings and...'

'How much?'

'A tidy sum.'

'Wow. Well done you.' Abi looked thoughtful. 'I can't see Dad minding if you're bringing some money in.'

'I'd like to think you're right but he's never liked me painting so can it be our little secret for now?'

'Oh Mum, I don't want to lie to Dad.'

'No, no, not lie. Just be a bit economical with the truth sometimes.'

They looked at each other and both broke into nervous laughter.

Abi placed her empty bowl on the table and settled back in her chair. 'So, whereabouts in London will it be?'

'Oh, some small gallery in the Mayfair district.' *Why did lies have to get bigger and bigger?*

Abi looked suspicious. 'So whereabouts does Aaron live in America? And why is he doing this exhibition in London?'

'He flits around. He's back in New York at the moment; we're going to Skype to keep in touch. But he'll be back here in August.' Wanda felt dreadful. It was like she was digging herself into an even deeper hole. She reached across to her daughter and held her hand. 'Listen, your dad has been through a lot, so let's not tell him about this just yet. Let him settle back in to home life first.'

'You're right. He won't be happy until he's back farming.'

Wanda knew they could not be sure if he would ever be able to return to full-time farming but simply smiled at her daughter. 'Now, we need to get up to the hen barn and collect the eggs before the egg man comes at four.'

'Oh no, is that the time.' Abi looked at her watch. 'Okay Mum, but we'd better get the rest of the shopping put away first.'

'I think that will have to wait; I've put the fridge stuff away.'

Abi was looking at her mother as if in awe. 'By the way Mum, I think you're brilliant getting an exhibition.'

'Thank you Abi.' A tear welled in her eye.

As soon as they had collected all the eggs and placed them in the trays in readiness for four o'clock Wanda decided it was safe to let Abi finish off.

'Don't worry, Mum,' Abi said stacking the last of the trays outside the barn door. 'I'll make sure the egg man gets them all.'

'Great, that means I can snatch a couple of hours up at my studio.'

'Yes, you'd better start painting.'

It was great having her daughter on board with her mission; it was definitely going to make life easier. 'You can leave the hens out; we can come up later to get them in.'

'Dusk. They have to go in at dusk.'

'That's right.' Wanda beamed at her.

But when Wanda actually got to her art studio, she had so much on her mind that she found it hard to settle. She still hadn't met Conor properly and he hadn't returned her call; maybe Sunday wasn't the best day. Martin had clearly been economical with the truth when it came to the insurance payout and the hiring of a replacement for Glen. What was he playing at? But then, she did have some sympathy for him; it couldn't have been an easy time for him and Fi. She shook her head trying to dispel all these thoughts so that she could focus on the task in hand.

What was she going to paint? She grabbed a piece of scrap paper and a pencil and sat back in her chair waiting for ideas to pop into her mind. Nature, it had to be nature. Magical. She sighed. Her mind had literally gone blank. She was never going to find inspiration in this shed. She stood up, put the strap of her camping chair over her shoulder, found a sketchbook, picked up her pencil and made her way through Rachel's Covert and into Lucas Wood looking all around her as she went.

The sun had got stronger and there was a marked contrast between sunlight and dark shade in the wood; Wanda would have welcomed a breeze. Wild honeysuckle was wrapped around branches and giving off a sweet scent. She could hear pigeons calling and the loud flapping of wings.

Down on the woodland floor, buttercups, clover and bright yellow ox-eye daisies were dotted around.

She reached Quercus and looked way up into the canopy. Very near to her a swarm of bright green caterpillars was smothering a branch. One of the wriggling creatures fell and spun a silk thread as fast as it travelled down through the air, clinging to the end of the thread itself so that it could climb back up to the branch. That was magical. She discarded her chair and sketchbook and grabbed her mobile to capture the moment on camera. Just in time.

Quercus was quiet. Wanda didn't like to start the conversation. It was at this point that she always doubted that she had ever heard the mighty tree's voice. Was it all in her head? But actually, she really wanted to ask Quercus something today.

Being in this place always gave her a sense of calm. She was even a little sleepy after a soporific lunch combined with the heat of the day. Pulling out her camping chair she found a relatively level piece of ground. As she sat down and made herself comfortable, she considered that she might snooze for a while. But she couldn't afford to be sleeping on the job! She had ten, maybe twelve, paintings to create before the 17th August to allow time for them to be shipped out to America. And they had to be framed. *Help.*

Why wouldn't Quercus talk to her? Perhaps she should initiate a conversation. Instead, she gave the tree a hug, wrapping her arms as far as they would go around its large ancient trunk. The lower part of the trunk was covered in green moss and white lichen and there were old and gnarled looking brown-grey mushrooms nestling in between the top of the roots.

She heard a sound; someone was approaching. *Not Martin, spying on her and demanding she started spraying something dreadful around, surely?* She turned around.

'Gilbert!'

'Wanda Taylor.' He stood, his feet bare, looking thoughtful. 'What brings you here?'

Wanda took a breath. 'I'm looking for inspiration. I need to do more paintings.'

'I've heard Glen is out of hospital soon. I'm surprised you've got time to paint.' His words were gentle even if they did hit a sensitive point.

'I haven't got time really. Just snatching an hour or two while I can.'

'So old Mr Taylor and his missus, they've gone home, have they?'

'They have.'

'It's hard to let go of a farm that's been your life.'

'Don't worry he's still giving orders over the phone.'

Gilbert laughed. 'That sounds like old Mr Taylor.' He used Quercus' trunk to steady himself so that he could lower himself to the ground, his bottom landing heavily on the woodland floor. It was quite an operation for the old man, especially as he still wore his heavy old mac despite the temperature.

'You should have my chair,' Wanda said, getting up.

'Sit yourself down young lady. I'd probably break that flimsy thing. Anyway, I'm down here now. Might as well stay for a while.' He shuffled his bottom and removed a stick from under one cheek. Wanda resumed her seat and after a long contemplative pause, Quercus spoke out of the blue.

'I thought you had finished with me, little lady,' he bellowed. 'Used me to get what you wanted and left me to cope with my resting years.'

'I said I'd visit,' Wanda protested.

'Gilbert, young man, you do tire so easily.' The tree was obviously not impressed.

'Yes, well, I'm not so young these days.' Gilbert smiled to himself as if to say, *C'est la vie.*

'When I was your age, I was just getting going. Ah, the good old days back in the seventeenth century when farming was a gentler pursuit.'

'What was farming like then?' Wanda was curious.

'They started growing more crops so that they could send food to the towns and cities, but nothing like the scale of today.'

'There were a lot less people in those days,' Gilbert chipped in.

'Many homo sapiens manufactured cloth woven from wool taken from sheep's backs. Some made a lot of money.'

'That's why there's such big churches in this area,' Gilbert told Wanda. 'Those who made money were trying to buy a place in heaven.' He chortled to himself.

'Yes, I've heard that. So nowadays we have intensive farming so we get the most out of every bit of land so we can feed the millions of people.'

Quercus roared with disapproval. 'No, no, no! What you are doing is destroying the soil, reducing biodiversity, killing vital organisms!'

'Isn't that why we add fertilisers though to improve the soil?' Wanda asked half-expecting some condescending retort from the ancient one.

'Oh, Wanda Taylor you have so much to learn.'

'Fertilisers contain chemicals that are bad for nature,' Gilbert explained.

'Oh dear. So what should we be doing?'

'Giving nature a chance!' Quercus boomed.

'I don't know. It's all so difficult.' Wanda felt despair.

'Not difficult.' Quercus said not enlightening them any further.

'What we need to do,' Gilbert explained, 'is stop using so many harmful chemicals and be gentler with the soil. Some farms have already adopted a no dig approach.'

'No dig?' Wanda was intrigued. It was a nice idea.

'Yes, it means the soil improves over time.'

'The worms would be delighted; you don't know how many complaints I've had from them,' Quercus chipped in.

Wanda sat back in her chair. This was quite a revelation to her. But she knew that the Taylors would think it was all a barmy idea likely to bankrupt them. 'I just can't see this happening. I feel so awful to think that we are slowly destroying wildlife.'

Quercus sighed heavily. 'It's homo sapiens that will die out in the end. The flora and the fauna and the whole ecosystem will thrive without you.'

'It's true,' Gilbert said with a serious frown. 'We are just causing the problem. Nature doesn't need us.'

'What a very sombre thought.' Wanda felt with absolute certainty that something had to be done. But how on earth would she convince Glen. She could not tell him she'd been talking to a tree.

Wanda's thoughts went back to her painting project; she hadn't sketched so much as a scribble. But all this talk of nature and biodiversity made her think. She just needed to look more closely at everything around her.

It was getting late when Wanda got up to the office. She searched the laptop for the details of the insurance payout. No one had told her how much they had actually got. Surely there must be some email correspondence? But she was struggling to find anything. She went over to the filing cabinet. The last bank statement to be filed was around the time she left the farm. What had Martin been doing with them? She checked the hanger marked insurance. It was empty. Martin must have taken the whole file and not returned it. It was maddening but the last thing she wanted to do was to call him. It was Sunday so she couldn't call the insurance company. But Richard, their accountant, didn't mind a friendly weekend call. It didn't take long for her to find out that the payout was a thousand pounds a week. That was enough to pay Lee and Conor, surely? And apparently they were paying out twenty-five pounds a day while Glen was in hospital, something that had never been mentioned to her. No wonder Martin had commandeered the whole file and wiped any evidence on the computer. It took a while for the injustice of the whole situation to sink in. She had been paying Lee out of her art earnings all this time. She took a deep breath to calm herself. There was no point in getting angry. She would simply put it right and start paying Lee from the farm account.

CHAPTER 19

Abi loitered at the main door of the milking shed waiting for Lee to appear. She had poked her head in earlier but he was busy hosing down and had not looked up. She wandered a little way up the track towards Low Meadow. It was a glorious sight in the sunshine; she'd not really noticed before. She took a photo on her mobile and posted it on Instagram. The caption read: *my new home* and she added a smiley emoji. She hoped Gavin would see it. It was two fingers up at him; she was doing okay without him. Or was she? The London crowd would probably think she was mad. She looked back to the milking shed and saw Lee walking across the yard to the house.

'Lee,' she called out. He stopped and turned towards her. When she reached him, she handed over the notes and coins that her mother had given her to pay him. 'That's enough until Friday,' she said.

'That's good.' He looked a little surprised. He checked her out, his eyes wandering up and down her body. 'Right then.' There was an awkward pause.

'Actually, Mum says we can pay you weekly by direct debit, if you like? You see the insurance money is coming in so...'

'Direct debit.' He looked impressed. 'Definite then.'

'Yes, it will be.'

'Okay, we'll give it a try.'

'Mum also asked would you be able to do some muck spreading on Cuttings Meadow.'

He looked thoughtful. 'It's possible. Thing is the cows take quite a time; I mean twice a day.'

'Right.'

'If I had some help that would be different. Cut the time quite a bit and then I could do muck spreading.'

'I suppose I could help you. Not mornings though.'

'Afternoons. You could give me a hand?'

'Yes.' *Was she mad?*

'You done it before?'

'Once when Dad went into hospital. Mum said I was pretty good.'

He grinned at her now. 'Right, so we'll try it today.'

'Today? Oh, okay. Yes, all right then. Four o'clock, isn't it? Oh, hang on a minute, that's when the egg man comes.'

Lee rolled his eyes. 'Sounds like you're a busy woman.' They both laughed lightly. 'I think you'll find the egg man knows what he's about as long as the barn's left unlocked and you text him. Your Mum's all for opening up and freeing the hens so they go everywhere.'

'She says they're happier that way and lay more eggs.'

'Well, there you are.' Lee seemed highly amused by it all. He stood there looking into her eyes, seemingly in no hurry to leave and then he said, 'I thought you lived in London with some high-flying job. What you doing here?'

'That sounds more like Lily. No, I fancied a change. Things were a bit crap so... I don't know how long I'll stay. Dad's going to be home tomorrow and Mum needs some help looking after him.'

'When do you think Glen will be back up and running?'

Abi looked down at the ground and kicked a stone with her trainer. 'We just don't know. It's all had a massive effect on him.'

'Poor Glen. Farming is all he knows. Still, sounds like there's a bit of girl power going on. Here to save the day.' He smiled at her and Abi laughed. 'Right well I'll come early this afternoon,' he said, 'and do the muck spreading before milking. Cuttings Meadow, did you say?'

Wanda was making the bed up in Lily's old room. They hadn't talked about it, but she had wondered if Glen would want to sleep on his own to begin with, given his fragile state. It had been six weeks since the accident. Six weeks they had been apart and not shared a bed. Admittedly, before then they had been like ships passing in the night, barely acknowledging each other's presence. Glen would always be asleep when Wanda went to bed and he would always be up for milking way before Wanda even woke up.

But now things were going to be very different. And for how long? He had said he missed her. She couldn't remember the last time he had said anything like that to her, revealing his feelings. He was so buttoned up normally, so focused on the farm. It was as if he lived in fear of something going wrong, things not working out, the farm failing all because of him.

Her mobile rang, interrupting her thoughts.

'Hi Fi, how are you?'

'Martin won't settle. He's driving me mad.'

'Oh dear.'

'It's not your fault. Anyway, I'm ringing about Glen. What time are you picking him up tomorrow?'

'I don't know yet. The doctor is seeing him today and he's being assessed. You know, "Can he do stairs", that sort of thing. He reckons he can.'

'Right. Good. Well, if you want me to pick him up and bring him back to the farm. I mean, I know you must be busy.'

'That would be really helpful.' Immediately Wanda had misgivings. Perhaps Glen would be disappointed if it was not her. Perhaps he would read something into it. 'Actually Fi, I'd better do it myself.'

'I'm sure he'd prefer it, if it were you. Well, look, I tell you what, I'll drive over to yours once you have him home. Then I can help out with anything you need.'

'Thanks Fi. I really appreciate that.'

'Anything to give me a break from Martin. He just doesn't know what to do with himself.'

'He should take up fishing or golf.' Wanda giggled as she tried to imagine her father-in-law doing either of those leisurely pursuits.

'That's just what I said.' Fi was animated now. 'And you know what he said to that? He couldn't think of anything more boring.'

They were both laughing now. Wanda was pleased that she was getting on better with Fiona now.

'At the time,' Fi went on, 'he was sat in an armchair staring blankly into the distance.'

'Fi, are you sure he's okay?' she asked gently. 'I mean, he's not a bit down, is he?'

Fiona sighed. 'He's very worried about the farm. He doesn't seem to be able to muster up any enthusiasm for anything else.'

Wanda had a thought. 'Is there any kind of club for retired farmers? You know, somewhere that they get together.'

'There must be I suppose. Not sure it would be up Martin's street, though. Perhaps I'll google it.'

With the farmhouse ready for Glen's homecoming, Wanda went out to the winter barn to find her two poorly cows with mastitis. 'Now Daisies, I have to do this so the vet can make you better.' She put on a pair of latex gloves and started to milk them by hand. One of them mooed loudly and raised her head. She jostled her bulky body as if she was tired of being in the pen. 'I'm sure it is a bit unpleasant,' Wanda said trying to calm them. 'But still, you'll feel more comfortable after.'

The vet, Nathan, appeared in the barn looking mildly amused.

'Here comes your medicine, Daisy.' Wanda met his quizzical expression.

'Right, I have the antibiotic,' he said as he walked over to her.

'Good. And remind me, are the rest of the herd all clear?'

'Yes, there are no signs. But you could treat the whole herd with antibiotics just in case. That would be belt and braces.'

'How much is that going to cost?' Wanda's tone gave away her outrage at the thought.

'Well, yes, it's expensive. But some farmers use antibiotics routinely so it avoids any complications.'

'It's funny how we humans are supposed to avoid having antibiotics unless strictly necessary and yet with animals...'

'True. Just telling you what the options are.'

'Thanks, we'll leave the rest of the herd if you don't mind.'

'Your decision,' he said.

'Right I'll leave you to it if that's okay.'

On her way up to Hungry Hill to water the potatoes, Wanda noticed a young woman near the tractor barn; she must have been sent by Bartletts. She went over to say hello and found her setting up the combine harvester.

'Hello, I'm Wanda.'

'Tanya.' She came over to Wanda and shook her hand.

'Ah yes, Fiona mentioned you to me. I didn't know you were coming today.' Wanda kept her voice light. She was never quite sure how the contract with Bartletts worked.

'I'm taking the combine out. We've got wheat ready on Mill Field.'

'I see.'

'Martin asked me to check on Hungry Hill as well. Make sure the pesticide has gone down.'

'Oh, so Martin called you?'

'Yes, he did mention that you were looking after things until Glen gets home. He said you needed his help due to your lack of experience.'

'Did he now?'

'Sorry, have I said the wrong thing.'

'No, I'm pleased you've enlightened me. Nothing I didn't already know anyway. Listen Tanya, Martin has retired. He's finding it difficult to let go but he really needs to for the sake of his health. So next time he rings will you tell him that Wanda has it covered.'

Tanya looked uncertain. 'If you're sure.'

Wanda was sure she could run things her way. 'Absolutely.'

'So, am I still harvesting?'

'Yes, that's fine. But no need to worry about Hungry Hill. I'm just going up there myself to water the potato crop.'

'Right you are.' Tanya had a frown on her face which said something different.

Wanda reached out and laid a hand momentarily on her arm. 'I'm sorry about the mixed messages. I will call Simon at Bartletts and explain the situation.'

'Okay.' She still sounded uncertain. Wanda walked away feeling exasperated; would Martin ever let go?

There was a long hose attached to the side of the hen barn which was new, probably something Martin had installed. Wanda set to work unravelling the hose so she could reach the far end of the field. Once she was set up and directing the hose to water one square after another, she found the experience quite meditative. Calming even. When all the lush green leaves of the potato plants were shiny with wetness she stopped. Next she opened the barn doors wide so that the hens could venture out if they wished. They might prefer the barn today in favour of the wet ground. As it happened they were all keen to waddle and squawk their way out of the barn; about time too, seemed to be their sentiment. The very sight of them breaking free put a smile on Wanda's face. They were avoiding the sodden potato crop and pecking round the edge of the field even heading towards the track.

'Not too far,' she called out as she followed some and cajoled them back towards the barn. 'Believe me, you're better off staying close to home.' They obliged and gathered around Wanda as she walked back.

But then she saw Martin approaching, making his way steadily up the track. Wanda took a deep breath and told herself not to be too unkind to him but she could already feel her heart beating faster, almost a sense of panic coming over her. This was not fair.

She decided to go in the barn and busy herself but actually Abi had been up earlier so there was very little to do. Maybe there would be a few more eggs. Martin appeared at the barn door. He wore a heavy frown and looked anxious and confused. Wanda suddenly felt guilty. She walked over to him.

'Martin,' she said in a soft tone. 'How are you?' *Why had she asked that? It was obvious.*

He sighed. 'I'm worried, Wanda. I'm really worried and coming up here has made things ten times worse.'

'Martin, I know I do things differently to you but if I'm managing the farm then I have to do it my way.'

'I can't stand back and watch you ruin what I and my son have built up.' His voice was scarily calm.

'Listen, Glen is home tomorrow so I promise I will discuss matters with him.' *Goodness only knew how that would work out. Would she be able to be totally honest with Glen?*

'He's not going to be able to keep an eye on you. Not to begin with. It's down to me.'

'Martin, you have retired. You have to let go of responsibility for the farm. Glen and I are taking it forward from here and maybe in a different direction.'

'Get the hens in now!' he ordered.

Wanda just looked at him and didn't say a word. He started crying silently, brushing tears away with the back of his hand.

'You openly defy me you wretched woman!'

Wanda concentrated on breathing deep and evenly and said nothing.

'It will be different when Glen is back,' he continued. 'You mark my words. I might be on the scrapheap but he's a Taylor through and through. He knows what's right for this farm.' He turned to leave, tears still flowing.

'You get these bloody hens in the barn now!' he shouted as he walked away looking like a broken man.

Wanda stood there stunned by his outrage. What little hope she had of making a go of the farm her way was stamped out by this man.

Glen had walked up and down five stairs successfully if rather slowly. He was encouraged to walk without a walking stick. The nurse said, 'That's good,' rather cheerily. Glen felt patronised. He was not a child. He was able to use the bathroom by himself now; at least that bit of dignity was no longer stolen from him.

'You do have a wife at home that can look after you, I believe.'

'We're farmers. She's having to run the farm.'

'I see. But do you think you'll manage?'

It was a loaded question. If he said no, he might have to stay in this godforsaken place even longer. He was desperate to be home again. And Abi was there. That gladdened his heart. He had always thought, that of his two daughters, she would be the one that might help out when the chips were down. Lily was too embroiled in her career but that was okay. She seemed to be doing very well for herself. Abi didn't seem to thrive in London. She seemed to pick the wrong boyfriends and her career had not really taken off. But she was a lovely girl, if not the academic kind, and it would be great to have her back at the farm.

'Yes, we'll manage.' He smiled at the nurse to give himself the best chance of escape even though he knew managing at home was going to be difficult.

He had been walking around on the ward for several days now, determined to build up his stamina. A couple of times some random member of staff had found him struggling and asked him where his bed was and could they help him get back to it. He did not want to be bed bound! He was going home tomorrow. In his dreams he was back being a farmer, driving the combine to gather in the harvest with a blue sky above. He'd always enjoyed those moments; somehow it made it all worthwhile. But in his waking hours he reminded himself what a hard life it really was. How on earth were they going to get through this? Wanda had told him very little and he had no idea how she was managing. His father had made many a disparaging comment but then stopped himself. He had even said once that Wanda had met some American guy through the gallery in town.

'What do you mean "met"?' Glen had asked, horrified by what his dad might be implying.

'Nothing. Forget it. He's been buying her art from the gallery that's all.'

'Why on earth did you mention it then?'

'I shouldn't have. Forget it. It was nothing.'

'What was nothing?'

'Look son, you concentrate on getting better.'

Glen decided to put the whole incident out of his mind. It was just too much. He knew his father had always been disappointed in Wanda because she had failed to embrace farming in the way he had wanted her to, expected her to even. But how they farmed was between him and Wanda now. He could not wait to be back involved and to fully understand what was going on. He knew his attempts to get back into the nitty gritty would be frustrating, given his limitations, but at least he would be able to try. The doctors had been pleased with his progress and said that gradually he would do more. But when he asked the vital question, 'Will I be able to get back to full-time farming?' they looked shifty and made non-committal remarks with some sort of positive spin but with the word, *maybe*, in front of it.

That afternoon it was hot and airless in the milking barn. What little rain there had been earlier had not cleared the humidity. Abi dare not breath in too heavily for fear of the smell of cow poo or urine filling her nostrils; she couldn't decide which was worst. The cows in their milking stations were being fed on pellets, munching away happily even though just relieving themselves of the twenty litres of milk should be incentive enough to be here. Kylie Minogue's voice blared out of the sound system as she sang, '*I should be so lucky*'. Lee was bare chested and sweaty as he carried out his work. His torso was muscled and tanned and Abi felt a small stirring inside. She shook any such thoughts from her mind and concentrated on the job in hand. She needed to stay focused so that she did not make mistakes. Lee had been kind on the odd occasion that something had slipped her mind. He would come right up to her so that she could smell his scent and say gently, 'See, this is what you do after the clusters come off,' as he placed the iodine cup under each teat of the cow's udder. Then she would be annoyed for forgetting that bit.

'Sorry, I meant to, I mean...'

'You're doing really well,' he would say generously. 'It's so good to have some help.' She'd cut short the smile she wanted to give him and get back on with the job. Next cow, disinfectant foam, then she could attach the clusters on to the udder to start milking. Check the appearance of the milk. What was she looking for? It looked okay to her. Like milk. Then she had to wait until the machine sensed that the flow had slowed right down and stopped. Lee would manage to start on the next cow whilst this was happening but Abi knew she would get confused and forget which one was which. So she just waited and in that time her eyes wandered over to Lee. Sometimes she'd catch him looking at her too and she quickly looked away, feeling self-conscious. She had not really noticed him before now but he was one fit guy. Of course, he wouldn't be right for her. Her mother had made the mistake of marrying a farmer; she wouldn't follow that same path. No, she would be going back to London anyway at some stage. When her dad was fit and well again.

When the last cows were on their way back to their new pasture Abi felt exhausted but elated at what she had achieved.

'You're a natural,' Lee said to her smiling. He was smeared with milk and dirt but did not seem to care.

'Hardly.'

'We all have to start somewhere. You did good. Shall I show you how we wash down?'

Abi's heart sank. She was dreaming of a cup of tea and a comfy chair.

'Tell you what,' he said somehow reading her, 'I'll do it today. You go and see the last of the cows in and close the gate.'

'Thanks, I'd like that.'

'You making me a cup of tea after?' he said with a cheeky grin.

'Might do,' she replied not at all sure if that was the best response in the circumstances.

'It'll have to be a quick one; I've got to get up to Sally's Grove shortly.'

'Yes, then,' she said. *How bad could it be?*

CHAPTER 20

Glen soon realised that being in hospital was markedly different to being at home. Of course, he'd had his every need catered for by the nurses when he was on the ward. Any attempt to get back to a normal life was exhausting. He really wanted his independence back more than anything. He knew deep down that without it there was no hope of him taking up the farming mantle again. But frustratingly, he had no choice but to bow to the help offered by his mother as well as Wanda and Abi. At first, he had slept most of the time and done very little.

He'd only called the doctors once when he had been a bit concerned about the level of pain he was experiencing. Dr Harris came out to the farm to see him the same day which surprised him. But it was good because he checked Glen over and left him reassured that everything was okay. The doctor told him that the drugs he was taking were most likely the cause of his tiredness and so Glen had decided to reduce the dose gradually during the last week. It was a difficult balance to strike but he certainly did not want to spend the rest of his life sleeping.

His conversations with Wanda were maddening. He had the distinct feeling she wasn't telling him everything. She was making out that all was well and he had nothing to worry about but he knew that was simply unrealistic in farming.

'So, no problems with the potato crop on Hungry Hill? We didn't know what to expect given that we haven't cultivated that field for many a year.'

'Well, the plants look green and healthy. I've been watering.'

'And spraying I take it?'

'I think you underestimate that field. Leaving it alone for so long has actually done it a lot of good, I reckon.'

'I don't see how.'

'Nature is a wonderful thing you know.'

'What are you talking about?'

She hadn't replied.

'So, we're in for a good harvest, are we? It must be just a couple of weeks now.' He tried to catch her gaze.

'Let's just wait and see, shall we?'

Glen sighed.

'Have some faith,' she said, not unkindly.

And so it was, whatever he asked her if it was about the farm.

As he considered his wife's behaviour since he had returned home, an uneasy feeling came over him. She had been jumpy, always in a hurry to go out. Not like the Wanda he knew. Was she really taking the farming seriously and working all hours? That was very hard to believe given her track record. Was she staying out to avoid him? Had she got used to be being on her own?

And he was sleeping in the spare room. When he'd first got home, she had said casually, 'Do you think you might sleep better in Lily's old room, just to begin with?' Perhaps she read the expression on his face because she quickly added, 'Up to you, of course. You know how you feel.'

He couldn't work out whether she simply did not want him back in their bed or she was genuinely concerned that his physical state meant that he would be better on his own. He had felt particularly fragile at the time, his rib area hurting. He had to take powerful painkillers to get by. Perhaps separate beds was for the best. For now.

That morning he had awoken to a sun-filled bedroom and felt like he had a modicum of energy; he decided that today would be the day he ventured out. After all, he had been home for two weeks. His mother was not due as far as he could remember and Wanda had said she would be out first thing. He would walk up the track to Low Meadow and see if he could get as far as the cows on their pasture. They would be back from milking by now.

Lucas Wood was quiet, the birdsong muted, just the silent fluttering of butterflies and the odd buzzing bee. Lush green was omnipresent with the sweet smell of honeysuckle which wound its way around every stem and branch in its path. Wanda stood back from her painting and decided it was finished. Or at least she would move on to the next one and maybe come back to this one. If there was time. If course, there wouldn't be time. She had just four weeks until her work had to be ready for the exhibition and had only done one painting. The very thought sent her into a blind panic, but that was only making things worse. She had to stay calm. She looked at her painting of the lime green caterpillar scurrying up its own spun thread, the sunlight behind it, one of Quercus' lower branches its destination. It was good. Good enough. Please God. She would show Aaron on their next Skype call. She started to pack up her things when Quercus spoke for the first time.

'Leaving me now, little lady?'

'Yes, I must. I've a hundred and one things to do.'

'A hundred and one? You will never succeed in one day. Just stay a few minutes more.'

Wanda looked up in to the bright canopy of the tree. The leaves were a vibrant green. 'You've been quiet until now.'

'You were concentrating. And you are likely to fail in your attempt to be ready for your exhibition so I left you be.'

'Thanks Quercus. So pleased you are gunning for me.'

'You make no sense to me. Now listen, I have something important to tell you.'

Wanda was intrigued. 'Well?'

'I'm getting good vibes through the mycorrhizal fungi network. Change is miniscule and slow but there is change indeed. A reversal of the fortunes of biodiversity seems to have begun.'

'Really?'

'I wouldn't lie to you about such a serious matter.'

'I know you wouldn't. I'm just amazed. Maybe it is down to me. I haven't been using pesticides since I have been running the farm.'

'That is so good to hear. But why the change of heart?'

'Well, I could see that they would be bad for the hens and they cost a fortune. Of course, if the potato crop is no good, I'm in big trouble.'

'Are we talking about Hungry Hill?'

'That's right.'

'Your crop is bountiful Wanda; mark my words.'

Abi shielded her eyes from the sun pouring through her window as she woke up, the thin curtain doing nothing to block it. She decided to pull on some shorts and a T-shirt and make her way up to the hens. They would appreciate being let out on such a glorious day. She had grown fond of the little feathered creatures already, even learning the names of the ones her mother had picked out as worthy of a name.

She even enjoyed the walk up the main track to the hen barn. Somehow the farm looked different these days. Once up there and with the hens released onto the field, she made a start on collecting the eggs. With both barn doors wide open there was just enough sunlight to see by without turning on the artificial lights. This was how her mum did it and Abi respected her ways so she did the same. She could see that it was a more restful pastime in this half light even though it might be a little more difficult to find all the eggs. Her mum had some quirky ways of doing things which probably her dad saw as wrong but what harm was there if you got results and you had happy hens.

On her way back down the track she saw her dad resting against the gate where the cows were grazing. That was a good sign. She walked over and stood beside him.

'Dad, you okay? Is this your first time up here since...?'

He was squinting into the sunlight and blinked as he turned to look at her. 'Abi, love, have you been sorting the hens out?'

'Yes, I've collected quite a few eggs already.'

'Thanks for helping out. It's brilliant having you here.' He was so different since coming out of hospital, all wistful and calm.

'Don't tell Mum, but I'm quite enjoying it.' She smiled at him.

'It has its benefits, this life. Just look at the view, the cows happily munching away on the green grass. But it's hard. I don't know if my body can take much more.'

'It's early days. You'll get better.'

'I'm sure things will get easier but I think it's unlikely that I'll ever be the man I was before the accident. Running a farm is hard slog and you need to be fit.'

Abi couldn't imagine her dad doing anything other than farming. He'd grown up on the farm; it was all he knew. 'Do you think you'd ever sell the farm?' It seemed unthinkable but with everything that had happened, perhaps it was a possibility.

He sighed long and hard. 'It may come to that. Your granddad would be heartbroken if I did. He'd say I've failed. All his hard work will have been for nothing.'

'That's not fair.'

'I can see his point. A lot depends on your mum. And you for that matter.'

Abi squirmed. 'Oh Dad, I don't think you can rely on me. I mean I am giving it a go but I can't see myself doing this long term. Like you say, it's a hard life.'

'I don't blame you. Do you think you'll go back to London?'

'I suppose so.' She thought about her life in the city, the awful presenter who expected miracles from make-up, the tiny flat and her hopeless relationship with Gavin. 'Actually, I'm not sure. I'm not really sure about anything except that every day I go up to the hen barn to collect the eggs and at four o'clock I help Lee with the milking. It's kind of nice not having to think beyond that. Living in the moment. I appreciate the countryside much more than I ever did as a child. London's different. The people are different. And as for Gavin, he's let me down, twice. Twice! What a fool I was to believe anything he said to me.'

'We all make mistakes. At least you didn't marry him before you found out.'

'Do you ever regret marrying Mum?'

He hesitated before he answered. 'Of course not.' Abi was not convinced but dared not push him further. She couldn't imagine her parents not being together and on the farm.

They stood in thoughtful silence watching the cows enjoying their pasture in their uncomplicated world. And then Glen said, 'I'd better get back to the house and have a sit down.'

'I'm walking back too. Do you need some help?'

'I'll manage. I've got to. But it's good to know you will be by my side.' He smiled at her.

'Would it be better to paint them here?' Saffy said as Wanda photographed a few of the Meadow Glamping hens that they had persuaded into a separate coop.

'It would and I will as far as I can. It's just the time it takes to get over here and being away from the farm.'

'Why don't you tell Glen about the exhibition? Wouldn't that make life so much easier? I mean you stand to make a lot of money, don't you?'

'Potentially. Right now, I just feel doomed to failure. I'm at least ten paintings short and Aaron is getting very twitchy.'

'So, tell Glen.'

'No! Not yet. I haven't told him about half the stuff happening on the farm. He seems to have given up asking. But then Martin will call him for an update and it all gets a bit awkward.'

'From what you've told me you seem to be doing a good job; what's the problem?'

'In Martin's eyes I'm doing everything wrong and the farm is bound to fail.'

'Why don't you paint some of *your* hens?' Saffy changed the subject, perhaps trying to be a little more positive.

'Because we only have two varieties, Goldline and Light Sussex. You have five and yours are so cute, especially these five. And this setting is lovely with the kitchen garden in the background. Actually, I might do some of your veg next, if that's okay?'

'I'll have to charge.' Saffy laughed.

'I'll pay you in bottles of wine and great company.' Wanda winked at her friend.

'You have a deal.'

Lee was playing it cool. He was polite and kind and even said things like, 'we make a good team,' when milking was done for the day. But he almost avoided looking at Abi at all. He was very focused on the job in a business-like fashion. He quoted stats at her like how good the yield was at the moment and what the price per litre of milk was today. It didn't mean a lot to her but she feigned interest.

Abi knew she had put him off any idea of a romantic liaison that first day she had milked with him and they had drunk tea together afterwards. All she had said was that she was badly hurt by Gavin and that she was a bit disillusioned with London and needed time to work out what she wanted out of life. It was probably a bit of a blow to his ego as he'd made it very clear he fancied her. The other big thing was that he was a farmer. He was cute and fun and she liked him a lot but he was still a farmer. There was no getting past that. She could almost see history repeating itself. God forbid.

It was a shame because helping him with the milking was becoming a bit of a chore. She would carry on doing it while her father was recovering from his op but she really did not want to be doing this long term.

'Oh damn!' The cow in front of her had just pooed.

Lee laughed. 'You'd better clean it up. Mop and bucket over there.'

'Can I just finish…?'

'No! You have to clean up straightaway. We can't risk contaminated milk.'

'Right.' She could feel her face reddening. The stench was awful. He was looking at her and dropped what he was doing.

'I'll do it. It's no job for a lady.' Was he mocking her? Still she wouldn't fight him for the task. She stood back while he cleaned it up.

'All ready for you madam.' He mimicked tugging a forelock.

'There's no need for that,' she said and immediately wished she hadn't. He was looking at her with serious eyes.

'You can't have it both ways you know,' he said. *What did that mean?*

'I'm just trying to help out.' She knew she sounded stroppy but didn't care.

'Sorry,' he said and gave her a tight-lipped smile. 'It's great that you're helping me, I just wish...'

'Wish what?' she dared to ask.

'Nothing,' he said.

They washed the milking shed down together at the end barely exchanging a word.

'Right, I'm going to close the gate on the cows,' he said. 'Are you coming?'

There was no need for her to go. It only took one person. But she thought maybe it would be a chance to clear the air; that would be good.

One of the cows was loitering on the track.

'Come on, girl.' Lee gave it a push in the right direction. The cow mooed and stumbled forward but then it picked up its pace and returned to the pasture. Lee was watching it carefully.

'Is it all right?'

'Yeah, I think so. It doesn't look lame anyway.'

With the gate closed Lee leant on it looking out over the field. Abi stood next to him not sure what to expect. Then he turned towards her.

'Fancy going to the pub tonight?'

Abi thought about it. 'Yes, okay.'

'The White Horse up the road all right for you, is it? Or would you prefer to go into town? I could drive.'

'The White Horse is good.'

'I don't know, Dad.' Glen was getting a little fed up with the frequent calls from his father. He was sat in the farmhouse garden under a shade drinking a mug of tea he had made. It had been a peaceful moment until his father called.

'Well don't you think you should ask Wanda? She should be giving you daily reports. I'd insist on it, if it were me.' Martin sounded agitated.

'Dad, I'm not a hundred per cent you know. I can only do so much. She tells me everything's fine so I just have to trust her.'

'Big mistake, that. Listen, I probably shouldn't have but I rang Karl earlier to see if Wanda had ordered the pesticide for Hungry Hill a couple of weeks back. He said he's not heard from her at all. We've had nothing from him since she took over.'

'Right.' Glen thought that was puzzling but there may well be a perfectly innocent explanation. He would give her the benefit of the doubt.

'What do you mean *right*? Aren't you worried?'

'Look Dad, I'll ask her when I see her but there's not a lot I can do right now.'

'No, well, I can see that. So, I was thinking I should come over. I can be your eyes and ears while you're getting back to full strength.'

'No Dad. We've been through this. You've already scared Wanda away once and I don't want that happening again.'

'Charming! After all I've done for you while you were in hospital!'

'Sorry, Dad, but you've got to let me be in charge now.'

'Fine, if that's the way you want it. Be it all on your head.' Martin ended the call.

Glen put his mobile back on the bistro table and blinked his eyes as he tried to recover from the emotions his father had stirred in him. He didn't want to believe a word Martin had said but it all fitted with Wanda's evasive answers to his questions. What was going on out there? Never had he felt more frustrated that the accident had left him a lesser man unable to even run his own farm. Tears came to his eyes. He never cried. But he just couldn't help it. He didn't hold back and cried out in agony and despair. What would become of them?

Wanda stood back and looked at her painting. She smiled realising she had made good progress in quite a short space of time. Although she didn't know exactly what time it was. She was happy with the hens she had chosen even though not one hen had kept still for more than a millisecond. She had sketched out the composition for her painting from one of the photos she'd taken earlier and had mixed a very pleasing pallet of colours to match the grey speckles, golden tan, soft blonde, pure white, and chestnut brown of her models. She had added cadmium red for the combs on their heads.

She left her easel and wandered into Saffy's kitchen garden in search of inspiration and soon came across an aubergine-coloured pea pod so dark it looked black from a distance. She had started to take some pictures when her mobile rang out.

'Glen, hello. Everything okay?'

'I don't know.' He sounded forlorn. 'You tell me.'

'I'll be home soon,' she blurted out and realised in the same moment she had failed to tell him that she would be going out in the first place.

'You're not on the farm then?' he asked.

'I've just popped over to Saffy's.'

'I thought you were rushed off your feet with farm work.'

'I am mainly. Listen, what time is it?'

'It's nearly seven o'clock. What are we having for dinner?'

'Gosh, I didn't realise how late it is. Right, I'll come back now then.'

Abi hadn't thought the pub would be so full on a Tuesday evening. There were people she knew from the village and they made a point of noticing her and, no doubt, the fact that she was with Lee. Perhaps they should have gone in to town after all. But at least here she could walk home as soon as she had had enough.

Lee grinned as he placed her glass of white wine in front of her and settled down with his pint. 'It's Sauvignon Blanc,' he said mispronouncing the words in a rather endearing way. 'They don't have no other.'

Abi took a sip. 'It's fine.' It tasted a bit odd; not what she was used to but this was a rural village pub.

'So tell me about life in the big city. I haven't been there myself apart from once on a school trip. I found it noisy and busy.'

'Well, there's a lot more to do than in the country. Bars, cafés, restaurants and shops. Lots of galleries too.'

'Right so you spend your whole time spending money?'

'Not really; we were pretty skint actually. Living in a tiny flat.'

'What work do you do?'

'I want to be an actress. Just haven't had my big break yet. So I've ended up as a make-up artist in television production.'

'Do you enjoy that?'

'Sometimes. But it can be hard work. Some of my clients expect miracles.'

'What so they look like Quasimodo but they want to look like Jennifer Aniston.'

Abi laughed. 'Exactly right!'

'Yeah, I can see that would be challenging. I think I'd tell them their expectations were a little too high.'

'That would go down well with this presenter I was making-up just before I left. She would have bitten my head off.'

'Nasty. So did you just walk out of your job then?'

'Pretty much. But I was only temping so I wasn't committed really. I did leave dragon face in the lurch; I got quite a few angry texts about that.'

'Interesting. What puzzles me is why you came back to the farm.'

Abi felt awkward. She took a deep breath. 'I just felt drawn in a way, to coming home. I mean, I was mainly running away from Gavin after I found out he'd cheated on me. Again. I was just sat in this tiny flat eating rubbish food on my own because my boyfriend was out having a good time with another girl and I'd had such a crap day at work, I just thought…'

'Get me back to those cows!' Lee laughed out loud and Abi joined in.

'Not exactly the cows. Though they're all right. When they don't poo in your face.'

'Agreed, crap is a downside of milking.'

'And in the city you don't always feel safe even walking the streets. I mean, take that terrorist attack last month on London Bridge. Seven people killed, just like that. It makes you question what you're doing there.'

'So, life is expensive, dangerous and the guys are lousy; pretty rubbish really.'

'When you put it like that. But also I wanted to see my dad. He nearly died you know with that accident. Makes you think.'

'Yes, I can see that. He's a good bloke, Glen.'

They sat in thoughtful silence until Lee said, 'Fancy another drink?'

Abi decided that the wine wasn't too bad after all. 'I'll get these.'

It wasn't even nine o'clock when Lee said that he had better get home. The time had gone so quickly. Abi felt relaxed and carefree as they wandered out and along the road back towards the farm. It was a beautiful evening, the sun low in the sky.

'Don't you live in the next village?' she asked wondering how he would get home.

'Yes, it's only a mile away.' There was a pause before he added. 'Fancy walking up Gorey Hill? We should just make it before the sun sets.'

'You going all romantic on me now, are you?' she asked probably due to the amount of wine she had drunk and with just a packet of peanuts to soak it up.

'On an evening like this it's a glorious sight. What do you say?'

It was still early. Why not? They were soon climbing up from the base of the hill. He picked up speed on the way and she did her best to keep up with him. By the time they reached the top she was panting.

'What's the hurry?' she cried out.

He was laughing and turned her gently around so that she was looking out over a beautiful pink sky with an orange sun just about to dip below the horizon.

'Wow.'

'Quite something, isn't it? Bet you don't get that in London so much.'

'We do have parks, you know. And Hampstead Heath.'

'Right and how often do you go there at sunset?'

Abi didn't answer, just stood and stared. It was quite a sight. 'Worth the climb,' she had to admit. He was standing close to her. He smelt sweet tonight, not his usual rugged self.

She turned towards him. He was waiting for her and took her in his arms, holding her close, and kissed her. It was lovely, she felt light-headed. But she didn't want to lose control. She pulled away and they were looking into each other's eyes. She was embarrassed and smiled.

'Time to go back?' he said softly as if he had no expectations of her.

'Yes, let's go.'

'I'll have to walk you home now, of course, as it's dark.'

She didn't argue.

When they reached the farm he said, 'You will be at milking tomorrow as usual, won't you?'

'Yes, of course.'

He took her hand in his and kissed it. 'Goodnight,' he said with a slight note of triumph.

She walked into the farmhouse dreamily. What had just happened?

CHAPTER 21

The more Wanda looked at the orange peel mushroom, the more enchanting it seemed. She had come across it by chance on the edge of the path above Rooked Meadow. There must have been at least twenty growing in a cluster. She couldn't believe her luck. She looked out over the field; this small pocket of land was full of gay abandon on this mid-August day. It was as if all nature was wild and free with pops of the bright colours of wildflowers here, there and everywhere. So different from the rest of the farm. As there were so many of these unusual mushrooms, she had decided it would be safe to pick just one when she was ready to put paint to paper. The mushroom had a thin fragile flesh of tangerine-coloured petals, almost forming a rosette, and it had very little in the way of a stem.

This was Wanda's twelfth work of art for the exhibition and Aaron had agreed that it would complete her collection on their Skype call yesterday evening. As usual she'd had to go round to Saffy's to make the call as she had no internet connection in her studio. Luckily Saffy was supportive of her mission, pleased for her even. Though there were moments when Saffy would look at her and Wanda knew what she was thinking but neither of them said anything. It was the elephant in the room; Glen didn't know about the exhibition. Aaron had said he was going to add her painting of Quercus making it thirteen, although he may mark it *sold* from the off as he was rather fond of it, and really wanted to keep it as part of his own collection. All the works were to be carefully packaged and ready to be shipped to New York by the 18th August, so she had just a few days to complete this last work and get it framed. Wanda was to fly out five days later, giving them two full days to hang the paintings before the exhibition started on the Saturday. Aaron was even hoping to have a private view on the Friday evening if they were ready in time. It all sounded very last minute.

Wanda felt really excited whenever she thought about it but then she remembered that Glen still knew nothing of her plans and she felt a knot in her stomach tightening. She even felt nauseous at times when her anxiety levels rose. Her justification for not telling him was that the right moment just hadn't presented itself. She knew it wasn't going to go down well but hopefully, when she told him how much she stood to make from the whole project, surely, he would be pleased for her.

It had been a very difficult time trying to juggle creating works of art with farm work and managing Glen. Luckily August was less busy than many months as the harvest had been gathered in and with the insurance still paying out, she had been able to spend the time she needed on this amazing project. Glen had agreed with her that they should let Conor go as he was really out of his depth. Instead, they had given more work to Bartletts and with Lee's increased hours they were just about managing. But Wanda had been up and out of bed from early, by her standards, to very late every day. She kept herself going with caffeine so that, when she did go to bed, she was still buzzing and could not sleep. Glen was now back in their bed at his suggestion but nearly always asleep when she crawled in, in the small hours.

Whenever he got the chance, Glen would snatch a moment to ask about the farm like over a meal shared with Abi not around. He would ask her questions that she didn't want to answer. He was also getting stronger and able to walk further which made him more dangerous. Luckily the potato crop had been harvested successfully, just as Quercus had said it would. It confirmed to Wanda that nature was amazing, miraculous even, and thank goodness because Wanda needed all the help she could get right now. Lee had kept on top of the muck spreading and the silage making for the cow's winter feed. Abi seemed to be helping him out more and more, even with the disgusting smelly jobs as she called them. No one was more amazed than Wanda. And she hadn't talked about going back to London for weeks. What was going on with that daughter of hers?

Even though poor Tanya was still getting orders from Martin, Wanda had managed to persuade Bartletts that everything should be done her way. She had lost count of the times Tanya had questioned what she asked her to do. She just had to play the upper hand and say that she didn't want to hear Martin's name mentioned again. Fi was on Wanda's side in that she was determined that Martin was retired now. The poor woman was holding on to a dream that they would enjoy some relaxing, leisure–filled years together. The trouble was that this new lifestyle seemed to make Martin's blood pressure rise, not fall.

Getting the paintings ready had been a tricky operation. As each one was completed and got the okay from Aaron on their Skype call, Wanda had taken it to a picture framer she knew who operated from a very rural spot in the middle of nowhere. Aaron had told Wanda to use the money from her advance for the framing costs, which was fair enough. The framer was not willing to store the paintings after he had done his work and so Wanda had the dilemma of where to put them. The farmhouse, was, of course, not an option. In the end she had come across Gilbert in Lucas Wood one day and asked him if he would help her out. He'd been happy to oblige but said he couldn't be responsible if they were stolen from his home. The security at his cottage was modest but Wanda felt she had no other choice.

There was some comfort knowing that she just needed to complete this last painting, get it framed and then she could contact Aaron's courier. They would be able to pick up the complete set of her work from Gilbert's cottage.

Wanda had promised she would cook for Glen and Abi that evening and they would sit down together as a family to eat. Maybe even out in the garden. It would provide the perfect opportunity to tell Glen about the exhibition. And tell him she must. Wanda's heart beat faster at the very prospect.

Glen had told Abi that he would be able to see to the hens that day. It would give her some time off. She had readily accepted his offer. He put on his old farming trousers and a T-shirt and set off, taking it easy as he went up the main track. There were harebells, purple blue and delicate, growing along the fence. He had not seen them before. Perhaps he had always been in too much of a rush to notice. He got as far as where the cows were grazing and stopped to have a good look at them and check they were all doing okay. Some were gathered under the shade of a tree, whipping their tails around to send the flies away, others drinking from the water trough. Glen considered going into the field but decided against it. He still felt vulnerable among them even though there was no bull. According to Wanda the A I. programme had gone well and they were all in calf. Lee seemed to be doing a decent job looking after the beasts and there hadn't been any complaints from the distributor about the quality of the milk so it looked like all was well. Strictly speaking Wanda should be more involved or Lee should be promoted to take on the responsibility of the herd. They were very lucky that he had assumed that role, despite what they paid him.

What was also very puzzling was how healthy the bank balance was. It was ludicrous that with him out of action they were managing to make more money. He would get to the bottom of it with Wanda that evening. She was obviously feeling guilty because she had promised to not only be home, but to cook. And she wasn't a natural cook like his mother.

Glen reached the hen barn and still felt okay. His pain wasn't too bad today. In fact, getting on with jobs took his mind off it. The first thing he noticed was a profusion of bright red poppies growing around the barn and into the field. That was unusual.

When he opened the barn door there were tens of hens gathered making a noise as if they were waiting to go outside. And the lights were not on but perhaps they were not working. Wanda had not said anything. He left the barn door open a little for light, found the switch and turned them on. They were working fine. Odd. Meanwhile some of the hens were beginning to make their escape outside despite the narrow gap. Damn it. He tried to get to the door but the hens were thick and fast around his feet. He struggled at first, determined to make his way, but the pain in his chest increased so he stopped and steadied himself, resting a hand on the side of the barn and took a breath. More and more hens were getting out. This would not do. It was all Wanda's fault; she had no regard for how the farm should be run. It was down to her that they didn't clip their wings so they could just fly away. She thought it was cruel. He felt so helpless as the hens filed out but he dared not move from his spot. He tried to calm himself, remembering the words of the doctor. Stressful situations were to be avoided. This should not have been stressful. His wife was responsible for this. He would have words with her. Strong words.

When most of the hens were out, he opened the barn door wide and went outside himself. He leant against the barn wall and slid down to a sitting position on the ground. It was a relief and he was finally able to calm his breath but what a commotion it had been. He would call Wanda.

She could come and sort this mess out. When she didn't answer, frustration overcame him and tears filled his eyes. What on earth was Wanda up to?

Abi wanted to make the most of her unexpected free time. She had until afternoon milking, or even all day if she texted Lee to say she couldn't make it today. He wouldn't like it and she would feel bad. She rang her mother.

'Can I borrow your car?'

'How long for?' Wanda asked.

'You don't need it, do you?'

'Well, actually, I do.'

'Oh Mum, the one day I have some spare time and you want to use the car again. What's the point of me being on your insurance?'

'Where do you want to go?'

'Anywhere out of this village! I thought I might go into Bury.'

'Will you be back for milking?'

'Haven't decided. Probably. But the idea of a whole day off from farming is rather yummy.'

'Mm. Well, I definitely need the car later. Probably about four-ish, so if you were back by then it could work.'

'All right then, I'll be back. Seems very early.'

'Keys are in the usual place in the kitchen.'

'I know.'

She hadn't told Lee that she had some time off. It had all been very last minute; Dad had only offered to do the hens the evening before. Her first reaction had been to text Lee on the off chance that he was free too. Being a weekday, it seemed very unlikely. And she was hankering after some girly company, truth be told.

Now she decided to look through her old contacts. Zoe was always a good laugh. Or maybe Amy. She sent Zoe a text.

Abi here! Long time no... Don't suppose for a mad moment you are free for lunch today in Bury? Abi x

It was only a few minutes before she got a reply.

Amazing crazy girl! What you doing here? Last I heard you were loved up in London. Working but IN TOWN so could squeeze an hour at lunch time? Say 12.30? Zx

Her day was looking good. Abi put on a pretty sundress and her sunglasses, grabbed her handbag and the car keys and made her way out. Lee appeared from nowhere just as she was about to get into the car. What was he doing here at the farmhouse?

'You look nice,' he said. He was standing just a short distance away from her looking quizzical.

She smiled at him half-heartedly. 'Just off to town. Meeting a friend for lunch.'

He came right up to her and put a possessive arm around her. He smelt of cows. 'I wish I was coming,' he said and kissed her lightly.

'Sorry, yeah, it was last minute you see. Dad offered to do the hens for me.' He still looked puzzled. 'And I knew you'd be working.'

'Working for your farm, actually.' He was clearly miffed. 'Your mum's got me fixing fences and making more silage. I only agreed to it this morning, mind.'

Whoops. 'Right, well I'll see you later.' She kissed him again by way of compensation despite the whiff of him.

'Well, you go and have fun then.'

She was in the car with the window wound down and the engine on when he said, 'You will be back for milking, won't you?'

'Yes, worst luck.'

'I see.' His expression was properly offended now. She drove off.

No. 5 Angel Hill was full but Abi had nabbed a table outside, albeit on the shady side on the pedestrianised street. Actually, the respite from the sun was welcome. Zoe strolled up on time.

'Abi!' she screamed across the street. Abi had forgotten how full-on this gregarious woman was. They were laughing as they hugged. 'My God it's been ages.' Zoe sat down. 'I need to know everything. What the hell are you doing here in town?'

Abi managed to persuade her friend that they should order food first and they both decided on a smoked salmon bagel and a pot of tea.

'We should be drinking something stronger than tea to celebrate.' Zoe clinked her cup against Abi's.

'You're working and I'm driving. How is the job going? Still at the same solicitors?'

'Yeah, same old, same old. Still on reception. But I quite like my work. It's a big practice so it keeps me busy.'

'Sounds like it's stress-free. I was a make-up artist in TV production.'

'Wow. TV.'

'Yeah, but what I really want to do is to get into acting. I used to do quite a few auditions but more recently I've been too busy working.'

'But make-up artist; that has to be fun.'

'Depends on the client. Some are real bitches. In fact, the men are much better. Apart from the ones who don't want any make-up until I tell them they are going to look dreadful on screen without it.'

'How funny! So what are you doing now? Is this a flying visit or what?'

Abi sat back in her chair. 'I don't know really. A lot's happened. My dad was badly injured by a bull.'

'Oh no! That's too awful.'

A waiter appeared with their food. 'Ladies.' He had a friendly smile. 'Enjoy.'

'Thanks. Starving.' Abi said and took a bite of her bagel.

'Food's always good here.' Zoe smiled. 'So how's your dad now?'

'He's back home and he's okay but he's not the man he used to be.'

'So have you got a farm manager in?'

'Not exactly.'

'By the way you've got cream cheese on your face.' Zoe pointed to Abi's cheek.

'I'm not surprised. This bagel is yummy.' They both laughed. 'Long story,' Abi continued, 'but we did have someone for a while but now my mum's sort of in charge and Dad does what he can. But the guy we normally have, Lee, is doing the milking twice a day and quite a bit more at the moment.'

'Well that's good.' Zoe looked at Abi with a quizzical expression. 'And?'

Abi squirmed in her seat.

'What are you not telling me, Abi Taylor?'

'I don't know really. I'm just not sure about anything, including Lee.'

'Ah!' Zoe cried out triumphantly. 'So you and Lee are an item.'

'Well, sort of.'

'You're not sure about him?'

'I like him, I like him a lot. He's good fun. We do the afternoon milking together and he's so sweet, helping me when I forget things. There's so much to remember.'

'Wow! Sounds like you're loved up. I remember when you were adamant you wouldn't get involved with the farm.'

'I know. And I still am really. I don't want to be a farmer's wife.'

'Whoa! Hang on a minute. You're considering marrying this chap?'

'No, no, no. It's just if we get involved...'

'You are involved,' Zoe pointed out.

'And it gets serious, then...'

'Is he crazy about you? You don't need to answer that. He is, isn't he?'

'I think so. And that scares me.'

'Oh, Abi, Abi, Abi. What are you going to do?'

'The thing is I came back because of Dad initially. Well that and my crap, now ex-, boyfriend in London. And because I'd just had enough really. Life in London isn't all it's cracked up to be. Lily's okay, she's got a brilliant job and actually half owns a flat with a gay friend of hers. But me, I was renting a tiny place with the rat, Gavin.'

'Bury St Edmunds is a great town if you're looking for an alternative.' Zoe was beaming with pride. 'I've got a flat now in the centre. Two bedrooms. Thanks partly to bank of Mum and Dad.'

'That's brilliant. You know, I've been wandering around town this morning and I was thinking what a lovely place it is. People are so friendly too. You don't get that in London.'

Zoe was still smiling but said nothing.

'Anyway, right now, the farm needs me.'

'You've got the day off though, right?'

'Sort of. Got to be back for milking at four.'

'Can't let the loved-up Lee down.'

Abi rolled her eyes. 'What am I going to do?'

Wanda was making fish pie. She was following a Mary Berry recipe, skipping any bits she didn't fully understand because time was short. Earlier she had whizzed over to the picture framers as soon as Abi was back with her car and dived into the supermarket on her way home. She had felt a sense of achievement handing over the final art work. Aaron's feedback on their video calls had been really positive. '*You've done it, girl!*' he'd said and Wanda had felt pleased as punch for a fleeting moment.

It had clouded over in the late afternoon and the air was thick with humidity. By the time Wanda had got the fish pie in the oven, she was sweating in the close atmosphere. Why had she not done a salad? Although she could see Glen turning his nose up at that. Farmers don't eat salad. She poured herself a glass of cold water from a bottle they kept in the fridge and went to sit outside in the garden. She gulped the water down and then lent back on her bistro chair and closed her eyes. She needed this moment just to breathe. She could easily fall asleep; she was so tired. But it was a good kind of tired, the kind you feel when you have a strong sense of achievement. She was proud; she had done it. She had produced the art work for her New York exhibition. It was the most amazing feeling. This evening she would have to tell Glen. It would be okay. Surely he would have to be a little bit impressed by what she had achieved.

Just then there was a loud crash of thunder and the heavens opened. Huge, warm droplets of rain smothered everything instantly. Wanda grabbed the chair cushions and ran inside.

The storm had cleared the air but the atmosphere, as they ate around the little bistro table in the garden that evening, was far from convivial. The table was too small for three people and Abi was slightly detached holding her bowl of fish pie and fork away from the table. Wanda sensed that they each had their own agenda and that despite being physically close together they were actually miles apart. At least the fish pie tasted okay and everyone was eating it without complaint. Abi was quite happy to say that she'd had a lovely day in town and thanked her father for going up to do the hens for her. It was a shame that she also shared that she had been so reluctant to get back in time for milking.

'But I thought you were getting to like milking with Lee?' her father said.

'It's okay. But it's every day. I mean if I had weekends off.'

Glen laughed. 'Farming is round the clock, twenty–four seven.'

Abi looked like she had some clear thoughts on that subject but decided to keep quiet.

'I need to talk to you about the hens.' Glen turned to Wanda, his expression serious now.

'Oh?'

'Yes, when I went up there the lights were off. And worse still the hens all managed to escape outside. There was nothing I could do about it. I can't overexert myself. The pain gets worse.'

'Dad, you should have said. I didn't know you still have pain.' Abi sounded concerned.

'It's something I have to live with.'

'I'm sorry Glen. Are the hens still out now?' Wanda asked.

'They will be. Some of them have probably flown off.'

'No, no they won't. I'll go up later and make sure they are all safely in.' Wanda hoped that would be an end to it.

'But that's not the point. Farm policy is to keep the hens in the barn and keep the lights on for maximum production.'

'Well, Glen, it's not *my* farm policy.'

'But it was what we all agreed.'

'I didn't agree. I'm just railroaded into doing everything the Taylor way. If I'm expected to run the farm, surely I get a say...'

'And that's another thing,' he interrupted her. 'When I rang you about the hens you didn't answer. Where were you?'

Wanda was so tired after what had been another long day. She really felt that she couldn't take any more. This was definitely not the evening to confess about the exhibition after all. But Abi was staring at her pointedly.

'Mum, I think it's about time you told Dad,' she said gently as if her words were not going to wreak havoc.

Wanda closed her eyes and took a deep breath.

'Tell me what?' Glen was more than agitated now. 'Is this about that American chap? Dad told me he thought you were carrying on. It would explain a lot about your absence all the time. Creeping into bed late at night.'

Abi was biting her lip. Wanda wanted to be beamed up into space.

'Well?' Glen demanded. 'Should I take your silence to mean you're guilty as charged?'

'No!' Wanda raised her voice to meet his. 'No, it's nothing like that.'

'But the American chap is involved,' Abi added unhelpfully.

'Listen, Aaron is in America. I have not been carrying on with him as Martin implied. I've just been doing some paintings for him.'

'For an exhibition in London,' Abi said. 'But don't worry, Dad, because Mum's going to make lots of money and that will help with the farm.'

'So you've been painting for this Aaron chap when you're supposed to be doing farm work. I don't believe it.'

'Not all the time.' Wanda reached for her wine glass and, realising it was empty, she took the bottle out of its wine cooler and poured herself some more.

'So what exactly has been going on?' Glen looked as if he was mortally offended and he was holding his ribcage with the palms of his hands.

'Glen, do you need more painkillers?' Wanda got up from her chair. 'I'll go and get them for you.'

'No! I don't want more painkillers; the side effects are dreadful. Anyway I've had a glass of wine.'

'But Dad, perhaps you should take them just now; you've only had a small glass.' Abi looked worried.

Wanda went into the house and got the tablets and a large glass of water. She took them outside and put them on the table in front of him but he didn't touch them. She sat down again, took a large glug of wine and said, 'Listen, I know I don't run the farm the way you would, but I have said now for some time that I will do it my way. And as for the exhibition this is something I'm doing for me and I've managed to keep everything going on the farm for which I think I deserve some credit. And I've got all the art work ready in time to be shipped.'

'Shipped?' Abi interrupted her, looking confused.

'I mean couriered.' Wanda hoped she wasn't blushing. 'And still I'm doing the wrong thing. We agreed that when Martin left the farm he wouldn't interfere any more but he has.'

'Only because he's worried.' Glen's knee-jerk reaction was so typical. 'He was telling me only today that he spoke to Bartletts and they've been told not to use any pesticides. What kind of crazy idea is that?'

'Martin is worried that he's losing control. But he can't control the farm if he's retired? Fiona wants him to stop his involvement.'

'I think Mum's right about not using pesticides,' Abi chimed in which surprised Wanda.

'We've saved a fortune,' Wanda pointed out.

'But all the crops will fail!' Glen's face was red; he was getting breathless.

'Right, that's it,' Wanda said, keeping her voice calm. 'This stops now. Look at you. You need to take some deep breaths and take those painkillers. I don't care what the side effects are. I think we should get you inside and comfortable.'

Tears were running down Glen's face. 'I'm not an invalid,' he said more softly now. 'I can't believe I've been reduced to this.'

'Take the tablets, please.' Wanda handed him the glass of water.

He took them and Abi and Wanda helped him to get to an armchair in the lounge.

As Wanda put the kettle on to make them all some tea the words to the song, *New York, New York* were resounding in her ears. She laughed nervously to herself. How on earth was she going to tell Glen that the exhibition was in New York?

CHAPTER 22

It was the first time Wanda had woken up in Brooklyn, and she spent the first few moments puzzled as to where she was. Then she remembered that she was in Aaron's spare bedroom. When she opened her eyes, she saw a sea of white.

The flight, the day before, had left her feeling groggy and when she had realised on landing that her day was still another five hours long, it was disconcerting to say the least.

'You'll be fine,' Aaron assured her when he picked her up from John F. Kennedy airport. 'Best to just go with it and by the time you go to bed you'll just sleep anywhere.'

'Anywhere?' That worried her. There had been no talk of a hotel booking and she hadn't liked to ask.

'Well actually, I hope you don't mind but you're kinda booked in chez moi.'

Wanda wasn't in the mood for riddles and her face obviously said as much.

'What I mean is, Wanda, my creative genius friend, you're staying at my apartment. Spare bedroom of course. I'm sorry you're not in a swanky Manhattan hotel but the budget didn't stretch.'

'Oh, that's okay,' she said, not at all sure if it would be that great. And if

Glen found out she'd be in even more trouble. The last few days leading up to her trip had been tricky to say the least. Glen, on finding out the whole truth, had gone crazy and overreacted to the extreme. He'd basically said that if she got on the plane their marriage was over. She put it down to the pain he still had and the frustration he felt; surely he didn't mean it? A sweet parting it was not. Abi had simply asked, 'Why did you lie Mum?' She had tried to explain that she felt bad about it all and wanted to break it to them gently. That didn't seem to help. At least Abi hadn't run back to London.

Aaron's apartment was on 4th Avenue and was in a block with a rather pedestrian feel from the outside, far from the elegant brownstone buildings they had passed in the car on the way here. Apparently it was just a ten-minute walk from the gallery.

Inside, his apartment was contemporary and minimalist with whitewashed walls and black leather sofas; it had the feel of a rejected male on a low budget. He watched Wanda's face as she walked into the place. 'Look, I'm divorced, it's a stopgap. But actually, I quite like this existence. There's something very simple about it which frees you up to just get on with life.'

'Very deep,' Wanda had responded, feeling like a zombie by this stage.

Now as she lay in this strange bedroom she could hear his Nespresso coffee machine making noises suggesting that Aaron was up and not in the one and only shower room. Wanda had not packed a dressing gown and Aaron had lent her a shirt, pale blue, washed and unnecessarily ironed. Given the difference in their heights, the shirt was pretty good at protecting her modesty.

Staying at Aaron's was better than Wanda had expected. He was pretty easy going and there was so much to do for the exhibition that she spent most of her time in the apartment asleep. By day two of dressing the gallery it was beginning to take shape. At the start, the room was nothing more than whitewashed walls and pale wooden floorboards. White was clearly a theme for Aaron. But, as he had pointed out, it was a good backdrop to display her work.

'Do you think we could have some pedestals with big vases of flowers to break up the centre?' Wanda suggested having stood back to see how the space was shaping up.

'Good idea,' Aaron shouted from across the room. 'Excellent idea. And I think a nice wooden table here in the centre where we could display some postcards I've had printed up.'

'Even better. What are the postcards?'

'I took some of your paintings for a hi-res scan as soon as they were unpacked so I could get giclée prints done.'

'Can I see?'

'Tyler, where are the prints?' Aaron spoke to a small young man who wore a cap which never seemed to come off his head.

'Boxes over there.' Tyler nodded.

'Courtney, can you source the pedestals and the table. We need something stylish; you know what I mean?'

'Sure thing. I'm on it.' She took her mobile from her pocket. Wanda had been surprised that Aaron had enlisted help; she knew the budget was tight. But realising what a perfectionist Aaron was, she was quite relieved.

Aaron was opening a box with the prints in. Wanda went over to take a look at them.

'See,' Aaron said looking pleased with himself.

It was odd seeing her art in miniature but they looked good. 'They're great. I really like them. I shall take one of each as a memento.' She smiled as she felt proud of her achievements.

It was nearly seven o'clock when Aaron decided he was satisfied that the four of them had done the best job they could possibly do. After much debate, mainly as a result of Aaron's indecision, the painting of Quercus took pride of place in the centre of the back wall of the exhibition. 'It will be the first work they see as they walk towards the display,' he explained. Wanda had pointed out that as it had a red sticker on it already that might be a bit off-putting. To that he had said he would sleep on it and decide finally tomorrow.

It was a balmy evening and the sun was still shining bright, but had fallen behind the tall buildings. They walked to an Italian restaurant just round the corner from the gallery. Aaron boasted that Italian food was actually better in New York than anywhere else as they had so many Italians living there. Piccola Cucina Osteria was small as the name suggested and rather quaint. There was just a half-wall between the diners and the chefs. The food must be good, Wanda surmised; otherwise it would all be very embarrassing.

She followed Courtney's lead and ordered the Bucatini all Sarda.

'It means pasta with sardines,' she explained helpfully.

'Sounds good.' Wanda liked Courtney. She wore shorts and a cropped top and could get away with it. Her long dark hair was tied back with a bright orange scrunchie. She had done a great job with the flowers. The long-stemmed white lilies she had managed to buy were not yet fully open so that they would be at their best tomorrow evening for the preview party.

Aaron ordered the wild boar. Of course, he did. A man that size had to eat meat or he might wither away. The chefs looked like two brothers, both lean with thin dark moustaches and wearing black T-shirts and soft trilby hats. They worked in unison with slick efficiency shouting out the odd thing in Italian. Wanda sat back in her chair and sipped her wine. She should savour this moment. Who knew what life had in store for her back home? Still no word from Glen, despite all her text messages. She'd had a reply from Abi who said her father was okay but hurt. Wanda did feel bad about leaving the farm for over ten days in all. She'd done her best to set up Lee and Bartletts to manage things and Abi had said she would do a bit more, emphasising it would just be while her mum was away. Wanda prayed that Glen would not get his parents back involved. But she knew that the likelihood of Martin barging his way in, with every reason to sound off about how terrible Wanda was, was too high.

'You excited about tomorrow?' Aaron was trying to attract her gaze.

'Sorry, miles away there. Of course I am,' she said wanting to add that at the same time she was terrified. What if the Americans didn't like her art? Still, this whole thing was Aaron's idea; he must know what he was doing.

The food arrived and was delicious. The banter was fun and Wanda laughed and forgot her cares for a couple of hours. She learnt from her new friends that New York had around five hundred galleries. Somehow she took comfort in that. She was just one artist exhibiting in one little gallery. It wasn't as if she was at the Metropolitan.

They rolled home well after ten o'clock which was quite late enough for Wanda after what had been a very long day. The streets were still alive and buzzing; this really was the city that never sleeps. Wanda was happy to fall into bed. Tomorrow was D-day.

The following day, having double checked that everything was okay and nothing terrible had happened overnight, like a painting falling down, Aaron turned his attention to drumming up punters for the evening opening. This meant him calling all those who had already said that they were coming while Wanda walked the streets with a handful of flyers to distribute. She had learnt by now not to make any comment on anything

Aaron suggested; he knew best. The day was overcast but dry and, after her initial misgivings and slight nervousness, Wanda began to enjoy her task. She found that going into independent shops and handing a flyer to the person behind the counter generally derived a pleasant response. Usually, *thank you lady*, or maybe *ooh, an art exhibition.* Some engaged her in conversation asking if she was the artist and being overly delighted to discover she was. This was certainly a friendly neighbourhood. After a while she started to hand out the flyers to people on the street. As soon as she spoke with her English accent they were interested.

The caterers arrived at the gallery at four-thirty laden with cool bags and boxes. They set to work assembling trestle tables at one end which Aaron had designated for hospitality. Having covered the tables in white linen cloths, they started to work in the small kitchen putting together an elegant finger buffet befitting a cultured event and placed the bottles of Prosecco on ice. All they needed now was punters.

At five to six, Wanda noticed that her *Quercus* painting still had a red dot on it. She decided not to say anything but just to stand in place at the entrance and pray someone would turn up. She was wearing an emerald green dress she'd bought especially for the occasion which she was now having doubts about. Was it too low at the front? Was the long length making her look shorter or were her killer high heels making her look sort of normal height anyway? The woman in the boutique in Bury St Edmunds had told her that it suited her well.

'You look amazing,' Courtney said and Wanda couldn't have been more surprised. 'You okay?' she asked now, looking puzzled.

'A bit apprehensive,' Wanda said apologetically.

'Come here,' Courtney said and hugged her which quickly brought a tear to Wanda's eye. 'It's going to be just fine. I've invited everyone I know; I've told them all that you're this hot new artist from little ole London,

England.'

'That's kind. Actually, I'm from Suffolk.'

'Really, where's that?'

'Not far from London.'

'Well, there you go. Best not to confuse folk with unnecessary detail.'

As Wanda laughed two well-dressed men, one wearing a yellow ochre cravat, walked into the gallery.

'Good evening gentlemen,' Wanda said brightly.

'Well, hello there. Are you?' The two men looked at each other and back to Wanda. 'You're not *the* Wanda Taylor, are you?'

This was ridiculous. 'I am, actually.'

'Wow. So great to meet you. Aaron has told us all about you. We are expecting great things.'

Wanda felt a thump to her stomach. She only had thirteen paintings on show. None of them were particularly big, certainly not the size of Monet's lilies. She was an amateur. She was a fake. What the hell was she doing here? 'I hope you're not disappointed,' she mumbled. 'Please help yourself to a drink.' She gestured to the drinks table. The exhibition might go down better with alcohol.

'Well thank you. From what I can see,' the taller one said, 'I think we are in for a real treat.' They beamed at each other and made their hip-swaying way over to the hospitality area.

After about half an hour the place was lively enough with a respectable number mingling amongst the paintings. Aaron took over on the door so that Wanda could circulate and answer any questions. She was still feeling nervous and was convinced she was going to accidently blurt out that Quercus was a talking tree. They would think she was mad. And she had promised Quercus that she would tell no one of their conversations. But how would he know, this many thousands of miles away. She couldn't be sure now that she knew something of the mycorrhizal fungi network. It was such an incredible thing that anything was possible. She'd only have to pass a tree in New York and her ancient oak tree back home would know about it.

'What inspired you to paint these wonderful images?' A woman with large spectacles and a walking stick asked her, bringing Wanda back to the room.

'Ah, well, it all started with Quercus, a four-hundred-year-old oak tree on the farm where I live.' Wanda waved an arm in the direction of her painting of Quercus.

'A tree with a name?' she asked looking amused.

'Yes, just a name I decided to give the fine tree, you understand.' Wanda laughed along with the woman. 'And it all went from there.'

'Magical nature,' the woman said thoughtfully, repeating the name of the exhibition. 'But is nature actually magical?'

'Oh yes,' Wanda said definitely. 'I mean, take the wood wide web, how amazing is that?'

Wanda was met with a troubled slightly confused expression but smiled at her anyway.

'Well, I must refresh my drink. Maybe it will help me to understand this art of yours. I must say it's all new to me.' And off she trotted.

It was getting close to eight o'clock when the party was due to draw to a close. Aaron had told her not to get hung up on how many sales there were this evening as it was simply a preview. But Wanda couldn't help thinking that if these people were going to buy, they would do so here and now. There were no red dot stickers. She took a deep breath and reasoned that there was a whole week to go. Just then one of the gay chaps, the first to arrive, approached her.

'Wanda, my dear,' he said close to her ear in a lowered voice, 'would you put one of your red dots on the painting of the orange peel mushrooms?' He was beside himself with excitement as he continued, 'I'm being discreet as I'm buying it as a little birthday surprise for Brandon.'

'How lovely, of course I will.'

'Thank you so much. I shall be back at the end of the week to collect it on my own.' He tapped the side of his nose. 'Do I need to leave a deposit?'

'Er, yes, I believe you do. Aaron is in charge of that side of things,' she said pointing him out.

'I'll be sure to have a word,' he said.

By the time the caterers had cleared up and they had got the room looking clean and tidy for the following morning, it felt late to Wanda and she was happy to walk back to Aaron's flat with him for a snack before bed. He told her on the way back that the purple pea pod painting had also sold that evening. He'd forgotten to put the red dot on it but he would do so first thing.

'So that's two paintings I've sold?'

'Yes, and I have the business card of a chap interested in two more,' Aaron said matter of factly.

'But that's brilliant. Why didn't you say?'

'Sorry, it's been a busy night. But Wanda, I told you not to worry. I have every faith we will sell them all by the end of the week.'

Wanda felt relieved. She would sleep easy tonight.

By the end of the week Wanda was loving New York. She had got to know the neighbourhood around Aaron's apartment and had come across some surprising finds. She was on first name terms with the brothers at the Osteria where they had returned twice as the food was so good and so reasonably priced. The jewel of Wanda's finds was an amazing vintage shop where they had a mixture of American and Japanese clothing including some beautiful kimonos and Christian Dior scarves. Wanda was very tempted by a turquoise kimono dress but then imagined herself on the farm in the exquisite garment and how ridiculous she would look. A moment of sadness and deep regret came over her all of a sudden. Was she living her best life? She shook herself out of such thoughts; she was just being silly.

There was still no word from Glen. She had given up texting him, calling him. Abi had said how much she missed her mum and was looking forward to seeing her. Her words sounded heartfelt as well. Her daughter had changed and it would be interesting to see how life panned out for her.

Part of her was looking forward to going home and part of her dreaded it. Perhaps Glen was going to follow through with his threat and end their marriage as soon as he saw her. It all seemed so terribly sad, particularly for him.

On her last evening in New York Aaron took her to The River Café which overlooked the East River, part of the giant harbour which flowed through New York, with a magnificent view of the Brooklyn Bridge to their right. It was magical but there was just the two of them. Aaron had explained that he wouldn't be inviting Tyler and Courtney because it was a Michelin star restaurant. He wanted to treat her and to thank her for all her hard work and what had been a very successful exhibition. Only one of the paintings was not sold and Aaron had said he would have no problem selling it to one of his dealer friends. Not only that but Wanda had been approached by two separate people who wanted to commission her to produce paintings for them. They had both gone into some detail as to what they wanted and Wanda had their business cards so she could get in touch.

Soft piano music played as Wanda ate shrimp and crab. It was all exquisite but she couldn't help thinking it would have been more fun with the others back at the Osteria. That thought made her feel sad. She was leaving New York in the morning. Aaron seemed to guess her thoughts.

'Sorry to be going home?' he asked.

'I am actually. I've had the most amazing time.'

'This is an awesome city. It is easy to fall under its spell.'

'I've done that all right.'

'But you must be missing your family. How is Glen getting along?'

'Good question. I've had no word from him all week.'

'What?'

'Before I came out he said that if I did this, if I got on the plane, our marriage was over.'

'Oh Wanda! That's awful. You should have said.'

'What difference would it have made? Anyway, I told myself he didn't mean it and that he'd come round and he'd answer one of my calls at least. But no.'

Aaron looked very concerned.

'Don't worry, I don't blame you,' Wanda continued. 'It was my decision to do this and I have no regrets. I've fulfilled a long-held dream. I'm just not sure at what cost.' She smiled despite everything and decided to snap out of this melancholy mood and raise her glass of wine. 'Here's to our success,' she said as cheerfully as she could manage.

'Thank you,' Aaron said sincerely. 'You are an amazing woman Wanda Taylor and it's a privilege to work with you. To success.' He clinked her glass with his.

CHAPTER 23

Abi was holding up a piece of card which read *Wanda Taylor, NY Artist of the year*. Wanda noticed the big smile on her daughter's face first, then she saw the sign and laughed and almost cried with happiness. She made her way as quickly as her little legs and large suitcase allowed her and was quick to hug her daughter who held her tight and said 'Missed you, Mum.'

Abi led the way out of the airport terminal to where she had parked her mother's car. She insisted on driving. 'No, Mum, you must have jet lag, it's not safe.'

Wanda smiled to herself and settled into the passenger seat. The sun had already set and it was a moonlit night. The drive from Gatwick would take just over two hours which was plenty of time to regale all the tales of her exciting trip. Abi was particularly interested in the vintage clothing store.

'Sounds wicked Mum, are they are on Insta?'

'Yes, they are actually.' Wanda was pleased she'd spotted that on a poster somewhere in the shop.

When Wanda had exhausted her news, she put her head back and it occurred to her that she could easily sleep; adjusting to UK time wasn't going to be difficult. She hadn't managed to nod off on the plane; she was just too uncomfortable and it was too noisy. But her daughter had other ideas.

'So, Mum, which do you prefer, New York or Bury St Edmunds?'

'What kind of a question is that? They are so different, but Suffolk is where I live.'

'It's just that it seems like you came alive when you were there and you really loved it.'

'What are you saying? Are you trying to get rid of me?'

'Of course not. I suppose, if anything, I'm worried you might up and leave.'

'What's your dad been saying?' Suddenly his threat to her before she'd left seemed very real.

'He refuses to talk about you really. But then Granddad Martin comes over and he's saying you got everything wrong on the farm when you were in charge and Dad seems to agree with him.'

Wanda's heart sank. 'Sounds like I don't have too much to come home to.'

'They've made a few changes while you've been away.'

'That's a shame.' Wanda didn't even want to think about it; her poor hens and what would Quercus have to say about it. Perhaps she should have stayed in New York? Maybe she would have been able to make it as an artist there. Aaron had said, half-jokingly she assumed, that she would be welcome to stay at his for a bit if she was stuck. As if?

For the rest of the journey they both said very little. Abi put the radio on to lighten the atmosphere but nothing was going to stop Wanda fearing the worst.

When Abi drew into the yard at the back of the house all was quiet and there was no sign of life. She went to take Wanda's case out of the boot.

'Leave it,' Wanda said and Abi looked confused. 'I'll bring it in later. I'd love a cup of tea first.'

Her daughter looked doubtful but left the case where it was. They both went through to the kitchen and Wanda put the kettle on.

'I think I'll go up to bed,' Abi said. 'I'm pretty shattered after all that driving.'

'Oh, stay and have a cup of tea with me.' Wanda was aware that it sounded like she was begging.

'But Mum, you and Dad need to sort things out.'

'Where is your dad? He'll be in bed at this time, won't he? It's gone eleven o'clock.'

'Not sure,' Abi said. She gave her mother another hug. 'Night Mum, good to have you home,' she said and turned to go upstairs.

Wanda sighed and suddenly felt very low. Just after Abi left, Glen appeared as if from nowhere. Had they planned this?

'Hello, do you want some tea?' Wanda asked, as if she hadn't just been away in New York for ten days.

'Yes, okay.' Had she caught him off guard? 'Then I need to get to bed; this is late for me.'

The tea made, they both sat at the kitchen table. He didn't ask her about her trip.

'So, how have you been while I've been away?' Wanda asked.

'Okay. The same. Not great. Dad's been helping out a lot.'

'I see.'

'Yes, we've got the farm back running as it should be. Mum's not very happy but it had to be done.'

Wanda closed her eyes and let out a long slow breath.

'Wanda, this marriage isn't working.' He said it calmly, quietly even. 'I told you I didn't want you to go to America and you openly defied me.' He looked crushed. 'I can't take any more.'

'But...' Wanda was flummoxed by this. 'But that's not fair.'

'I'll tell you what's not fair; you spending time with another man, this American chap. He seems to be more important to you than your own husband.'

'That's not true. Your father jumped to the wrong and ridiculous conclusion that I was having an affair with Aaron. I have never been unfaithful to you; you have to believe me.'

'You went to America to be with him.'

'I went to New York to put on an exhibition of my art work. It was an opportunity of a lifetime. My relationship with Aaron is purely professional.'

'I still think you were wrong to go. I told you what the consequences would be if you got on that plane.'

'Oh, for goodness' sake! We're not living in the Victorian era. I have a right to follow my own dreams.'

'That's just it though, isn't it? Your own dreams are nothing to do with me or this farm.'

Was that true? Wanda didn't know any more. Anything else she might have to say, she had already said before and more than once.

'Right then.' She couldn't quite believe this was happening. Was her marriage really over just like that? She tried to look into his eyes but he was staring into his mug. She was finding him very difficult to read. 'So do you want me to go?'

'You can sleep in the spare room tonight.'

'So, you're not throwing me out at midnight. And tomorrow?'

'I think it's best you go.'

Wanda finished her tea and then got up; she looked around the kitchen. 'Where's the key? To the back door.'

'It's on that hook over there.' He pointed. Wanda had a vague recollection that the key had been kept on that hook by her in-laws when they were in residence many years ago.

'Right.' She snatched the key off its hook. 'Can't wait to get rid of me, can you?' Tears burst from her eyes.

Glen looked confused. 'I didn't say that. Where are you going with the key?'

'I'm going for a walk. I don't want to be locked out of my own home.'

'But Wanda, it's late. It's not safe.'

'It's not late in New York. Anyway, why do you care about what happens to me?'

'I do care. Of course, I do. Don't go out now. Please don't.'

Wanda stared at him through her tears, held on to the key for a moment and then left. She locked the door behind her.

It was a beautiful balmy night and Wanda immediately knew where she was headed. Halfway up the main track she reached Low Meadow and saw the daisies, some of them munching away still, on the pasture. Some of them looked up and over to her. One of them mooed loudly.

'I've missed you too, daisies!' Wanda yelled out.

As she got nearer Lucas Wood the night suddenly seemed darker and a shiver went down her spine. Was she afraid? Not long now. It would be great if Gilbert was around, but no doubt it was far too late for him. She quickened her pace and finally reached Quercus. Relieved she fell against the mighty oak's trunk, laying her cheek on its knobbly bark.

'Hello Quercus, I'm back.' Nothing from the tree. 'You were a great hit in New York, but then you probably know that.'

Just then the breeze rustled the leaves of the lush green canopy. Was that all Quercus could manage at this time?

'Hello Wanda Taylor.' The voice was calm and made Wanda smile with relief. 'Why the visit under the night sky when homo sapiens are more likely to sleep?'

'I just wanted to be here with you for a while. Things aren't going too well for me right now.'

'Things aren't going well for you. Huh! These lands have had to put up with a barrage of chemicals while you have been fulfilling your human dreams on another part of the planet.'

'I'm so sorry Quercus. My influence is zero around here and it's going to get worse. They want me out. Gone.'

'You are going? Where? We need you.'

'I don't know where. I've no idea what I'll do. Maybe I should get back on a plane to New York.'

'Do not desert us, Wanda Taylor.' The voice was stern.

Wanda looked up into Quercus' branches. She felt overwhelmed with sadness.

'Wanda, if you abandon our cause, I, and many other organisms, will surely die.'

'Die? But you are not even in your declining years yet?'

'I fear I will be denied that privilege.'

'What a dreadful state of affairs.'

'Don't move away to another continent, Wanda. I'm begging you.'

'I won't,' Wanda said timidly knowing she had no choice but to leave the farm.

Seeing Quercus had not made Wanda feel better as she'd hoped. If anything she felt worse. The house was dark when she got back and there was no sign of Glen; he must have gone to bed. Wanda went up to the spare room to find that the bed had been made up for her. Had Glen managed that?

She had a restless night and ended up falling into a deep sleep around three o'clock and then oversleeping in the morning. It was gone ten o'clock when she looked at her mobile screen. Thoughts of Glen, her marriage being over and the devastation the farm was causing to nature whirled around her head once more and she decided she could take no more. She would talk to Glen and try and make him see sense.

Abi was in the kitchen making toast. 'Morning Mum, still on NY time?' She smiled. 'Oh God, you look awful.'

'Thanks, that makes me feel so much better.'

'Sorry, Mum. Probably the jet lag. You just looked so great yesterday.'

'Must be the Taylor farm effect.' Wanda knew from her daughter's expression that she should not have said that.

'How did it go with Dad?' she asked sounding upbeat regardless.

'He says our marriage is over and he wants me to leave.'

'God, Mum, that's worse than I thought. I mean I knew he was mad with you for going to New York, but...'

'I've never really fitted in here,' Wanda said speaking her thoughts out loud.

'Don't say that.'

Wanda sighed. 'Do you know where your dad is?'

'He's gone out. He said he will be out all day.'

'How will he manage that in his condition?'

'I saw Granny Fi turn up. I think she might have taken him to their place.'

'Oh great! So, they're all in on it.'

'Mum, I don't want you to go. This is your home. And this place is not the same without you. If you do go, I can't see me staying. I think I might go back to London. Try for one final time.'

'What about Lee?'

'He won't like it, I suppose.'

They gravitated towards each other and hugged, holding each other tight.

'Don't go,' Abi begged.

'Don't you go either.'

Glen obviously didn't want to talk to her today. He had made it clear that he wanted her gone; what choice did she have? With a dry mouth and a confused sadness, Wanda grabbed some clothes and toiletries, her dressing gown, a paperback and her hairdryer. She couldn't see clearly through her scratchy eyes and it was difficult to think straight. She would have to come back for anything else she wanted. She knew her suitcase was still in her car.

She decided to keep her house key, leaving it behind made the whole thing seem so final. She somehow managed to get her stuff and herself into the car and found a tissue to blow her nose. This would not do. She would drive to Ben and Saffy's; they would be pleased to see her, surely?

Ben answered the door. 'Hi Wanda.' He looked puzzled. 'Were we expecting you?'

'No, sorry. I've just got back from New York and well, I, erm.'

'Oh yes, of course. How did it go?'

'Good, yes. It went well.' She knew she sounded deflated. He was clearly distracted.

'Saffy's just picking Toby up from the train station; he's staying for a few days.'

'Right.' He still hadn't invited her in. 'Well, any chance of a coffee?'

'Yeah, I suppose so. You might have to make it yourself. I've got some glamping customers turning up any minute.'

'No problem.'

'Actually, it might be better if you came back tomorrow.'

'Sure.' She had to tell him. 'Actually, Glen's kicked me out. Apparently, our marriage is over.'

Ben looked startled but at that moment his mobile rang and he had to answer it. 'Okay, so where are you now?' he said to the caller. Wanda was still outside the door and it had started to rain. Ben was preoccupied with giving directions so Wanda snuck in and went through to the kitchen. Saffy had a rather expensive-looking brand of ground coffee in her cupboard and she decided to just help herself. What the heck. After all, she was alone in the kitchen. Ben appeared having finished his call.

'Did you just say that it's over between you and Glen?'

'Yes.'

'Sis, don't be ridiculous. Glen needs you more than ever.'

'It's him that's ended it!' she shrieked.

'What is he thinking? Do you want me to talk to him?'

'Ben, right now I've got jet lag and I've had a dreadful night. I'm exhausted and I'm fed up of thinking about what a complete mess my life is.' She paused to try and compose herself.

Ben gave her a concerned smile now and hugged her as much as any man hugs their sister. 'Sorry sis'. No really. I'm so sorry.' And Wanda burst into tears. Again.

CHAPTER 24

Later that morning when Ben and Saffy finally accepted what Wanda was telling them about Glen asking her to leave the farmhouse, they were really nice to her. It didn't help that their son, Toby, was home for a few days and they obviously wanted to spend a bit of time with him. Also, the glamping site seemed to be very busy and glampers were coming up to the house with queries about this and that. Life goes on around you even if you are having a crisis, Wanda thought to herself.

She ended up having a lazy day, just helping out a bit in the kitchen garden, harvesting some tomatoes and cucumbers, a bit of weeding and then some watering. It was good to feel useful. By six o'clock she was sat at the garden table with a glass of wine and a bowl of peanuts while Saffy cooked dinner for them all. Toby appeared with a beer in his hand and sat tentatively next to her.

'I hear you've just been to New York.' He sounded impressed.

'Yes, I had an exhibition of my art work there.' Right now Wanda could not quite believe that the last couple of weeks had actually happened.

'Get you, Aunty Wanda. I didn't realise you were that good.'

'No, well, I was pretty amazed too.'

'So did you sell any of your paintings?'

'All but one. And Aaron reckons he'll be able to pass that one on to a dealer friend of his.'

'That's brilliant. So, you must be loaded right now.'

'Not exactly. I suppose I've got a bit of money coming my way but when you're homeless and you've no idea what you're going to do next, it kind of takes the edge off it.'

He looked embarrassed. Wanda decided to rescue him. 'So how's your uni course going? I suppose you don't go back until the end of September. You're doing a degree in Sports Science aren't you?'

'That's right but I've got a flat share now with some mates so I'm London-based. I've been working in hospitality through the summer to earn some money.'

'And do you enjoy that?'

'Yeah, well, there's a lot of temporary work available at one-off events. It's quite a laugh really and the pay's not bad.'

'Sounds like you're doing really well. Getting some work experience before you graduate is a valuable thing to do. I wish I had.' Wanda was wistful.

It was another warm evening and they ate outside. The atmosphere was mellow and Wanda couldn't help thinking that this family was far more relaxed than her own. When the light faded Saffy lit some candles. There was raucous laughter coming from a group of girls outside one of the yurts. 'That will be the hen party,' Saffy told them.

'So, what do you think you'll do now, Wanda?' Ben asked and Saffy gave him a hard stare as if to say, *Don't ask her that.*

'Goodness knows,' was all she could say in reply.

'You should go back to New York,' Toby suggested. 'You were obviously a hit there. Americans love an English accent.'

Wanda smiled at the innocence of youth.

'Things will work out,' Saffy said, 'you'll see. Glen will come to his senses.'

Wanda realised then that she was really very hurt by the way he had treated her. It wasn't fair. Did she actually want to go back? She had now had a taste of the life of an artist; perhaps that was the path she should take.

There was a yurt free for one blissful night only. After that the glamping site was fully booked until mid-September. With Toby home until he went back for his third year of uni there really was no room at the inn.

It was a shame that it had clouded over by the time Wanda lay in her comfy bed and looked up through the top of the yurt; she couldn't see the stars this time, just darkness. Fitting really, she reflected. She couldn't think straight about what tomorrow might hold. This whole episode was exhausting. Luckily, she soon fell asleep.

It was Saffy who suggested she moved in with her parents at Orchard Cottage. 'After all, it will only be temporary,' she emphasised as she busied herself making breakfast. 'And Ixworth is just down the road.'

It didn't feel like a temporary situation to Wanda. It felt like she was doomed. She had some of the money from her art sales and more to come but it seemed reckless to spend it on a hotel. She thought long and hard about asking Carolyn if she could stay with her again, but in her heart of hearts, Wanda knew she would rather pay rent for her own place than lodge with Carolyn again. Also, Aaron hadn't mentioned Carolyn once in New York. Wanda had been tempted to sound him out by asking him outright if he intended to keep in touch with her. But the time had whizzed by and she'd concluded that he must have just seen it as a fling.

Saffy didn't exactly throw her out after breakfast but it was obvious that she and Ben were busy with the glamping site and also wanted to spend a bit of time with Toby. Wanda reluctantly rang her father.

'Oh Wanda, I am so, so sorry to hear that,' he said, clearly shocked after she'd laid the facts bare. There was the sound of a kerfuffle at the other end of the phone and suddenly Rita took over the call.

'Wanda, what is this nonsense? I know you and Glen have had your differences but this is ridiculous. The poor man; it's not long since he came out of hospital. He nearly died in that terrible accident. You do remember, don't you?'

'Of course I do, Mum. As I said to Dad, this is Glen's decision.'

'I don't believe that for a moment. The man isn't thinking straight. I know he was upset about you swanning off to New York with that American man. Fi's told me all about it.'

'I didn't swan off with him. I went over on my own. He lives there. He exhibited my work in a gallery.' It was hopeless trying to explain.

'Yes, well whatever the detail, you can understand why Glen wasn't too happy about the whole thing.'

Wanda despaired. She couldn't possibly move in with her parents into their bijou abode; she would go mad.

'You will have to go back to the farm and beg,' Rita continued.

Just then Wanda heard her father's voice again. 'Give it to me. It's my mobile. You're upsetting Wanda.'

'Oh for goodness sake,' Rita said and Graham had evidently reclaimed his handset.

'Wanda, my love, where are you? Where are you now? Shall I come and get you?'

'I'm at Ben's. I have my car and some of my things. I'm not destitute yet.'

'Of course you're not. But you said you can't stay there.'

'No. Maybe I'll buy a tent and see if they'll let me camp in their grounds if I promise not to scare the other campers.'

'That doesn't sound very practical long term, does it?'

Wanda sighed deeply.

'Listen,' her dad said, 'I'll drive over there and we'll make a plan. Okay? Tell Saffy I'm on my way. Won't be long. You make yourself one of those fresh coffees you like and sit in the garden. That is if it isn't raining there; it seems to have just started here.'

'You're rambling, Graham,' Rita shouted in the background.

'Yes, I'm rambling so I'll be on my way. Don't go anywhere Wanda, will you?'

'No, Dad, I won't run off.' *Where would she run to?*

Wanda smiled to herself as she did what her father had suggested and made herself a fresh coffee. Wanda had confessed to Saffy the day before that she had opened the packet of superior-looking coffee granules. 'Oh good,' Saffy had said laughing, 'I was wondering when that would get used up. One of the glampers bought it for us as a parting gift.'

Wanda decided to sit under the umbrella in the garden, mainly to avoid getting too wet in the light rain shower.

It was only half an hour before Graham appeared. What was so lovely was that he just behaved as if everything was normal. He had always been calm in a crisis; the polar opposite of her mother. He suggested they had a drive out to Bungay where they could get a spot of lunch in a pub. He was happy to drive. As Saffy was busy with some new arrivals, Wanda left her a note so she knew why her car was still parked outside and off they went.

Graham took the scenic route and it was not long after they had set off that the sun came out. He said very little, allowing her to sit back and soak up the scenery. It was all a bit odd but Wanda decided that she would enjoy the ride; what else could she do right now.

Just before they reached the town, they drove past a sign for Fen Farm Dairy. Wanda had heard of it but had never really taken much notice.

'Slow down a minute, Dad.'

'What's that you say, love?'

It was too late. 'Nothing.' She only had time to notice two small huts that were painted black and white like the markings of a Friesian cow. It looked like the farm was selling produce from them.

'You spotted the dairy farm,' her dad was saying now. 'Raw milk they do there. We could stop on the way back if you like.'

Why would she be interested in another dairy farm? 'No need,' Wanda said.

Bungay was quiet but then it was a Monday. It was a quaint little town with a lot of Victorian architecture and what may have been a bandstand but was now a café. You could tell Bungay had a strong sense of community from the notice boards. There was a poster advertising a weekend of family fun at the playing field. Wanda had only visited the town once before, or was it twice, and that must have been when Abi and Lily were young.

Graham parked in the main town car park and they walked up to the pub that he had in mind.

'Won't it be closed today?'

'No, I checked. Apparently it is the only one that is open in Bungay on a Monday.'

'Have you been before?' she asked considering that Hobson's choice might not serve the best food.

'I have, yes, and it's not bad. Traditional pub fare.' That could mean anything coming from her father but Wanda was just happy to have his company today. He was a good antidote to the drama going on in her life.

Wanda settled on a salmon dish with noodles which she hoped would be a safe bet. She went for a soft drink so she could keep a clear head; the wine had flowed last night and rather a lot of it in her direction. Graham waited until they were both settled with their food before he broached the subject of her life and what she might do with it.

'Do you think it's worth trying to talk things through with Glen? I mean it sounds like you haven't properly talked things through and tried to rescue the situation.'

'I was thinking that too, when I woke up on Sunday morning, but by the time I got downstairs he'd scarpered to his parents for the day. Or so Abi thought. Not the sign of a man up for negotiation.'

Wanda watched her father as he tucked into his burger; none of this was his fault but she needed him to understand. 'Listen, Dad, Glen actually threatened me with ending our marriage before I went to New York. What I mean is, he said that if I went it was all over.'

'I see.'

'I just thought that he was being really unfair. I mean this was the chance of a lifetime for me. I was convinced that he would see sense eventually.'

'Mm.' Graham sipped his half pint. 'Well, we are where we are.' He looked like he was deep in thought. 'Do you want to go back? I mean, to the farm. Do you really want to make a go of it?'

'I don't know. I think I do but Glen seems adamant.' The truth was she was conflicted; what Quercus had said to her at midnight on Saturday had stayed with her and she felt a strong pull towards the farm for that reason. 'Not as things stand. I mean not with the Taylors in complete charge: spraying crops within an inch of their life, caging the hens.'

'So that's a no, then. I mean the Taylors are in charge, aren't they, by default. It's their farm.'

Wanda smiled at her father. 'Does the fact that I've been married to

Glen for thirty years not mean anything? I mean it's Glen's name on the title deeds since he officially took over.'

'Good point.' Her father looked troubled now. 'But it is their farm. I'm sure that's how they see it.'

'Then I give up now. Game over.' Wanda put her fork down and sat back in her chair. The salmon was okay; nothing like as good as the food she'd had in New York but not bad.

'How about going back to Bury and making a go of it with your art?' he suggested, 'I mean you've got a successful exhibition under your belt now.'

'Suppose I did, where would I live?'

'Ah, now, I was going to come on to that. Now don't bite my head off but I really think the best option would be for you to move in with your mum and me,' he raised a flat palm to her as she nearly exploded, 'just temporarily. Until you're sorted with somewhere else. Maybe you could rent in Bury at first. You liked being in town, didn't you?'

Wanda took a deep breath. 'The truth is, I don't think I have much choice. I'm sorry if that sounds really ungrateful but you know what Mum's like.'

'I do and I shall have words with her, don't you worry.'

Wanda let out a giggle. 'You, Dad? Stand up to Mum?'

'I will and I shall. Oh, look you know what's she's like but really you should take no notice of her.'

They were both laughing now.

'So, what do you say?' Graham asked, an expectant expression on his face.

'Okay, but just for a few days.'

On the way back Graham pulled into the forecourt of Fen Farm Dairy and parked up. 'Let's take a quick look,' he said.

Wanda could see the dairy had a herd of Montbéliarde cows, just like their own dear daisies. Their eyes were bright and they were all jostling for position in the pen outside what must be the milking shed. The farm was indeed selling produce from two huts at the front which were set up like kiosks and they were advertising raw milk. It was self-service with vending type machines.

'This is interesting,' Wanda said.

'Shall we get some?' Graham read the instructions and grabbed an empty bottle. 'I think we can fill this with the raw milk.'

'They've got cheese as well. I've heard of this Baron Bigod. It's like brie, apparently.'

'Let's get some of that too, then.'

'Can we get two lots? I'll leave one at Saffy's as a thank you for last night.'

They put their purchases in the boot of the car under a blanket and set off back to the glamping site to pick up Wanda's car.

Rita was out when they got back to Orchard Cottage. She'd left a note about a W.I. meeting; she would be back about six. It was warm enough to sit in the garden and Graham got out two of their more comfortable chairs while Wanda insisted that she would make the tea.

'I don't want to be treated like a house guest,' she said. The truth was that she wanted to somehow keep busy. She didn't want to be left alone with her thoughts for too long. Perhaps she would try and make a start on one of the commissions she had got in New York. But where would she paint?

'You're right, you should make yourself at home,' Graham said when they were both sat down with a cuppa.

'Dad, is there anywhere I could paint while I'm here? A couple of the

Americans that attended my exhibition have given me commissions.'

'That's brilliant. This art thing is really taking off for you, isn't it?'

'Well, yes, I suppose so. Although I've never had much success in this country.'

'That could change. But where could you create without upsetting your mother?' He looked thoughtful.

'There isn't anywhere, is there? That's the trouble with downsizing,' Wanda pointed out.

'Well you'll be in the spare room but there won't be enough space to paint and sleep when the sofa bed is made up.'

'You've got a sofa bed in there now?'

'Yes, love, it was your mum's idea. It means we've got a bit more space when it's just the two of us. You see your mum uses it as a sort of craft hobby room.'

'Oh Dad, this is never going to work. Mum's losing her hobby room and I'm sleeping on a sofa bed.'

'It's a good quality one. It's comfy, I promise. You'll be fine.'

Wanda closed her eyes and tilted her face up to the sun that had just come through the clouds. 'What has my life become?' she said before laughing nervously.

'The way I see it, you've just had a very successful exhibition in New York and your life has hit a bit of a crossroads. Why not take a bit of time out before you decide what you want to do next? I mean you can stay here for as long as you want.'

Just then Rita appeared. 'Wanda? What are you doing here?' She was wearing a loose floaty pink kaftan and had matching pink lipstick, not a look that Wanda was used to seeing on her mother.

Graham leapt up as he glanced at Wanda. 'Rita, can I have a word with you inside?' He had a knowing look and nodded his head in the direction of the French windows.

'Surely you can say whatever it is in front of Wanda?' Rita sat down in the chair her husband had just vacated. 'Is it wine o'clock yet?' she said gaily.

Graham looked agitated.

'Don't worry, Dad, I can take it.'

'What do you mean? What's this all about? You're not staying here, are you?' Rita sounded worried.

Graham let out a cry of frustration. 'Rita, why do you always have to say the wrong thing?'

'So, you are staying?' She looked at Wanda.

'If it's not too much trouble. Just for a few days,' Wanda added quickly.

'We don't have much space since we moved in here. I've often wondered if we did the right thing.' She looked wistful.

'We've talked about this over and over,' Graham said clearly annoyed. 'This house is just the right size for us at our time of life. Anyway Wanda needs somewhere to stay and I for one, think that...'

'So you haven't sorted things out with Glen, then?' Rita interrupted him.

'She hasn't had the chance!' Graham threw his arms up in the air in despair.

'Mum it's over with Glen. I wanted to try and make things work but it's him that's resolute on us splitting up.'

'But what have you actually done to try and save your marriage?' Rita turned to Graham. 'Any chance you could pour me a glass of the Pinot Grigio in the fridge?'

Graham sighed the sigh of a downtrodden male. 'What about you, Wanda? Are you ready for a glass of wine?'

'I'd better not; I might be driving.'

'Where will you be driving to?' he asked which was a good question.

'Over the edge of a cliff at this rate.' Wanda laughed after she'd said it, just in case they thought she meant it and decided to lock her in a padded cell. Graham ignored her and disappeared into the house mumbling about getting another chair out.

'Of course you can stay here for a couple of nights,' Rita said almost through gritted teeth, 'but I do think you need to at least try and work things out with your husband. I mean, how on earth is he managing after his accident?'

'Well, Mum, you would have a better idea than me, with a hotline to Fiona.'

'Fi is really not happy that Martin has had to get back involved with the farm while you were away. She's convinced he's going to have a heart attack.'

Graham had got another chair out and appeared with the bottle of wine in a cooler and three glasses. He started to pour and Wanda decided that a small glass wouldn't hurt. When they all had a glass in hand, Graham raised his to Wanda, 'Here's to the artist; congratulations on the success of your exhibition.'

'It's a shame it was at the cost of your marriage,' Rita added.

Graham turned on her. 'For goodness' sake Rita! Why can't you have a little empathy for once?'

'Oh well if you're going to be like that.' She stood up and walked inside taking her wine with her.

Wanda couldn't quite believe that this was going to be her home before she could sort something else out; she'd be happier in a war zone.

'Just ignore your mother,' Graham said sitting back in his chair and getting comfortable.

'Dad, I do appreciate what you are doing for me here but I really can't see this working.'

'You'll have to stay tonight though, won't you?' He turned to her with a look of concern.

'Yes, I will stay tonight.' She imagined herself trying to sleep on a bench in the Abbey Gardens in town, that being the only alternative. She was fifty-two; what had become of her?

It was nearly three o'clock in the morning and Wanda had given up trying to get comfortable on the sofa bed. Getting ready for bed had been quite a performance. It had taken her a long time to extinguish all the artificial light in the room. There was a clock radio on a small table that flashed the wrong time continuously, an old television in the corner on standby and some sort of night light which came on as soon as it got dark. This room was clearly not designed to sleep in. Unplugging everything had proved tricky as there was so little room to manoeuvre now that the sofa bed was made up. With her big case she had taken to New York open in one corner, and a wardrobe too she just about had enough room to stand up. The curtains were paper thin and hopeless so the moonlight came shining through. Finally, after tossing and turning, she had eventually fallen asleep. By two o'clock she was awake again.

Her attempts to get back to sleep were failing. She had tried lying on her back in semi-supine, deep breathing and meditation but all to no avail. The disturbing dream she had woken up to played over and over in her mind. In it Quercus had given up the fight against chemicals and withered and crumbled before her very eyes. As the ancient tree turned black and was reduced to a pile of ashes it let out a deep roaring cry of pain. She had stood there shouting, *No, no. no! This cannot happen!*

The oak tree's demise set off a series of events causing death and destruction to the wildlife all around the farm and beyond. She saw the orange peel mushrooms turn dark grey and shrivel to nothing; the potato crop on Hungry Hill was devastated to the ground and all the hens lay dead on the darkened foliage.

Wanda knew it was just a dream but she actually shed a tear and felt deeply saddened by the images in her mind. She tried to tell herself that Quercus was fine and all would be well but she feared for the tree's life. Quercus had told her in no uncertain terms that there was a real danger to wildlife from the chemicals being used on the farm, but was the tree exaggerating?

She got up, fed up with her painful back, and decided to go down to the kitchen and make herself a cup of tea. As she crept down the stairs in her dressing gown, she heard snoring coming from her parents' room. Her eyes had become accustomed to the dark so she didn't turn any lights on. She put the kettle on and made herself a mug of tea. There was chamomile tea in the cupboard and she considered whether it might help her get back to sleep. But she knew she hated the taste, so she opted for her usual English breakfast.

The tea made, she opened up the French windows and walked into the garden. It was just about warm enough to sit out in the night air. It was a cosy traditional garden with a small terrace and perennials including burnt orange rudbeckias, pink asters and hydrangeas in the borders around a small lawn. It was all very neat but not about to win any prizes at Chelsea. Her dad would be the one who kept it tidy; Rita was too busy with all her activities.

When Wanda had gone up to bed the evening before she had found a few watercolours, that her mother must have painted, at the back of the wardrobe behind a box of craft materials. One was a Suffolk landscape with a big sky, another a few wild flowers in a jar on a shelf. She had used a pale timid palette of pastel shades and created a series of watery images. Rita had never mentioned to Wanda that she had tried some painting, perhaps because she had always been so disparaging of Wanda's desire to be an artist.

As Wanda sat there sipping her tea, she considered that her parents were very conventional. They had married, had two children, stayed together through thick and thin, retired at the sort of age you are supposed to and downsized into a cottage in a pretty village where the biggest scandals played out amongst the members of the village hall committee.

No wonder they had struggled with some of her life choices. Quercus would describe them as people without an aura, without an affinity with nature. They were the sort of people who would make Quercus stand silently in their company and not reach out.

Quercus. That's what she kept coming back to. The words of the huge ancient oak were etched in her mind; she just couldn't ignore them. She almost felt a sense of duty to do something to save the tree, the biodiversity in it and around it and the living organisms in the soil that the Taylor family farmed. It seemed like an impossible task but one that, crazily, she felt compelled to take on.

Finally, she felt a sense of peace. Had she found her purpose? Her tea finished, she yawned and stretched and knew that now she could sleep. Even if it was on a lumpy sofa bed.

CHAPTER 25

Wanda woke up again at eight o'clock; she may just have had enough sleep. The important thing was it was becoming clear to her what she needed to do.

Her mother was commandeering the one and only bathroom. 'Sorry, love I'm having a shower,' she shouted through the door. 'There's a cloakroom downstairs.'

Wanda rolled her eyes and did what she could in the tiny cloakroom which had a very powerful air freshener with a sickly-sweet smell that made her choke. A fake lavender plant was covered in dust. Why did people have these things? She dressed quickly in yesterday's clothes, having not had the will to try and find something different in her NY suitcase, and went in search of breakfast. Her dad greeted her in the kitchen. 'Morning Wanda, did you sleep okay?'

'Sort of. In the end. Not really.'

'I saw the empty mug,' he said, his eyes kind. 'I'm sorry we're not better sorted for guests, well, not long term anyway.'

'I've only been here one night.' Wanda giggled.

'You seem brighter today.'

'Yes, I am. Dad, can I use your laptop please? After breakfast.'

'Yes, of course you can. I've got it set up in the lounge on a little side table.'

He insisted on making her a cup of tea and getting what she needed for a bowl of muesli and then sat next to her at the small kitchen table which was crammed into one corner.

'So, what have you got in mind?' he asked.

'I need the internet to do some research.'

'Oh, right, so is this for these commissions you've got from the Americans?'

'No, no, nothing like that.'

Wanda smiled at her father as she tried to work out what she could tell him of her plan.

'Job hunting perhaps?' he guessed. Reading her expression he tried, 'Looking at rentals in town?'

She decided to bite the bullet. 'I'm going to research how we could make Capel Farm an organic farm, not using pesticides and fertilisers.'

Graham looked astounded. 'That's a bit of a change from yesterday, isn't it?

'Yes, you could say that.' She laughed nervously now. 'Listen Dad, I know it sounds like a bit of a mad idea and it's going to be very difficult to persuade Glen that it is what we should do, but I know in my heart it's the right way forward.'

'What about your marriage?'

'Well, I guess this will either break it for good or save it.'

'Good for you,' he said and seemed satisfied that she knew what she was doing. 'And if there's anything I can do to help.'

'Thanks Dad, I appreciate that.'

By lunchtime, despite the rather slow wi-fi speed, Wanda felt she had enough to make her case. She wrote out the words she wanted to say to Glen in longhand, scribbling bits out and re-writing until the page was such a mess she started again on a fresh piece. This time she got it all down and was pleased with how it read.

She rang Abi.

'I hear you've moved in with Granny and Granddad.' Abi managed to sound sympathetic.

'Yes, well, just for a couple of nights.'

'It's good to hear from you,' Abi said with a tone of regret.

'How's your dad?'

'Struggling, I reckon. Granny Fi's been over but she's not happy. She's told him off for throwing you out.'

'Thrown out, was I?'

'Sorry, Mum.'

'It's okay. Listen, I want to talk to your dad. Do you know when he'll be at the farmhouse today?'

'He'll probably be in and out. He can't do too much at once but he keeps trying.'

'Do you think this evening might be best?'

'Maybe. Granddad Martin did call in earlier and said he was going to call a meeting around six. He wants me to be there.'

'That sounds like the last thing we need.' Wanda closed her eyes in disbelief.

'Yeah, Mum, I know. What are you planning to say to Dad?'

She had an idea. 'I will tell you but Abi, can you meet me in town today?'

'Middle of the day, yes, but you've got the car.'

'How about I pick you up at twelve?'

'Great.'

'Will you walk round to the front of the farmhouse so I can scoop you up without driving into the yard?'

'Okay Mum, I'll be there.'

Wanda drove into town and headed for St John's Street. She was browsing in one of the charity shops when she came across a copy of *Silent Spring* by Rachel Carson. She could not believe her luck. *All paperbacks fifty pence*, the sign read. From what she had read online about this book, it warned of the devastating consequences of using pesticides in farming. The chemicals used, with particular mention of DDT, were killing many living organisms, and becoming an integral part of the food chain. Of course, the agrochemical industry was incensed by it. They fiercely defended their products and in turn their massive profits. Despite some substances being declared poisonous to man, it always took rigorous testing to prove this before governments would act to ban the substance. Of course, little was done to stop the growth of this industry in the meantime.

With her purchased copy in her handbag, Wanda went into the café on Angel Hill for a coffee. She still had a bit of time before she was due to pick Abi up. Sipping her latte, she started to read. The message was immediately stark and shocking. It was amazing that this work had been published way back in 1962.

Abi looked troubled when Wanda picked her up at noon.

'Everything okay?' Wanda asked as she drove back in to town.

'Oh Mum, there's definitely going to be a family meeting this evening. Lee's been invited too. And Dad wants me to go. He says that I've done an amazing job helping out on the farm and he wants me to become a full-time permanent member of the team! With a salary.'

'Eek. How do you feel about that?'

'It doesn't feel right. It's not what I want.'

Wanda didn't ask any more. She waited until they were both sat at a small round table in a corner of The Bay Tree café back on St John's Street, with their lunch order taken by one of the waitresses, before she placed her hand on Abi's.

'I've had an idea.'

'You're not going back to New York, are you?'

'No, nothing like that. It's to do with the farm.'

'I think you're best well out of it. In fact, wherever you end up I might be moving in with you at this rate.' Abi looked apologetic.

Wanda smiled kindly. 'I want to change the farm. I think we should farm organically. Stop using pesticides because they're destroying biodiversity and ruining the soil.'

'Really?' Abi said with disbelief in her eyes. 'Where's this come from all of a sudden?'

'You know I've never liked using chemicals. Anyway,' Wanda produced her copy of *Silent Spring* and laid it on the table in front of Abi. 'it's all in this book, the harm that they are doing to our soil and the planet.'

Abi frowned as she picked the paperback up. 'This looks old.'

'It was published in 1962.'

'So how come it's relevant today?'

'But that's the point. It is! Farmers are still using poisons to kill pests which, in turn, kill many other organisms including birds and fish.'

'But why? Why hasn't anything been done about it before now?'

'Because farmers like your father aren't interested. They think that the most important thing is to farm the land intensively, to maximise the yield from every inch of soil, obliterating the so-called pests as they go.'

Abi was thoughtful now. She sat back in her chair. 'But Mum, how are you going to convince Dad that this is the right way to go?'

Wanda produced her sheet of paper with her speech for Glen carefully written out. She handed it to Abi. 'Here, read this.'

Abi read it, serious faced. When she got to the end, she placed it carefully on the table in front of her. 'I think you're right. We should go organic. A hundred per cent. But I just don't know how you'll persuade Dad, not to mention Granddad Martin.'

Wanda sighed. 'Granddad Martin is meant to be retired. He's like a bad penny!'

'Mum, you are so right. I back you all the way. But I just have no clue as to how we would do it.'

Wanda fidgeted awkwardly in her chair. 'Me neither, really, but I believe we can find a way.'

The waitress delivered their sandwiches and a pot of tea. Wanda realised she was hungry. 'Thanks,' she said before turning back to Abi. 'So, if I go to your dad with this, will you back me up?'

'Yes, Mum, I will. I don't actually want to stay at the farm as things stand. But with this,' she picked up the piece of paper, 'I might be tempted.'

Glen was in the garden, his head resting back on a chair. Was he asleep? Abi approached him cautiously. He looked up and immediately saw Wanda right behind Abi.

'Dad, we want to talk to you,' Abi touched his arm gently. 'Mum's got something she wants to say about the farm.'

'I've heard enough from her.' He was grumpy. Perhaps they had woken him. 'Anyway, we've got the meeting tonight for talking.'

'I'd really like to talk to you before then,' Wanda managed an assertive tone and picked up a chair so that she could sit opposite him. She had her prepared speech in her hand.

Glen looked confused but not angry.

'Surely you can just listen,' Abi pleaded pulling up a chair too.

He eyed them both suspiciously but said nothing.

'May I?' Wanda put her reading glasses on.

'Well, I'm intrigued, I'll give you that,' Glen said. He coughed and held his chest with one hand.

'Are you okay?' Wanda asked.

'This is as good as it gets.' He flitted his eyes up to the sky.

'Right, well here we go.' Suddenly Wanda's mouth was very dry and she couldn't speak.

'I'll get you some water, Mum.' Abi disappeared and came back with a glass. Wanda took a gulp.

And then she read.

'We have been married for thirty years and I know I haven't been the farmer's wife you wanted me to be. It has taken me until now to realise why. And it's not about my art, although that is important to me and it always will be. It's because I don't agree with using chemicals on the land and I don't agree with caging hens or separating cows from their calves at birth.

'We have both strived to make this farm work using your father's values and the end result is that it simply isn't working. We are facing financial ruin. Those are your words, not mine.' She looked him straight in the eyes at that point and could see she had his attention

'When something is not working, it's not about trying to do the same thing but harder, it's about making *changes* and doing things differently so that we can expect a better outcome. Martin means well but he hasn't moved with the times. More and more farms are moving away from the use of costly chemicals and some are becoming organic farmers.

'The use of fertilisers, pesticides and fungicides is destroying our soil, killing off many living organisms which is reducing biodiversity and having a harmful effect on our ecosystem. Even the ancient trees in Lucas Wood are suffering as a result.'

Glen's eyes widened at that point but he seemed interested and said nothing. Abi was looking at her mother with pride.

'This way of farming is not sustainable,' Wanda continued. 'And it is not working. To make matters worse, the chemicals end up in the food that we eat and that is harmful to our health.'

'It's time for a change,' she continued before taking a deep breath to calm herself. 'I think we should go for organic certification and turn Capel Dairy Farm into an organic farm. From what I've researched so far, it would take us about two years. There are conversion grants available; I'm not sure how you apply for them or how much we'd get but we could find out. In the meantime, we could still produce milk, eggs and crops; it would just be without using chemicals. And don't forget that the cost of pesticides and fertilisers is huge, so we will be saving money there.' Wanda tentatively looked at Glen. He seemed more bemused than anything else.

'And I'm happy to invest the earnings from my art to the cause and,' Wanda raised her voice as she could see that Glen was itching to say something, 'I think we should sell direct to the public.'

'Now you really have lost it,' Glen interrupted.

'Hang on a minute.' Wanda raised a palm to try and halt any further comments until she had finished. 'Fen Farm Dairy, just outside Bungay, do it from self-service sheds at the entrance to their farm and I've had a look at their website; it looks like a vibrant and profitable business.'

'I know where you mean,' Glen said, 'but they make cheese and yoghurt on the premises. It's a completely different business to ours.'

'We don't even have a website,' Abi added.

'But we could have a website and maybe even a dairy. Anything's possible with a bit of vision and a willingness to change. I mean, why sell eggs to the wholesaler for nuppence when we could sell organic free-range eggs direct to the public for a tidy profit? We could set up a farm shop; more and more farms are doing exactly that nowadays.'

'But it could take years until we start making a profit.' Glen's expression was pained. 'More importantly, we haven't a clue how to go about it. I mean if we stop using pesticides, we're going to have weeds and pests everywhere and damaged crops.'

'What I have learnt through my research is that if we continue to use chemicals it will lead to the decline of many species, including pollinators, soil organisms and the natural enemies of pests,' Wanda said pleased with her detailed knowledge. She continued despite Glen's startled expression, 'So you see, intensive farming isn't sustainable in the long run.'

'All very worthy,' Glen retorted. 'But it doesn't alter the fact that with organic farming you end up producing a lot less and have to charge a lot more for it. I mean is there a demand for expensive food?'

'There is,' Wanda said, though not really sure of her ground and her voice gave her away, 'a growing demand,' she said praying now that there was.

'There definitely is,' Abi said. 'I mean supermarkets are beginning to stock more organic veg. Apparently in France they have lots of organic produce in their shops.'

'France?' Glen questioned.

'We're still part of the EU,' Wanda said.

'We voted to leave! Last year.' Glen was, perhaps rightly, exasperated by that comment. 'And that means the UK will be coming out of CAP; that's our EU subsidy down the drain which is half our income!'

Abi was fired up. 'All the more reason to come up with a new way of doing things. I mean if we carry on the way we are, it's going to be very difficult to replace that EU subsidy money.'

'Exactly,' Wanda exclaimed.

Glen was thoughtful. That was a good sign. 'We're going to need a lot of professional advice. How much will that cost?'

'We can talk to other farmers who have already turned organic, which won't cost anything. There are quite a few in Suffolk alone; you would be surprised. They have been through the process of getting organic certification so we can learn from them. There's also this Organic Research Centre who have lots of experience they can share. They've even produced a handbook we can get.'

'A handbook?' Glen was incredulous.

'Yes, a handbook. It costs thirty quid.'

'A handbook for self-destruction?'

'Don't be so negative, Dad. A handbook sounds like just what we need.'

'Answer me this.' Wanda swept an arm around indicating the surrounding farmland. 'Is this what you want? Does this make you happy?'

Glen sighed. 'I thought it did, once,' he said quietly, peering down at his lap.

'Dad, I think Mum's idea is brilliant.' Abi pulled her chair nearer to him. 'It feels right. And it would transform the farm into a better place. I, for one, would be tempted to stay. But I'm sorry I don't want to be part of it as things stand. It just seems wrong.'

Immediately Glen looked hurt but then he sighed with resignation and put his head back. 'I don't know. I'm outnumbered here, clearly.'

'You think it's a good idea, don't you?' Abi's eyes were bright, full of hope. Glen sat in quiet contemplation for a few moments, then tears sprang from his eyes. He raised a hand to cover up his crying. Wanda smiled gently at her daughter. They both waited patiently.

Finally, Glen said, 'You two really believe this is what we should do, don't you? I must admit I admire your tenacity, courage even. You make quite a formidable team. And you are my wife and my daughter, my family.' He paused to wipe his eyes. 'I've no idea if this is going to work, but you know, I don't think I have a lot of choice and I am willing to give it a go. Like you say, it's too much of a struggle the way we've been doing things. I can't go on like this. I'm broken since the accident.' He looked up at them, his eyes almost pleading. 'And with you two on board I think there's hope.'

Wanda beamed. At last. 'It's the right decision. It won't be plain sailing but this time I think we can enjoy the journey.'

'Yes, and it's absolutely the right thing to do for the planet and future generations,' Abi said and Wanda didn't hide her surprise at her daughter's enthusiasm.

'Time to celebrate.' Abi got up and walked into the house.

Wanda's eyes rested on her husband and he gazed back at her and smiled.

'Does this mean I can move back home?' Wanda asked quietly.

'I've missed you,' Glen said and reached out to take her hand. He pulled her over and she sat carefully on his lap.

'I've missed you too,' she said and they kissed for what seemed like the first time for a very long time.

Abi appeared with a tray laden with a bottle of wine and three glasses. 'Oops. Enough of that,' she said embarrassed.

'We are married,' Wanda pointed out.

'I'm not supposed to have alcohol with my painkillers.' Glen said.

'You don't take as many these days, do you?' Abi pointed out.

'That's true. In fact, I haven't had one today.'

'Well, there you are,' Abi handed him and her mum a glass. 'Anyway, one small glass won't hurt.

'To the organic future of Capel Farm,' Wanda said and she thought of Quercus and how pleased the wood wide web was going to be but not too loudly as she was still on her husband's lap.

That night Glen persuaded Wanda that she could lay her head gently on his chest so that he could hold her as they fell asleep together.

'Are you sure,' she said. His eyes were full of love for her.

'Come here,' he said and she kissed him before she rested her head as he'd suggested with the gentlest of touches.

'It's okay,' he encouraged her, holding her tight.

She could hear his heart beat and felt safe in his arms. Today was the first day of a new beginning.

CHAPTER 26

The following day the three of them sat round the dining table. They knew they had a monumental task ahead of them but enthusiasm was high. Glen had the laptop from the office upstairs and was browsing the internet. Wanda had told him to start with the Organic Research Centre website which she knew had lots of useful information on it. Hopefully it would help Glen to start to work out how they would go about this seismic shift for the farm.

As she'd watched him in the garden the evening before, when they'd celebrated the decision they had made, she could see in his eyes that he found the whole thing bewildering. It was like he was being swept along this path fearing the unknown but compelled to go along with his wife and daughter. But it also looked like a weight had been lifted from his shoulders. When he'd called his father to cancel the family meeting, Wanda had heard him stand up to Martin for the very first time. 'But Dad, this is my decision, mine and Wanda's. We own the farm now.'

Graham had brought over his laptop for Abi to use.

'Your mother's interested in what you're doing,' he said to Wanda as he handed it over. 'I've tried to explain and she thinks I'm talking rubbish.'

'Tell her we are going to grow crops in accordance with the moon phases from now on.' Wanda couldn't hold back a grin.

'You're not, are you?'

'No, Dad. We're going organic.'

Abi took the laptop. 'Thanks Granddad.' She opened it up straightaway. 'I can start thinking about building us a website.' Wanda wasn't sure if it was too soon for that but it was so great to have Abi on board she wasn't going to say anything to upset her.

They had tentatively agreed that their first aim was to work out how they could carry on with the business as usual, farming the same mix – dairy, eggs and crops – but moving in an organic direction. In actual fact, the first thing they found themselves doing was working out exactly what turning into an organic farm meant. None of them really had a clue how to go about it.

After some time, Glen looked up from his screen. 'This organic malarkey is complex to say the least. There's a whole science behind the production of the seeds you might use for growing crops. They are actually producing plants that don't need inputs, so that means fertilisers and pesticides, and can cope with unpredictable weather.' He blinked before opening his eyes wide. 'And there's other stuff too which I can't really get my head around right now, but it sounds pretty amazing. God knows how much it all costs.'

Wanda was reading about how you might go about getting funding to convert to organic. The Countryside Stewardship scheme seemed to be a possibility but the application process looked like a minefield. The more she read, the more she felt completely out of her depth.

'We need to find out what Capel Farm would be suitable for first; I suppose what I mean is, what we should produce going forward.' Wanda pulled a face indicating how scary it all seemed to her. 'And then we need help with the actual application process; otherwise we might not be successful.'

'Changed your mind?' Glen spoke genially in a *told you so* kind of way.

'No! Never. Crikey, we've only just begun. Rome wasn't built in a day.'

'Just how much money did you make in New York from your paintings? I've no idea,' Glen asked.

'Erm, well, let me think, including the advance I got, although actually I've spent some of that, it must be close to fifty thousand pounds.'

'That's a tidy sum.' He looked at her, clearly impressed. 'I had no idea we were talking that sort of money. That's the Americans for you.'

'Actually, I reckon I could command similar prices in this country after my recent success.' Wanda tried not to sound narked, but she was a little. 'And I have two commissions as well, as a result of the trip. But, of course, I will need to spend some time working on them.' She smiled and looked pointedly at her husband to add emphasis.

'We need to build that into our business plan,' Abi said. 'Mum must be able to spend some of her time on her art which will generate additional income; it will be really good to have during the set-up phase. Which is going to be two years, I reckon.'

'That could work,' Glen conceded and then looked thoughtful. 'So, is it a business plan we need?'

'Yes, I read somewhere you have to have a business case,' Abi said, looking through some notes she'd made.

Glen raised his eyebrows. 'I hope you're not expecting me to write that.'

'I think we should all do it together,' Abi said.

Wanda sighed. 'It's not straightforward, is it?' After a moment's pause, she added, 'I think I'll go and do the hens,' and got up. 'All this internet browsing, fact finding stuff, is driving me crazy.'

'But I do the hens.' Abi smiled at her mother.

'You wouldn't normally complain,' Wanda pointed out. 'Anyway, you're better at the research side of things.'

'Me? I'm not a farmer.'

'I'm here,' Glen said, 'surely together we can work it out?' He looked at Abi.

'Yeah, Dad, we'll crack this.' They all laughed making the most of a lighter moment.

By lunchtime Abi and Glen were screen weary and needed a break. Wanda was back from the hen barn and Abi helped her prepare some lunch for them all. Glen suggested that they eat outside as it was a nice day.

They were back at work in the dining room at two o'clock when Lee turned up. He walked into the room looking slightly nervous and turning to Abi for clues. 'Well, I'm here, like you said. What on earth is going on?'

Everyone looked at Wanda so she explained that they were going to move to organic farming. Lee listened intently.

'So do you still want me or not?' He looked confused now.

'Yes, definitely,' Wanda said. 'We are going to continue to produce milk, eggs and some crops while we go for organic status but we will have to do things a bit differently. As far as the herd are concerned, we must not use fertilisers on the pasture land.'

'That's pretty much what we've been doing,' Lee interrupted her.

'Yes, but I think we'll need to go a lot further,' Glen said. 'I mean introduce herbal leys, adding different species into the grass, that sort of thing.'

'Not something I've done before but I'm willing to learn.' Lee kept glancing at Abi nervously.

'Great. And when it comes to forage for winter feed, we need to make sure that we don't use any fertilisers, pesticides or any chemicals at all,' Glen said and Wanda was impressed. 'We need to decide whether or not we go for a hundred per cent grass-fed, which would mean dedicating more land to produce forage. But if a hundred per cent is not possible, we can supplement with grain rations.'

'So would we buy in organic grain?' Abi asked.

'I suppose so.'

'Nothing but grass all year round would be tough, unless you don't bother with any other crops,' Lee suggested.

'Yes, well, we're very much in the planning stages,' Wanda said. 'That's just one of many decisions we need advice on.'

'Wanda's right,' Glen said. 'We're going to have to get an expert in.'

Wanda stood up. 'Do you want a cup of tea, Lee?' She yawned. 'I think I need the caffeine.'

'Wouldn't mind a cup.'

When she returned with a pot and four mugs Lee was telling them about a farm in Norfolk where he'd worked.

'Yeah, so Home Farm are organic but not dairy. All arable.'

'That's interesting,' Glen said. 'I'd like to pick your brains, if that's okay?'

'Better still maybe they wouldn't mind if we both went up there,' Lee said looking at Glen. 'I mean show us round and tell us about their crop rotations.'

'That would be perfect,' Wanda said as she poured the tea.

'Yes, I'd like that,' Glen agreed. 'Now, while I think of it, another matter is the breed of cow we milk. I mean I'm reading that most organic dairies use Holsteins or Jerseys or even a crossbreed of the two.'

'What do you mean; get rid of the Montbéliardes?' Abi looked horrified. 'What would happen to them?'

'Hang on a minute,' Wanda interjected. 'We chose the Montys because their milk is very good for cheese making. So why not find a local organic cheese producer? Longer term, of course?'

'I like that idea,' Abi said. 'We can't get rid of the daisies.'

'You can't be sentimental in farming,' Glen said with a serious face.

'You might have to make allowances, with the girl power on board.' Lee winked at Abi.

Glen laughed. 'You're right there, mate. We'll be calling this place *Daisy Farm* next.'

'What a brilliant idea,' Abi said.

'I love it, but perhaps we should concentrate on other stuff,' Wanda said. 'Lee, we want to put you in charge of the dairy side of things,' Wanda continued even though they hadn't really agreed this as a family but Glen didn't seem to object.

'I can't be relied upon since my accident,' he explained. 'I hope to be able to help out more with the milking at some stage.'

'Right, well, it's fine with Abi helping in the afternoons.' Lee said.

Abi took a sharp intake of breath. 'That's temporary though. I mean I see my role as more about managing the website and the distribution side of things, setting up a farm shop for example.'

Wanda was proud of her daughter. 'All this change is going to take time. There's so much to learn.'

'I know a graduate from the agricultural college,' Lee said. 'He's looking for dairy herd experience and we wouldn't have to pay him too much. What do you reckon?'

'I think we could try him out,' Glen said, 'and if he works out, we could get him doing the milking with you a few times a week.'

'Good idea,' Abi said a bit too quickly. 'How about every afternoon,' she added with glee.

'Can't wait to get away from me,' Lee said resentfully. 'Think you're management now, do you?'

'It's not like that at all,' Wanda said. 'We're all in this together. Abi just wants to spend some of her time building us a website and other stuff.'

'The milking was always a temporary help out,' Abi said in her defence.

Wanda didn't know if the relationship between Abi and Lee would last but she knew that Lee was an asset to the farm she didn't want to lose. 'Listen, Lee, what we're doing here is going to bring about a lot of change and we really want you to be part of it.'

'I'm in, really I am. It's a bit more interesting than some of my other work.'

As the days turned into weeks, there was an energy about the place; they all had a new sense of purpose. Glen had a spring in his step, even if he still needed to rest a lot of the time. Now he could feel useful by sitting at his desk to learn more about the direction they wanted to take the farm in. Wanda was chuffed to bits that her plan was actually beginning to happen. Even though they all knew that they had challenging times ahead, the atmosphere on the farm was entirely different.

Martin's reaction to the news had been predictable. He thought they were all nuts. But Glen had managed to persuade him, with his mother's help, that it was the right thing to do for the farm and also for himself. It was hard for his father to accept that Glen was never going to be the farmer he had been before the accident.

'You've got to understand that having Wanda and Abi on board makes a huge difference to me. I need them, I really do,' Glen explained.

'I can see you need to try a different approach. I only hope it works out for you,' was the best response Martin could offer.

Wanda knew that he expected them to fail but wiped that thought from her mind. She needed to be positive about this new beginning. It had to succeed. Fi had come round and hugged Wanda hard thanking her for what she was doing. 'It turns out, Wanda, that you are exactly what this farm needs!' She laughed as she said it and Wanda couldn't help joining in, if nervously.

'I don't think Martin feels that way,' Wanda said.

'Martin is retired. Even if I have to watch him like a hawk, he's going to slow down. I've actually found a retired farmers group that meet in Bury once a week. He pooh-poohed the idea at first but I made him go along to try it out. And guess what, he came home full of it!'

'I'm so pleased, Fi. And what will you do with your time?'

'Your mum's getting me involved with the W.I. and a few other bits she does.'

'Good.'

'But I did want to say...' Fiona looked shy all of a sudden. 'This farm shop you are planning to set up.' She hesitated.

'Yes?' Wanda was surprised by this level of interest from her mother-in-law.

'Well, if you want someone to help out in any way, I'd be happy to volunteer my services.'

'Oh Fi, that would be brilliant. Thank you. We will bear that in mind when the time comes.'

'Just part time, you understand.'

'Of course.'

Lily called. 'Mum, what is going on? Abi tells me you're going organic.'

'Yes, that's right.'

'But I thought you were focusing on your art these days. Was that exhibition in New York really a great success?'

'It really was, yes, thanks.'

'And now you're practically running the farm and making massive changes. I can't quite believe it. What's come over you?'

Telling her daughter that she had been talking to an ancient oak tree was not an option so instead she said, 'I just listened to the land and realised there's a better way.'

'Oh yeah? Sounds like you're away with the fairies.' Lily laughed.

'Yes, the fairies; they helped too.'

'Mum, you're stark raving wonderful.'

'Thank you, Lily, I'll take that as a compliment.'

'Actually, Mum, I do think you are pretty amazing. I mean, all that you've achieved. When Dad had his accident, I was convinced you'd end up selling the farm. But no, you've turned things around.'

Wanda was not used to praise from her daughter. She didn't know how to respond.

'Even more amazing,' Lily continued, 'Abi is staying on full time. I never thought that would happen. Or is it something to do with this Lee bloke?'

'I have a feeling it is much more to do with the new venture.'

Vicky, the adviser from the Farming and Wildlife Advisory Group, was a youngish woman dressed just like a farmer. Wanda took to her immediately.

'Would you like a coffee in the kitchen to start with?' Glen asked.

'I'm keen to walk the farm first, if that's okay,' she said. 'I'd like to get a sense of what your vision is for the future.'

Wanda panicked. What was their vision?

'We want to know how we could transform the farm to organic,' Glen came to her rescue, 'so we are producing organic milk from our Montbéliarde cows, or another herd if you think we should change it, and...'

'Let me stop you there. So your vision is to have an organic dairy farm;

let's sort out the detail as we go along.'

'And egg production,' Wanda added hastily. 'We have two hundred, a mix of Goldlines and Light Sussex and they are free range, kept in a barn overnight.'

'Great, I'd like to see that. Anything else?'

'We have some crops at the moment,' Glen said, 'some for forage, some veg. We're thinking of possibly getting the cows to one hundred per cent grass-fed, but that would take up quite a lot of our acreage.'

'Okay, I think I have a reasonable idea of what we're talking about. Do you want to show me around?'

'Let's do the cows first,' Glen said. 'I have to tell you, I had an accident a few months back but I'll do as much of the tour as I can.'

'I'm sorry to hear that.'

'I can take over if Glen gets tired,' Wanda said. 'Actually, it was my idea to take the farm in a new direction.'

'Well then, you are essential to this outing.'

'I suppose I am.' Wanda felt pleased with herself, if a little nervous.

Vicky was impressed with their pasture system, moving the cows daily to keep the grass growing without the need for fertilisers. 'These fields would be perfect for a mix of cover crops, herbal leys, etc.'

'Would we be able to use antibiotics if any of the cows get sick?' Glen asked.

'You'll find with time that with herbal leys, the cows get better nutrition which will boost their immune system and so the need for antibiotics is lessened.'

'That sounds good.' Wanda smiled.

'But if a cow does get sick?' Glen asked.

'Then you would take them out of milking until the drug is out of their system, usually six days. And, of course, the general use of antibiotics as a prevention tool is out of the question.'

'Good,' Wanda declared with emphasis.

When they got as far as Rooked Meadow, Vicky's eyes widened. 'This looks good. How long have you been wilding this bit of land?'

'Most of my lifetime,' Glen said, 'as far as I can remember.'

'And why was that decision taken? Was the soil poor here?'

'Closeness to the wood which casts shade, but otherwise it seems to be a quirk of the way my grandfather farmed. And my dad decided to leave it alone too. But it seems like a waste, doesn't it?'

'On the contrary, this area is helping biodiversity and carbon sequestration. Along with the wood too, I suspect. This is just the sort of thing that helps you to get a grant.'

Glen looked amazed. 'You get money for having a field you've done nothing with?'

Vicky laughed. 'Absolutely. You could add in additional wild flower seed to make it even better.'

'It looks amazing in the spring,' Wanda said. 'Full of colour and insects, butterflies.'

'Well so far I'm impressed,' Vicky said.

'Shall I take you up to the hen barn?' Wanda asked. Glen felt able to go with them; it was obvious that he was impressed with Vicky.

By the time Vicky left, Wanda was buzzing with excitement.

'She talked a lot of sense,' Glen admitted. 'Better than I expected.'

'Oh Glen, I really think this is going to work. The more I heard her talking, the more I'm convinced that we are doing the right thing.'

'Good!' He laughed. 'It's great to see you so enthusiastic about the farm.'

'Yeah, I am actually. This feels so right.'

He went over to her and hugged her. 'Wanda, the farmer, who'd have thought.'

'Wanda, the organic farmer, if you don't mind.'

Gilbert came to the farmhouse early one morning; he had heard talk of the changes down at The White Horse in the village and found Wanda in the kitchen clearing up after breakfast. He didn't take his well-worn gaberdine mac off.

'Well, I'll be blown. What a turn of events,' he said grinning all over his lined, weathered face.

Wanda smiled mischievously. 'Well Gilbert, it was you who said I should listen to the land.'

'Did I say that?' His face lit up.

A giggle burst from Wanda's mouth.

'What do you know?' Gilbert played along. 'Miracles do happen. You been up to Lucas Wood recently?'

Just then Glen appeared at the door. 'Gilbert, old man.' He nodded to him respectfully.

'Good to see you fully up and about, young Taylor. Nasty those Jerseys.'

'I'm not too bad now. What's all this about Lucas Wood?'

'Lucas Wood?' Gilbert questioned as if he hadn't just mentioned the place himself.

'I found inspiration for some of my paintings up there,' Wanda said quickly to take the heat off the old man.

'It's a very inspiring place,' Gilbert added. 'Worth a visit every now and then.' He winked at Wanda. Glen looked bemused yet again.

'Anyway, I'm off to Risby Farm with Abi,' Wanda said to change the subject. 'We're checking out their organic egg production.'

'I won't keep you then.' Gilbert lifted his old felt hat and nodded his head towards Glen. He was about to turn to go when he hesitated. 'It's good to see you two, well you know, together, united so to speak.'

Glen gazed at Wanda in awe. 'Turns out my wife is a force to be reckoned with.'

'She certainly is,' Gilbert agreed and Wanda felt herself blush.

CHAPTER 27

At dusk, with Gilbert's words heeded, Wanda offered to go up to Hungry Hill to get the hens safely in to the barn for the night. Abi was more than happy to have some time off. It was a cool cloudless autumn evening and the sunset was beautiful with the sun a ball of warm orange against a big salmon pink Suffolk sky. The hens seemed a little reluctant at first so she talked to them as she always did.

'Snowball, you lead the way, please. Set an example. And you, Delilah, show the other Goldlines how it's done,' she said to her newly appointed leaders. As if by magic they obliged. She could swear that they understood her or at least they responded to her calming tone of voice.

With the barn door closed and bolted, Wanda made her way along the top of Cuttings Meadow. She could see the cows in the distance. Where the path dipped down, she veered right into Rachel's Covert. There was her old art studio. She had fond memories of the place going back to when the girls were babies. Now she was allowed to paint in Lily's old room which she had turned into her new studio. Lily had been a bit put out when she'd first heard about it. Where would she sleep when she came home for the weekend? They would think of something, Wanda had said, not giving it any thought at all at that precise moment, her head was so full of the farm. But it seemed that the more Lily discovered about everything her family were doing at Capel Dairy Farm, the more enthralled she was. It was almost as if she felt she might be missing out.

Lucas Wood was a little eerie as the light faded, but Wanda knew that Quercus was not far away now and she would be there soon. There was a definite autumnal feel with the hazel trees already flame red and orange. Leaves were falling fast and carpeting the path. She heard a fallow deer barking in the distance and hoped it was okay. Dark green ivy smothered tree trunks and rose hips and crab apples provided pops of colour amongst the fading greens.

When she reached Quercus, the first thing she noticed was that the tree still had a full canopy of green leaves; the oak tended to hang on until November before the leaves turned golden brown. There was something wonderful about the longevity of this majestic tree, to think that it could live for a thousand years or more. That was, of course, if man treated it well. As usual the tree was quiet at first apart from the rustle of its leaves in the breeze. Wanda looked up the broad, wizened trunk into the canopy and the night sky beyond, in awe of this marvel once more. She hugged the tree as far as her arms would allow, resting her cheek on the bark and felt an overwhelming sense of peace. The battle was over, she was reunited with Glen and most importantly the farm had a future which would save her ancient friend.

'You came then.' Quercus sounded old and weary.

'I've been busy, very busy, but then Gilbert reminded me.'

'My messenger delivered. Good.' There was a long pause before the tree added, 'So what are you going to tell me little lady? There is news; I can feel it through the fungi network. Tell me what I need to hear, pray do.'

'Yes, I have the most wonderful news. Capel Dairy Farm is going to become an organic oasis; there will be no more chemicals.'

'Just in time. Or rather too late for many organisms. But in the years to come it is possible that the order of nature may be restored once more.'

'We're going to be doing all sorts of things like having herbal leys and deep-rooted cover crops and an eight-year rotation. I don't really understand it all but I hope you are pleased.'

'How did you persuade the Taylor family? They have been so merciless in their chemical spreading ever since the 1950s.'

'It wasn't easy. I think in the end it was as much about saving my marriage as saving the farm. And Glen's accident with the bull; it has changed him significantly.'

'The bull did a good thing then? And sacrificed its own life.'

'I'll never think of it as a good thing. But that's an interesting way of looking at it. Maybe I owe that bull my marriage.'

'And I owe my declining years to you, Wanda Taylor. What a wonderful little lady you turned out to be. Just goes to show that size doesn't matter.'

'Is that a joke, Quercus?'

'I don't understand what a joke is, but if you mean am I being very serious, you are correct.'

CHAPTER 28

December 2019

Wanda looked around the new farm shop with pride. The dairy section was stocked and ready to sell organic milk, yoghurt and some exciting cheese products, courtesy of local artisan makers – the milk provided by their own dear Montbéliarde herd. Then there was a vegetable section with some of their new home-grown range of red cabbage, Brussel sprouts, parsnips and celeriac combined with vegetables grown by neighbouring organic Suffolk farmers. Above the display of organic eggs ran the video from a live webcam following the free-range lives of the hens. Rhode Island Reds, with their beautiful reddish-brown coat of feathers and shining black tails highlighted by hints of green, had been added to the Goldline and Light Sussex birds, as well as Orpingtons with fluffed-out blonde feathers, short legs and a curvy, short back. The Daisy Café at one end of the shop would be serving coffee, tea and locally produced organic pastries and cakes.

Adorning the walls of the farm shop and café were works of art, including one of an ancient oak tree named Quercus; Wanda had painted the mighty tree a few times now, much to Quercus' delight. She was chuffed to bits that they were selling her work alongside the produce of the farm. She had found a local firm who could produce giclée prints of paintings so they had prints to sell of all her magical nature-themed works at a more affordable price. With the PR that Abi had organised locally after her New York exhibition, Wanda had made a name for herself as an artist. Aaron had not only facilitated the two commissions she had come back with but had arranged several more in the last two years. It thrilled her that she was able to paint now with Glen's blessing.

There had been so much hard work to get to this point but she had loved every minute of it.

Abi appeared carrying a large box that was almost bigger than her. 'I've got the holly and mistletoe here.' She raised her voice so that she could be heard from behind the box.

'We're cutting it a bit fine,' Wanda said laughing.

Abi plonked the box down in the centre of the shop. 'Just over an hour to go until we open,' she said playfully tapping her watch.

'Until the *grand* opening! This is such an improvement on the vending self-service shed.'

'It's going to make a massive difference. Remember how we started with an honesty box for the eggs? In this day and age!'

'It worked though, didn't it? We made some money.'

'Thanks to all those posts on social media that I sent out. They really put Capel Farm on the map. Our Rhode Island Reds are Instagram stars.'

'You've been wonderful, darling. Now what are we doing with all this?' Wanda picked up a sprig of mistletoe.

'Well, I thought we'd just spread it around the shop over the displays; make it look more Christmassy.'

'Right you are.' Wanda was doubtful but having tried a few options she began to get creative. She stood back from the egg display. 'I like it. Tasteful and not too OTT.'

'Exactly.'

Just then Lee walked through the door still in his wellingtons from milking. He looked around him in awe of the brightly lit shop. 'Looks like you've been busy.'

'Don't come right in!' Abi was quick to say. 'We don't want a muddy floor.'

Lee looked offended and stayed put on the doormat at the entrance.

'How did the milking go this morning,' Wanda asked nicely.

'All good. One a bit lame; I sorted it.'

'Oh great, thanks for that. Are you coming to the opening?' Wanda asked and Lee looked straight at Abi who was busying herself with placing holly on the egg display.

'I'm sorting the hens today as you're all busy,' he said.

'Why don't you come down when you've finished.' Wanda walked over to him. 'You've worked really hard; you deserve a break.'

'Thanks Wanda, I might just do that.'

'You'll have to change,' Abi said. 'I mean clean clothes.'

'Yes, ma'am; I'll make myself respectable for the customers,' he said, his tone embittered. 'Better get on.' He smiled at Wanda and she smiled back before he turned and left.

'You should be kind to him,' Wanda implored. 'He's a real asset to the farm.'

'I know Mum, but it's over between us, has been for over a year now.'

'You broke his heart,' Wanda said and immediately regretted it.

'He wasn't right for me. I'm not going to marry a farmer.'

Wanda went over to her daughter and gave her a hug. 'You did the right thing,' she said. 'Right now, we'd better get a move on.'

With the Christmas decorations all in place, and the box they came in hidden at the back, Wanda asked Abi, 'Did you hear back from Lily? Does she think she'll make it on time?'

'She's trying her best and she'll definitely be here at some point.'

'Who's picking her up from the station?'

'No one. She's driving up. She's bought herself an electric car.'

'Electric? Will it make this far?'

'Apparently so.'

Fiona burst through the door looking a bit flustered. 'So sorry I'm late.'

'You're not late,' Wanda said eyeing the large wall clock they had installed in the shop mainly because Wanda never wore a watch.

'There's only thirty minutes to go. Where's Glen?' Fiona asked.

'He's coming. Don't worry. Now let me show you what's what in the café.' Wanda took her mother-in-law's arm and steered her to the other side of the shop

'Is Rita coming to help me?' Fiona asked after Wanda had finished explaining it all.

'Yes, but why don't you phone her just in case she needs reminding.'

'Surely she won't forget on such a momentous day?'

Wanda raised her eyebrows. 'What about Martin?'

'He promised he would come, probably towards the end. He's quite the man of leisure these days.'

'That's a good thing, isn't it?'

Fiona nodded. 'As soon as he'd accepted that you were going organic, I think he felt really out of it because everything changed.'

'But does he think we've done the right thing now?'

'Not sure he'll ever admit to that.' Fiona looked at Wanda and smiled. 'I can see you have, though, so well done you.'

At precisely eleven o'clock, a green ribbon was tied across the main doors. Quite a crowd had gathered, huddled together for warmth. It was a clear and icy cold December day and not one for long speeches, Wanda surmised.

Glen looked very smart in chinos, a pale blue shirt and navy blazer and Wanda considered that she fancied him more now than the day she had married him. The less strenuous life of a desk-based manager was doing him the world of good. He handed Wanda a pair of scissors.

'Thank you all for coming to the opening of our little organic farm shop.'

'Not so little!' someone in the crowd shouted.

'We are very proud of what we have achieved as a family at Capel Daisy Organic Farm.' She couldn't help grinning at Glen who grimaced at their new name. 'I know you're all freezing and can't wait to get in and so, I declare the farm shop open!' She cut the ribbon and everyone cheered and started to make their way in through the doors.

The day flew by as shoppers browsed the goodies within and delighted in watching the hens pecking and foraging away on the live film. As they had decided to offer every customer a free hot drink, Fiona was kept very busy and Graham made a pretty good assistant in the absence of Rita who apparently wasn't feeling too good. They also did a good trade in warm pastries and muffins provided by a local baker.

Glen helped Abi out on the till until well into the afternoon but then decided to make his way back to the house for a bit of rest. Wanda chatted away to customers and was in her element. She soon realised that Abi had turned her into a social media celeb; everyone recognised her. It was quite nice having the attention and the praise for what they had accomplished in two short years. Everyone seemed very pleased with the local organic offering.

Lee turned up looking shower fresh and very smart and seemed happy mingling with customers and answering their questions about the dairy herd and the new organic ways.

At four o'clock they finally closed the doors on the last customer. Martin had just turned up and joined the rest of the Capel team as they headed back to the farmhouse for hot soup and crusty bread to celebrate their success. Wanda was pleased that Lee joined them. Glen was in the kitchen when they walked in and the soup was already warming. Wanda went up to him and threw her arms around him and kissed him.

'Thank you darling,' she said.

'What for?' Glen asked. 'Putting the soup on?'

'Everything. Our new lives.'

Lily walked through the door at that precise moment. 'Typical,' Abi said. 'Arrive after all the hard work has been done.' She went over and hugged her sister.

Wanda thought it was safe to slip away when the gathering was in full swing. She put on her big coat, woolly scarf, gloves and wellington boots and started up the track through Low Meadow. She carried a torch so that she could find her way, but the moon and the stars were also lighting her path. It was a bit lonely with the cows in their winter shed and not out grazing on the pasture but she kept going until she reached Lucas Wood. It really did seem like a mad thing to do but she was compelled to visit her old friend.

As soon as she reached Quercus she hugged his mighty trunk. 'How are you today? Do you feel the cold?'

Quercus took a moment. 'I feel the cold and the warmth of the sun but most of all I feel life.'

Wanda was not sure how to respond to that. 'Is that a good thing?'

'It is the most wonderful feeling. All life around me: the fungi network restoring itself, biodiversity beginning to return. I feel hope. Hope for the future has returned. Thank you, Wanda. You learnt the lessons I taught you and you went forth and transformed Capel Farm.'

'It's been a pleasure. It's so much better to be doing good rather than harm.'

Just then Glen appeared. He looked frozen despite being suitably wrapped up.

'Glen! What are you doing here?' Had he heard her talking to Quercus?

He smiled broadly as he walked straight up to her. 'I could ask you the same thing.'

'Oh, just fancied a walk, you know. Clear my head.'

'You come up here to paint, don't you. This is your ancient oak tree.' He looked up into Quercus' canopy.

'I do, yes. I find it calming.'

'I've been reading that trees give off pheromones which make you feel good.'

'I'm sure that's true.'

'Well, much as it's a lovely spot, it's freezing up here.' He smiled.

'Yes, let's head back now.' She held his gloved hand and they set off together.

'Bye Quercus,' Wanda said lightly.

'You're talking to a tree now, are you?'

They laughed together and Wanda snuggled into Glen's side and laid her head on his arm.

ACKNOWLEDGEMENTS

As you can imagine, much research was needed before I could start writing this novel. Whilst I had a strong interest in farming and food production, I had no farming experience. So I would very much like to thank those who provided help and guidance.

My research journey started when I sent a tentative email to Suffolk farm, Fen Farm Dairy. What a lovely bunch of people work there. They kindly set me up with a Zoom meeting with owner, Jonny Crickmore, and he educated me on all things dairy farming and answered all my questions. I even attended a milking session at his wonderful farm which was an invaluable experience – see chapter one!

I have scribbled much of this novel at a shared working space, @inc in Bury St Edmunds which has proved to be a very supportive environment. There I met Cate Caruth who put me in touch with Martin and Rachel Soble at Whitethorn Farm, Carey, Hereford, HR2 6NG. They have an organic farm and put me in touch with the right organisations to create the last part of the story.

Marc Middleton, Insurance Advisor, was really helpful in providing an insight into personal accident insurance for farmers.

I also have to say a big thank you to Anna Beames, Chief Executive Officer of Suffolk FWAG – (Suffolk Farming Wildlife Advisory Group) who was so generous with her time and helped me to shape the transformation from intensive to organic farming.

Finally, my husband, Tony, has been there for me every step of the way.

THANK YOU

Thank you for reading The Artist, the Farmer and the Ancient Oak.

I hope you have enjoyed Wanda's tale. I would be very grateful if you would leave a review on Amazon. This would help others decide if they want to read this book.

I love to hear from my readers so please send me a message through my website and blog:

https://www.gillbuchanan.co.uk/

or my Facebook Page:

https://www.facebook.com/gillbuchananauthor

ALSO BY GILL BUCHANAN

The Long Marriage

Forced out of his job and not ready for retirement, Roger can't believe his wife's career is about to take off. At the same time his best friend is having some kind of mid-life crisis and having an affair with a much younger woman. Roger's whole world has turned upside down and he hasn't a clue what to do next.

Unlikely Neighbours

Alex loses his job at 49 and is forced to downsize; he has no plan B and seemingly nothing in common with his neighbours. Chloe, he wrongly assumes is an air hostess, Becky has a small child which is not really his thing and Sheila gives him some very odd looks. Will they come to his rescue?

Forever Lucky

A London middle-class family suddenly fall on hard times when Dad dies unexpectanly. When his secret gambling habit is revealed, Katie finds herself having to consider the unthinkable – selling the family home.

Birch & Beyond

The sequel to Forever Lucky, Katie's further adventures as she navigates life after her husband's untimely death.

The Disenchanted Hero

Inspired by the true story of Molly and Guy who fall in love against all odds as World War 2 rages around them. This is a love story that ends in tragedy and creates a rift between father and son. Will a heroes return trip to Anzio bring them together again?

ABOUT THE AUTHOR

Gill Buchanan started writing in her early forties and soon realised that being at her keyboard, creating characters and delicious storylines, was where life became thrilling and fun.

She now lives in Bury St Edmunds in Suffolk which she considers to be the best town in the country and has no plans to leave.

When she's out and about she is always fascinated to get into conversation with new people, especially if they have shared experiences. Even better if they are a bit different, eccentric even! It makes for a richer life and feeds her creative mind.

She writes in the genre of Contemporary Women's Fiction and her stories always have humour, poignancy and a feel-good factor by the end.

Her novels make the perfect holiday read or for anytime you just want to relax and be entertained with a book.

Printed in Great Britain
by Amazon

27529134R00182